CABLE HARBOR

Also by Donald Bowie

Station Identification:
    Confessions of a Video Kid

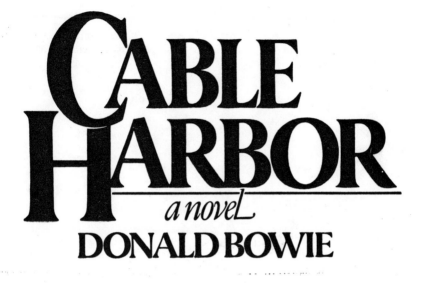

CABLE HARBOR

a novel

DONALD BOWIE

W. H. Allen • London

A Howard & Wyndham Company

1981

All characters in this book are fictional, and any resemblance to persons living or dead is purely coincidental.

Grateful acknowledgment is made for permission to reprint the lyric from "We'll Sing in the Sunshine," published by Lupercalia Music Publishing Co., Inc.

For Harvey Klinger,
who unfailingly gives
100 percent, but takes only 10

CHAPTER ONE

During the winter there was an epidemic of male menopause. Male menopause is an indisposition that is catching in cold weather: a young, supple, raw shoot of leg, spied in the bleak offices of February, is like the advent of spring itself; it's adolescence regenerate, a tender prodding of crocus at hardened old sod. And so, over the winter, there were sudden uprootings in well-established marriage beds.

When summer came, some of those whose beds had been undone in winter took to deck chairs. In Cable Harbor, a couple of the new divorcées were at the Bath Club, in their deck chairs, by 9 A.M. every morning, including Sundays and holidays. They had nowhere else to go, and nothing better to do. Laura Damon, who was *single*, felt sorry for the divorcées. There were so many of them this year, it seemed to her, and there was no comfort to be had in numbers. Calling the role, in her mind, as she walked into the Bath Club and saw all those orphaned faces, Laura frequently became depressed. There was Linda Keller, who had been married to Dr. Keller (he was having a pool built for his receptionist/bride). And Vivian Black. She'd been married to Joe Black (a lawyer now living wth a paralegal). And Ruth Hollis, who used to be married to Sam Hollis, the Ford dealer (he was sleeping with some dame he'd met snowmobiling; she had been cross-country skiing, and she bent over to tighten one of her straps—innocently enough perhaps, but Ruth maintained that any person who goes out on a golf course in stretch

1

ski pants is looking to have goggles trained on her). And these three were just last winter's victims. There had been four divorces among the Cable Harbor crowd the winter before.

The winter of the four divorces was the same winter that the townie kids started breaking into the big summer houses and drinking the liquor and screwing around. The kids never took anything, but people would find broken glasses and burnt matches in their living rooms, and upstairs the beds would be all messed up, the sheets just about tied up in knots. Which is likely to happen to the sheets, Laura figured, when a bunch of kids are coming of age in them. In a freezing house they've broken into, with a space heater radiating like a toaster on their little bare bottoms.

Sometimes Laura pitied the townie kids, the natives, the real down-Mainers. It was true that they were born into an all-natural, organic life-style, what with the lobster fishing and the woodstoves and the L. L. Bean duck shoes that were actually used for duck hunting. But most of them never got out of Cable Harbor. They never did very much with their lives—except in the wintertime. And what they did during the winter anybody could do any afternoon in New York; Laura wondered how it was possible for a down-Mainer to commit adultery. Did they even know the language? Laura couldn't imagine a liaison with hot whispers coming out in that down east twang:

"Ya lahk hit whan ah do that?"

"Ayuh."

Still, it went on up here, in the absence of the summer people. Every winter.

The ravages of the last winter in the city were nearly spoiling this summer for Laura. She hated going to the Bath Club and having to step over all those divorced bodies. Vivian Black's body especially. Vivian had lost a lot of weight right after her divorce, and she'd gone into therapy and taken up yoga. There she'd be, standing on her head and talking about some new insight, while you were trying to get at the hose so you could wash the sand off your feet. And Vivian was relatively together; you could literally fall over Linda Keller when she was in one of her trances, staring at the fair-weather clouds as if she could see in them the prospect of renewed January.

It's not fair, Laura thought. All these women in their early forties who chose marriage over a career *before there really was a choice.*

2

And then they wind up getting dumped. And feel helpless because they don't have a career and don't especially feel like opening up a dress shop. (Vivian was actually thinking of opening a dress shop, and credited her therapy group with giving her the courage.)

Laura was twenty-six. She knew that she had a real choice to make. She had not been married, and she had not embarked on a career—she had been *working*, but that wasn't the same thing, in Laura's estimation, as *embarking on a career*, like those women who seemed to be walking along Park Avenue with every single one of their sails hoisted. Laura felt she still had a number of options. But it was pretty nearly time to choose. Laura had a girl friend who was thirty-one and single. This summer that friend was opening a dress shop.

There was only one Cable Harbor divorcée who never made Laura feel guilty about having options open to her—Marie Cartey. Marie had been divorced three years before; she was forty-four, and she was living as though she, too, had important choices still to make. Because she lived and dressed that way, tourists visiting Cable Harbor often speculated that Marie might be an actress doing summer stock (the New Yorkers thought she might be one of Norman Mailer's ex-wives).

Since late June, Marie and Laura had been staking out a corner of the Bath Club for themselves. There on the edge of the deck they would sit and talk and eat tuna salad on wilted lettuce. Marie always brought a thermos of lemonade and vodka. Laura sipped and Marie, frankly, drank. She admitted she drank; if you drank, Marie maintained, you didn't get divorce mixed up in your mind with widowhood, the way the girls on Valium did—"tranquilizers are for grief," she liked to point out, "and liquor is for unwinding . . . after work—or after your marriage."

One afternoon at the beginning of July, Laura, having picked her way through the thin brown bodies on pallets, and Marie, having opened her thermos, were contemplating life as it appears in direct sunlight.

"I wonder if we're getting too much sun for our skin?" Marie said. Laura was perched in the middle of her deck chair, with her arms wound around her legs and her chin resting on one knee. The sun was striking her dark blond hair and her shoulders and arms, but Laura was not burning, though her skin was as fair as Marie's.

3

She was deeply tanned, except for the pink that dappled her nose and her cheeks.

"I suppose any amount of summer sun is too much," Laura said to her friend, "especially when you combine it with alcohol."

"What if you get too much sun, drink too much, and smoke two packs of Vantages a day?" Marie asked. She pulled a fresh pack out of her beach bag. Without lifting her chin from her knee, Laura considered the question for a moment and then replied, "The odds are you wind up looking like an old Navajo squaw. And when that happens, I suppose you either get a face-lift or start wearing a lot of turquoise jewelry."

"That might be fun. You could rent a house in New Mexico and live like Georgia O'Keeffe. Or could you? I think there was a western division of the lost generation running around in the Rockies once. Georgia O'Keeffe and Ansel Adams and those people. But now there's just John Denver and Gerry Ford's condominium in Vail." Marie exhaled a stream of smoke through her nostrils. She seemed to be allowing the West to be blown dustily away.

"I don't think you'll ever have to move to New Mexico, Marie," Laura replied. "You have a good complexion—oily skin. You might never get deep wrinkles. A few laugh lines maybe."

"I'll have laugh lines all right—under my earlobes."

"Don't be silly. I can't imagine you ever needing a face-lift."

"I might not at that," Marie reflected, "if I move to England. It'd be nice to live in London. In a city with a climate like a facial, all that lovely moisturizing fog. And another nice thing—whenever you have to go out for a quart of milk or anything you can put on a wrinkled trench coat and feel just like Ingrid Bergman. I wonder which would be better, Ansel Adams in a dry climate or Roberto Rossellini in the fog?"

"God, has Vivian gotten thin," Laura said.

"That's what's called the lean and hungry look," Marie replied. "I've been telling her there's no nutrition in Valium. Did you know she wants me to open a dress shop with her?"

"I'd heard about the shop," Laura replied. "But I didn't know she wanted you to go in with her."

"Vivian would like to raise an army," Marie said. "She has the basic training all mapped out: divorce, diet, therapy; forward, *march*."

Vivian's lean and hungry look explained to Laura in an intuitive

4

way why everything the woman said lately seemed to be just flipped at you with a snap, like a remark passed by one of the queens in a slick new deck of cards.

Laura had been doing some serious thinking about what was in her own cards. She knew she was becoming restless, and she feared becoming too restless, slipping into that nervous tapping of perfect fingernails that is one of the distinguishing characteristics of the privileged unhappy. As a Damon, Laura had been privileged to spend most of the summers of her life in Cable Harbor, in a cottage of twenty-five rooms. In the course of those summers she had grown up among other grandchildren in tennis togs, grandchildren who, if they were lazy and self-indulgent enough, could spend the rest of their lives being gently supervised by the trust officers of Morgan Guaranty, who are the best baby-sitters in the world.

Not wanting to be a big baby all her life, Laura had gone to school with serious intentions. Most of the girls at Wellesley had also been serious. They had applied themselves. Most of them had already had their engagement pictures published in the *Times*—as a result of their serious application. Laura's application, which apparently had been misdirected, landed her in a publishing job. From which she had been fired in April. The publisher replaced her with a man. The word was that he wanted to run a macho outfit. The idea was a source of bitter amusement for Laura. A *macho* publishing house. What a laugh. Considering that only seventeen people in the continental United States read books anyway, and of those seventeen, fifteen are women.

Half daydreaming, Laura said to Marie, "When I was a kid, I used to have all these romantic ideas about European men. Londoners with umbrellas. Romans who pinched. But this maid we had kind of spoiled it for a while. She was German—Pennsylvania Dutch. Once she put a hex on the milkman, because he left a fresh note for her in a bottle. Anyway, this maid told me that when European men go away—like on a business trip or something—they ask you for your panties or your blouse. And then they take them out on the train or the plane and sniff them." Marie blinked.

"Do European men really get off on that?" Laura asked. "I mean, is it stimulating for them to inhale your perspiration stains?"

"That sounds more like Los Angeles to me," Marie replied. "Out there they use cocaine as talcum powder."

"Oh," said Laura. She closed her eyes and began to daydream about Europe—the two weeks she had spent on the Italian Riviera the summer before. Nothing Laura remembered from that vacation seemed better than just sitting on the steps of her rented house in Portofino with a glass of Soave. During the two weeks, there was but one brief romance.

Laura met Hans in a waterfront café. She drove back to his hotel with him in his new BMW, which he said was a *Bayemvay*. He was tall and exotic, and he wore the tightest jeans Laura had ever seen on a man. His long hair and beard reminded Laura of the Dutch Masters cigar boxes in restaurant showcases. Hans said, in bits and pieces of English, that he lived in West Berlin and worked for an architectural firm. Laura didn't care what he did for a living: what mattered was that he reminded her of the wild pirate who used to climb up to her window when she was little and sick in bed.

Hans began undressing as soon as he got Laura inside his hotel room. Laura realized later that he had not even given her the time to appreciate, romantically, the view of the moonlit harbor. Hans just stood there in a tiny pair of briefs and told her, "I vant to fok you, hey-huh?"

"Couldn't we finish the discussion we were having first?" Laura asked. "Why the dollar is so weak and the mark is so strong, remember?"

"Ah—my English. It's ah-bad. It's nuts so gud, huh? Ve talk latar." Big grin. Come on, *all I want is to fok you.* Was this the way the Dutch Masters got Manhattan from the Indians?

"I like de vay your boops go."

Laura looked down at her breasts.

"I fok you now, huh?"

Laura felt as though she was making a fool, or worse, an international tart (something General Foods might package as a midnight pick-me-up) out of herself. Still, it would be undiplomatic simply to walk out the door. Shrugging, Laura undressed. Was there any way she could introduce some sense of tenderness, of affection, into this situation? Or would she have to allow herself to be victimized by this pirate? Looted sexually? Come on, girl, she urged herself, think of a fantasy situation. Embroider something.

The Berlin Wall. Of course, that would do it. As she unhooked her bra, Laura imagined Hans scrambling through the darkness, with searchlights waving at his heels. There he was, at the base of the wall, hurling upward a rope with a grappling hook on the end. Now he was shinnying up. Oh no. The East German secret police. Machine gun fire. Dear God, he was hit, in his shoulder. But he made it over to the other side where sexual freedom and Laura were waiting for him.

Hans scooped up Laura and burrowed his shaggy head into her breasts.

God, Laura remembered gloomily, the guy's body had been hard as a rock. What did he do? Work out by lifting his *Bayemvay* over his head? Laura did not like hardened men. Steely types. Macho publishers. It was one thing to have muscles, but it was something else altogether for a guy to be so thick with maleness that no warmth penetrated. Twice in her life Laura had thought herself in love. In the delirium of what she now knew to be infatuation, Laura had, for a time, felt as though she were consorting with Mercury. The Greek god whose ankles were winged, winged to ruffle your heart when your lover was going out for the Sunday paper, his shirttail hanging out boyishly in back. Winged to sweep your soul skyward until—one day it was bound to happen—you came too close to the sun, to the white light in which everything that was uncertain flared cruelly clear, and, in a flurry of feathers, you came down with a thump.

There had been no quicksilver in Hans. He was thoroughly down to earth, an earthmover that gripped and thrusted. Right after he climaxed—and that did not take very long—Hans got out of bed and switched on the light. He looked at Laura helplessly, like a little boy who has messed his pants. He pulled a pair of baby-blue pajamas out of his suitcase and stepped into the bottoms.

"I hope you dond tink I'm crasey, but I cand sleep widoudt dem." God, baby-blue pajamas with a draw string and everything. Hans went into the bathroom and began brushing his teeth. Laura was trying so hard not to giggle that her own teeth felt full of tiny bubbles. What a fine romance this was—the Roman Spring of Laura Damon. Things weren't supposed to work out this way, but then how were they supposed to work out? Only that afternoon Laura had seen a woman with four long loaves of bread under one arm and a child who looked as if he were going to the urchin academy under the other arm. The poor woman was all in black, probably because she was pregnant again. There seemed to be no end of ways a woman could be put through the wringer.

7

Laura's uncertainty about the way things were supposed to work out had made her appear to many of her friends wistful, if not lost. What puzzled Laura most about herself was that she had figured out a lot of things, but so far she had been unable to figure out exactly where she was going with her life. Now that she was out of work, Laura was afraid that she might start to drift. There were so many slow currents you could get into—and then just glide lazily along. Especially here, in Cable Harbor, in the summer.

A few days ago, before the heat really set in, Laura had wandered down to the harbor. She had in mind to sit on the rocks and read her book, an old paperback copy of *The Women's Room* that her sister had bought the year before she got married. Laura found herself unable to concentrate on Mira's problems, though. Shifting about on her rocky perch, she idly studied the delicate layering of the pink and gray granite around her. The old boulders, tumbled about by a glacier in another eon, looked like so many porcelain petticoats frozen in the exaltation of a cancan. Solid stone swirling. The water eddied in and out below Laura. Locks of seaweed rose and fell with the inhale and exhale of the tide.

Gazing out at the harbor traffic, Laura followed the progress of the lobstermen's boats, the little craft she had always thought were so cute, with their bows upswept and pointed like an old man's pocket handkerchief. She paused at the sight of a young fisherman just in after his day on the water. His chest was bare. It was criss-crossed with red suspenders. The fisherman was very young—no more than twenty. He had long, curly blond hair. Poseidon in red suspenders. Laura was warmed, on her rock, with desire. Absentmindedly, she began to nibble on the binding of *The Women's Room*.

It was late November, according to the calendar on the wall of the cottage that Laura presently saw in her daydream. It was getting dark, and the young fisherman had not yet returned from the sea. Laura's heart was softly lit in waiting, her love reaching out like a kerosene lantern in the dark. It grew later, and later still. Windswept branches cracked against the walls of the cottage. Laura returned again and again to the cast-iron stove to stir the clam chowder she was keeping hot. Gradually, she was growing frantic. Then, suddenly, the door slapped open and there he stood, framed in the lamplight, his yellow slicker shining and his curly blond hair stuck to his forehead by salt spray. Laura would run to him, snuggle against the cable-knit sweater she'd made for him herself, smell the sea in his damp hair. Later, she would warm his body next to hers under an enormous quilt.

Well, Laura reflected, I've had crazier fantasies. The fisherman *was* cute, but kind of dumb, probably. Still, he was decent subject matter for one of the personal fictions Laura liked to retreat into, since reality was often enough a tabloid that ought to be passed by on your way out of the supermarket. Smart or dumb, most of the people Laura's age seemed to have made up their minds about what they were going to do with their lives. In a way, Laura was grateful that she had proven to be an exception—life still held out a promise, vague and equivocal though it might be. Laura's sister, Melissa, was evidently satisfied that life had kept its promise to her; she had never held down a real job, but now she had a husband and a baby and a big house in Greenwich and she was happy.

Of course, there was the line Laura had overheard in the powder room of the Bath Club during a dinner dance: *Chuck used to say he married Melissa for her money, but now he says he really loves her.* If that was the case, Melissa had come out ahead on her investment. But Laura had no business head when it came to love. Buying a husband was a proposition as untenable, in Laura's view, as macho publishing: such things wouldn't be possible if there were pills to take for penis envy.

Feeling rancid with sweat and suntan oil, Laura said to Marie, "I've got to get into the pool. Coming?"

"No, not right now," Marie replied. "I don't have the energy. I feel middle-aged today."

"Well, you won't be middle-aged officially until the day when you can't pull the zipper in the back of your bathing suit all the way up."

"It won't be official until then? Even with a three-martinis-a-night handicap?" Marie looked disappointed.

"You'll just have to be patient," Laura said. Climbing out of her deck chair, she realigned the seams of her bikini where it was creeping up her leg. She skipped over to the deep end of the pool, crouched, and dove in. She swam underwater, with her eyes open.

Near the surface, children's legs dangled. The nubbly little legs reminded Laura of shrimp. Sunday, on the beach, she had come upon a swarm of tiny shrimp—no doubt just hatched—that where snapping over the hot sand toward the ocean. The shrimp were springing from a clump of drying seaweed. Cupping in her hands as

9

many of the minute creatures as she could, Laura began carrying them to the water. As she swam underwater now, Laura was thinking how ironic it was that you could eat a shrimp cocktail in the evening and save hundreds of baby shrimp from dying in the afternoon. The fact that people could live with contradictions like that probably explained a lot of marriages in Cable Harbor.

With the water chortling in her ears, Laura let herself rise to the surface. She floated there, putting her legs through the motions she had learned for a Bath Club water ballet twelve years before. Laura dipped her head in the water again—the chlorine helped the sun streak her hair. Gliding over to a ladder, she lifted herself out of the pool. Then she stood under a shower for a minute, amid a group of children who were sticking in their sandy feet.

Settling back into her deck chair, Laura said to Marie, "Well, are we going to head for London or Taos or where are we going?"

"No," Marie replied flatly. "No exotic places. I don't think American women should get involved with European men or the Mexican food they make in Taos—it's hard enough to hold on to a guy without having to deal with diarrhea all the time."

"You're probably right," Laura said glumly. (She hadn't achieved an orgasm that night with Hans, and the next day she was running to the bathroom every five minutes.) Trying to think of something perky to say, something along the lines of the sentiments you read inside the greeting cards that picture pastel little girls in huge sunbonnets, Laura came up with, "I suppose everybody is getting ready for the fashion show."

"Of course they are," Marie said, as though she were replying to a silly schoolgirl. "With Saks doing it this year, who would dare miss it?"

"What was the theme?" Laura asked. "I forget."

"Half sizes are beautiful," Marie said. "Are you modeling this year?"

"No, I am *not* modeling this year. I said last year if they asked me to wear the wedding gown three years in a row I'd absolutely refuse. So this year they've asked me to model a bridesmaid's dress. I said, 'No, thanks, I've already got a closet full of them.'"

"Maybe Arthur will wear the bridesmaid's dress," Marie reflected.

"That's not a very nice thing to say about one of your best friends," Laura admonished. "Why, just the other day my mother was saying how Arthur and Herbert have one of the best marriages in Cable Harbor. She thinks their house is beautiful, too."

"There they have no choice in the matter," Marie said. "Gay men have to live in beautiful houses. It's part of their destiny. Like it was part of Pat Nixon's destiny to pick out tailored clothes. I used to have this dayworker who couldn't understand how Nixon could be such a crook 'when his wife dresses so beautifully.' That's exactly what she said. Pat Nixon dressed beautifully and Arthur and Herbert live in a beautiful house. Maybe it all has to do with your idea of your own value as a person. Like Vivian says, 'If Parke Bernet thinks something is worthless, they tell you, *It would only have decorative value.*' That's what Pat Nixon had, and that's what Arthur and Herbert have—*decorative value.* It's not fair, of course. But then none of us get to set our own prices in the marketplace, do we?"

"Well, it's true their taste is part of Arthur and Herbert's appeal," Laura replied. "Though they are capable of little lapses. I can't imagine what Arthur had in mind when he put those parrots in the kitchen, in cages, right over the counter. Every so often I get this morbid feeling that he keeps them in the kitchen so he can stick one in the Cuisinart whenever he wants to make a pâté."

"I assume you're coming to their party tomorrow night," Marie said.

"Wouldn't miss it for the world," Laura replied. "You know, Marie, this might actually turn out to be a fun summer. Let's see, there's Arthur and Herbert's thing tomorrow. The fashion show is coming up. And at the beginning of August the Williamses are throwing that big party for Instant Replay."

"That should be the highlight of the season," Marie said. "A cocktail party for a horse. And to think my ex-husband used to put horses into his hamburgers. I've certainly come a long way, haven't I?"

Marie had been married to Dan Cartey, the eldest of the two Cartey brothers. The Cartey brothers had begun with a hamburger stand. They turned the hamburger stand into a fast food chain by borrowing more money than they could ever repay; then they sold the chain to a conglomerate for twenty times the amount they had borrowed. Not long after the merger Dan went through male menopause. As Marie put it, "He decided he wasn't getting enough kicks. So he went on a nationwide tour of hotel rooms—with a Rockette."

"Oh, I didn't tell you what happened yesterday afternoon when I was leaving here, did I?" Marie asked. Laura shook her head no.

"Talking about Arthur and Herbert just now made me think of it. Anyway, I was out in the parking lot and I saw two of the little boys—about ten, they were, and one of them was Sandy's kid—and they were *wrestling* with this *man*. I said, 'Hey, what's going on?' and Sandy's kid says, 'We're wrestling. Father Jack wrestles with us all the time.' That was when I recognized this guy—he's one of the priests from St. Agnes's. He just looked at me sheepishly and started tucking in his shirt. Can you *imagine?* I didn't know what to do, so I went home and called Arthur."

"What did he say?" Laura asked.

"I said, 'One of the priests from St. Agnes's is *wrestling* with all the little boys. What should I do?' So Arthur says, 'Call the police. There's nothing worse than an ordained pederast.' So I called the police and they went up to the church and had a word with Father Jack. Arthur told me that there was a cardinal they all used to call *Minnie* who liked boys too. Minnie's dead now, but they replaced him with another chicken queen. Arthur wouldn't tell me which archdiocese it was. He said it's wrong to remove all mystery from the ceremonies of the Church."

"If I were gay," Laura reflected, "I mean if I were a gay *guy*—I could never be a lesbian, not the way I bowl—I wouldn't go after boys. I'd look for men my own age. Older men, even."

"That's the effect of years of tuna salad without mayonnaise," Marie pointed out. "You wouldn't be willing to squander all that weight loss on youth. Most gay men are practical that way too—Arthur says, 'I draw the line when I see them on a skateboard.' Say, do I sound like a fag hag?"

"No," Laura replied.

"Oh yes I do," Marie said. "I admit I'm a fag hag. Being a fag hag is like being an alcoholic. The first step toward a cure is admitting to the problem. The next step, when you're a fag hag, is to drop your subscription to *Architectural Digest*. Actually being a fag hag is not so bad. Arthur says girls like me have been following him around for years. He said one little girl started tagging along behind him in the fourth grade. The next year the school promoted her to a public relations job."

"I wonder if I should try getting into public relations," Laura said.

"Sometimes I get jealous of Arthur and Herbert," Marie said. "I envy them the companionship. They *do* have one of the best marriages in Cable Harbor. But of course they have always had the advantage of not being able to have any kids."

There was a burst of applause from the pool. Apparently some acrobat was performing on the diving board. Marie extended her neck to investigate. Her mouth fell open and hung there for a long moment, and her eyes widened.

"Marie!" Laura said with alarm. "Are you all right?"

"Yeah . . ." Marie muttered. "Yeah . . . I'm okay." She wiped her face with her hand. "I was just sort of bowled over there for a minute . . . by this terrible wave of horniness."

"Oh," said Laura, her breath returning. "I understand. Vivian was just telling me the other day how she gets them too—hot flashes."

"It wasn't that," Marie said. "It was *that*." She tossed her head in the direction of the pool. Laura looked across the deck to see what had given Marie her turn. She saw, and her heart sank.

"Good grief," she said. "What was that dive he just did? A quadruple half gainer? How old is he? Twenty-one? Do you suppose he'd be interested in an older woman?"

"That vision is Jamie Lawrence," Marie said. "He's twenty-four, actually. Isn't he gorgeous? And what a body. This is the first time I've seen him in a bathing suit. It's so refreshing to see a handsome man around here. I've gotten so sick of bloated fish bellies wrapped in *The New York Times*."

"Where on earth did he come from?" Laura asked.

"Don't you know? You've been around here long enough . . . at least your family has. He comes from old, old money. His grandfather is the Lawrence that owns Cragmere. I'm sure you know who they are—she has these six-foot-high cheekbones and she's never dyed her hair or anything and the old man always looks like he just crawled out from the bilge of some Hinckley sailboat, which nine times out of ten is exactly what he did just do."

"I didn't even know the Lawrences had a grandson," Laura said.

"They kept him hidden in the bilge with their old Topsiders," Marie replied. "Actually he just got out of Harvard Business, I hear. Before that he was at Yale."

"He never came here before in the summer," Laura said. "I'm sure. I would have noticed."

"He had an English mother," Marie said. "They keep their kids in pens—public schools. I imagine young Jamie spent his boyhood summers on some Scottish moor, firing shotguns at gamebirds, deer, touring high school girls from Hewlett."

"I wonder what he's doing here now," Laura said.

"They say he's living in a tent on the edge of his grandfather's property. Want to go camping?"

"I musn't stare at him," Laura said, "I'll get carried away."

"Oh, come on, Laura," said Marie, "you've never gotten carried away by a guy, before, have you?"

"No," Laura admitted. "You're right. I've never really been carried away. I've been picked up a few times, though."

Marie reached for her cup of spiked lemonade, which was nearly empty. Through the prism of the plastic, she studied Jamie Lawrence like a jeweler looking for a flaw in a diamond. She said, speculatively, "He must have been on the swim team at Yale. He's wearing racing trunks. That's where he must have learned to dive like that—on the Yale swimming team."

"Swimmers always have such beautiful bodies," Laura said. She sounded warmly appreciative of the fact, like a child hearing the happy ending of a story.

"Male beauty is such an extravagance," said Marie. "Having a beautiful man around is like having a raincoat lined with mink. It's enough for a raincoat and a man to be functional. Plain. So you can wear anything with them."

"I suppose he knows how good-looking he is, doesn't he?" Laura said impatiently. "He'd have to know. People must stare at him."

"Like you're doing," Marie replied. Self-consciously Laura reached down and pulled her beach towel up over her legs. She'd always thought that her ankles were chunky. Every time she began to think that she might be pretty, her instep tripped her up. But wasn't that always the way? You had to be vulnerable somewhere. Or you could be vulnerable all over the place; you could be a hundred pounds overweight and have a face full of pimples—and yet never once be seriously wounded by life. Or you could live in southern California and be beautiful and invulnerable—seal up even your pores with suntan lotion and hide behind your sunglasses when you saw somebody coming. Or you could move north to Marin

County and go into analysis and stop worrying about your ankles and your weight and maybe even stop shaving under your arms.

With the wheel of vulnerability having come, in her mind, full circle, Laura concentrated again on what Marie was saying.

"Jamie sure is a walking Winston ad," Marie said. "I think if a guy with his looks ever approached me—even looked at me the way those Winston guys stare at you from the billboards—I'd lose twenty pounds on the spot. Or else I'd turn into a pumpkin. And be thrown from an overpass by my ex-husband and the kids."

Shaking his shaggy head, Jamie Lawrence emerged from the water.

"I think Arthur and Herbert should invite Jamie to their party tomorrow," Marie said. "What a lovely idea that would be. There'd actually be something to admire besides the furniture and people's dresses."

"It's kind of short notice, isn't it?"

"No it isn't. What does a man have to do to get ready for a party but roll on some Right Guard? If he's at the party you can go after him, Laura."

"No, thanks. The publisher who pushed me out of my job—Mr. Machismo—was a Harvard Business alumnus. One rejection from Harvard Business is quite enough."

"I wonder if he comes to the party, I wonder if any of the members of the *corps de réjection* will go after him?"

"Vivian might," Laura said. "Since her therapy group has given her all that fresh confidence. I think Vivian is really capable of anything at this point. The other day she told me she's been sleeping with a gun under her pillow."

"Vivian's got a *gun?* With bullets in it?"

"She told me she keeps it loaded all the time," Laura replied.

"Once I bit a bullet," Marie said. "I was only eight. My uncle was sixteen and he had a .22 and I was in love with him. So I bit one of his bullets . . . and I broke my tooth. I hope Vivian knows that bullets are hard and they hurt. I don't think she's ready to handle bullets. They're sort of a . . . capsule version of reality."

CHAPTER TWO

Marie and Laura lingered on at the Bath Club until it was nearly empty. They agreed on a basic principle: if you're going to make a career of idleness, it's best to try to put in a normal working day. That way you don't get bored.

As they were folding their beach towels, Marie said to Laura, "People don't realize what a serious business tanning is. It takes a lot of application."

"Of aloe vera lotion," Laura added.

"No, it takes more than that," Marie replied. "Getting a tan is like setting up a business. At first you have to be on the job every single day. You can't even take weekends off. But then eventually you can get away with just going to the beach a few days a week. To maintain your base."

"Sometimes the whole process seems . . . a little frivolous somehow," Laura said.

"Whimsical, maybe," Marie said as she packed her thermos bottle in her Fortnum and Mason picnic hamper. "You should know the difference between a frivolity and a whim. You were fired from your little publishing job because of somebody's whim, weren't you? Our lives are governed by whims. Sometimes they seem like serious intentions, I admit—especially when lawyers get ahold of them."

"Whims," Laura mused. "Frivolities, fancies, follies. It's a lightweight world, I guess. Especially for women."

"If God had meant us to be taken seriously He wouldn't have

allowed us to be dressed in crinoline when we were little girls."
Marie closed her picnic hamper with finality.

"But I want to be taken seriously," Laura said.

"Correction," Marie replied. "You dream of being taken seriously.
Myself, I prefer fancies and follies and frills. Fortnum and Mason
picnic baskets. Arthur and Herbert's parties. Sitting on this deck.
And why not? So many things that people pretend are serious are a
waste of time. Living luxuriously . . . luxury itself . . . what is it but
an expensive waste product? So why not enjoy it while we have it
here, before the final disposal of all the waste products is upon us?"

"Hedonist," Laura said.

"I speak as one who has bitten the bullet," Marie replied.

When Marie finally arrived home around five-thirty, she poured
herself a vodka and tonic and walked out to her poolside cabana,
where she picked up the telephone receiver. She dialed Arthur and
Herbert's number. Herbert answerd.

"Guess what," Marie began. Herbert said he wasn't very good at
guessing games. Figuring out who was on the line, Arthur picked up
an extension in another room and broke in: "I'm great at guessing
games. When I was a kid I used to play a guessing game with my
mother when we were out riding in the car. You remember how you
used to play games in the car when you were a kid—to pass the time?
Well, instead of that geography stuff where you name a city that
ends in *r* and the other player has to think of a city that begins with
r, my mother and I used to try to guess the ages of all the other
women drivers. I was very good at that guessing game. I still am."

"I bet you can't guess what I've got in store for you," Marie said.
Indeed Arthur couldn't guess, though he tried groping in the dark
for a couple of minutes—hinting at things young adolescents do to
each other when they turn out the lights at their parties.

"Time's up," said Marie. Sounding as though she were modeling
him in clay with her hands, Marie then began to describe Jamie
Lawrence. When the description was complete, Herbert said, "If
he's as good-looking as you say he is, Arthur will certainly want him
to come."

"I'll even make up an extra bed for him," Arthur volunteered
enthusiastically. "In fact, I think I'll make up several beds and place
them in strategic places, like ashtrays."

"Now see what you've started, Marie," Herbert said. Talking with

Marie, he could have passed for a leading man setting up a comic situation with Doris Day. Everyone agreed that Herbert was distinguished-looking. Some of the women at the Bath Club had said that Herbert looked just like the pictures of Hubert de Givenchy in W. Many of Cable Harbor's widows and divorcées were still setting their sights on Herbert, even though they knew what his relationship with Arthur was. The women sensed that Herbert's homosexuality was a matter of preference. And preferences are always subject to change. Arthur, on the other hand, appeared to be homosexual by nature, not by inclination: a hairdresser, as opposed to one of Doris Day's leading men. Arthur was worth consulting about questions of taste, but he wasn't the type with whom any woman in her right mind would dream of consorting. Arthur was spoken for sexually—you could tell by his slight lisp.

"This is so thoughtful of you, Marie," Arthur was saying. "We told you that you didn't have to bring anything. Still, I've always loved B.Y.O.B. parties—when it means *bring your own boy*. How old did you say he was? Twelve? If he lives in a tent he must be around twelve. It might be a little awkward having an available twelve-year-old boy at the party—when we haven't invited any clergy."

"I told you he's twenty-four," Marie replied.

"Then why's he living in a tent? I thought only twelve-year-olds and people who sort of do up their two weeks' vacation in Saran Wrap go camping."

"The oriental rug dealer who stuck you with that dry-rotted Oushak probably lives in a tent," Herbert put in.

"Jamie is probably trying to find himself," Marie explained.

"What a coincidence," said Arthur. "I found a part of myself when I was sleeping in a tent in my parents' backyard. And I was only eleven at the time."

"You mean you started abusing yourself when you were eleven," Herbert specified.

"Why shouldn't I have? I'd certainly taken enough abuse from other people. What was I supposed to do all by myself in a tent, sensitive little boy that I was, shunned by my peer group and all? All these silverfish got into my stack of comic books, so I couldn't read out there." Recalling other details of his boyhood, Arthur nervously combed his bright blond hair with his fingertips. From a

18

distance, Arthur still looked like a boy. Seen more closely, he looked boyish, for a man of forty, as a man of eighty will sometimes look cherubic; such looks occur when the aging process softens rather than sharpens.

"How are you going to invite him if he has no phone? He probably doesn't have a phone, living in a tent." Herbert was being practical, which was one way he felt he complemented Arthur—or at least neutralized his influence.

"I'm going to drive out there and ask him in person," Marie announced.

"That's not extending an invitation," Arthur advised, "that's looking for a rendezvous."

"Don't be ridiculous," Marie said. "This kid couldn't possibly have any interest in me."

"How do you know?" Arthur persisted. "Plenty of young guys go for older women. Experience. Anne Bancroft. Remember *The Graduate?*"

"Sure I remember *The Graduate*. But I also saw *Moment to Moment.*"

Herbert said, "Listen, Marie, don't you be shy. You just drive yourself straight out there and go ahead and invite him. Look him right in the eye."

"No, for God's sake don't do that," Arthur shouted. "Never look them in the eye. Never, ever. Unless they're already toying with your front buttons, of course. Don't listen to what Herbert says, at any rate. He doesn't know anything about approaching people. He never went to the bars. What does he know about cruising? Listen to me, Marie. Wear dark glasses and a scarf. Pretend you're Jackie O. shoplifting in Bamberger's."

"My resolve is weakening," Marie said. "I'm losing all the self-confidence I had built up. And I just finished my vodka and tonic."

"You've got to steel yourself," Arthur insisted. "Nothing is more formidable than youth and beauty. That's why Alexander the Great conquered the world where Napoleon and Hitler failed. Alexander was *pretty*."

"You're making me a nervous wreck," Marie replied. "I've got to make myself another drink."

"Where are you?" Arthur asked.

"Out by the pool," Marie said.

19

"If you're feeling faint inhale some chlorine," Arthur suggested. While Marie was at the bar, Arthur and Herbert conferred briefly.

"I hope you're going to behave yourself if this kid does show up," Herbert said.

"What do you mean? My behavior is always exemplary."

"Exemplary for a neurotic queen, maybe," Herbert shot back. "Well, at least this kid would be better than the little hustlers you pick up in Key West. If by some fluke he likes you, you won't have to pay to get his teeth straightened or to send him to computer programing school."

"I always leave them better than I found them," Arthur answered self-righteously. "A lot of queens can't say as much for the way they leave a toilet seat."

"You should always leave the toilet seat *down*." Marie had come back on the line. "That shows you were taught good manners at home. Where were we?"

"We were trying to figure out the best way to approach this Jamie Gorgeous," Arthur filled in. "How about a nice Catholic confessional? Go with sin on your mind and hope to be forgiven."

"That would be a waste of time," Herbert said. "Beauty is always unforgiving. It's ego given too much encouragement."

"He's right there," Arthur conceded glumly. "Maybe you could wear a pair of mittens and attach the invitation to one of them with a safety pin? Really, Marie, I hardly know what to suggest. I just hope this little latter-day hippie decides to come after he's put us all through such anxiety. I hope he doesn't have to get out a rush order of sandals or something."

"He isn't a hippie sandalmaker," Marie said. "I told you he comes from a lot of money. He's a *Lawrence*, for God's sake. He's even been to Harvard Business."

"Money too, huh? He really is perfect. How depressing."

"Nobody's perfect," Herbert insisted.

"I'm sorry to contradict you, darling," Arthur replied. "But there are perfect people. Sights to behold. Perfect people exist so you can have somebody to seek if you haven't found Jesus—or if you don't have easy access to a choirboy."

"Maybe I'll have a big glass of vodka and Amaretto tomorrow morning instead of orange juice," Marie said. "Then I'll be kind of glazed—waxed like the floor—so it won't matter if he tramples me underfoot. What the hell? I'll just plunge right in."

"Now you're talking," Herbert said.

"I guess that's the thing to do," Arthur agreed. "Plunge right in. I always go to the baths with that attitude."

Having arrived at a consensus, Marie and Arthur and Herbert concluded their conference. After Marie hung up, she sat staring at the pool for a while. She wondered how Arthur and Herbert had managed to stay together for twenty years. They were so different. Arthur was such a conventional queen: self-absorbed, preoccupied with youth and beauty, promiscuous. Herbert, on the other hand, was sensitive, quiet, probably very affectionate and . . . loving. Marie thought there were probably two sides to homosexuality. It seemed there were two sides to every story, except the ones the nuns told when she was in parochial school. But for two such different people to survive, together, on opposite sides of the emotional fence, in a life-style that was fenced off anyway . . . Marie could not quite fathom it. It was one of those mysteries of human relations that you could not even begin to fathom until you got to the bottom of your glass. Then you had to have another. And when you'd finished that one it didn't seem to matter whether you penetrated the problem or not.

Marie's ex-husband, Dan, had not bothered to tell her that he would be flying into Cable Harbor on Tuesday. He didn't want to have to answer her questions, especially her questions about money and the business. She had a way of adjusting the figures he was responsible for according to his successes, though he never made any such adjustments to allow for his miscalculations. Marie had made it clear to Dan that she felt granting him the divorce was, for failure, allowance enough.

Dan had avoided coming to Cable Harbor, even during the summer, since the divorce, but now he was here on business, making a kind of courtesy call on an investment. The investment was an unfinished resort hotel, a steel and granite framework that had been erected on the site of the old wooden Perry House, a holdover from Cable Harbor's Victorian heyday, which, when it was finally razed, was already breaking up like a ship of porches in a gale.

The new Perry House had become a mystery to the people of Cable Harbor. There it sat, in the middle of its meticulously maintained lawns, continually unfinished. The hotel had been half-done for three years now. Some were speculating that the developers—

the Cartey brothers and other unnamed parties—were playing a waiting game, hoping to use the granite shell they had built for condominiums should the town fathers ever agree to make way for them. One wag had suggested, to the amusement of none of his listeners, that "they're circling the campers—and the condos are coming." Should that have proved true, the cavalry of detached-dwelling owners was drilled and ready.

Yet nothing was happening. There were no confrontations, no appeals to the zoning board. Just the sprinklers turning quietly on the new Perry House's green but empty grounds.

Dan climbed out of his twin-engine Cessna. One by one, five Japanese businessmen emerged after him. They followed Dan across the runway single file, like five black crows watchfully sidestepping along a telephone wire. One of them aimed his Nikon at the hazy hills in the distance, but he did not break rank to do so. A Cable Harbor cab—a station wagon with a cab's white comb light stuck in its roof and an interior that smelled of laundry—met Dan and his inquisitive companions at the edge of the landing field. They got in the cab and were driven out to the site of the Perry House. Dan began to show the visitors around. They were interested in everything, and seemed to see postcard views—to look at and think about sending back—everywhere. The Nikon whirred. Heads nodded, and notes were taken. One of the Japanese businessmen got his foot wet by a lawn sprinkler and laughed like a delighted child.

They came upon the body outside one of the Perry House's first-floor rooms. The dead girl's backpack lay next to her hand, which was chalky and coolly inanimate, like a mannequin's hand. There was a moment of pure surprise and silence.

"Ah," said one of the Japanese businessmen.

"Ooohh," said another. "She must have been hitch . . . hi-kah! Very dangerous!"

Dumbfounded, Dan wrestled with his thoughts. He half thought he should ask the one with the Nikon if he wanted to take a picture.

Tuesday morning Marie was up at ten o'clock. Pouring herself a big glass of orange juice, she added to it enough Finlandia to instill self-confidence. After she finished her juice she went back upstairs and picked out the best of what she called her "Petunia Pig goes to Palm Beach" caftans. With that she decided to wear a pair of simple

22

emerald earrings, a cabochon emerald ring, and her platinum Piaget with the jade face. On the whole, the look was right for the occasion, Marie decided: She had gotten herself up like a Polynesian princess on her way to be thrown into the volcano so the pineapple crop wouldn't fail. But what the hell?

Ready for anything except a direct stare from blue eyes, Marie backed her Porsche out of the crushed-marble driveway. Heading up the shore road, she felt pretty much in control, though she did tend to accelerate erratically whenever she felt the spur of anxiety in her side.

There was a hardware store NO TRESPASSING sign posted at the beginning of the dirt road that led into the acreage Jamie Lawrence's grandfather had settled on him for the summer. The sign at the main entrance to the Lawrence estate said, simply, "Cragmere." The lettering was incised and gold-leafed, and of a style common to the sterns of yachts. Funny how a NO TRESPASSING sign can be more inviting than a gilded name, Marie thought. There was something unspoken in those estate signs the old-line Wasps used, those nice, polite names and archaic, gentle hints like "private" and "no motors beyond this point." What was it they were trying so politely to say— "No Irish need apply?"

Ignoring her social insecurities and caking the Porsche with dust, Marie bulldozed her way down the dirt road. The land on either side of the road was unspoiled—as the Lawrences' money was, no doubt, always fresh and fragrant from the bank, and crisp as a cucumber. The road crossed exposed granite ledge in places. The whole point of land that the Lawrence estate encompassed was granite and trees clinging to granite; the roots of the pines and maples seemed only to have gotten a grasp, not to have embedded themselves. The wind was everywhere in Cable Harbor, but out on this point the ragged forest and the leaning grass looked constantly away from the sea— were turned away by wind and blowing salt water, forced back by the shouldering of the sea.

There were few proper beaches in Cable Harbor, but there were many cold stone alleys between the ocean and the land that were always littered with blanched branches and seaweed torn off the bottom, like clumps of soggy carpeting. Marie wondered what kind of a kid would want to live out here, where the granite was serrated by the Atlantic. Where small animals with eerie eyes surprised you at night in the road. Maybe he didn't like people. Otherwise he could live with nature the way everybody else did, domesticating it in clay pots. Marie screeched to a stop as soon as she saw the campsite. The tent was bright blue and geodesic, too slick to be army surplus. That would figure; L. L. Bean probably stocked it. Next to the tent was a beat-up Volkswagen van, and standing next to the van was Jamie Lawrence. He was washing it. Marie was suddenly slapped with the fact that Jamie was not wearing a shirt—or *pants*. All he had on was a pair of Jockey briefs. Swallowing hard, Marie tried to remain calm. If I don't have a fatal heart attack here and now, she told herself, I will get out of the car and start talking to him just as normally as I would if he were wearing pants. Things did not go black, so Marie got out of her car.

Pausing as he was about to dunk his sponge in a bucket of water, Jamie said, "Hi."

"Hello there," Marie replied in a voice that sounded as though it came from one of those schools of poise where young girls try to maintain their posture with books on top of their heads.

"I'm Marie Cartey. You must have seen me around the Bath Club."

"No," said Jamie, putting down his sponge so he could shake hands, "I don't think I've seen you before, but I'm glad to meet you anyway."

"I've seen your grandmother and grandfather from time to time. They're awfully sweet."

Picking up his sponge, Jamie began to swab one of the van's hubcaps. It was a gesture that clearly implied, *Well, what do you want?* Marie panicked. She couldn't think of anything to say, but she knew if she didn't say something she was going to faint. So she blurted out the first thing that came into her head.

"I think it's a riot that you don't have any pants on."

Jamie looked puzzled: not embarrassed, just puzzled. Marie's cheeks were roasting.

"What I mean is—I mean, I wasn't trying to make you feel awkward or anything—what I meant was, it was just so perfect for you to be standing there in your underwear when I showed up."

"Why should I feel awkward?" Jamie said. "My underwear is white—so what?"

"I'm sure that's exactly the way the Stevens boys feel. About their underwear. Do you know the Stevens boys?"

24

"I know the family," Jamie replied.

"Um," Marie muttered. "Anyway. What I think I'm trying to say is—is—a couple of weeks ago one of those Stevens boys was standing outside the barn that their parents have finished off as a guest house. That's where they live in the summer, the Stevens boys, with their motorcycles and surfboards."

"Uh-huh," Jamie said.

"So there he was, standing by the barn door. This Stevens boy. In his underwear." Marie paused while the significance of what she was saying materialized in her mind.

"It was Sunday morning and everybody was just leaving St. Agnes's. All us good Catholics, that is. And this Stevens boy was standing there in his Brooks Brothers boxer shorts, watching all the Catholics going home from church. I'm sure he didn't feel the least bit uncomfortable. We were the ones who felt awkward. The Catholics. I mean, we were all dressed and he wasn't, but somehow *we* were the spectacle. You can't possibly imagine what it's like to sit through a mass with a hangover and then have to get in your car and drive right by some Harvard guy in his underwear."

"I think one of the Stevens boys has a carpenter's license now," Jamie observed. "My grandmother hired him, I think, to work on the house."

Marie sat down on a rock.

"In other words, he's become a carpenter?" This kid must think I'm nuts, she thought. But Jamie did not think that Marie was crazy. He was thinking that she was like the forty-year-old widow he had slept with when he was sixteen. She had turned her huge house in Westport into what amounted to a foster home for minority children. She slept with Jamie because she was grateful to him for helping her, at the club, with her tennis serve. Though Marie's manner was like that of the Westport lady, Marie seemed to be getting entangled in her intentions.

"Why is it that when you kids don't do anything serious you always become carpenters?" she was wondering aloud. "Or you paint houses or mow lawns. Summer job stuff. Handyman stuff. Why don't any of you become commodity brokers and trade only in organically grown soybeans? Or you could open environmental auto dealerships." Why am I cross-examining this nice, sweet kid about his life-style, Marie asked herself.

Jamie shrugged. Then he said, "I don't know. A lot of guys think they want to be doctors or lawyers. Then they get into smoking dope. Then they want to be carpenters."

"You can compromise," Marie said. Compromising used to be part of growing up. Do you know what my oldest son manufactures?"

"No, I don't."

"Ceramic bongs. He's twenty and he didn't go to college. He got through Mount Herman—barely."

"What he's doing sounds interesting."

"One of the pipes he makes is in the shape of a gnome. Like something out of Tolkien. My son says they appeal to young housewives, so I said, 'Maybe Tupperware will add them to its line.' Oh well. At least he's not a carpenter. Am I boring you terribly? I know I must be boring you. I didn't come all the way out here to do that. I wanted to invite you to a party. Tonight. I know this is short notice but . . ."

"What kind of a party?" Jamie asked.

"A dinner dance with lots of people," Marie replied. "People from around here. People like me. We're all a bunch of nervous wrecks, I'll admit, but we can be nice to be with when we have a few drinks and start to relax."

"I don't know," Jamie said. "I haven't been going to a lot of parties lately."

"I'm not asking you to go to a lot of parties—just this one."

"Would I have to dress up?"

"You might want to wear a pair of pants."

Jamie laughed. Marie laughed, too. With her tension finally receding, she peeked at him from under her false eyelashes, which she had been using as a veil. He sure was beautiful. He looked as though he might have been made by Michelangelo—to Arthur's exacting specifications.

"The party is being given by two friends of mine," Marie said. "Arthur and Herbert. They live in the old Cleveland house. You must know where that is?"

"Yes, I do," Jamie said.

"Why don't you come at seven or so? Cocktails start at six-thirty, and they'll be serving a buffet sometime after eight. You can bring along a friend if you'd like."

"I don't know that many people around here," Jamie said. "I think I'll just come by myself."

"That'll be fine. I don't think you'll have any trouble meeting new people at the party."

"Thanks for inviting me," Jamie said.

"It was my pleasure," Marie replied. "Well. I really do have to be going now. Have fun washing your car." For a brief, irrational moment Marie imagined herself being washed in a tub by Jamie. Taking an awkward step backward, she reached for the handle on the door of her Porsche. She got into the car quickly.

"We'll look forward to seeing you tonight, then," Marie called out as she started the car.

"Right," Jamie said. "I'll be looking forward to it, too." As she pulled away, Marie tried to catch a last glimpse of Jamie in her rear-view mirror. In your dreams, she was thinking, you always see a figure like that waving good-bye, and you swear you'll see him again the next time you visit Hawaii—or wherever it is—but then you never ever do make it back. What happens? It's not that Hawaii drops off the map, but somehow it doesn't stay the same, either. A recollection from the couple of years she'd spent teaching grammar school popped into Marie's mind: the way the kids used to set the globe spinning. That inflatable Rand McNally map of the world— the kids would twirl it like a top, until every place you could land on the globe got lost in a pastel blur. That was what happened to Hawaii; it spun away from you. Every magic moment you could ever experience, every place you landed—all of it vanished eventually, became submerged in the endless revolution of days and nights in which the world turned, faster, ever faster.

CHAPTER THREE

Laura seemed to be spending the day in her room. Her room was on the third floor of Blenheim, which was one of the three Georgian-style mansions in the Damon compound. Laura's grandfather had built all three of the houses; he had completed the last one, for his younger son, just before he folded up the Monopoly board and died. The Damon houses stood in a row on one of the hills that rose around the harbor. Like enormous Saratoga trunks, the houses were each fitted with spacious compartments for summer things. At the beginning of the summer the houses were opened, and at the end they were closed. Much of what happened between the opening and the closing was simply forgotten by the Damons and their friends, like stuff made of straw that is not taken back to the city. So Laura could chance upon, in a drawer, a swimming ribbon she had won when she was twelve. She might find on a library shelf a program from a summer stock production starring a has-been actor who had died a year ago. Laura did not enjoy rummaging in her family's summer house: there were too many reminders of overlapping seasons. The house, which slept through every winter, could awaken you to any July or August day within a span of twenty years. Today Laura was reluctantly searching her closet for something to wear to Arthur and Herbert's, something that would make her ready for one occasion that the house would not shut away.

Stumped by her wardrobe, Laura decided to consult her mother. Whenever she was consulted by one of her daughters, Mrs. Damon feigned flattery and surprise. Asked by Laura what she should wear, Mrs. Damon launched a preface: "Wear? What should you wear? I hardly know what to suggest. It is your life, after all. You girls are responsible for yourselves at this point. It was years ago that I gave up calling people's houses to find out where you were."

"I don't think we have to put my choice of a dress into some kind of historical perspective," Laura said. "Think hard, will you? What would look really good on me? Marie Cartey's inviting this terrific-looking guy from the club over to Arthur and Herbert's and I'd like to look—well, *nice*."

"What is he, a lifeguard? I hardly ever go near that club anymore. They used to have the loveliest luncheons, lobster salads. And white linen tablecloths with water goblets and decent silver. What do they serve now? Tunafish salad sandwiches on paper plates. It's appalling the way that place has gone down."

"This guy doesn't work at the club," Laura said. "He's a member."

"A member? Well, who is he?"

"The Lawrences' grandson Jamie."

"The Lawrences!" Laura took some satisfaction in her mother's reaction—she wouldn't have sounded more surprised had one of the marble cherubs in the garden emptied his cornucopia in her lap.

Mrs. Damon had to be sure that what she had just heard was correct.

"A Lawrence. He's actually a Lawrence? You're sure he's not a tennis pro? Or a textbook salesman?"

"Mother, have you been sneaking chocolates again?" Laura asked. "No, don't tell me. I know you have. You always feel guilty about it and then try to compensate by being sarcastic about other people's weaknesses. So what if I was dating a textbook salesman? He wasn't really a textbook salesman anyway; he was just doing that to have something to do. Now he's living on eight acres in Baja California, and sometimes I wish I were there with him."

"Forgive me if I sounded sarcastic, dear, but you must admit that a boyfriend with a listing in the *Social Register* is not exactly what you've accustomed me to. Or your sister either. I suppose she's happy in her marriage, but I can't get used to the way your brother-in-law— my son-in-law—sort of smirks, as though he's come up with a winning lottery ticket. Anyway. What's done is done, isn't it? Let's think about what you're going to wear."

"Let's."

"Goodness. I haven't felt this needed in years." So saying, Mrs. Damon plunged into Laura's closet.

Years before, when Laura's sister, Melissa, announced, at the age of fourteen, that she was going out with a golf caddy, Mrs. Damon had thrown up her hands, given her her own telephone line, and left for two weeks at a weight reduction spa in Arizona. At eighteen, both Melissa and Laura would receive, as every Damon grandchild did, one million dollars plus the interest that had accumulated since birth. From then on, the trustees would see to it that they didn't do anything too foolish. Which was the best one could hope for, Mrs. Damon had concluded.

Melissa had gone to Pine Manor for two years and then married a tennis pro. Who bought himself a new Alfa-Romeo not a month after the wedding. Laura had just been shopping around, her mother assumed, looking for a similar bargain. The idea of her meeting a Lawrence, somebody endowed with an Ivy League education and a legacy from forty different factories, was breathtaking.

At length Mrs. Damon produced a dress. Holding it out on its hanger, she showed it to Laura and said, "I think you should wear this. Definitely." The dress did make the most of what Laura had . . . because it was low cut.

"Do you have the right jewelry?" Mrs. Damon asked. "Would you like to borrow my pearls?"

"I don't think jewelry will impress him very much, Mother. I don't think he's that kind of a guy—he's living in a tent."

Mrs. Damon lit up with recognition.

"Oh, of course. I know exactly who he is now. I heard he was planning to come up here and live in a tent. Lydia Hamilton told me all about him one afternoon when we were shopping in Bendel's. The poor boy."

"What do you mean, 'the poor boy'? What did Lydia tell you about him?"

"What I heard was that he was an only child. His parents were divorced years ago. I never knew them. Anyway, after the divorce his mother—she was English—she became one of those ladies who travel. You know the type. They always have sunglasses on, those sunglasses with the big lenses that look as if butterflies lighted on their eyes."

30

"Yes, I know," said Laura impatiently.

"Well, it seems that a year ago this Lawrence boy was visiting his mother at her hotel in Venice. I think she was staying at the Gritti Palace—for the life of me I can't figure out why those ladies who travel like Venice so much."

"Because it's sinking slowly."

"Oh yes. That's probably it. Anyway, they were having lunch out on the balcony, and he went in the room to get something—I don't know what—and when he came back outside there was his mother, still in her chair, *dead*. Of a stroke. She was only in her fifties, Lydia said."

Laura was silent.

"And that wasn't the only thing. Lydia said that not long after the divorce the father was drowned in some sailing mishap. They didn't find the body for six months. When they finally did find him, the only way they could identify him was by his gold belt buckle."

"He's sort of an orphan, isn't he?" Laura said.

"Let's just say he's become independent at an early age—through a very tragic set of circumstances, there's no doubt about that."

Laura suddenly felt worn out. She said, "Mother, I think this dress will be fine. I think I'd like to rest now, for a while."

"So anyone can understand why the poor fellow likes to be off by himself somewhere. Isn't it nice that he's starting to go out around here?"

"Yes, it's nice. I don't know what's wrong with me. I feel exhausted."

"Oh, that will never do. Looking exhausted. You wouldn't want to show up at Arthur and Herbert's looking like some straphanger on the subway."

"What would you know about subways, Mother?"

"Enough. Actually a woman can look very respectable riding the subways—nowadays, now that everybody has to have a career. But you never want to look like a tired straphanger. You should always have a good book to read. Whether or not you actually read it is beside the point. Just so long as the book is open and you look absorbed in it. Awake. Louis Auchincloss is wonderful for achieving that kind of look. He rides the subways himself, you know."

"Should I bring a book to the party, then?"

"No, just get some rest. Put your head on the pillow and try to get some sleep. Sleep makes everybody look better." Mrs. Damon closed the draperies, which trailed along the floor like imperial gowns. As soon as her mother left the room, Laura stretched out on the bed.

So Jamie Lawrence was an orphan. Of course, he had his grandparents, but they were probably not very supportive if they were anything like the rest of the old people in Cable Harbor—holding themselves up with canes and cocktails. Life certainly could be unkind. Closing her eyes, Laura tried to nap. She was almost asleep when she heard her mother hollering in the hallway.

"She was what? No! She wasn't! Raped! And *murdered!*"

Marie was thinking of writing a guide to male menopause. After returning home from her visit to Jamie Lawrence's campsite, she made herself a vodka and tonic and once more occupied her mind with the project. Chapter One would be *Warning Signs*. Item: when they let their gray hair curl over their ears, you're in trouble; when they dye it black, you're finished. Item: when they start picking out their own clothes at Barney's or Wilkes-Bashford, you're in trouble; when they start receiving gifts of shirts from Bloomingdale's you're finished. And so on.

As Marie was debating about whether she should make lunch or drink it, Arthur called.

"Is he coming?" Arthur asked.

"Of course," Marie replied. "I'm irresistible."

"Oh, good," said Arthur. "I'm glad that's settled. Do you have any idea who did it?"

"I did, of course. I was very persuasive."

"Did you use a blunt instrument or what?"

"No, I used my natural charm."

"I didn't know your charm could be fatal."

"What are you talking about, Arthur?"

"The murder, what else? The girl hitchhiker. You don't mean to say you haven't heard about it?"

"No!"

"Then you better sit down. For one thing, it was your ex-husband who found the body. On the grounds of the Perry House. He was showing around a group of prospective buyers, I guess—and there she was. This dead girl with a knapsack. Now, either she fell out of a hot-air balloon that was trying to cross the Atlantic or the wrong car stopped for her."

Marie was speechless.

"Everybody's up in arms," Arthur said. "Literally up in arms, Marie. It's as if Paul Revere rode through town this morning yelling 'Rape!' Vivian Black called five minutes ago to tell me she's bringing her gun with her tonight—in her evening bag."

Stammering, Marie said, "Arthur, I was . . . out driving today . . . alone. In my car. What if . . . what if I'd broken down and somebody, a stranger had stopped to . . . to . . ."

"I once met a truckdriver that way," Arthur said. "I thought he was gay, but he turned out to be a born-again Christian. That's why he was so solicitous about my flat tire. You can't go through life asking *what if*, Marie. Or pretty soon you'll be afraid to venture out of doors."

"That's just it," Marie replied. "Most people are afraid to go outside the door. That's why they keep coming up here in the summer. Here it's supposed to be *safe*."

Herbert had concluded that being gay does not have to limit you to gay places. He liked living by the ocean, but he did not like the Fire Island Pines or Key West, which he said were not resorts but sandbars (with the accent on the bars). Determined to find a summer place where only the gulls screeched, Herbert discovered Cable Harbor one day in the real estate section of *Town & Country*. At first Arthur was hesitant, but he loved the house and eventually came to enjoy the idea of being one of the token gays in a rich little summer enclave: a New York pansy in a hotbed of Waspy geraniums.

The house Arthur and Herbert bought was an Italianate villa built around the turn of the century. Despite the dark brown shingles and the stone foundation with moss growing on it, the house's cream-colored latticework and swirling staircases projected an air of opera. Inspired by that air, Arthur proceeded to make a stage set of every room. He installed modular seating covered in cranberry velvet and a large pool with a mosaic on the bottom. Where there had been oak panels, Arthur installed mirrors. Theatrical lights twinkled even on the ceiling of the kitchen. After six months of construction, Arthur was satisfied—for a while (Herbert maintained that Arthur, like any other hermit crab, had a primal need to get into bigger and better shells).

At any rate, the Cable Harbor house was yet another showcase for the fabric design firm that Arthur and Herbert owned, and it rapidly became a social centerpiece. Since the redecorated house was an overindulgence, nobody felt shy about going there to drink. So Arthur and Herbert's parties, which were curiosities their first summer in Cable Harbor, were now highlights of the season.

Arthur was concerned that tonight's party might turn into the last page of an Agatha Christie novel, with everybody sitting in a circle waiting for the murderer to be pinpointed, so he told George and Marjorie Hanson, who were catering the party, to pour everyone doubles and plow through every group of anxious low talkers with the canapé trays. Arthur was sure that Marjorie, at least, would not hesitate to overwhelm someone with an hors d'oeuvre. The first time he used them for a party, Arthur had walked into the kitchen while Marjorie and George were having a fight. George was standing by the sink all red in the face and Marjorie was throwing dinner rolls at him. Marjorie's hair was all piled in the wrong place and her pink uniform had popped two buttons in the front, so that she looked like Dolly Parton dressed as a waitress. Discreetly leaving the kitchen, Arthur went back to the party and told a number of his guests that Marjorie and George were a pair of American classics and he was never going to hire anyone else. After that, George's catering service zoomed in popularity, though neither George nor Marjorie ever figured out why.

George had been working all day to set up Arthur and Herbert's latest dinner party. The process was especially aggravating this day, because a lot of things went wrong. Not enough ice had been delivered. The lobsters proved to be two to three pounds apiece, whereas Arthur had specified pound-and-a-half ones—"arranged on the plate sort of squatting on their tails—you know, George, like in *Swan Lake*." Only four girls were available to serve, and one of them had a summer cold and was sniffling loudly. Every so often George had to sit down in order to lower his blood pressure. He was wandering around that afternoon in the kitchen with a two-and-a-half-pound lobster in each hand when Arthur came in to see how things were going.

Biting his lower lip, George gestured hopelessly with the groping live lobsters and then blurted to Arthur, "They're too big, too big." He pointed with one lobster to a vat of scallops and almost shouted, "They're sea scallops. I ordered those nice little Digby Bay scallops and instead they send me these abortions."

"Relax, George," Arthur said. "The mob can eat lobster Newburg, as Marie Antoinette would advise us if she were alive to do a Julia Child segment. And the scallops we can spread on Herbert's rose bushes. When the night crawlers come out they'll think Herbert's running a fat farm."

"See, I told you not to get so upset," Marjorie said. "Over big scallops."

"Then get started with the lobsters," George demanded, and he thrust a lobster at his wife, who was standing behind him. The lobster seized one of her breasts in its claw. Shrieking, Marjorie batted at the lobster with her spatula. George turned to watch in an oddly detached way as his wife pranced about the kitchen, screaming and swatting, with the lobster clinging to her front like an angry baby.

With the chaos in the kitchen finally under control, and the big party tent huffing on the lawn like a stout British matron, Arthur was now settling into his characteristic host's complaisance. Out on the road, the policeman Arthur and Herbert had engaged to direct traffic adjusted his cap.

Just after six-thirty, the automobiles the policeman had been hired to usher began arriving. Many of the automobiles were marked according to an old code—or were unmarked, but still easily identifiable. The wooden station wagons from the twenties and thirties represented seasoned money, enough long-term affluence to preserve a "beach wagon" at a summer house until the vehicle passed from utility to high style, as old Nantucket baskets do. Arriving in a new station wagon did not necessarily mean one was nouveau riche, though. Most of the new station wagons were distinguished by a broad red or beige stripe directly under the side windows. The striping was a caste mark for cars that went back to the days when black Packards had to be picked out in parking lots by their livery. On the doors of some of the arriving Cadillacs and Mercedes were hand-painted monograms, discreet initials like those that appear on the pockets of Brooks shirts, and that provide, socially, the same kind of identification. Among the arrivals were a couple of old Fords, a 1956 sedan eccentric with extra stoplights and gauges, and a 1953 convertible. These old but unblemished Fords were used only in Cable Harbor, in the summer, by owners too far along in years and too secure in their positions in life to care about appearances on the road. They wanted long wear, in their clothes and in their automobiles. It was to the two old Fords, and to an elderly, immaculate black Cadillac, that the policeman tipped his hat. Like all the natives, he knew a thing or two about the summer crowd.

Standing by their front door, Arthur and Herbert followed the progress up the path of their first guests.

"Here comes Flash Donahue," Arthur said. "Who's she leaning on?"

"Looks like Mrs. Lee," Herbert replied.

"It's Amanda Lee all right," Arthur agreed. "I guess this is her evening to keep Flash on her feet. Isn't it heartwarming the way the boozy old girls look out for each other? It really is a lot like the Pines." Arthur stuck his head inside and shouted to George, "Get set to pour. The ladies probably haven't had a drink since five-thirty and they're all afraid that they're going to be murdered in their beds."

George, who was approaching the french doors with twenty pounds of ice, nodded his head vigorously. Arthur's voice seemed to be coming at him from the far end of some dream corridor that he, George, had been waxing for days, until the smell of wax and the constant rubbing, rubbing, in circles, had put him in a trance. Marjorie had seen her husband in what looked like trances all the time of late; he would just stare at string beans, let the shallots simmer until they blackened. And then he'd come out of it and be in one of his rages again. Marjorie blamed the heat in the kitchen in the summer. Sometimes her whole boy felt parboiled.

Homing in on Arthur and Herbert with her watery eyes, Flash Donahue said, "Here we are—oh, it's so nice to see you again."

"It's nice you could come, dear," Arthur replied, taking the old lady's frail hand, which he had described to Herbert as "different from an ordinary hand; like the carcass of a hummingbird, you might say."

"Don't we have an exquisite evening?" Mrs. Lee said, and then, fumbling in her mind with the damper of the day's frightful discovery, added, "Considering what's going on."

"I think it's a simply elegant evening," Flash added. *Elegant* was her favorite word. She used it to distinguish between wealth and poverty, good manners and rudeness, blue sky and clouds.

"You two boys look as elegant as the evening," Flash said.

36

"Wasn't that terrible about that poor young girl? Nobody seems to know who she was. I say it's all the welfare. That's what's doing it."

Arthur smiled reassuringly. And to Flash Donahue and Mrs. Lee his smile, and his elegant appearance, were reassuring. Looking at Arthur, you could hardly believe that there were in the world such things as welfare. Arthur was wearing a blue blazer with eighteen-karat gold buttons, white trousers of paper-thin wool, and shoes made of leather that was as pliant as lettuce. On his wrist was a Corum watch fashioned from a twenty-dollar gold piece, and on a finger he wore a cabochon emerald the size of an olive. Arthur dressed to spite the straight world; he felt it was a matter of principle that the clothes on his back should cost as much as a New York city cop earns in a couple of months.

"I believe in basic values," Arthur liked to point out. "There are those who think they're upholding basic values when they set upon gays in the street with baseball bats. And of course they are; think of what's being defended when you shoot a Harvey Milk: motherhood, Christianity, machismo. But there are higher ideals than those even, and I dress the way I do to defend one of them, the loftiest American ideal of them all, everybody's fundamental belief in . . . *things*."

Herbert disapproved of Arthur's spiteful materialism, his abiding faith in the transcendence of greed, so he kept the gold Rolex Arthur had given him in a drawer most of the time, and winced when his lover appeared in a getup that made him look like a fey bookie. Few in Cable Harbor sensed that Arthur, in his exhibitions of extravagance, was sticking out his tongue at the straight world. Most people found him and Herbert charming—and certainly not at all threatening.

"They accept us," Arthur told Herbert, "because they have money and power; therefore they don't need victims—they have no desire to make somebody *pay*. And of course there's no telling what some of them might have been doing when they were in prep school."

Secretly Arthur was pleased to be accepted by the Cable Harbor crowd; acceptance had eluded him during his boyhood, especially during gym classes, where he was bullied and felt lost on a strange planet governed by those who could throw a football. But in the social atmosphere of Cable Harbor Arthur could breathe freely. He was in his element. And when Arthur and Herbert threw a party

37

everyone came. Anybody who chose not to risked missing the latest trends. Being able to manipulate those trends was for Arthur a way of connecting—which was something he had never been able to do with a baseball and a bat.

By seven-thirty most of Arthur and Herbert's guests had arrived. Flash Donahue had finished three drinks and was wandering around like the problem child in a nursing home. Laura, who had arrived at seven, was telling Marie, who had just walked in, how nice she looked. Marie had not quite recovered from the jolting news Arthur had given her. She said to Laura, "I've got to get a drink right away. All afternoon I kept picturing Dan as some kind of Bluebeard, piling up dead Rockettes in the Perry House."

Nobody saw Jamie Lawrence coming in. When people became aware of his presence, there was, in his path, a parting of the waters. Up and down looks. Herbert saw Arthur spotting Jamie at almost the same moment he noticed Jamie himself.

Uh-oh, he thought.

"My God, what an incredibly beautiful boy," Arthur whispered.

"Now, you behave," Herbert warned him. "This isn't a gay bar, you know."

"All the world's a bar," said Arthur, "and the people merely bottle openers."

Marie caught sight of Jamie on her way back from the bar.

"Whoops—he's here," she said to Laura. "Do you want me to introduce you?"

"I'm not so sure I want to meet him," Laura replied. "If he's been to Harvard Business, he might be capable of murder—how do I know? It often works that way in New York. Harvard men get into publishing firms and then they start taking little earnest copy editors out to lunch and then after lunch they murder them—in their earnest little studio apartments on East Eighty-first Street."

"Oh, don't be so paranoid, Laura," Marie admonished. "I'm sure what happened to that girl Dan found was her own fault."

"The earnest little copy editors are probably to blame for what happens to them, too," Laura said. "At least partly. They do it by the book, poor things."

"Well, I've got to speak to him even if you don't want to," Marie declared. "After all, I did invite him." So saying, Marie stood on tiptoes to pick out Jamie Lawrence in the crowd and then embarked on her mission. Laura sat down to think about life.

Seeing Marie, Jamie smiled and said, "Hi, how are you?" He appeared to be a bit self-conscious. He was drawing on the Mexican tiles of the terrace with the toe of one of his Topsiders.

"I'm so glad to see you made it," Marie said. Before she could say anything more, Arthur materialized.

"Is this ou-ah gentleman callah?" he inquired.

"Arthur, this is the young man I told you about, Jamie Lawrence," Marie said. "Jamie, this is Arthur Conrad, one of your hosts." Arthur and Jamie shook hands. Over by the bar, Herbert was watching. It was amazing to Herbert how swiftly Arthur could cut through a crowd when he wanted to get next to somebody like Jamie Lawrence—who could move in any faster? The shark fin from "Jaws," perhaps. Or an N.Y.U. girl with an Actor's Equity card.

Flash Donahue, who seemed to be guided in her wanderings by the note of a foghorn only she could hear, suddenly came upon Arthur from the rear. She looked puzzled, as though she had no idea what she might have done with the last fifty years of her life.

"Arthur, I don't think I brought the right bag tonight," Flash said. She held up for everyone's inspection her gold lamé evening purse. "Is this bag appropriate, do you think?"

"Gold is always appropriate, darling," Arthur replied. "We're living in one of those eras when everybody should wear a lot of it— seeing how you never can tell if you're going to have to flee across some national border in the dead of night."

Flash was relieved for a moment, but then apprehension shook her by the shoulders again. She said to Arthur, "Have they found out who killed that poor young girl yet?"

"No," said Arthur, "but they're working on it. That sniffling girl who's walking around with the caviar tray is actually an FBI agent."

"How did you ever get her on such short notice?" Flash wanted to know.

"J. Edgar Hoover recommended her to me years ago—one night when I ran into him at the Continental Baths."

"It's nice to know things are under control, isn't it?" Flash remarked to Marie. Marie smiled. Flash said, "I believe I'd like a little more to drink. George mixes up the most elegant Manhattans." And off she went, a bit unsteady on her feet, but evidently confident that the security at Arthur and Herbert's house was tight.

"There's nothing wrong with growing old so long as you can do it with dignity," Arthur observed. "Imagine, she's buried three husbands—that we know of." Not quite looking Jamie in the eye, Arthur said, "My husband is standing over there, by the bar." Pointing out Herbert, he added, "I haven't buried him yet. In fact neither of us is likely to have to be buried. We're entombed in life together. We also have a business partnership, which really seals the tomb. Any gay marriage that lasts until both partners are past forty is inevitably an entombment; ideally you should play it like the last act of *Aida*. Tell me, Jamie, do you think marriage is practical in this day and age?"

"Yes, I think it's practical," Jamie replied. "It's a reasonable expectation. I've always thought of it as a logical step. The first step you take is when you start going out with somebody. Then maybe you start sleeping with somebody. And then the next step is to get married."

"Let's see if I'm taking these steps right," Arthur said. "Step one is social life. Step two is sex life. And step three is marriage, which provides a home life."

"Don't forget step four," Marie put in. "Step number four is divorce, which is the night life."

"So you think marriage is practical," Arthur went on. "Straight marriages, I assume. Herbert and I have a gay marriage. To have a gay marriage involves the same number of steps, but it's trickier, because you're going up the down staircase. Do you think gay marriages are practical?"

"Sure. They're probably more practical in city apartments than they are in other places," Jamie replied. "Because most city apartments don't have staircases."

Pressing the point, Arthur said, "Then you don't object to gay marriages on any principle other than the floor plan of the honeymoon suite?"

"No," Jamie said. "I don't."

"Hm. I may well become a gay divorcé," Arthur concluded. "Listen, you two hold the fort for a while. I'm going over to get Herbert and we'll work our way back here so you can meet him, Jamie."

"Arthur is too much, isn't he?" Marie said to Jamie as Arthur headed for the bar.

"He does seem to have a lot of nervous energy," Jamie replied.

40

"I think he'd be uncomfortable if a conversation went on for more than five minutes without a punch line in it. Maybe he's afraid that if this cocktail circuit ever collapses, people with bridge tables will take over."

"I have that same neurotic fear myself," Marie said.

"So did my mother," Jamie said. "That's one reason why she went to Italy."

"My mother used to have bridge parties," Marie said. "She served M&M's. You know, that melt in your mouth rather than in your hands. No chocolate mess."

"My mother went to parties at Peggy Guggenheim's house in Venice," Jamie replied. "There weren't any M&M's. But a lot of the people there looked as though life had slipped through their hands. That's what my mother said about them. Maybe it's better to have a chocolate mess, huh? That way at least you have something to show."

"No, you have to hide it," Marie said. "No chocolate messes. That's what society is all about—white gloves pulled on over the sticky fingers."

CHAPTER FOUR

"The kid is extraordinary," Arthur was telling Herbert. "Not only is he gorgeous but he's intelligent too."

"Plato used to talk about that kind of hypothesis, I think," Herbert said. "The idea of beauty and brains together has been tantalizing since ancient times."

"Did Plato believe such a combination was actually possible?"

"I think he did," Herbert said, drawing on his scotch for insight. "I think his conclusion was that if you ever run into a combination like that you should try to get him for a lover."

"If only I were younger," Arthur said.

"You're still relatively young," Herbert replied. "You don't think like an old queen yet. You're not popping into the bars in the afternoon with your dry cleaning under your arm."

"I wonder if they're still making martinis over there," Marie said. Politely taking the hint, Jamie said, "I'll check. Gin or vodka?" Marie had an urge to say, "Jet fuel," but instead she replied, "Vodka, please, with just a teensy bit of vermouth and a teensy bit of ice."

As Jamie hustled off on his errand, Marie noticed that he hadn't bothered to stick his feet all the way into his Topsiders. Either that or he'd worked his way out of them while he was talking. His heels were scrunching the backs, so that he was wearing the Topsiders like slippers. How cute, Marie thought. How sweetly adolescent. He isn't even comfortable in those ratty Topsiders. What he likes, basically, is to be naked. Unconsciously, Marie wiped her hands on her dress.

While Jamie was at the bar Vivian Black sidled up to Marie. Vivian was dressed like Carmen Miranda without the fruit hat, and there was a telltale bulge in her evening bag.

"That fellow you were just talking to certainly is handsome," she remarked.

"Do you have a cigarette, Vivian?" Marie asked.

"I thought you were trying to quit."

"I thought I was, too, but the resolutions we make are always subject to circumstances." Trying to keep her eyes on Jamie while he was at the bar, Marie was ducking and dipping like a boxer.

"Am I in your line of vision or something?" Vivian asked.

The alcohol that Marie had consumed before she left for the party, combined with what she had just drunk, was beginning to operate in her on the principle of an air surge oven.

"I just adore his little ass," Marie said.

"Huh?"

"Oh, don't say 'Huh' like that, Vivian, for God's sake. You sound like a seventh-grade girl who's six feet tall. I'm talking about Jamie over there, the handsome fellow I was just talking to. He's getting me another drink. Look at him. Look at his ass. I love their asses when they're that age. They're so little and cute."

Vivian reflected. Then she decided, "I'm not all that anal. I have to do all my own dusting now, and I can't say I enjoy it very much. If you're anal you're supposed to thrive on housework. There's a woman in our therapy group who loves it. Doing housework, I mean. She's anal retentive. That's why she has trouble getting along with her kids. She's so afraid they'll break something. One of the women in our group who's been through est told her she had a feather duster up her ass. I thought that was kind of an uncouth thing to say, whether you've been through est or not."

"What a heroic little butt he has," Marie went on. "Admit it, Vivian, that is one irresistible ass. You've got to admit it. You're a Celtic woman like I am and you know as well as I do that what we Celtic women want is warriors, with muscles in their rumps."

"I really am not sure," Vivian replied, with forlorn sincerity in her voice.

"You're just feeling insecure," Marie said. "I feel that way too sometimes. But I'm never insecure about my sexual desires. I'm as confident about sex as Sister Don Bosco, my sixth-grade teacher, was. Only our gears are different. Sister Don Bosco was always in reverse and I'm always in low, which is the stump-puller gear. I learned that in driving school when I was sixteen."

"I wish I had your self-confidence. I wish I were a little less frightened, especially at night. And I *practice* assertiveness."

"If you want to build up your self-confidence, Vivian, why don't you get yourself a new outfit? You're the one who's been talking about opening a boutique. So dress like you mean business. Get yourself a new Calvin Klein dress and a pair of Gucci sandals and a little pearl-handled Baretta."

"Sh-shh-shhh," Vivian interrupted. "Don't tell the whole world, Marie. I'm very sensitive about my gun." She clutched her evening bag to her breast protectively. Jamie was returning with the drinks.

"Here comes your gallant young friend," Vivian added. "I'll just make myself scarce so you can have him to yourself."

"Have him to myself?" Marie repeated as Vivian was moving away. "If I were to have him all to myself it would be a greater victory than any that's been won before in the history of Weight Watchers."

Alone in the middle of the party, Laura was amusing herself with a fantasy. She had returned to New York and taken the only job she could get: cleaning lady for a small publishing house in the East Forties. One night while she was cleaning she heard a noise. Then the transom above the office door opened and a box was pushed through. The box crashed to the floor and a thousand-page manuscript flopped out. There was the sound of running feet outside the door. Laura took home the manuscript and edited it that very night. It turned out to be *Sweet Savage Love*, only better written. The book became a best seller and Laura was promoted from charwoman to assistant editor.

A week later, James Thurber's grandson came to Laura with a book idea. It turned out to be *Jaws*, only it was better because Laura did most of the writing herself. She was promoted to editor in chief right after the movie came out. Laura went on a trip to the West Coast, where she met a rich woman who had taken the Famous Writers' School course. The woman had written a book that she wanted Laura to see. It turned out to be *The Thorn Birds*, but it was better because it was set in New Zealand, which is a nicer place. Laura was promoted to publisher. Laura began to look like the rich woman from Los Angeles. In fact she started to look like the woman on the cover of *Scruples*—veil and all.

Laura was invited to speak at the graduation ceremonies of Harvard Business School. She wore an academic robe, but she kept on her expensive hat with the veil. Laura did not begin her speech until there was absolute silence. When it was quiet enough for her, she surveyed all the bright young men coolly. Up and down. And from side to side. Then, measuring her words carefully, she said, "Can you type?"

Marie was swallowing her vodka martinis without giving them due consideration. She realized that she was on the verge of becoming irresponsible, and she realized that she did not care if she acted responsibly or not. What difference would it make if she made a fool of herself? There were casualties all over the battlefield. Every day another divorcée got blown away.

"I think they're starting to serve," Marie said to Jamie. "I wish I had more of an appetite—for food. Are you hungry?" Smiling at Marie, Jamie said that he wasn't. He was enjoying Marie's company. She was motherly in her concern for his stomach, yet girlish in her wide-eyed fascination with him. Though Marie was not skinny, Jamie felt in her person the bones sticking out; obviously she was half-starved romantically. It took only a little attention to nurture her.

Catching the sympathetic look on Jamie's face, Marie ventured a confidence.

"I'll tell you a secret," she said. "My ex-husband is the murderer. He works for Spectre. All our restaurants are just fronts—for Spectre. You see, my ex-husband was seduced by a James Bond movie. He sold out to Spectre and ran off with a Rockette who was a Soviet secret agent. That's how the Vietnam War got started, you know. Kennedy liked Ian Fleming."

"I thought he liked Marilyn Monroe," Jamie said.

"His fantasies were probably political *and* sexual," Marie said. "It's sometimes hard to distinguish the difference. I think it was Kissinger who said power is the greatest aphrodisiac."

"I think that's especially true in Italy," Jamie said "that blurring of sex and power."

"And in France they've dumped the political fantasizing altogether, since De Gaulle died. Now it's nothing but sex, sex, sex. The way it is in New York. Except when Mayor Koch is on TV."

"But you can't be sure if Mayor Koch is asexual or just politically independent," Jamie put in.

"That's a point to ponder," Marie agreed. A faraway look came into her eyes.

"My husband was never into politics," she said. "But he sure was into sex. He ran off with a Rockette." Marie paused to drink. Then she said, "Now, most women, when their husbands run off with a Rockette, would turn into the Phantom of Radio City—if you can imagine that. It isn't too hard: black circles around the eyes, white ghostly faces, Playbills from the Saturday matinees. But not me. My life is only just beginning. Do you think it's possible for a woman to find romance after forty? That was the existential question that Helen Trent posed. And I think it's a question that makes Sartre and Kierkegaard look like lightweights."

"Who was Helen Trent?" Jamie asked.

"My alter ego," Marie replied. "You mean you really don't know?" Jamie shook his head.

" 'The Romance of Helen Trent' was a soap opera. On the radio. Which I remember because I'm forty-four years old."

"You don't look it."

"You *are* sweet." Marie reached out to pinch Jamie's cheek, but her hand faltered and instead she picked a thread off his polo shirt.

"I feel a little light-headed," she said. "I think I want to go in the house and lie down for a bit. Arthur and Herbert have guest rooms up on the third floor that used to be servants' rooms. I think I'll just go up there and lie down. Open the window and let in the air." *What on earth do you think you're doing?* Marie's conscience sputtered.

"Sounds like a good idea," Jamie said. One foot was out of its Topsider altogether, Marie noticed.

"Doesn't it, though? I don't want to put you to a lot of trouble or anything, but do you suppose you could bring me up another drink in a little while?" *You are out of your mind. Stop this. Stop it immediately.*

46

"Sure. Be glad to."

"I hope you don't think I'm trying to take advantage of you." *Maniac. Lunatic. You'll be humiliated.*

"No, I don't think that."

"I didn't think you would. You're so sweet. And so gallant. Okay, then. See you in a little bit?"

"Sure."

" 'Bye."

" 'Bye."

Hail Mary, full of grace, the Lord is with Thee.

Marie climbed the brick steps and walked bravely through the french doors. Realizing that she was very, very drunk, she concentrated hard on where she was going. But her heavy concentration provided no more than a loose rudder. The modular furniture seemed at sea; Marie had to navigate around it to get to the kitchen. Arthur and Herbert had installed at one end of the kitchen a stainless-steel restaurant refrigeration unit with multiple doors. Which door had the stuff behind it? Where had Arthur said he kept it? Just "in the refrigerator." That was all Marie remembered.

"Looking for something, Mrs. Cartey?" It was Marjorie Hanson.

"No . . . no, thanks, Mrs. Hanson," Marie replied. "I just came in here to get a tonic."

"George has tonic outside. Where is he? Off in the woods somewhere again? Lately he can't keep his mind on what he's doing five minutes." Marjorie wiped her hands on her big chef's apron; preparing, apparently, to do battle, she then rolled up her right sleeve and searched the counter for missiles.

"I'll wing these cucumber slices at his ears, one by one," she vowed.

"No, no, no, don't do that," Marie said. "I didn't even ask your husband, Mrs. Hanson. I came in here to get a certain special kind of tonic that Arthur keepsh"—damn it, she thought, I'm slurring words—"in the refrig-sure-*rator*."

"Oh, then George isn't asleep at the switch again."

"No,no,no,no."

"That's a load off my mind. But George is really getting terrible that way. He's a typical man, though, I suppose. The reason these truckdrivers run off the road all the time is that their minds are on 'Charlie's Angels.' Or those filthy dirty magazines. What men need is to have sex taken away from them every so often, the way you have to treat a child who gets a drum set and then bangs on it all day long."

"A drumming in your earsh—*ears*," Marie reflected. "I've never thought of it that way before—desire, that is. But men aren't entirely to blame for the way they are. They manufacture so many millions of sperm, and the sperm swarm in their heads, I imagine, like mosquitoes, and so theresh—*there's*—this constant itch that men have . . . I've got to look for my tonic."

"Go right ahead. I think TV shows like 'Charlie's Angels' are just encouraging those sperm to multiply. It's disgraceful."

Marie began to unlatch the doors of the refrigeration unit. Prune juice. Granola. Wheat germ. What looked like eggplant spread. This had to be Herbert's food locker. Marie opened another door. No luck. All lettuce. She tried yet another door. A pitcher of Kool-Aid. A half-eaten Kron macadamia nut bar. Skippy peanut butter. This had to be Arthur's space in the refrigerator. And sure enough, there they were, right in back of the peanut butter: four little amber bottles sealed with white plastic. The bottles had no labels, Arthur said the stuff had been made up in San Francisco by a private chemist, and that these poppers were the best you could get, pure, prescription-quality amyl nitrite. Marie had been invited by Arthur to try it—"the best aphrodisiac in the world other than Warren Beatty," he had said. Marie had replied that she had no reason to try it. Now she did.

Pocketing the little bottle, Marie sidled past Marjorie, who said, "What a funny little tonic that is."

"Did I say I was after tonic?" Marie said. "This isn't. This is . . . for the mosquitoes."

"Didn't George run the insect foggers when he was supposed to?" Marie slipped out while Marjorie, threatening to *get him when he comes back in here*, chose her weapons, this time radishes.

Climbing the stairs, Marie felt with each step as if she were descending into a deep well. She was dizzy with drink and nerves. But she knew there was no turning back now. The kid was a gentleman. And what gentleman, other than Herbert, would refuse a lady's bed? But what if somebody caught them? If Vivian walked in on them they could always make it look like yoga. But what if it were somebody, anybody else?

48

Well, so what? Big deal. A part of Marie felt as complacent about all this as a wicked child. Lodged in Marie's memory was the spectacle of a little girl whose teacher she had been. *The little girl who ate construction paste.* The children had been making Christmas cards out of colored paper. Sequined ornaments and roughly triangular trees. And this one little girl, a pretty little thing, was making a big mess. The construction paste was caked on her fingers. And she started licking it off. Slowly, and with enormous relish. Until her little fingers shone with spit. Marie was aware, as she climbed the stairs, that she was descending—or perhaps ascending—to the level of that little girl whose wanton snacking she had witnessed so many years ago. Suddenly Marie felt capable of sucking Jamie Lawrence's cock.

Arthur had papered the walls of the middle guest room with green Korean grass cloth. The bed, all brass curlicues and paisley bolsters, suggested anything but a good night's sleep. The room was the World of Suzie Wong.

Leaving the door ajar, Marie struggled out of her girdle. She kicked the girdle under the bed and then sat down on the spread to take off her shoes. Free of the restraints of fashion, Marie heaved a sigh. *Freedom.* No marriage. No responsibility. No guilt. No girdle. Ah, to have your hips unbridled at last.

Marie felt as though she had abandoned her old body and entered another. This new, unbridled body had a mind that didn't care about unfaithful husbands, or whether or not the kids went to college and got married and provided grandchildren. This mind and body had no home cooking concerns; all of that stuff was pushed onto the back burner where it belonged. This mind and body would have no problems in a relationship with a younger man. In fact this mind and body might even be able to get up and go jogging with him in the morning. That was how together Marie felt.

But then she began to feel queasy. Picking up a book of matches engraved in gold with the name of the house—Last Resort—Marie lit a cigarette, the emergency smoke she had borrowed from Vivian. A feeling something like a dip in a roller-coaster ride came over her. All the drinks Marie had swallowed suddenly seemed to be loaded on a tray that she was unable to balance on her shoulder. Marie rested her head on one of the paisley bolsters and closed her eyes.

Marie's mother had always liked to talk about people going on

49

pilgrimages. A pilgrimage—the kind of expense-paid vacation the Church would give away if it ever brought bingo to morning television—would ideally be a group trek up a stony hill in your bare and bloody feet. Well, here I am, Mother, Marie thought, at the end of my pilgrimage, unbloodied and unbowed. I've come a long way to reach this room. And now my soul is going to take a nice, warm bath. I'm not going to be ravished. I'm going to be cleansed and purified. In spite of you, Mother; in spite of you, Sister Don Bosco; in spite of you, Daniel Cartey.

Fishing for the bottle of amyl nitrite, Marie began to pick at its plastic seal with her fingernails. The seal was tight, worse than what you'd encounter on a stubborn bottle of catsup. Marie set her cigarette in an ashtray. Taking the bottle in her teeth, she ripped at the seal. It stretched and began to peel away.

Mrs. Lee was acting as spokesperson for Flash Donahue, who was supposed to be chairing the upcoming fashion show but so far had managed only to bend a coathanger. Mrs. Lee was talking to Jamie Lawrence.

"We've been looking for an attractive young man to act as a sort of escort for the ladies as they come off the ramp. Someone to assist by taking their hands. And Arthur suggested you."

"That sounds like pleasant work," Jamie said. "And you say it's for a good cause?"

"A very good cause."

"Okay, I'll be glad to help out."

"Oh, that's simply marvelous."

Marie carefully unscrewed the popper bottle. The cap came off with a faint hiss.

"They shouldn't be allowed to drive cars or own property," Arthur was telling Flash Donahue.

"Who shouldn't?" Herbert asked.

"Welfare recipients, obviously," Arthur replied. "And the same rules should apply to Italian soccer players. Once you reach a certain degree of heterosexuality you should be declared incompetent." Vivian had come upon Laura, who was meditating among the tea roses and had started a conversation with her.

50

"Marie says I should assert myself with a new outfit," Vivian said.

"All you need to assert yourself," Laura responded, "is a Cartier compact from the twenties. One of those snappy Art Deco models. You can snap it shut with a clack in elevators and everybody around you will know how blasé and hardened you are."

At the bar, George Hanson was mixing drinks mechanically rotating bottles and glasses in a rapidly revolving sequence that looked like the pattern of a square dance. All evening George had been watching the breasts of the women guests. Gulping when one of them leaned over and her breasts puffed outward, slipping in his mind through the sharp shadows of cleavage. Nobody, not even Marjorie, had any idea that George was sexually obsessed. An anarchy in his head, a pandemonium of fish market invoices and Propa-ph falling in the sink and Marjorie's demands, had given way to one clear, compelling siren song. *Tits*. George often put himself to sleep at night saying the word over and over to himself. Tits, tits, tits. The very word was luxurious forming in his mouth. Nothing else mattered as much. It was as though in his middle years George had slipped into an adolescent fixation; he was constantly building boob models in his mind, and the glue was going to his head. Boobs, tits, knockers, breasts, all in pairs, two to each set: they filled every shelf; they dangled from the ceiling.

Gingerly putting the bottle to her nose, Marie took deep breaths, as Arthur said you should, inhaling first through one nostril, then through the other. The stuff entered her sinuses like a mist of ginger ale. Nothing happened. Then abruptly, the room depressurized. Marie's head felt like a balloon into which someone with hot breath was blowing. Swaying, she lost her grip on the bottle. It fell onto the bedside table, and its volatile contents spilled over the ashtray where Marie's cigarette was burning. The chemical ignited in a flash.

While he was at the bar ordering Marie's drink, Jamie Lawrence noticed a good-looking girl. The girl was talking with a very tanned, fortyish woman who had a lot of gold bangles on her arms. That one is pretty nice, Jamie thought. The good-looking girl reminded him of Botticelli's *Venus*. He undressed her mentally and stood her in a seashell, on which she rose from beneath the sea. Or got out of the tub. Naked and soaking wet, in any case.

"There's a woman in our therapy group who's been through est," Vivian told Laura. "She says I'm eating myself up with penis envy."

The paisley bedspread caught fire while Marie was trying to beat out the chemical flames with it. In a panic, she fell back against the brass headboard like a moth pressed to a screen. The bottom seemed to have dropped out of time; for perhaps five seconds she was unable to move.

Then, her reflexes returning, Marie jumped up and grabbed the cut-glass decanter on the bureau. She hurled the contents of the decanter at the flames, but instead of extinguishing them, whatever was in the decanter made the flames flare even more fiercely. Dumbly, Marie looked at the empty decanter. Her hand was sticky. Good God. It wasn't water. It was *Cointreau.*

Yelling "Fire," Marie fled the room. She tripped in the corridor and her knee thudded into the carpet. Thick as the carpet was, the hardwood underneath it struck like a hammer. Marie somehow got up and hobbled to the stairs.

"Fire," she shrieked. Waving and limping as if she were in a three-legged race, Marie started down the stairs.

When she reached the foyer, all out of breath and streaked with sweat, Marie was on the verge of fainting. Laura and Vivian were waiting in the foyer, in front of the door to the powder room, when Marie appeared. They saw her at the same moment, and their mouths fell open and their eyes widened in an accord of astonishment.

Marie sagged to the stairs. Vivian grabbed at the clasp of her evening bag. It flashed into Marie's mind that Vivian was going to pull her gun out. And then Marie fainted.

CHAPTER FIVE

"Arthur, we've got to clear everybody out of here quickly," Herbert whispered.

"What on earth are you talking about?" Arthur replied.

"There's a fire. Up on the third floor. The fire department is on its way." Arthur peered around one of the ivy-garlanded tent poles in order to survey the house.

"What fire? I don't see any fire."

"It's in one of the guest rooms. The detail cop tried to handle it with a fire extinguisher, but it had too much of a head start."

"You say the fire department is on its way?"

"Yes."

"Well then, what's the big deal?" Arthur set down his drink and cupped his hands to his mouth. He shouted out, "Everybody. Can I have your attention, please? Everybody. Attention. Please." The rumble of the party stopped. Arthur continued. "I have an announcement to make. We're all going to have to confine ourselves to the tent for a while because the house is on fire." Anxious murmuring began. First a murder—*in Cable Harbor*—and now *the house was on fire?* As if stirred by some Jungian race memory of the French Revolution that was generic to their class, a number of women clutched the jewels at their throats.

"This party now has a disaster theme," Arthur announced. "It's *Towering Inferno* time. Somebody tell Ida to play *There's Got to Be a Morning After.*" As if on cue, the sirens of the Cable Harbor volunteer fire department were already wailing in the distance. Giving stage directions, Arthur said, "I'll need three or four able-bodied men to help get the piano out on the lawn. We can't have a party without music." The tennis pro from the golf club and three tennis-playing husbands brought the piano screeching out onto the terrace. Ida the piano player, a Mount Holyoke girl with glasses who looked ready to consecrate her life to library science if only she could get out of this, had to sit down again and play requests like *Smoke Gets in Your Eyes.*

The first piece of firefighting equipment arrived. It was a 1948 Mack that looked like a red Kitchenaid Mixer with wheels and a bundle of thick gray cord. Arthur yelled to the firemen, "You fellows be sure to get drinks from George." By now smoke was puffing from the dormer window on the third floor, "just like the old Camel sign," Arthur observed with delight. Trailing hoses, the firemen tramped into the house. Upstairs, the sound of enthusiastic breakage began. A particularly loud crash came from the burning room, and the partygoers oohed, as though they were watching fireworks. A bit of smoldering chintz sailed from the window. Then a fireman's head poked out. He waved. Everyone cheered and applauded.

Bearing a plate full of lobster with the Newburg sauce scraped off and spinach salad, Vivian sat down with Arthur.

"Your poor house," she sympathized.

"It's worth the redecorating to have a bunch of firemen here," Arthur replied. "I've always wanted to see some of them in action."

"What's happened to Marie?" Vivian wanted to know.

"She's in Herbert's study with him, apologizing all over the place, I suppose," Arthur said. "Don't forget that Marie had a Catholic girlhood. She still has a need to confess and be forgiven. And Herbert still has guilt feelings about being gay, so they complement each other rather nicely. Marie confesses and Herbert receives her confessions. On the whole, Herbert prefers to receive confessions of love, but any little confidence will do, as long as there's an air of absolution."

"Marie does seem to be drinking an awful lot lately, though," Vivian said. "It worries me."

"Her life is in transition right now," Arthur replied. "Making transitions can be treacherous."

"Don't I know it," said Vivian. "Getting from one stage in your life to the next . . . even from one experience to another. The leader of our therapy group says that for a lot of us it's a rocky road even to reach an orgasm."

"No orgasms without your rocks," Arthur agreed.

"I just don't want Marie to get into real trouble with her drinking," Vivian said. "She reminds me of that old fairy tale, 'The Red Shoes.' You must remember that story. The one about the girl who puts on a pair of red dancing slippers and can't get them off again. The slippers won't let her stop dancing. Day and night she dances . . . until she dies. I forget what happens to the red shoes."

"Were they Capezios?" Arthur asked.

"Herbert ought to tell Marie to take a nice hot bath," Vivian said.

"Now, there's an idea," Arthur replied. "I've been thinking of installing a hot tub up here. Your therapy group could use it. I understand they're great for staging little psycho dramas. Like holding your mother's head underwater until she explains why she made you ashamed of your privates when you were a child."

"Oh, Herbert, I could just die," Marie was saying. She was sitting on the Chesterfield sofa with her fists pressed against her eyes, and Herbert was dabbing her forehead with a cool, damp facecloth.

"It was an unpredictable chemical reaction," Herbert said softly. "An accident."

"Oh, sure it was . . . like Mrs. Murphy's cow starting the Chicago fire by upsetting a lantern with her tail. Probably Mrs. Murphy told her the bull was coming over later . . . and she got all excited. I can relate to that. The restless horniness of an old cow . . . that leads to a general conflagration."

"I wish you'd stop putting yourself down all the time, Marie," Herbert said. "You're a very wonderful, very worthwhile person."

"Don't waste your time trying to build me up," Marie said. "I'm not worth the effort. I'm nothing but a wreck. I'm a ruin. And I spread wreckage everywhere I go. I'm a Helen of Troy . . . without the looks . . . and without the parade of . . . Trojans? Following me."

Unmasking her eyes, Marie blinked at Herbert. He was trying to suppress a laugh.

"That didn't come out the way I meant it to," Marie said.

Herbert laughed out loud.

"I know it. I know I'm ridiculous," Marie said. "I'm a pathetic, comic figure." A tear rolled down her cheek. Herbert wiped it off with his fingers. Reaching over, he hugged Marie.

"I'm so sorry I cause all this trouble for everyone," Marie said. "When I was little . . . I'd go along with my mother to the hairdresser's. And while she was getting her hair done, I'd go around with a magnet and pick up all the loose bobby pins on the floor. They all said how I'd be such a wonderful homemaker when I grew up . . . because I did such a good job picking up bobby pins. . . . I'd keep my house neat as a pin, they said. But I can't keep anything neat. Even though I have a maid now. Is that what life is? Do you just keep making bigger and bigger messes?"

Herbert got up and walked over to the wall. He touched a picture frame, and it glided upward, revealing a steel door. Twisting the combination lock on the door, Herbert opened it. He removed a file folder and flipped it open to show Marie what it contained.

"These are the records on this house," he said. "Everything Arthur and I have spent up here; it's all in alphabetical order. I also have in this safe part of my coin collection, which I've been cataloging. There are also a couple of stacks of new hundred-dollar bills. Everything is as neat as a pin. But it doesn't represent happiness, Marie. Just organization. Dry accounting . . . that's locked up in a fireproof safe, where there's not even air to breathe."

Pulling a matchbook from Lutèce out of his pocket, Herbert flipped up the cover with his thumb and held the row of matches out to Marie, as if to prove his point.

"Look," he said. "There's nothing neater or more organized or more pat than a matchbook—when it's fresh. But it gets pulled apart, bit by bit. Eventually it all goes up in smoke. But if a matchbook stays in somebody's pocket for a while, it may get to go to a few parties; it may even get left by the bed in some exotic hotel somewhere. So even though it winds up pulled apart you can at least look at it and say it's been around. And that's something."

"What are you trying to tell me?" Marie asked. "What should I do? Start a fire in a hotel room in Singapore?"

"No, Marie. I'm trying to tell you to stay the way you are. Be one of the people whose hair is always down because she can't be bothered trying to locate bobby pins anymore. Don't be on your knees . . . picking up after yourself. You've outgrown that. Be glad that you have."

Laura, who looked apprehensive, approached Vivian and Arthur. She said, "I was just thinking, Arthur—those parrots you have in the kitchen. Do you think they're all right?"

"The fire's upstairs," Arthur said. "I doubt there's any smoke in the kitchen. Don't worry about them."

"I think I want to go see for myself," Laura said, and she went off on her errand of mercy.

"Laura's so humane," Vivian observed. "Maybe that's why she's never been married. She's the type who would do the dishes the night he tells her it's all over."

Laura pushed through the kitchen door. The parrots resided in bamboo cages among the ferns and space-age kitchen cabinets. There was no smoke in the kitchen, and the parrots were eyeing everything with their usual cocked heads. Marjorie was still there running things. She asked Laura if she wanted some mosquito repellent too.

"No," Laura said. "I just wanted to check on the parrots."

"Oh, they're fine," Marjorie said. "I think they must know something I don't—they're not working for a living. How is Mrs. Cartey? They warn you about those aerosol cans. But I can't imagine how such a little bottle of 6-12 could . . . and why do they keep it in the refrigerator?"

"I guess it's highly concentrated stuff," Laura replied.

Marjorie shook her head in a kind of general disbelief. "Think of it. Mr. Conrad refusing to let the party end even with the house on fire. I guess parties are pretty important to the gay boys."

"Arthur says he goes to parties and bars for the same reason some people look at apartments when they have no intention of moving—so you can appreciate how well off you are . . . at home. Marie Cartey told me he said that to her. She said he said every party and every bar is a religious experience—sort of like Christ wandering in the desert. He said all the gay bars are full of gay Christs."

"That sounds sacrilegious to me," Marjorie replied. "But still you can't say much against Mr. Conrad. He's the soul of generosity."

"He is, isn't he?" Laura concurred. "Well, I suppose I'll get back to the party now."

"Have a good time," Marjorie said. "I should get out there myself, to check on George. See that he isn't sitting reading *Penthouse* or something."

Laura felt silly because she had been so concerned about the parrots. Still, there was enough guilt in the world without finding Arthur's exotic birds all flopped over on their backs in the morning. Laura wandered over to Herbert's greenhouse and sat down on an overturned clay pot to be by herself for a while. Propping her chin on her knuckles, she contemplated the black moss between the white marble stepping-stones that shone in the moonlight.

The party had certainly turned out to be bizarre. Laura wasn't one to revel in such nights, the way Arthur did. Ten years before, when Laura was still in her teens, she had been introduced to down-East decadence, and as was the case with European decadence, it simply wasn't Laura's style. She had gone out with three boys. Since one boy's family was away, the four of them went to his house to shoot pool. Halfway through the first game, Laura realized that she was the object of a three-way hustle. The more beer the boys drank, the more pointedly interested they became in Laura. They fell over each other to help her make her shots. They grinned at her. They leaned on their pool cues in adolescent caricatures of macho poses.

After the billiards, the boys decided, at 3:00 A.M., to go skinny-dipping in the pool. They invited Laura, but she demurely volunteered to go to the kitchen instead and whip up some scrambled eggs. Knowing that Laura would have a clear view of the pool area from the kitchen window, the boys turned on the floodlights. And Laura looked. She couldn't resist; it was like in *Hud*, when Patricia Neal pauses at the kitchen sink when she sees Paul Newman with his shirt off. Dishes or no dishes, eggs or no eggs, desire is desire. Facts are facts. Brazenly naked, the three boys shouted, pushed each other, sprang up and down on the diving board, and exchanged wisecracks that produced guffaws. Laura knew that she was being talked about; they were probably trying to figure out who had the best chance with her. That would be a pointless discussion, because Laura had been evenly, diplomatically pleasant and noncommittal to each of them. Nobody was going to get grass-stained tonight.

Laura was sure that most of her girl friends—her sister, for that matter—would be out by the pool handing out towels if they were in her position. It wasn't modesty that kept Laura in the kitchen, though; it was a kind of pride, a schoolgirl's daydream, perhaps—

you don't hand a bath towel to just anybody. Virginity might not be precious anymore, but certain intimacies were, in Laura's mind. At sixteen, Laura was sure of herself in this regard at least: you'll never be able to construct anything if you casually scatter the little building blocks of love.

When Laura and her three frustrated boyfriends left the house at six, in her Mustang, the streets of Cable Harbor were still mostly empty. On Ocean Drive, Laura swerved sharply to avoid a robin who flitted into the path of the car, but she was not quick enough. The bird thumped into the grille. Laura stopped. There was nothing she could do. Tenderly, she picked up the broken robin and set it on the shoulder of the road. The boys told Laura, "Forget about it. It wasn't your fault." One of them put his arm around her to console her. This is what I get for staying up all night with these guys, Laura thought. If I'd been home in bed I wouldn't have hit that poor bird.

Before she finally did go to bed, a little after seven, Laura stood in front of the sink staring at the faucets. Boys run hot and cold, she was thinking. Either they're horny or they're not. But we girls, we turn on to *warmth*. So we suffer over dead robins. Laura washed her face with warm water and went to bed, but the daylight was so strong in her room that she couldn't sleep. So she got up after two hours, exhausted herself by playing tennis, slept a little in the afternoon, and vowed not to get caught up in wild nights anymore.

Remembering the robin she had killed in the unnatural act of driving down the road at 6:00 A.M., Laura could now at least console herself with the knowledge that Arthur's parrots were safe and sound.

"Hi," somebody said. Laura looked up. It was Jamie Lawrence.

"This is kind of a crazy party, isn't it?" Jamie said. "Do you mind if I pull up a flower pot and join you?"

"No," Laura replied. "I'd like some company." I'm melting, Laura thought. Damnit. If only there were some way you could be attracted to a man and not show it. Stop *radiating*, she commanded herself. Stop *smiling* like a little idiot. Remember, this guy is a Harvard M.B.A.

"I'm Jamie Lawrence."

"I'm Laura Damon."

"I don't know many of the people here. Mrs. Cartey invited me. She was going to sort of introduce me around—but she got distracted."

"That's putting it mildly. Poor Marie."

"You know her?"

"She's a good friend, yes."

"She was going to rest awhile upstairs. And I was going to bring her a drink. But the fire department got there first. With water. Which I assume she doesn't drink all that often."

"Well, she's divorced . . . and she does drink a little too much. It was one of those cases where part of the solution became part of the problem."

"There's a lot of divorce around here, isn't there?"

"Yes, there is. And now there's been a murder. I think I liked it better when all this town amounted to was simple, nonviolent, daytime soap opera."

"Maybe it's the red tide," Jamie said.

"The what?"

"The red tide. You know. The microorganisms that make shellfish toxic. Maybe murder is a form of red tide. Always out there. How do we know that distant roar we hear up here at night is the waves breaking? It could just as easily be the sound of the red tide . . . rushing through the cities."

"That sounds like one of the horror stories I used to hear when I was a kid," Laura replied. "Something awful floating to the surface. But it turned out to be just a bar of Ivory soap, if I remember the ending rightly. Say, what are you trying to do, make me afraid of the dark?"

"No," Jamie said. "I was only trying to identify the fear that's in the air here . . . in these waters . . . wherever. Red tide seemed as good a way of labeling it as any. There was a time when most of the people in this country thought mainland China was the red tide."

"And all it turned out to be was part of the Bloomingdale's catalog," Laura added. "Wouldn't it be nice if all our fears wound up on the shelves in Bloomingdale's? If nobody got any closer to actual violence than going into Bloomingdale's bookstore and picking up something by Truman Capote?"

Laura noticed that Jamie's polo shirt was open, revealing his chest. A giddiness came over her.

"I assume you're the Jamie Lawrence who's living in a tent," she said. "Are you a hiker, too?"

"I see word travels around here," Jamie replied. "Yeah, I'm living in a tent. But I'm not a hiker. I did do some hiking when I was living in England, but now I'm kind of turned off by the back-packing crowd. The *Rocky Mountain High* shit. I can't deal with people who burst into song when they reach the summit."

"I know what you mean. When I saw *The Sound of Music* I wanted to chase Julie Andrews across that alpine meadow with a riding lawn mower."

"You got it. Too much fresh air and glowing good health can be sickening. Every time I see one of those Sunkist Orange soda ads I want to swear off Frisbee playing forever."

"Right. And it's not just those pimple-free adolescents that drive you crazy. What about the romantic idealizations of family life that they put on TV? 'Eight Is Enough.' Blech. I like a realistic view of the way people interact in a family unit—like when Mike Wallace has somebody really *cornered* on 'Sixty Minutes.'"

She looks English, Jamie was thinking. He recalled a cockney girl he had met in a theater queue in London. The girl had bright red rouge on her cheeks and was wearing lipstick that looked plastic. And she was irresistible, bubble gum packaged in a damp Shetland sweater, a lollipop that licked back. Jamie was seventeen at the time. Now, seven years later, he had not forgotten the cockney girl. The night he spent with her in London had been transfigured into a primary sexual response; as he looked at Laura, who was sexy in the same way as the cockney girl, Jamie was becoming more and more interested.

"After all, it's in your family that you first learn that reality is what other people want, and idealizations—daydreams—are what you want—" Laura was cut off in mid-sentence by the expression on Jamie's face. There was no mistaking the meaning of it. Laura blushed.

Jamie eased his arm around her.

"Oh dear," Laura said.

"What's the matter?" Jamie asked.

"Nothing. Well, actually, something. You went to Harvard Business, didn't you?"

"How'd you know that?"

"Oh, a little birdie told me."

"Marie told you?"

"Yes, she finds out things about people. It's one of her hobbies."

"What else does she know about me?"

"After Harvard Business, it's mostly speculation."

"Marie should start a stamp collection," Jamie said. "I think she needs something to keep her occupied."

"That's exactly what my mother's dog groomer said about her Westy—'Tippy should start a stamp collection so she won't be chewing herself all the time.'"

"I don't think I'm following you. I asked you if something was the matter and you said I went to Harvard Business. Does that create some kind of a problem?"

"Not really. It's just that I'm a little wary of guys from Harvard Business. I was fired from my job by a Harvard M.B.A. I was working for a publishing house and they brought this guy in and he decided he wanted more of a male organization. So I was one of the people who got the ax."

"That's sex discrimination, isn't it?"

"Not the kind that can be proved. Anyway, what happened to me—and some things that happened to a couple of girl friends of mine—sort of made me wary of Harvard Business graduates. Women go off with them and are never seen or heard from again. One or two have turned up years later . . . in country clubs in Westchester . . . drunk."

"You can't condemn a whole race of people for the actions of a few," Jamie said.

"I'm not, I'm not," Laura replied. "But you can't blame me for being a little . . . wary."

"You shouldn't be. All business schools do is make charts of the paths that the guys with jungle instincts have been following for years. But they don't turn out many guys with a sense of the jungle. They turn out organization men . . . who look for abandoned burrows. Your girl friends probably got stung because they went into the burrow without sniffing around first."

"You're really quite metaphorical," Laura observed.

"My mother used to send me first editions of Byron," Jamie explained. "And Shelley. And Ezra Pound. She was into metaphors of frailty . . . and self-destruction . . . and exile."

"Your mother must have been a remarkable woman," Laura said.

"She once told me that in a previous life she was the wolf who nursed Romulus and Remus," Jamie replied. "She was living in Florence at the time. With a Scottish art student about my age."

The gentle pressure of Jamie's fingers on her arm almost made Laura shiver.

"You're certainly not a typical Harvard Business type," she said. "Whatever prompted you to go there?"

"The family foundation," Jamie replied. "Somebody has to run it. Since my father died they haven't been doing much besides give grants to college professors who operate Xerox machines."

"That's only natural, though, isn't it?" Laura said. "Higher education *is* Xeroxing, isn't it?"

"Yeah, I suppose so," Jamie said. The expression on his face was again unmistakable. Laura sat still but lurched inside. Suddenly Jamie's presence—there in the dim light, next to her—was overwhelming. Laura felt herself being enveloped; she felt as though she were going to fly out of her skin. And then he did it. He kissed her.

When she caught her breath, Laura said weakly, "My, but you do that well. Whatever prompted you to do that?"

"Errant desire."

"Goodness. Desire among the rose trellises. I feel like the heroine of a Regency romance. I don't suppose you've ever read one of those, have you? But they're reassuring to large numbers of women nowadays—because the sex is put off until after the end of the book. . . . Tell me, do you always act this way with strange women?"

"No, sometimes I hang around museums—dangling one of the volumes of Shelley that my mother gave me."

"What do you do about women who aren't vulnerable to fallen Romantic poets?" Laura asked.

"You mean the sort of woman who goes to Harvard Law?"

"Yes."

"I used to ask them if I could carry their books for them," Jamie replied. He kissed her again. And Laura felt herself yielding. For now, anyway.

"Two of the guests just said good night," Arthur told Vivian. "Laura and that Lawrence boy. I said to him, 'Be sure and come again.' I told him, 'The next party we have, we're going to torch the gazebo.' "

"Oh, please, Arthur, no more mayhem," Vivian pleaded. "It's getting to be too much. Murder. Arson. Everybody trying to score at cocktail parties. I don't know what the world's coming to."

"Have you ever been in a bar trying to score when the music suddenly stops?" Arthur asked.

"No, I haven't," Vivian replied.

"Then you've never experienced limbo," Arthur said. "Take my word for it. We need loud music and we need a certain amount of mayhem. They provide shelter."

"It seems silly to be driving two cars," Laura said.

"Is it okay to leave your car here all night?" Jamie asked.

"Sure. That's one of the things Arthur likes most about throwing parties. The next day he walks around to see what people have left behind. Once he found a pair of pantyhose that way."

Jamie opened the door for Laura. There was nothing boorishly preppie about the gesture—he seemed unconsciously solicitous. Still, having car doors opened for her was not what Laura was used to— or wanted—in her relationships with men. She had become accustomed to letting herself into cars. And more often than not, she did the driving.

Jamie turned the ignition key and the van rattled to life. It was a typical old Volkswagen, with an engine that accelerated with a noise like a fusillade of popguns.

Out on the shore road, Jamie glanced at the rearview mirror and said, "Looks like we're going to run into a snowstorm." So saying, he jerked the mirror out of its mount and handed it to Laura. Then he reached over and opened the glove compartment. Inside were some maps. And some coke.

Balancing the rearview mirror on her lap, Laura measured the cocaine into six fine lines with a razor blade. She handed Jamie a straw, and held the mirror just under his chin. Putting the straw to his nose, Jamie drew in a line and passed the mirror back to Laura. She followed suit.

"This isn't cut with anything, is it?" Laura asked. "There's no quinine or anything in it, is there?"

"No," Jamie replied. "It's pure."

"How did you ever get such wonderful stuff?"

"My roommate at Harvard Business was Colombian," Jamie said. "We keep in touch."

"I'll never say anything again about Harvard Business . . . *connections*," Laura resolved.

Jamie just smiled.

CHAPTER SIX

When Vivian returned home from Arthur and Herbert's party she made her usual rounds. First she locked the front door behind her (it was a dead-bolt lock that had to be opened with a key even on the inside). Then she went around checking the sliding doors, which were jammed with aluminum crossbars. And she pulled all the draperies. Vivian's house was directly on the harbor, but its single occupant saw to it that it was never a beacon for anyone—except when she was out and the lights were on their automatic timers.

Laura had to go to the bathroom, but she realized that Jamie's tent wouldn't have any plumbing. Climbing out of the van, she said, "Where's the bathroom? In the bushes?"

"There's a Porta-John right over there," said Jamie, pointing. Sure enough, there it was: a white fiberglass outhouse that looked like the nose cone of a rocket.

"My grandmother had it sent over from a company that supplies construction projects," Jamie explained. "It was her idea to do it. She said, 'Camping out is fine—but there are limits.'" Laura felt grateful that Jamie's grandmother was aware of people's limits; perhaps she was one of those matrons who don't like waiting in line to use the ladies' room at the Met. She said, "I'll be right back," and headed for the Porta-John. Though the john was only about fifty feet from the tent, Laura still looked about her in the moonlight before she went inside. Even in her coke-induced euphoria, Laura was aware of the long shadows around her, the trees, the bushes. Where somebody could be hiding. It was terrible to be looking over your shoulder in Cable Harbor, to feel exposed, the way you feel on a subway platform late at night. But a girl had been killed. Who was going to be next? Son of Sam thought a dog was telling him to kill people; up here there might be a giant lobster or something calling out to some lunatic from the ocean depths.

For six years Vivian had been taking Valium. Her doctor in New York lectured her about it constantly: "That stuff is psychologically addictive. You'll be taking it every day, you wait and see. The day you don't take it you'll immediately get depressed." Then Vivian had found out from one of her girl friends that the doctor himself had been an alcoholic—and psychologically dependent on Valium at the same time. He had admitted as much to some of his patients, though with Vivian he had kept his counsel—except to tell her *no*. What a hell of a nerve. The only thing worse than the preaching of a reformed drunk had to be the bunk Dr. Callahan was spouting: a reformed nervous wreck has all that much more nervous energy to use to browbeat you.

The doctor in Cable Harbor was different. His office was in the double parlor of his old federal house; when Vivian went there she felt almost as comfortable as she'd felt when she was a child going to visit her grandmother. Dr. Wallace looked like some quizzical character actor out of the thirties. With his high gloss, pomaded hair, and habitually pursed lips, he could have stepped right into Edward Everett Horton's shoes and prescribed a cocktail for Fred Astaire.

Dr. Wallace was beloved in Cable Harbor for his sympathy, his modest fees, and his habit of walking into restaurants with his stethoscope hanging out of his jacket pocket. When Vivian went to him and saw that he was a chain smoker, she had a feeling he wouldn't be self-righteous about Valium. He wasn't. With Dr. Wallace prescribing for her, Vivian had gone from ten milligrams of Valium a day to eighty. With the result that her system sometimes brought her up short in the middle of the night—or even in broad daylight. My God, Vivian would suddenly think—for no apparent reason—am I going to be able to deal with the crowd in that store?

66

Can I even get myself across the street? The feeling was like a loss of blood in the brain.

Even after she started with the Valium, Vivian was nervous driving a car. Sometimes she grew edgy walking the dog; what if he got away from her and ran out into the traffic? Vivian was told by her analyst that her irrational fears probably were rooted in a childhood experience in which Vivian felt exposed and vulnerable. Trapped, somehow. But Vivian was never able to put her finger on one particular event. She did recall, though, that as a child her hand had been shaky. Sometimes she would rattle her cup like a feeble old woman. And she still would tremble occasionally: when somebody was watching her pour, or light a candle, or when she was trying to hold the little plastic plate in her mouth for a dental X ray.

Two years before her marriage ended, Vivian had gone to a photographer for a passport photo. At the time she was taking fifty milligrams of Valium a day. That was not enough to keep her from freezing in front of the camera. Her mouth started twitching as the photographer said "Smile." Staring at his hand, which he was holding out to one side, his thumb poised to trigger the shot, Vivian fought to get control of the expression on her face. But she couldn't. In the photograph she looked as if she'd seen a ghost.

Inside the Porta-John was a battery-powered lamp. Two mosquitoes were hovering around it, so Laura didn't waste any time. The toilet flushed with a blue swirl, the way a toilet in an airliner does. Laura felt a bit airborne anyway—that certainly was incredible coke.

Bringing along a flashlight, Laura and Jamie walked out to the edge of the cliff. Far below them the black water stirred, sighing in its rhythmic sleep. Impulsively Laura shone the flashlight upward. The beam rose perhaps a hundred feet and then stubbed itself out in the sky. Craning her neck, Laura followed the pole of light to its vanishing point under the handle of the big dipper.

She said, "Is it true that when you shine a light at the sky it keeps on traveling . . . right out into space?"

"I think that's true," Jamie replied. "It keeps on going until it hits a planet, or else it continues to move away from us—forever . . . which was the way my mother described the process of growing up."

Not knowing quite how to respond to that, Laura flicked off the flashlight and nestled against Jamie's chest.

"Sky," she whispered. "Endless sky. And endless sea. There's so much beauty up here. But people get used to it all and then they become indifferent. They miss all the beauty. It's too bad people are like that—indifferent. It's hard to recognize more than two kinds of people these days: the indifferent, and the violent."

"A lot of people just pretend they're indifferent," Jamie said. "But inside they're going bananas. When I was a freshman at Yale I knew a guy who never bothered to open a book, he was so indifferent. At least that was the impression he gave. But then one day he threw a package of tomatoes at a philosophy professor—the whole package—he didn't even bother to take off the cellophane. The next day he left for Paris. I think he's still there, trying to become a concert flutist."

"Sometimes you realize that the kids you met in school had more to teach you than the professors," Laura said. Jamie was stroking her hair thoughtfully. Laura was aware of his heartbeat. He kissed her. In the kiss Laura felt magic: the scarf flies from the sleeve, unreeling by the yard, intertwining, until the bolt, the very bone inside you, is bare.

For an instant, a small white scratch appeared in the sky.

"Oh," said Laura, "a shooting star. That means another soul has gone to heaven. Remember 'The Little Match Girl,' by Hans Christian Andersen? She was always seeing shooting stars, poor thing. And then one night the star was hers. She froze to death. Trying to keep warm . . . by lighting her matches."

"The shooting stars above, the red tide below," Jamie said.

"I feel safe now, though," Laura said. "Whether there's a murderer at large up here or not. I feel safe out here . . . with you. Is that naïve, to feel that way?"

"No, it's romantic," Jamie said. "Let's go back to the tent."

"Yes, let's," Laura said.

Vivian's daughter, Samantha, was spending the summer on an archaeological dig in England, the purpose of which, as far as Vivian could determine, was to unearth Roman kitchen utensils and sleep with the French boy with socks drooping over his ankles whose photograph had come in the mail at the end of June. Vivian's son,

Stan, was in Denver with a beard and a Jeep. So he wasn't going to be around either. Her ex-husband, Vivian imagined, was probably commuting between the city and Kismet. With all those swinging types who went jogging on the beach in bikinis and gold chains. She wondered if that dirty-minded little paralegal ever joined him in the city for lunch. Probably she did, and afterward they'd walk arm in arm up and down the aisles of Saks, she pointing out to him all the things she wanted.

Realizing she was going to be alone in the house this summer, Vivian had decided to buy the gun. It was the only answer to that nagging question *what if somebody breaks in—while you're all alone in the house?* If they want to, they can get at you. Vivian was well aware of that. You could have three locks on the front door and a bolt on your bedroom door, but they could still find you. It was like the old trick of boxes within boxes. All you have to do is keep opening them. But the joke is on them if when they uncover you, in the innermost box, they find out you've got a gun.

"You can't barricade yourself enough," Marie had told Vivian. "Very few women can. Ideally the wall between you and danger is your husband's chest. Look at the armor Joan of Arc wore: the breastplate was nothing but an impression taken from some guy's pectoral muscles."

Lately Vivian had been making an effort to discipline herself. She stopped herself from knocking on wood before going out to drive the car in the rain. She cut down a little on the pills, and tried to keep her mind on projects: picking off dead geraniums, polishing the silver, conjuring up images of herself running a business—putting a customer's American Express card through the machine without betraying herself with a tremor. If only there were enough distractions, maybe one day she could put away the pills altogether.

But Vivian knew she had to proceed cautiously. There was schizophrenia in her family. She had a forty-five-year-old cousin who spent every day sitting in bus terminals. He'd take a bus to a city an hour or two away, sit in the terminal for a few hours, then move on to the next city. He was running from the spies who were after the State Department secrets he had with him in a shopping bag. Vivian hoped she'd never get to that stage. With a little luck and a little support—*knock on wood*—it wouldn't happen to her.

Before she went to bed Vivian made sure the white caution light on the burglar alarm system was working, and she picked up the telephone to see that there was a dial tone. The alarm system was connected to a siren that would sound even if the house current failed (there was an emergency battery pack). When the alarm was ringing, a call automatically went out to the police station over the telephone wires—but of course that wouldn't do much good if the telephone wire leading to the house were to be cut. Which was why every night Vivian made sure she could hear a dial tone. Without that dial tone, the little "emergency" panic buttons that were almost as numerous in the house as light switches would be useless.

It was two-thirty before Vivian finally got into her nightgown and put her gun in the Sheraton stand beside her bed. Even with the drinks she didn't feel very sleepy. She couldn't stop thinking about what had happened to Marie. What a terrible experience. But maybe once she recovered from it she'd be more willing to talk about the two of them getting together and opening a dress shop. Maybe even an antique shop. Vivian certainly knew enough about antiques. She'd been buying at the country auctions for years. She had a subscription to the *Maine Antiques Digest*. So she even knew all the inside dope about the business.

One kind of shop that was out of the question, though, was a gift shop. No Lucite towel racks, please. No pretty place mats. Running a shop like that was really just a form of extended hostessing. Maybe, if Marie would go along with the idea, they could open a hybrid shop: an antiques store with fresh floral arrangements that were also for sale. Or a dress shop with a bar. Now *that* was a hot idea. Kir for the size sixes, Perrier for the size sixteens.

Thinking about drinking Perrier reminded Vivian of a bad dream she'd had the week before. She remembered that in the dream she was drinking—something, maybe just water—but she was swallowing much too fast. So fast she was drowning. And then, when everything was going black and she was nearly out of her mind with terror, she woke up with her lungs snatching for air. It was all just nerves. That was what Dr. Callahan said. And Dr. Wallace thought it could be nerves too, though he thought she might be allergic to something—mold spores, perhaps, or house dust. Sometimes allergies could cause shortness of breath. And it was true, Vivian had been allergic to things as a child. Once a bee sting had sent her into convulsions. Valium couldn't help you if you got stung by a bee, that was for sure. It couldn't do a thing against allergic reactions. Valium was only good for gut reactions.

Vivian wondered how Marie would react if she told her that she'd rented shop space. Maybe she just needed that extra push. Imagine me trying to push somebody into doing something, Vivian thought. I must be making progress. All her married life Vivian had needed to be nudged herself. She was afraid of flying, and though her husband told her she was foolish and insisted on their taking vacations, still, every time the plane took off, Vivian had her fingers tightly crossed. She would hide her hand under a magazine so her husband couldn't see.

The moonlight was making the tent iridescent. Jamie held back the flap. Inside there was a large air mattress made up like a bed. Laura went in, and curled up on the down comforter. Jamie sat next to her. He looked at Laura as though he were seeing her in a dream he could not quite believe. He took her in his arms. Languidly, luxuriously, they sank into each other.

Vivian hoped that all the excitement of the party wouldn't make her restless. She could do without any vivid dreams tonight, although she'd been fortunate in that respect lately. A naked man had stood by her bed, for a few moments, a couple of weeks ago. But that was it. Gradually Vivian's plans for opening a store and echoes of conversations from the party began to scatter themselves randomly in her head. She was slipping rapidly into sleep when she heard the noise.

After a few minutes, Laura and Jamie parted, briefly, to undress. What was usually awkward for Laura was this time effortless; she whisked off her clothes with her fingertips, as if removing crumbs. And then they were naked together. The feel of Jamie's body made Laura's skin electric: every pore was alive with the current. She felt along the curve of his strong back, her hand seeing for her, the way the blind come to know tangible art. Yes, said her fingertips, he is what I thought, a *sexy* Wasp.

Laura and Jamie rolled over and over on the comforter. In the grip of one another, they were nearly frantic; it was as though their hearts, confined by their bodies, were struggling to get through to

71

each other. Their hands and their lips sought any entrance, any access to that vital warmth. Finally there was but one way.

When he entered her, Laura lost her mind. Her soul was heaving. Her breath came in rushes. She felt herself streaming away. Her fingers burrowed into the comforter like tendrils.

The noise went through Vivian like a shock, like one of those muscular spasms that jerk the leg.

Jamie arched his back. He opened his mouth. For a minute his pulse was only in his cock. When the moment was over, Jamie settled gently back upon Laura. He breathed again. He was covering her, but Laura felt no weight at all.

Vivian felt as though a cold steel comb were being dragged along her scalp. She sat up in bed. Rigid. Listening. There was a rustle in her walk-in closet. The door to it was ajar. It sounded as if someone was inside, going through her things.

God, am I going to die now? Vivian thought. Oh, not now, please. Not like this. She was shaking. Her spine, her shoulders, the back of her neck—they all felt like tin twisting in an icy wind.

A squeal came from the closet.

Vivian reached with her fluttering hand for the drawer where the gun was. The drawer flew away in her grasp and everything inside fell on the floor. Vivian threw herself against the wall and slapped the panic button with her palms again and again. She shut her eyes tightly and prayed "OhhhhmyGodohmyGodohmyGod."

On a panel in the Cable Harbor police station a white light had begun to wink. The dispatcher radioed a patrol car.

"I think we may have a problem at the Black house," he said.

"Got ya," the officer behind the wheel replied. His partner turned on the Christmas tree on the cruiser's roof, but not the siren—they always responded to burglar alarms silently, in hopes of catching the perpetrator in the act. Through the early-morning blackness the cruiser rushed, its flashing light catching leaves overhead as the sun catches small fish in shallow water.

Vivian was hunched over on the floor. She was pressing her temples with her fingertips, trying to keep her face hidden from the horror, the horrible squeal. But she heard it again. It was louder. It was right at her ear. And then Vivian felt the sharp teeth sinking into her shoulder.

The police officers pulled up a few feet short of Vivian's driveway. They got out, and drew their revolvers.

"That her car in the driveway?"

"Don't know. I think so. Ain't that a New York plate?"

"Yeah. I think it is. Orange. Hard to tell." The two men quietly circled the house, trying the doors, checking the windows.

"Lights on down the street," one of them noted. "Must've heard the alarm. Been goin' long enough. If anybody was here, they must've cleared out."

"Let's try the front door again." It was locked.

"She's here. Her car is here. Ring the bell." There was no answer.

"You wanna go back to the station and get her key or you wanna go through one of the windows?"

"I think we better go through a window. I expect she's got insurance."

They broke a small pane in Vivian's kitchen door.

"Shit. I can't open it this way. It's one of those doors that you gotta open with a key on the inside."

"Wanna try a window?" The windows all had locks on them that required a key. There was no way they could be opened by reaching through a broken pane.

"Well, I don't see what we can do except go on in through one of her sliders."

"Those are mighty expensive."

"Expense don't matter in an emergency."

They picked the doors that opened off Vivian's bedroom.

"Christ, she's got a bar across it."

"Break it all out, then. But be careful you don't cut yaself."

"There's a picnic bench over there. I'll use that. That should knock it out as neat as you please."

The window fell out as gapingly as a front tooth. Parting the draperies, the policemen pointed their flashlights in the room. They stepped inside, their feet crunching the broken glass. Then they saw Vivian on the floor. Then they saw something else.

"Chrissake, watch it, watch out!"

"Duck!"

The first shot exploded a jar of vitamin E cream on Vivian's dresser. There wasn't time to get off a second shot.

"That, as they say, is that," Arthur said. The last of the guests had left, and Arthur and Herbert's house was silent. Everything seemed to be coated with a film from the party; even the Deco chairs in the dining room, which were of polished rosewood, stood in the 3:00 A.M. haze like so many smudged glasses.

"People aren't smoking cigarettes as much as they used to, are they?" Arthur noted.

"I didn't notice the cigarettes—with the house burning," Herbert replied.

"Yes, that was a distraction, wasn't it? How long did it take you to hear Marie's confession?"

"I don't know," Herbert said. "We were probably in there a half hour or so." Pouring himself a glass of sherry, Herbert surveyed the damage to the living room. Then he lifted his glass in a half-hearted salute to life as he knew it, like a person of uncertain health leaving on a sea cruise.

"Guilt is such a handicap," Arthur said. He had picked up an empty glass and was squinting at it. "Who the hell was wearing this pink carnation lipstick?" he added.

"At least guilt feelings are evidence that there's a soul resident in the body," Herbert said.

"Are they?" Arthur replied. "I think of guilt as a sentimental attachment to the sorrows of home."

"Since when have you ever felt guilty?" Herbert inquired.

"I haven't at all . . . in recent years," Arthur said. "My mother used to try to make me feel guilty. And a high school Latin teacher I had. She was a pathetic creature, really, my Latin teacher. She wasn't married, and she had to support her mother, who kept having heart attacks regularly . . . to coincide with school vacations, I imagine. So all Miss Cooper had in life was her little bit of power, in the classroom. She was very demanding. And very uninspiring. She tried to make us feel guilty if we didn't satisfy her demands; she thought reading Caesar in translation was immoral. I still have a little residual guilt left in me, perhaps. Because of Miss Cooper."

"You still feel guilty because you read Caesar in translation?"

"No, I feel guilty because I didn't put a wet paper towel in the seat of Miss Cooper's chair."

Herbert looked at Arthur as if he were regarding him from the railing of a departing ship; Herbert appeared drawn and in need of a muffler about his neck, lest whatever private consumption was eating away at him should go through all his stores.

"Let's just bring a few of these glasses out to the kitchen, shall we?" Herbert said.

"Did you hear Marie's confession in the closet?" Arthur asked.

"What?"

"I mean did you go into the closet and have her whisper through the keyhole?"

"No, as a matter of fact I sat next to her on the sofa."

"Technically, that's not the way you're supposed to hear a confession," Arthur pointed out. "You're supposed to have your ear to an opening that the penitent whispers through. Physical anonymity is essential. Papal infallibility ultimately depends upon ignorance of the body, you realize."

"I don't choose to ignore Marie's body," Herbert replied.

"And you don't have any guilt feelings about touching her, either, do you?"

"No, I don't."

"I was afraid of that," Arthur said. "Okay, let's get rid of these glasses."

It was clinging to his arm. With a furious swipe he hit his arm against the frame of the sliding door and scraped it along the jagged edge. It fell off and he stamped on it. His partner said, "Get it, get it, get it! Christ!"

"Sunufabitch. I cut myself, I think. And I think it got me. Call an ambulance, quick. We gotta get her to the hospital. We gotta get me to the hospital." He saw a piece of glass in his arm. He pulled it out. Then he started to bleed.

CHAPTER SEVEN

"I understand there was a fire last night," Dan Cartey said.

"That's right, there was," Marie replied. "And there was a murder the day before yesterday."

"What caused the fire, carelessness?" Dan asked.

"Yes, my carelessness, as I'm sure you know. A lot of thing are caused by carelessness. Household fires. Social diseases. School bus accidents. Hitchhikers getting raped and bludgeoned to death. It hardly pays to get out of bed in the morning." Marie had a bad headache. She took another sip of her bloody mary, which was half vodka. Talking on the telephone with her ex-husband always gave Marie a headache, or worsened the one she already had. Such conversations as the one she was now having also had a tendency to make her itch under her arms; the irritation neutralized her antiperspirant, it was a toxin to the lymph nodes, fluorocarbons flying in your face.

"We don't even know yet if the girl was raped," Dan pointed out. "We'll have to wait for the coroner's report before we can be sure about that."

"Everybody is assuming she was raped. Her clothes were all . . . disarrayed, weren't they?"

"Nobody looks neat with a broken neck," Dan replied.

"Maybe she was hitchhiking with a long scarf on, like Isadora Duncan."

"No way," Dan said. "We found her right by the hotel."

"God, what a way to wind up."

"That's one thing I wanted to talk about, Marie. I'm kinda concerned about how you're going to wind up. You could have killed yourself last night. How much is it going to cost to repair the damage to that place, do you have any idea?"

"Herbert said he and Arthur won't let me pay for it. Arthur likes having an excuse to redecorate anyway."

"Speaking of redecorating, Marie, don't you think the bills for the work you're having done on that house of yours are getting a little steep?"

"Look," Marie replied. "Part of our agreement was that I could get a house up here and fix it up the way I want it."

"What do you want, Versailles?"

"No, I just want to live comfortably, and right now I want to have something to do. Fixing up this house right is keeping me busy until I find some way to occupy myself permanently."

"From what I was told you came pretty close to occupying yourself permanently last night."

"What do you care?"

"Don't get like that, Marie. I care about you. I really do. What happened was . . . just one of those things."

"What things?"

"You know what I mean."

"No, I don't. And I'm curious to know. When your husband takes off with a younger woman after you've been married to him twenty years, it can't be just one of those things. It's probably a number of very specific things: stretch marks, cellulite, gray roots."

"Come off it, Marie."

"No, I'm serious about this. I want to know. I may have to go to a clinic to find out—some spa where they put you through a combination of therapy and gynecology, rig you up in a sling with your legs spread and then get you to talk about your problems. I'm sure if I can find a spa like that, Vivian Black will go along with me. Then again, she wants me to go in with her on a dress shop. I may do that with her instead."

"Now that sounds like a worthwhile project."

"As long as we're talking about projects, would you mind letting me in on the deal with the Perry House? What are you doing with that place anyway? I hope you realize that the town's going to be up in arms now that there's been a murder right on the grounds. They're going to be yelling 'Derelict building!'—'It's a menace to the community!'"

"The Perry House is no menace. It's simply unfinished. What's already up is entirely in accord with the terms of the variance and the building permit. The fieldstone façade is entirely consistent with the character of the town, like it was supposed to be."

"Well and good. But finding people murdered is not consistent with the character of the town, Dan. It's consistent with condominiums. It's 'Hawaii Five-O'—people getting murdered in high-rise condominiums along Waikiki Beach. You know, that's what everybody thinks you have in mind, Dan. They think you want to turn the Perry House into condos, and they'll fight you tooth and nail."

"I know what the crowd up there thinks. If I worried about what people think all the time, I'd be nowhere. What do you suppose those Japanese investors I had along with me thought when we found that dead girl? What kind of an impression do you suppose that made?"

"I can't imagine."

"It's easy enough to imagine. The Japanese are plenty smart, Marie. They know the score. They see a dead body on your property and right away they're going to assume you're connected with a carting company from New Jersey."

"Are we connected with a carting company from New Jersey? Is the Perry House part of some scheme to get gambling legalized in Maine? Is that it?"

"I'm not saying, Marie. But I will say that there are a lot of places in Maine that are as poor as Atlantic City used to be."

"You'll never get away with it. Condominiums, casinos, Hadassah groups—they're never going to let all of that get up here. They'll go to the barricades. They'll claim wild blueberries are vital to the ecological balance. They'll have the lobsters declared an endangered species. They'll put through five-acre zoning. You'll never get the best of them, Dan. They have connections all over the place. This one was ambassador to the Netherlands. That one was Secretary of the Navy."

"You just let me handle any problems that come up with the Perry House," Dan said. "And concentrate on keeping your own house in order. No more fires, huh?"

Marie said nothing.

"And watch the drinking, okay?"

"What drinking?" Marie replied, eyeing her glass, which was empty and mottled with tomato juice—it looked almost like a red moss. (That was the best thing about your first drink of the day; it slowed you down so you noticed things; it stopped the nervousness; you could see more clearly; you could even begin to reflect on things; be expansive just looking out the kitchen window, be wise enough not to be concerned about the night before.)

"You know what drinking."

"Don't talk to me like a child. If you want to talk to me like a child do it through your lawyer."

"You're getting defensive."

"No, I just think lawyers should earn their money every so often. Why don't you tell your Japanese investor friends that we know about them bludgeoning dolphins to death on the beach? So if they find one dead hitchhiker over here, they still haven't got much room to talk. Nobody's perfect."

"That's right, Marie, nobody's perfect."

"It's just one of those things."

With a sense of reassurance in the knowledge of human imperfection, Marie hung up. And then she went to the bar to fix herself another bloody mary.

It was a little past 6:00 A.M. As Laura lay there, yesterday's events crowded her mind, like shoppers filling up an elevator. She turned sideways, and saw a heroic male head with tousled hair. The elevator rose thirty stories. Laura felt in her heart something like what happens to a person's ears at high altitude. God, was he good-looking. God, what a night. But now what? Laura began to make some mental notes:

1. It's still very early.
2. I'm in a tent.
3. I'm in a sleeping bag.
4. I am naked.
5. There is a very handsome guy in the sleeping bag next to me. He is also naked.
6. But he's still asleep. Sigh.

7. I've been out of work since April and this certainly isn't helping me to find a new job.
8. My mother wanted me to go shopping with her this morning.
9. Marie is probably trying to call me—no, she's probably still asleep, but when she wakes up she'll be all upset about the fire and then she'll be trying to call me.
10. I bet if I just nudge this handsome guy he'll wake up and want to do it again.

She nudged him. Jamie murmured in his sleep. He turned over, and his arm wound around Laura. He squeezed her gently. He was awake. Laura smiled. She heard her sleeping bag unzipping. And in the wink of an eye his body was next to hers; Laura felt as though she were hung up in a Christmas stocking: in over her head with the best new toy any girl could ever get. Oh, pick up your needlepoint patterns by yourself, Mother, Laura thought.

When Laura woke up again it was past eleven. It was warm inside the tent now. It felt stuffy, almost like being inside a polyester blouse. She wondered if her mother was worried about her. There had been a murder, after all. And she had not come home last night. This was the only drawback to good sex: afterward reality had a way of redoubling itself.

Turning her head, Laura saw that Jamie was awake. He was looking at her. With his blue eyes.

"Good morning," he said.

"Good morning. Did you sleep okay?"

"Mmmm-hm."

"I slept beautifully. Would you like some coffee?"

"Mmmmm. Maybe later." He was playing with her hair.

"You don't want a cup of coffee now? You sure? I don't mind making it. If there's a coffeepot around here." Laura looked about her and added, "Coffeepot? I don't even see a hot plate. Goodness. This is so confusing. A woman needs a kitchenette at least—the morning after—or she's going to feel confused about her role. Her sexual role. I feel like a stewardess adrift on a life raft."

"Okay, you can make some coffee if it'll reassure you to do that," Jamie said. "Here, you can put on my shirt. There's a Coleman stove under the lean-to in the back. And a small refrigerator. My grandmother had them run an electrical cable out here. So she'd be sure I drink my orange juice and the bacon doesn't spoil."

"Your grandmother thinks of everything," Laura replied. "I love her."

Shucking off her sleeping bag, Laura pulled Jamie's polo shirt over her head, put on her panties, and then got up. Jamie yawned and stretched. Laura blinked as all that power uncoiled itself; it certainly wasn't what she was accustomed to first thing in the morning—how many females were? Except for Mrs. Mountain Lion in her den.

"What's in the refrigerator?" Laura asked.

"Eggs, milk, butter, bacon, steak, lettuce, tuna salad."

"Maybe I can put together an omelet."

Opening up the outdoor kitchen, Laura went to work. The coffee-pot turned out to be one of those old-fashioned ones with the glass knob in the lid. This is just like "Little House on the Prairie," Laura thought. Or Willa Cather. Well, not so much like Willa Cather. Pioneer coffeepots, yes, but no Michael Landon, no Jamie Lawrence. Maybe Willa Cather could have worked for the guy who fired me, Laura mused—she did wear men's clothes.

Scooping some coffee into the tin filter, Laura added water from the hose that Jamie's grandmother had no doubt supplied along with the electricity. She hoped the coffee wouldn't taste like Rocky Mountain espresso or something. Jamie appeared. He wasn't wearing a shirt, and the morning sun flashed on his muscles as on the brass gong in *Spartacus* or *Ben Hur* or another one of those chiseled-chest epics. Jamie was wearing a pair of Adidas jogging shorts that fit him the way an adolescent girl holds a love letter to her breast—cleaving and fluttering at the same time. Laura tried to keep her mind on breakfast. But Jamie sneaked up on her and tied his arms around her waist.

"How can I cook—like this?" Laura protested. Weakly. Jamie tightened his grip and began to nuzzle her neck. Laura dropped her spatula.

"The coffee's almost ready," Laura said.

"It'll keep," said Jamie. His lips were at her ear.

"Gee. This isn't at all like *The Little House on the Prairie*. I read all those books when I was a kid and it's funny—you learn all about what it's like to keep house, but you don't have any idea what it's like to play house."

"Mm-hm. You want to play house with me again?"

81

"Mmmmmm. Yes . . . yes . . . yes. Mmm. I wonder how the *prairie* ever got plowed."

"The whole house smells like a charcoal grill," Arthur said.

"That's your imagination," Herbert replied. "You can't smell a thing down here. Even up on the second-floor landing you have to really sniff around to detect anything."

"Then maybe I actually do smell a charcoal grill. They're advancing on us, a little each year, like the killer bees. The charcoal grills are on the march. Pretty soon they'll take over and suburban attitudes will be everywhere. Then we'll all have to start living like a couple of dykes. Meet somebody in a bar and go home with them and put two hamburgers on the charcoal grill. And be monogamous for thirty or forty years. What an idyllic prospect."

"Oh, stop driveling."

Arthur wiped his mouth with a linen napkin.

"Not dribbling—*driveling*," Herbert repeated.

"I drivel, you snivel," Arthur replied. "We're a little like the Constitution in that respect. We have a system of checks and balances." Sighing wearily, Herbert got up from the table and began to put things in the dishwasher.

"As long as you're redoing the third floor," Herbert said, "why not pick up some stuff for this kitchen? I wouldn't mind having a few copper pans, the French ones, that you hang on the wall. I could use them, and they'd make this place look more like a real kitchen—instead of a yogurt bar in Bloomingdale's."

"A yogurt bar in Bloomingdale's? God forbid. If that's the image this kitchen has got we're going to have to do something about it. I know. Next week we'll have about a dozen people over and serve a saddle of lamb with Louis Vuitton initials all over it. I bet Marjorie could do the initials with little pastry puffs."

"How can we have a dinner party if you're in the middle of redecorating?"

"We had a party last night while the house was burning, didn't we?" Arthur picked up Herbert's eighteenth-century Chinese Export lighthouse coffeepot with the sepia American eagle on it and poured coffee into his Minnie Mouse mug.

"Minnie Mouse wears such enormous shoes," Arthur observed. "They're like small boats. Or large clogs. Did I tell you my dentist wears clogs?"

"I don't know why you have to have a gay dentist too."

"Because I always look for the union label. That's what the Ladies' Garment Workers tell us to do and they know what they're talking about. Always buy gay when you can and don't be like those queens with the Japanese houseboys. Who are taking jobs away from American houseboys. So my dentist wears clogs because it's the only way he can relax at the profession. Did you know that dentists have the highest rate of suicide of any professional group?"

"No, I didn't. But I can understand why. All that fear and anxiety coming at you from that chair every day."

"Not to mention the bad breath some people have. To make a long story short, my dentist's father is in his eighties now and he's senile. He was once a dentist himself. He still practices, in the rest home, by removing his dentures and clicking them at the other patients. So I think his son has a perfect right to wear clogs if he wants to."

Pleased with himself for having completed, in his brief narrative, a life cycle of sorts, Arthur drank his coffee.

"Aren't you running late?" Herbert asked.

"The plane doesn't leave until one," Arthur replied.

"I don't know why you have to make a special trip to the city just to pick the fabrics," Herbert said. "You know every pattern we handle by heart. You could do the whole thing over the phone."

"Actually that's an excuse," Arthur replied. "I want to spend a day or two in the city so I can go to the Mine Shaft. I think I left a couple of glasses in the sink when we left the house. So I could wash them out while I'm there, too. Once you put on a pair of Rubbermaid gloves to wash out the crystal, then you might just as well keep the gloves on and go to the Mine Shaft."

"Don't you ever get tired of fooling around—in dives like that?"

"I might get tired of the Mine Shaft if I had had a normal adolescence. But I didn't. I had a gay adolescence. Which was a long period of dreary confinement, interrupted only by one experience at summer camp when I was thirteen. So now I've got to make up for lost time. Psychologically, everybody at the Mine Shaft is my age: sixteen, and in the backseat of the car at the drive-in movie."

"I've heard this story before, I think. Tell me, when are you planning on growing up?"

"Maybe never. Our generation was kept back so many grades.

When gay kids start going to the junior prom together, then maybe there'll be less business for the Mine Shaft."

"I think you're just trying to justify sexual greed," Herbert said.

"Sexual greed? If that's all the Mine Shaft amounts to, then the suburbs have already taken over New York."

"If you insist on going to the city I suppose I'll have to drive you out to the airport pretty soon. Hurry up and finish your coffee."

"It's not the airport. It's the air*strip*. That is one of the advantages of this place. It's too small to support an airport."

"So is the Pines," Herbert pointed out, "but out there it doesn't seem to make any difference."

"On the contrary. The Pines supports several airports . . . or several airline stewards . . . I forget which."

"You're in quite a philosophical mood today, aren't you?" Herbert said as he started the dishwasher.

"Big, dramatic interruptions in the stream of human events always have that effect on me," Arthur replied. "Natural disasters, murder at the Perry House, fire in the upstairs: just about anything can set one philosophizing."

"Including adolescent sexual frustration."

"That, I believe, was the origin of philosophy. Didn't Plato suggest in one of the dialogues that Socrates didn't put out?"

"Philosophy and religion both have their roots in our fear of mortality," Herbert said. "Which is something you should bear in mind when you're wandering around those river bars late at night."

"You're right, I know you're right," Arthur agreed. "Wander around the river late at night and you risk . . . about as much as you risked going to gym classes when you were in junior high."

"Watch out, that's all I'm saying."

"We'd better get going. It's twelve-thirty now."

"Are you listening?"

"I'm listening, I'm listening. Don't be worried about things all the time. The Mine Shaft isn't nearly as menacing as it'd like to be. It's a family place, really. The last time I was there I saw a nice boy who was wearing a yamulka. Of course it was black leather."

But Herbert couldn't help worrying about Arthur. He worried when he knew Arthur was going to bars. He even worried when Arthur got on a plane. Today, as he always did, Herbert waited until the plane that was carrying his lover was safely out of sight. Entrusted to the tenderness of the summer clouds.

84

So much of life, Herbert thought, was a flip of the coin, the opposite sides of which were joy and sorrow. Sometimes, in your life, you just spun until the coin landed on one side or the other, as Marie seemed to be doing now. Sometimes you turned up a bad penny. That was what Herbert knew had happened when he fell in love with Arthur. Arthur was a well-circulated bad penny: one side of him a vain profile and the other side a personal monument as large in scale as the Lincoln Memorial. The trouble with monuments erected to oneself, Herbert realized, was that they so often serve as tombs. Complaining all the time about gay marriages being a kind of entombment, Arthur had somehow avoided in his own mind the solitary entombment that is a fact of death. And he also refused to see that the bars, with their constant call to change partners, were empty spaces for the dance of death.

Thoughts like these depressed Herbert. They led to other, more depressing thoughts: what if Arthur picked up some hustler with a knife, some lunatic who would tie him up with a lamp cord or a necktie and . . . Look at what had happened to that girl. In Cable Harbor yet. What makes people get into cars with strangers? Get into bed with strangers, for that matter? Why couldn't people make homes for each other and stay home, in front of the fire, where it's safe and secure? Then again, maybe it isn't safe and secure anywhere anymore. Maybe the nuclear holocaust will be tomorrow or next week when you're standing in the supermarket with a Perdue chicken breast in your hand. Helpless. Maybe we're *all* in a dance of death.

No, Herbert couldn't accept that. It was too apocalyptic. It sounded like the Jehovah's Witnesses. It was just another excuse. Why, when you love someone deeply, do you . . . do they . . . have to keep making up excuses?

CHAPTER EIGHT

Right after breakfast George Hanson went out to his workshop. From the kitchen window Marjorie hollered at him, "You're not going to spend the whole morning working on that birdhouse *again?* By the time you get it finished the purple martins won't be nesting anymore. And what'll we have? A bunch of low-life sparrows, that's what we'll have."

"I got nothin' against sparrows," George hollered back.

Rolling up the garage door, George unlocked his workshop, went inside, and locked the door behind him. The previous owner of the house had built the room onto the garage and had used it as a playroom. There was still a plywood bar and a pair of barstools with red vinyl seats oozing stuffing. Into this playroom Marjorie had dumped everything she considered playful: a Jim Beam bottle in the shape of a building and a streetlight lamp with a hobo who looked like Red Skelton hanging on for dear life. There was a Miller beer sign over the bar, and the other source of illumination, which was next to the lawn glider that served as a sofa, was a ceramic flamenco dancer who looked as if he might be banging his heels on bathroom tiles—such was his pastel glaze.

Against one wall George had set up his workbench and tools. Resting on the workbench was the purple martin house: five pieces of sanded wood. That was as far as George had progressed with his project. His real interest in being in the workshop he kept locked up in the bar.

Trembling with anticipation, George slid open the bar and pulled out his 8 mm projector. He set up the projector on his workbench, focusing it on the white wall opposite. The painting on black velvet of a matador that was Marjorie's souvenir of the Cape hadn't hung on that wall for months.

In the kitchen, Marjorie was listening to "Get It Off Your Chest," which was the local radio talk show. She felt especially sharp this morning, and a mild thrill, something similar to stage fright, was coursing in her. Everybody who called in was talking about the murdered girl and the Perry House. Old Mr. Tucker, the retired lobsterman, was railing against the lenient judicial system, which, along with the Rockefellers, was part of a conspiracy "to tear down our country all the time."

"They let them go right out in the streets again, just as though nothing at all had happened. When what they oughtta do is lock 'em up and throw away the key. And I want you to know that I'm a veteran of World War I." Old man Tucker always concluded his speeches that way, reminding everyone in tones that sounded as if they were echoing in the halls of Montezuma that he had fought in World War I and therefore knew whereof he spoke.

Mrs. Booth was the next one to call. She was the wife of Sanford Booth, who owned the grocery store. Mrs. Booth was always sticking up for farmers and saying they weren't to blame for food prices. The oil companies were. Mr. Tucker always agreed with her there. But he thought that supermarkets were conspiring, too. Mrs. Booth had an opinion on almost every subject. She had a pretty good opinion of herself too, Marjorie thought. (Mrs. Booth was the only listener, other than Marjorie, who called "Get It Off Your Chest" so frequently that the show's host was on a first-name basis with her.)

This morning Mrs. Booth was holding forth on the murder. She was saying, "Only last winter one of my boys was out hunting and he found something mighty suspicious. Way out in the woods it was, in a little clearing."

"What'd he find?" the host asked.

"He found an old air mattress, you know, like the campers outdoors use. And under this mattress he found somebody's Turkish towel. Now, I for one would like to know what a mattress and a bath towel are doing out in the middle of the woods. I'd have been afraid to look under that mattress, for fear that somebody might be buried under it. In a shallow grave."

Always pushing the panic button, Marjorie thought. She's got some imagination. That nonsense she was talking last week—about the flying saucers. Anybody in a flying saucer who saw the chopped meat they carry in that market of theirs would head back to their own planet fast enough.

Marjorie felt ready to step into the spotlight. She picked up the phone and dialed.

"I don't know why anyone would be surprised to find a mattress in the woods," she began. "You can't go out blueberrying but what you don't find little settlements the kids have made—with beer cans. That's what they do, they go out in the woods with their beer cans and their marijuana and probably some of them even bring mattresses. It wouldn't surprise me any. It's one thing to complain about how the courts handle criminals, but it's another thing to be worrying about the Supreme Court when your own kids are out in the woods doing Lord knows what. I won't name any names. But I know a mother whose daughter got terrible poison ivy—on her bottom. What a way to find out. The heartbreak.

"What Cable Harbor needs is a community center where the kids can go and hang out. We need to be thinking what we can do, right here in Cable Harbor, to change things for the better, rather than worrying about flying saucers and the Rockefellers. The Rockefellers don't worry about us and we shouldn't be worrying about them. Rich people don't care about working people very much; they brush us off, like flies. We're just flyspecks on a banquet table as far as they're concerned. And I've been around the food business long enough to tell you that there are plenty of fancy restaurants where the rich get flyspecks in their food. Not everybody is as careful as George and I are. But it doesn't matter. The rich don't know about the flyspecks and their digestion isn't upset. So what do you do? Where you can get away with it you put out flypaper; you make it sticky, and then all of sudden you're noticed. 'Cause you're all in one place and sticking to it."

God, I'm really flying now, Marjorie thought as the words poured out of her. "What I'm trying to say is that the people of this town, if they felt like really sticking together, could make a lot of trouble if they wanted to. For one thing they could find out exactly what's going on with that Perry House. They could demand to know.

That's what town meetings are for, in case anybody's forgotten. And one more thing. One more thing about the rich. They don't like pests buzzing around them. They'll flick you off the easiest way they can. Maybe somebody might even be persuaded to donate the Perry House as a community center. What would they have to lose? They write off all those things on their taxes anyway."

"You sure are wound up today, Marjorie," the host said. "When you get goin' on a topic there sure isn't any holding you back."

Marjorie loved it when he kidded her that way. She blushed and played with the back of her hair self-consciously, like a giddy teenager. Almost immediately the studio phones began ringing. Old man Tucker was the first caller after Marjorie.

"I say that gal is makin' a hell of a lot of sense. I say she should be voted onto the board of adjustment. Maybe she should even be mayor. And I want you to know that I was a member of the board of adjustment in this town in the year nineteen hundred and twenty-six."

Marjorie felt as if she had just stepped down from the podium at the Academy Awards. Everybody had been listening to her. All eyes had been on her. Old man Tucker's voice was another ripple of applause. Marjorie's chest swelled with pride in spite of herself. Anybody could impress people—men especially—with expensive clothes or an expensive hairdo. But it wasn't everybody who could sound like Margaret Chase Smith.

Old man Tucker had scarcely finished when a new caller came on the line. The voice was one Marjorie had not heard on the radio before. It sounded like one of the summer people: talking and yawning in the same breath. And the voice was a little thick, too, as though whoever it was who was calling had had a few drinks. Marjorie strained her ear until the skin on the side of her face felt tight.

"I've heard that foreign interests are getting involved with the Perry House," the voice was saying. "Now, I'm not going to tell you what nationality these foreigners are—but who's been buying up all the prime farmland in the Midwest? And who's been driving up the price of co-ops in Manhattan? And paying six million dollars for houses in Beverly Hills? Not the Fiji Islanders, that's for sure."

"Ma'am, are you trying to say that the Arabs want the Perry House?" the host asked.

"Draw your own conclusions," the voice replied. "I just think it's one thing to have to pay the fortune we pay for gas, but it's another thing to have them elbowing you off the road in their Rolls-Royces—right here in the state of Maine."

Marjorie could almost hear old man Tucker thundering in his kitchen at that.

"Do you have any proof that the Arabs want to buy the Perry House?" the host asked the caller.

"I know for a fact that the Japanese have been at the Perry House already. And if the Japanese come, can the Arabs be far behind?"

Marjorie was sure she recognized the voice now. It was the woman who had started the fire. It was Mrs. Cartey.

Vivian's dream began with a circle of sparks whirling in the red night. The circle widened quickly. It became a porthole. And Vivian was drawn through the porthole into a day that was like a blue bell jar. She was standing on grass. She was in front of the Cable Harbor cottage that her parents had rented when she was a child. There was no sound. No birds singing. No wind. Nobody talking. The hydrangea bush was in full bloom. The puffy white blossoms looked like cotton candy. Standing there in the silence, Vivian reached for one of the flowers. And in the reaching out she felt tenderness extending from her heart, a great, soft, widening tenderness that almost filled the blue bell jar of day.

Before she touched the blossom Vivian woke up. She did not know where she was. She tossed her head from side to side. Her eyes ran up and down the walls and across the ceiling. A woman in a white uniform appeared.

"Where's this place?" Vivian rasped. Her mouth was dry. Her tongue seemed to be drying her words like a blotter.

"You're in the hospital, Mrs. Black," the nurse said. "Don't be concerned. You had an accident, but you're being very well taken care of and you're going to be just fine."

Vivian was seared by her memory. She reached for her shoulder and felt a thick bandage. Then she began to cry. The nurse hurried to get the doctor.

When Vivian came to again her head was thick with medication, but she knew that she was in a hospital bed. She was aware of what had happened to her; it was an awareness that she wanted to shunt to the back of her mind, though, a grim awareness that belonged in the gray area where cancer's seven warning signals were stored.

Vivian began to wonder how, only a little while ago, she could have thought that the crack in the plaster was a bug crawling. The doctor appeared in the oversized doorway. Smiling when he saw that Vivian was awake, he came in to reassure her. Vivian asked him for a Valium. The doctor told her that he'd have the nurse give her a shot later. Vivian didn't know whether to trust him or not; she'd learned to monitor her own nerves. What would a stethoscope and a look under her eyelids tell him about the frequency at which she'd been operating?

Right after the doctor left Vivian's room, the telephone rang. It was Linda Keller. Speaking in a voice that a mother might use to address her child's skinned elbow, Linda said, "Vivian, you poor little thing. I almost died when I heard what had happened to you. How *are* you?"

"Right now I'm still a little groggy," Vivian replied.

"What a *terrible* summer this is turning into. Some poor girl getting murdered. And now you getting attacked by—"

"I'd rather not talk about it right now, Linda," Vivian said. "I've gone through something that was . . . pretty bad. But if the alternative is being murdered . . . I guess there are worse things that can happen to a person than what's happened to me."

"Oh, definitely, there are much worse things. You could lose an arm in an accident and the surgeons might not be able to reattach it. Just *anything* can happen. One of my best friends in the city has been keeping one of her children in *the* most expensive institution for I don't know how many years. He's a complete vegetable."

"I feel better already," Vivian said.

"I'm coming right up there to see you," Linda promised. "Just as soon as I call a few other people and tell them about this. You poor little thing."

"Yes," Vivian replied. "All right, Linda. Thanks for calling." With relief, she hung up. Gazing longingly at the flexible straw in her water glass, Vivian tried to picture a team of doctors rolling Linda Keller into the operating room. Where they would take the flexible straw and, clinically, shove it.

Since the vodka was only watering down her depression, Marie decided she needed to talk to somebody. So she called the Bath

Club and had Laura paged. She wasn't there. Marie called the Damons' number. Laura's mother was summoned to the phone by the maid.

"Oh, Mrs. Cartey," Mrs. Damon said. "I'm so relieved that you called. Have you by any chance seen Laura?"

"Not since last night," Marie replied.

"Well, she didn't come home last night," Mrs. Damon said. "And I'm a little concerned about her, frankly."

"She didn't . . ."

"No, she didn't."

Marie knew that her voice was wavering. Trying to modulate it, she said, "I'm sure that . . . she's all right. Wherever she is. Could you please have her call me when she gets home?"

"Yes, I'll make a note of it. If you see her, you'll let me know, won't you?"

"Yes, I will. Thanks."

"Oh, you're quite welcome, Mrs. Cartey."

" 'Bye now."

"Good-bye."

Marie hung up. She stood there for a moment, feeling as though she were dangling from the telephone cord. She decided to call Arthur and Herbert.

"Arthur's already left for New York," Herbert said when Marie asked him, as calmly as she could, if the two of them were managing to cope with the awful mess she'd made.

"Oh dear," Marie said. "He's left you to shift for yourself in that disaster area?"

"I'm used to shifting for myself, Marie. In any relationship somebody stays home to wipe off the counters and somebody does . . . the errands."

"Mischievous errands, usually. You send them out for a quart of milk and they look for it in an erotic toy store. It's so goddamn hard to keep house. To keep it all together. While you're keeping the home fires burning and heating up the hot chocolate, out there in the night somebody is tipping over the outhouse."

"And in the end we homebodies have to shift for ourselves. Gloomy prospect, isn't it, Marie, to find yourself put away on the kitchen shelf, like an old Waring blender—in the age of Cuisinarts."

"Don't you go calling yourself outmoded, Herbert. In my opinion you're as sleek and attractive as a Braun coffee maker."

"Why don't you come over and have a cup of coffee with me, Marie. We can commiserate together."

"I've got a better idea. If you can come over to my place tonight, I'll cook dinner for you."

"Okay, you're on."

"Oh, terrific. I'll be buried in the pages of Craig Claiborne all afternoon."

"Why don't you make something out of Julia Child? Her recipes are homier. You don't feel self-conscious about licking your fingers when you're making a Julia Child recipe."

"All right, Julia Child it'll be. Home cooking for a pair of old homebodies."

When Marie hung up, her heart was palpitating. Dinner with Herbert. Just the two of them. When Marie was a little girl, her father had shown her how, when you rub a balloon on the rough sleeve of your jacket, you can make it stick all by itself to the ceiling. That was the way Marie felt now—rubbed just right, and adhering to a surface where you might make contact, but, you would think, never be able to make anything stick. Could Herbert actually be interested in something more than dinner? Or was this feeling of weightlessness only the after effects of the amyl nitrite, or the bloody marys? Marie had wondered for some time now if Herbert's kind eyes might be looking on her with something more than sympathy. But there was no time this afternoon to wonder. Get cooking, Marie told herself. Light the gas. Kindle again the flame of hope.

Marie was in the middle of making cold carrot soup when Linda Keller called.

"Marie, I just got back from the hospital," Linda said (even though she was recently divorced from a physician, she still did volunteer work for the hospital), "and—oh, this is so horrible I can hardly bring myself to tell you about it—are you feeling okay? After the fire?"

"Yes, yes, I'm okay. What is it? What's happened? Not another murder, I hope?"

"It's almost worse than that. Last night . . . Vivian Black was . . . *attacked* . . . by a *rabid bat*."

Laura had meant to call her mother first thing—right after she had her coffee—but the first thing she did this morning turned out to be a repetition of the last thing she'd done the night before. Day and night mixed. And the coffee sat until three in the afternoon. When she finally finished her first cup of coffee, Laura said to Jamie, "I really do have to call my mother. You know how parents can be—if they don't know where you are and they haven't heard from you, they assume you've been in an auto accident or you're lying helpless somewhere." Jamie was rocking Laura back and forth in the rope hammock he'd strung between two trees. Laura's coffee cup dangled by its handle from her little finger.

"Come to think of it, I *am* lying helpless somewhere," Laura said.

CHAPTER NINE

It was around four when Laura finally told Jamie that she absolutely had to call her mother *now*.

"I can just see her," Laura said. "She's probably pacing up and down—in her dressing gown. Whenever she has something to worry about she forgets to get dressed. Or she keeps the dressing gown on deliberately, so the sweep of it will add to the drama."

"I understand," Jamie replied. "My mother was like that." Laura suddenly remembered that Jamie had lost his own mother—and his father, too. She wanted to reach out and touch him, to reassure him somehow, but she did want to make that telephone call. And after they'd already made love three times, even a gentle squeeze might seem a bit heavy-handed.

So Laura swung her legs off the hammock and went over to the telephone, which Jamie's grandmother, with her usual thoughtfulness, had provided.

"Thank God," Mrs. Damon sighed when she heard her daughter's voice. Laura pictured her mother at the phone, sagging and exhaling, as she always did when part of the burden of motherhood was lifted from her shoulders. It was a marvelous performance to witness, Laura realized when she thought about it objectively—that massive droop that came with the lifting of any portion of the awful weight of responsibility; anyone outside the family who saw the performance would probably think Laura's mother hung her dresses on an ox yoke.

"I was nearly beside myself with worry," Mrs. Damon went on. "I was about ready to call the police."

"Oh no," Laura moaned. "You know better than that, Mother. I'm a grown woman, remember? I've been to Europe by myself five different times. I have my own apartment in New York. I worked for a publisher."

"Yes, I know all that. I just wish that you'd worked for Scribner's or Lippincott's. Instead of that other old place. That *slick* place. I bet there isn't one person in the Scribner family or the Lippincott family who's ever . . . who has . . ."

"Ever *what*, Mother?"

"Who has ever lived with somebody. Without being married to them. . . . Oh dear . . . I shouldn't have said that. Please don't take that the wrong way, dear."

"Oh, lordy." Laura felt fifty.

"Just the same, I'll bet that Scribner's has never published a book about people living together. Or using motel rooms either."

"Mother, I am not in a motel."

"Oh, you aren't?"

"No."

"Dear me. I'm so sorry, dear. I hardly know what I'm saying. After that murder. Where are you, anyway?"

"At a private campground."

"A campground! Wherever? Whoever? Heavens, I hope you're not with some character, are you? Some person who's traveling on a motorcycle. Some drifter with a beard and a black leather jacket. These people can be anybody. You never know."

"I've been with Jamie Lawrence, Mother. Remember him? He's living in a tent this summer." There was a profound silence on the other end of the line. Laura calmly examined her fingernails. She smiled to herself. The very telephone line seemed to be shimmering in the summer air, like a harp string.

Speaking in the fairy-godmother voice she had adopted yesterday afternoon, when Laura first mentioned the name Lawrence, Mrs. Damon said, "Oooh, what a lovely time you must have had. To stay out so late. You must have danced every dance."

"We didn't dance at all," Laura confided.

Mrs. Damon cleared her throat, which was usually one of her ways of registering disapproval, but this time there was no conviction in the brief *ahem,* only an indication of willingness to swallow—in this context—anything at all.

"No dancing, hm? Well, I'm sure you had a wonderful time anyway."

"Yes, I did."

"And I gather the party isn't over yet?"

"No. It's still going on. I don't want it to end."

"Perhaps it never will."

"Well . . . I'm afraid it has to. I should be out looking for a job right now."

"A vocation, dear. Try to think in terms of finding yourself a vocation."

"A vocation? Mother, this wasn't the sort of evening that would make a girl think in terms of becoming a nun."

"I didn't mean be a nun. I meant think about having a vocation. A life's work ahead of you. Fighting the good fight. You don't have to become a nun, but you might consider a little traditional sort of . . . religious ceremony. To start you off right."

"Mother-r-r-r-r."

"Laura. Heavens. Don't *growl* so."

"Mother, you know exactly how I feel about *that.*"

"Oh dear. I don't know what we're coming to. You . . . your generation . . . talks about *marriage* the way we used to talk about *sex.*"

"Mother, I'm going to have to go now."

"Oh, Laura, don't cut me off. I'm sorry I even hinted at . . . it."

"I'm not cutting you off. But I do have to get back to my date."

"Oh, of course. A man doesn't like to take a girl to a party and then have her run off and leave him standing there. I know if I were a man I wouldn't care to be left cooling my heels. They like to *be with you* for the evening . . . the day . . . however long it is."

"I should be home sometime tomorrow."

"There's no rush, dear. Do you want me to send over a different dress? Do you want your luggage?"

"Don't worry about it, Mother. I'll see you tomorrow."

"All right. Good-bye, dear. Be careful, now. Anybody could break into a tent pretty easily, I'd think."

"I'm perfectly safe, Mother."

"Yes, I suppose you are, dear. It's a lovely feeling, isn't it. I

97

remember, after your father and I were first ma . . . well, your friend will look out for you, won't he?"

"Good-bye, Mother."

"Good-bye, dear. And *good luck*." After Mrs. Damon hung up she remembered that Mrs. Cartey had been trying to get Laura. She wondered if she should call back, but Laura had not given her the telephone number, and trying to get it from information or Mrs. Lawrence would be . . . unseemly. She didn't want to be a nagging mother, after all.

Laura felt a bit annoyed with her mother, but it was a peculiarly satisfactory kind of annoyance. While talking, she'd been bitten on the leg by a mosquito. Scratching the bite was deeply satisfying as well. A puppy digging his ear with his hind leg might get the same pleasure out of scratching—but Laura doubted many people could. At least not many of the people in the Cable Harbor crowd. The itch was there all right, but who could get at it?

Marie was standing in the middle of her kitchen with a greased pan in one hand and a glass of vodka in the other. The dreadful news about Vivian had combined in Marie's mind with the ingredients for making paupiettes of trout mousse with leeks to produce distraction. Marie was cooking in a daze. As soon as she heard about Vivian, she had called Herbert and asked him to come over early. She told him she didn't want to be alone. But Marie had started drinking heavily even though she knew Herbert would be coming over soon. And now her right hand felt a little numb—usually that only happened the next morning—and she was fumbling with things because her fingers felt like the spokes of a whisk.

Straining, Marie focused on the leeks, trimming off the tops and bottoms with a squint and a jab, so that she looked like an old lady trying to thread a needle. At least with this cooking to do there was something to focus on besides fire, bloody murder, and bats. As long as she was cooking and drinking, Marie knew, none of that would sink in. Marie had been trying for some months now to keep things from really sinking in. She wanted to live blithely on the surface, to skim over the pond without thinking about the green gills and the muck below.

If that meant living like some kind of a swinger, fine. Swinging was relative anyway. Flash Donahue would probably think a swinger was someone who plays bridge every afternoon. And Vivian, God help her, probably thought swinging was a kind of therapy they used on the West Coast. For Marie, swinging was putting your best hip forward, and devil take the hindmost.

After lunch Marjorie went to Booth's market to pick up a couple of items. Walking into the store, she saw with displeasure that Evelyn Booth was behind the counter. Evelyn irritated Marjorie in a number of ways. First of all, she was one of those fatsos who prided herself on weighing a ton. Second of all, she always had to have the last word. She was always settling people's hash with the same sort of self-satisfied wheeze that no doubt you could hear from the cushion whenever she sat down. And third, there was that other fat slob of a sister of hers. If they weren't birds of a feather. The brother-in-law owned a taxi that smelled on the inside like a Gerber's baby food jar left out in the sun. They'd had about ten kids. And the oldest was the brat who'd taken Jennifer off into the woods where she got that awful case of poison ivy. Considering the family he came from, Jennifer was lucky she hadn't gotten worse. Marjorie wouldn't have been surprised to hear of hoof and mouth disease in the Booths' Salisbury steaks.

Fourth and—privately—the most irritating thing of all about Evelyn Booth, she was Marjorie's rival on "Get It Off Your Chest." So when she spotted her, Marjorie made a point of sailing *right by* the register. What a lousy selection of crackers they had in this store. Ritz crackers and Wheat Thins and Carr's biscuits lumped in for the summer crowd. But what could you do when you were all out of an item and in a hurry, what choice was there?

Unfortunately there was no way to avoid Mrs. Booth on the way out.

"Old man Tucker was in," Mrs. Booth remarked. "Said to me, 'That Hanson woman sure does talk sense.'"

"Did you happen to hear me?" Marjorie inquired aloofly.

"No, right after I talked I switched the station. On the other station they was doin' an hour of Loretta Lynn."

"You don't say. Well, it's too bad you missed me today. I had a thing or two to say about the Perry House."

Mrs. Booth hit the total bar and ripped off the tape. It was a wonder there was room behind the counter for the change drawer to slide out—with her big fat stomach sticking out. As Marjorie was putting her money back in her bag, Mrs. Booth said, "I wouldn't be worrying about an old empty shell of a building when people are getting bitten by bats. My cousin Lester, he's the cop, you know, and last night he was bitten by a bat. Along with one of the summer people. Both of 'em in the hospital. How do we know that flying saucers aren't stirring up the bats at night? Or maybe smugglers are sending them out of their caves. So they got a place to hide their drugs."

Marjorie's nostrils widened with disdain. "Flying saucers are a myth," she said, and scooped up her bag.

"They are, are they?" Mrs. Booth called after her. "Well, all I know is my brother who drives a potato truck out of Presque Isle found a woman's pocketbook standing upright in the middle of I-95 at three in the morning. Her car was off to the side of the road with the door open. Probably left her pocketbook in the middle of the highway when the flying saucer took her away."

"Oh, bullshit," Marjorie muttered to herself as she went through the door.

Dan Cartey often wondered if there was a day coming—a week from now or maybe within the next six months—when running an American business would be exclusively a matter of obtaining foreign capital. Lately he felt as if he were some kind of corporate tour leader—"We'll be stopping the limo here, gentlemen, so you can enjoy the scenic overlook" (two acres of warehouse in Secaucus, New Jersey). Still, 30 percent of the action was 30 percent, and the more capital the better; so long as the parent company kept expanding at the waistline, the Cartey Brothers' piece of the coattail would look increasingly better cut.

Sitting behind his massive rosewood and stainless-steel executive desk, Dan himself appeared to be a model of pinstriped substance. He looked younger than his forty-six years, because his smooth shirt collar seemed to carry over to his face. There was no evidence of wear and tear in Dan's face—just an Oxford quality, which is self-assurance overriding the years, and a calm about the eyes and mouth that indicates confidence that everything can be sewn up with a single stitch.

What with the ugly business up in Maine and Marie causing

problems again, Dan was in no mood to receive further communiqués from that neck of the woods. The call to Marie this morning might, with luck, have the effect of slowing her down for a while. Since the divorce she'd been running around lighting short fuses which then fizzled. Now she was evidently working with longer fuses and incendiary devices. Which was a great way of attracting attention to the Cartey name and, inevitably, to the Perry House.

One thing about women, they made you grateful to be in business. When he was married to Marie, Dan often felt as liberated walking into his office in the morning as he had when he was a kid hiding in a cardboard box. Her gripes he could leave at home in the sink with the empty coffee cups. It became more and more confining to be at home as the anniversaries accumulated. Finally the office funneled into the evening, and one evening, at a cocktail party, Dan met a girl.

She was a hostess sent over to help make things pleasant for three Arabs who were interested in franchises, which they collected like stamps. The girl, whose name was Lois, had come to New York hoping to be a dancer. Instead she had been picked up by a modeling agency and was supporting herself by sitting on the hood of a revolving car at the auto show.

"Mark my words," Dan said to Lois. "You'll get your chance. You'll be a dancer, you wait and see."

Lois waited patiently in the apartment Dan rented for her on East Fifty-second Street.

After Lois had been waiting a year and a half, Dan and Marie were divorced.

But the terms of the divorce settlement kept Dan tied to Marie, in a kind of marriage of inconvenience. Whenever Dan was reminded of this inconvenience, his mood altered for the worse. So when, right after lunch, he received yet another call from Cable Harbor, Dan was exasperated.

"Now what?" he barked.

"Mr. Hopkins the realtor," his secretary replied.

Mr. Hopkins was on retainer from Dan's organization to act as a watchdog for the Perry House. He saw to it that the grounds were kept up and the sentinal lightbulbs in the unfinished rooms kept burning. Today he was calling because he thought he smelled trouble.

101

"I was listening to the radio today," Mr. Hopkins reported. "And I heard something that I think you oughtta know about."

"Oh, and what was that?" These Mainers who always had to take you on a hayride before they got to the point. Damnit.

"Up here they have a talk show where people phone in an' say what's on their minds. It's called 'Get It Off Your Chest' an' that's exactly what the people do."

"Terrific."

"Course they have a set of rules you're spost to abide by. No personal attacks, and no attacks on religion or businesses."

"FCC regulations, I'm sure. And . . . ?"

"I think what I heard today comes pretty near to violatin' one of those rules."

"What'd you hear?"

"I heard a woman—a woman a lot of people listen to around here—sayin' they oughtta all get together and put out some flypaper for the rich to get caught in. Those were her words exactly. And that's a fact. She said we better call a town meetin' to determine exactly what's goin' on with the Perry House. It's my opinion that she was trying to get people to believe somethin' fishy is goin' on. An' the mood people are in, they're liable to go right along with her thinkin'."

"This is just what I need to hear right now. Who the hell is this dame?"

"Mrs. Hanson. She's the wife of George Hanson, the caterer. He's a funny one, but he puts up quite a meal. The summer people like yourself all use him."

"Does my wife use him?"

"That's the other thing I wanted to tell you. There was another woman called in who sounded a lot like your wife. She said the Arabs wanted the Perry House. Them and the Japanese."

It had taken Herbert a while to get Marie calmed down. She had called half hysterical. *Nobody knows where Laura is. If something's happened to her I'll go out of my mind.*

"Didn't you know she went home with that Lawrence kid?" *No. She didn't.* Marie's hysteria changed pitch, and she began wailing that she'd made a bigger fool of herself than she'd thought. *How could I have ever kidded myself that he had any interest in me?*

102

Here I didn't even know I'd been shot down. God, I can't even get shot down gracefully. I have to sag to earth in flames, like the Hindenburg. Marie began to cry bitterly. Herbert told her, "Look, Marie, make yourself a drink and sit down. I'll be right over."

I already made myself five drinks.

When Herbert heard that, he hurried.

He parked his modest Mercedes diesel next to one of the terra-cotta vases that were spaced around Marie's crushed-marble courtyard. All the ornamental plantings around Marie's house were as green and beveled by clipping as any you might see on an English country estate. Too bad, Herbert reflected, that they didn't contribute to the atmosphere in Marie's place some of that calm complacency of the English upper classes. Maybe that came from a long tradition of the lord of the manor cheating with boys instead of chorus girls. Certainly that would be Arthur's opinion, if anyone solicited it. Herbert smiled ruefully to himself. Arthur should only know how predictable his opinions were after all these years.

Herbert rang Marie's doorbell. She came to the door herself; the maid had gone to her sister's, she explained, to spend the evening baking cookies for the church supper.

"They do the whole thing, ham loaf and all, for three dollars a person," Marie said. "How's that for setting an example? We really must learn . . . all of us around this town . . . to be more *economical* . . . with our money, our emotions. There's altogether too much waste and *oops* . . . spillage." (Marie slopped some of her martini out of her glass as she let Herbert through the doorway.)

It was obvious to Herbert that Marie was very drunk, but he could also see that she had made a sober effort, at some point in the day, to make herself look attractive. And she had succeeded. She was wearing a beige silk dress and long amber beads, and she'd pulled her hair back so that her large blue eyes and small perky nose were the focus of your attention. She might have been crying earlier, but now she was clearly trying to keep herself in one presentable piece for Herbert's sake. No stray hairs tonight. No more bewailing fate. Herbert was touched to see that Marie had made such an effort. For him. In spite of everything. When was the last time Arthur had made a special effort—to do anything for *my* sake? Herbert wondered. It had been so long he'd forgotten.

Marie's foyer was as formal as the shrubbery outside. On the floor marble tiles put down in a black and white harlequin pattern echoed under the heels of Marie's and Herbert's shoes, much as people's steps reverberate in a museum; in Marie's house the echoing of the marble served to introduce the high ceilings, the carved moldings, and the English Queen Anne and Chippendale furniture within. Marie gave Herbert's straw boater to the Moor who stood by the door holding a tray for calling cards, and then she said to Herbert, "Let's go sit out on the sun porch. We can have our cocktails with the Boston ferns . . . who are really pleasant company . . . they're so earthy and damp . . . for Bostonians, that is."

"Fine with me," Herbert said. He followed Marie through the living room and out to the porch. Settling into one of Marie's antique wicker armchairs, which was as cozy and as complexly engineered as an old English pram, Herbert accepted with a smile the martini that Marie poured him from a full-to-the-brim shaker. He had a sip, and then he set down his glass on the Canton garden seat—a friend among Marie's furnishings in Herbert's eyes: the blue landscape sketched on the porcelain barrel always had a calming effect, as only a Chinese or Japanese landscape could, with that peculiarly oriental vision of scenery in utter silence.

"Macadamia nuts?" Marie offered.

"Ah, yes, thank you. These are Arthur's favorite, you know."

"Naturally. Does Arthur like *anything* that's inexpensive?"

"He's had some pretty cheap tricks over the years."

"Poor Herbert. I don't know how you've put up with that all these years." Marie swallowed some of her martini. It went down the wrong way, and she started coughing.

Clearing her throat after the coughing fit was over, Marie said, "Ulp. I sure sound tinny, don't I? If I keep coughing like that I'll have to move to Miami Beach and sit at the bar in the Fontaine-bleau. And have my hair bleached . . . without putting any toner in it."

"You okay?" Herbert inquired, leaning forward with a physician's appraising look on his face. "Are you okay . . . after last night . . . and all you went through today?"

"I'm okay, I'm okay," Marie assured him. She touched her neck as if it were slightly unfamiliar. "So when will Arthur be getting back from the city?"

"Who knows? These little junkets usually take a couple of days. But they've been known to last a week."

"Depending on who he hooks up with, huh?"

"That's right."

"How's the martini?"

"Cool, limpid, smooth, and probably it'll go to my head. It's an Arthurian drink, you could say."

"You and Arthur—umph"—Marie suppressed a burp—"ah—you know, a lot of people can't figure out how you two . . . how you ever . . ."

"Got together? Sometimes I wonder myself. Sexually, I'm happier with women . . . actually. I enjoy it more."

"You do? Then why ever . . . ?"

"Why Arthur? Because, I suppose, in some convoluted way, he's a father figure."

"A father figure? Are we talking about the same Arthur Conrad? He's such a . . . a child. A spoiled little boy. How can he be a father figure—erp, excuse me, Herbert—for anyone like you? You're so mature-acting—and dignified."

Rotating his martini glass slowly between the palms of his hands, Herbert thought for a couple of moments before answering Marie's question. Then he said, "The fault, dear Marie, is not in our stars, but in ourselves, that we are underlings."

"That's Shakespeare, isn't it?"

"Yes, I've always liked the rhythm of that line, and the sense of it. Let's see if I can paraphrase it for you: the fault, dear Marie, is not in our parents but in ourselves that we are always their children. Underlings."

"I don't understand . . ."

"Arthur is a father figure for me, Marie, because my natural father wasn't. He was only the voice of authority. And a loud voice it was. He was one of those men who make jokes in the office and then scream and yell at home. Of course, home wasn't *always* just screaming and yelling. Every year we'd take a vacation. And then it was nice and peaceful and quite at home. Because my father would be screaming and yelling in a hotel room."

"Oh." Marie had another sip of her martini and looked guiltily at a Boston fern.

"You see, Marie, I need masculine affection."

"That's very hard to get."

"Perhaps. I lived with a woman for a year. I tried very hard to be affectionate. And gentle. But she wanted it a little rougher. So she

105

started seeing a truckdriver. And then she developed a yeast infection . . . in her vagina."

"A yeast infection? In her vagina? Hm. If I knew you were coming I'da baked a cake."

"So I left . . . it was pretty messy. The whole thing. For a month she thought she wanted me back and called eight or ten times a day. A year later I met Arthur. But not in a bar."

"And on Arthur you pinned your hopes."

"Yes."

"Hope is scattered everywhere around here, isn't it? You can walk along the beach and pick up little bits and pieces of it, all different colors . . . and worn smooth by constantly being thrown up on the rocks."

"This is getting depressing. Let's change the subject, Marie."

"What shall we talk about, then? Vivian's tragedy? Laura's triumph? My baptism in flames? Art? Opera? The weather . . . or should we just go upstairs and fuck before dinner?"

"What?"

"I'm sorry, Herbert. . . . I wouldn't have said that . . . but I've been at this . . . sauce all afternoon, and sometimes . . . you start to say something and before you know it you're sliding down a hill on a sled."

"Actually, it's a nice thought," Herbert said, smiling. "Maybe we're entitled."

"What do you mean? Herbert, I was just kidding."

"No you weren't. Arthur was talking about the Constitution this morning, about how, when you've lived with the same person long enough, there are checks and balances, emotional guarantees . . . but there's also a Declaration of Independence that says 'When in the course of a relationship one partner leaves the other to his own devices—the one who's left has a right to the pursuit of happiness too.' "

"I'll take the Fifth Amendment on that one."

"Why?"

"Because I'm a lonely woman. And loneliness tends to incriminate you."

Herbert stood up and held out his hand to Marie.

"You get bills from the Holiday Inn on your credit card, invoices that you have no alibi for . . ." Marie went on. There were tears in her eyes.

"Let's go upstairs together, Marie," Herbert said.

"But what if Arthur finds out . . . ?"

"I'd call and consult him," Herbert replied. "But I'm sure I'd be interrupting something. Come on, Marie. Let's go celebrate Independence Day."

CHAPTER TEN

"Oh, Herbert, what have we done?" Marie said.

"We've made love," Herbert replied.

Marie smiled and stuck her forefinger between her lips, so that she looked like one of the bashful babies who decorated the rim of the soup bowl she'd used as a child.

"Tee-hee," Marie said.

"Tee-hee what?" Herbert inquired. His hair was messed up, Marie noticed. It made him look so boyish.

"Tee-hee, I was just thinking I should say to you, 'Oh, Herbert, it was never like this before,' but I can't say that because it was like this—once."

"When was that?"

"When I was a freshman in high school and I went to the junior prom with Sam Flint, who was the president of the dramatic club and a big star. We danced the Charleston and everybody stood back and watched us. And applauded afterward. I never saw him again socially . . . after the prom. I suppose he's gay and living in New York. Like all the other sensitive men."

"Arthur is gay and living in New York and he's about as sensitive as a snapping turtle. You shouldn't generalize, Marie. Every time you generalize, a possibility that's out there somewhere withers up and dies. It's like what happens to fairies when children say they don't believe in them. Tinkerbell begins to flicker."

"I'm not that way at all," Marie protested. "Far be it from me to close off any possibilities. . . . I always looked on you as a possibility. And now look where I am . . . in bed with you. Before dinner even. Tinkerbell wasn't flickering, in case you weren't aware of it, honey; she was *flashing*."

Laura and Jamie had now been together almost twenty-four hours. They'd had hamburgers and a salad for dinner, and then they'd made love yet again. It was ten after ten. Jamie was dozing, with his head resting in Laura's lap. She was wearing one of his Brooks Brothers shirts, which was generously made; there was almost enough broadcloth to pass for a shirtwaist, and Laura felt comfortable in it. She also felt comfortable with Jamie's head in her lap. Too comfortable. I've got to go back to the house tomorrow morning, Laura thought. How could I have stayed here even this long? Jamie moved his head a little in his sleep, so that when Laura glanced down at him she saw his profile. What incredible grace. The line from his forehead to his chin might have been drawn by Picasso or Cocteau—there was beauty and sensuality in every curve. *The line seems almost to undulate, to breathe.* Laura lightly traced in the air, with her finger, the outline of Jamie's face. All great art is body talk, she thought. And that is how I could have stayed here this long.

But enough is enough. Life goes on, Laura reminded herself. That girl down the hall from me on East Eighty-first, the one in 7B—what was her name? Clara? Yes, Clara. The one with the public relations job. I wonder if she's still with the same outfit. She's probably home now, right this very minute, making herself a pot of that mint tea she likes so much. Clara Gilbert. Now I remember. Clara Gilbert was her name. And always with the mint tea. That's what I need to do. Go back to Eighty-first Street and make a big pot of mint tea and then go out and find myself a job. Maybe in PR.

Laura imagined herself calling up Liz Smith with all kinds of choice information: Diane Keaton looked radiant last night at a screening of Robert Altman's latest. . . . She really does look radiant in person, Laura thought. Much more striking than in her movies. Probably Woody Allen toned down her looks so he'd be believable walking down the street beside her. Laura wondered if she had ever appeared radiant. She wondered if Jamie thought she looked radiant when he came up to her at the party. Or did he just think, she'll do for tonight? When would women ever get over worrying about being attractive to men? Even somebody Flash Donahue's age, with her fifty different handbags and her rouge that looked like a red sunset on each cheek, the last glow of daylight in the veil of wrinkles . . . even Flash Donahue was still vain.

The saddest thing about all this worrying about being attractive was that you couldn't win even if you were attractive. Men like a variety of attractions, and so many women are willing to stand, each in her own little booth, offering kisses for free. Not even collecting a dollar for a good cause. You'd think with so many of us getting fucked over all the time, we could at least raise a little money for Channel 13. Or maybe earmark a nickel of each dollar of alimony or child support for "Sesame Street," which makes it easier when you're raising kids alone. Some good should come of it all. Because you sure as hell can't rely on attractiveness or men. You need a *job*.

Having read herself that lecture, Laura tried to decide whether to shift her leg, as it was growing numb from being in one position so long. She decided not to. She didn't want to disturb Jamie. She wanted his head resting in her lap. How exasperating these tender feelings were. What a pain affection was. Things like that interfered with rational thought processes. One thing was clear to Laura, though: there was no future in this. Doing it with some guy, no matter how handsome and rich he may be, leads nowhere. Except to doing it some more. Until he feels like doing it with the next woman who happens along. Look at Marie. Look at Vivian. Look at all of them.

With the exception of Mother. She was an exception, Laura had to admit that. Mother and Daddy were happy. They had been happy. But the risks weren't as great for them. They'd married late in life, for people of their generation, and Daddy was already entering that stage where he liked to light a pipe and survey his property, his past accomplishments, the dessert dishes. Laura knew because in the home movies where she appeared as an infant, her father was already sitting in his chair at the dining room table with the look of a man whose digestion is establishing the pattern for his retirement. Maybe the secret was to look for an older man. If they have enough energy to get out on a squash court they have enough energy for another woman. But when they grow contemplative, with the pipe and all, you're pretty safe.

110

Jamie Lawrence was probably great at squash and tennis. And he didn't seem at all contemplative, except when he was talking about his mother, or when he wanted to do it again, and would start eyeing thoughtfully whatever part of you his shirt wasn't quite concealing. Oh, dear, thought Laura. What should I tell him? What should I do? Should I say, "It's been terrific? I had a wonderful time? I'd love to see you again? Call me?" Or should I say, "It's been lovely, but I have to be getting back to the city, so we probably won't be seeing . . ." Oh, God, I'd just like to sit here with his head in my lap forever. But how do I know he wasn't thinking before he dozed off . . . maybe he was thinking, "Man, I sure got a lot of action out of this one." They can be like that. So smug and pleased with themselves. I wish I could think straight. Thinking in this situation is like trying to get a lid off a jar with both your hands wet.

Laura sighed. She felt as though that was what life amounted to, maybe, a sigh. Oh, why don't you get tough, girl? she asked herself. Why don't you just play this thing by ear? If I play this right, I could be sleeping with him the whole summer. And wouldn't that make autumn in New York bittersweet? It would take three pots of mint tea just to tell Clara Gilbert about it. How did that golden oldie go, "I could never love you . . . the cost of love's too dear." Yes, that was it. . . . "But though I'll never love you . . . I'll stay with you one year . . . and we can sing in the sunshine . . . we'll laugh every day . . . we'll sing in the sunshine. . . ."

"Then I'll be on my way," Laura thought, and she moved her leg to make herself more comfortable.

It was ten-thirty and Marie and Herbert still had not eaten dinner. Marie had decided that this was *Tea and Sympathy*, but she was not Deborah Kerr. Guilt and embarrassment overcame her, and she wrapped herself up in the sheets and told Herbert, "I must look great to you, all sweated up and swathed like this—why don't we pretend it was all just an unfortunate occurrence at a health spa? A mixup in the assignment of the steam cabinets? That's believable. I could believe that. The two of us thrown together in the heat and humidity, all light-headed from the decompression of weight loss. We just didn't know what we were doing."

"I did," Herbert replied.

"You did? I was afraid of that. You were too good not to have

111

known what you were doing. But I keep thinking of Arthur. I keep thinking I've betrayed him."

"Arthur doesn't take sex personally. Why should I? Why should you?"

Marie wrapped herself up more tightly and said, "I hate these conflicting emotions. Conflicting emotions are murder. Once, when Dan and I were making love, I banged my elbow against the headboard just as I was reaching an orgasm. How's that for a two-pronged fork?"

Herbert tugged playfully on Marie's sheet wrap. He said to her, "Come on, Marie. Get out of those swaddling clothes. Sheets were never designed for a coverup."

Marie pondered that point for a moment and then said, "Yeah. You're right, I suppose. Wrap yourself up in the sheets or smooth them out afterward, it doesn't make any difference. You can never cover up your trail. Every unmade bed in Cable Harbor is a potential Watergate, isn't it?"

"Yes, and the politics are even more sordid, as things usually are on a personal level."

"Still," Marie said, "I'd hate to wind up like my Aunt Kathleen."

"What's she got to do with hiding under the sheets?"

"Oh, nothing, nothing. In fact she was the exact opposite." An image of Aunt Kathleen in the hospital came back to Marie, poking itself under her chillingly, like a cold bedpan.

"She was in the hospital dying of cancer. And even though she was on her deathbed, she was still trying to show herself off to every man in the room. Dr. Fitzpatrick and everyone. She'd hitch her johnny up and pull the sheets down off her so that her bare thighs stood out and pretend she wanted to show her new incision. And she'd say to her own brother-in-law stuff like, 'You wanna see where they operated on me? You're a big boy now, so you won't mind if you happen to see my twitcher too. Right? You won't mind, willya?' Her *twitcher*. Can you imagine? Thank God it was buried with her."

"Your aunt must have been made of sturdy stuff to be that horny when she was at death's door."

"I don't know. It may be a natural part of dying. I've always thought the death wish is nothing but lonesome horniness. A coyote's howl."

"Well, Marie, then we certainly know we're alive. Right now I'm not lonesome and I'm not horny."

"Then you're in a state of what used to be known as wedded bliss. Ready for some dinner?"

"That would be nice. Are you up for cooking?"

"Am I ever. One thing you should know about women, honey, if you're going to start fooling around with them, is that nothing gets those old gas burners lit up faster than a nice warm . . . afterglow."

So saying, Marie shucked off her sheet, put on her bathrobe, and, whirling around once on tiptoe, headed down to the kitchen. Herbert put on his briefs and went into Marie's bathroom. It was a Sherle Wagner bathroom, with brown marble fixtures so sculpted as to elevate the performance of bodily functions to quiet contemplation and aesthetic delight—a sensation that inspired Marie to tell some of her friends, "When I go to the toilet I feel like I'm looking for shells on the beach . . . and when I step out of that marble shower I feel like I've actually got a statuesque body; it sort of Florentines you."

In the cool elegance of Marie's bathroom, soothing himself with the tap water that plashed from the gold dolphin faucet into the oyster-shaped marble basin, Herbert allowed Arthur to reenter his thoughts. Taking Marie to bed had been a spontaneous idea, and Herbert had simply acted on it. Seized the moment. Herbert distrusted spontaneity, though. In his life he had never done anything spontaneously; what he had done was swim underwater for a long time with want held inside his chest, and then finally he had had to ripple the surface in order to breathe. That was what had happened tonight, with Marie. Now would come the consequences. And always they seemed to be important, if not dire—these consequences that came from raising your head and seeing daylight.

Marjorie felt that it was time to confront her husband with the fashion show; at the rate he was going, they'd be lucky to show up at the tent with a couple of packages of Oreo cookies. So she decided that as soon as she got back to the house she would ask George if he'd worked on the menu suggestions while she was gone.

She found him in front of the sink. George was looking into a roach trap, holding it up to the light so he could see more.

"Be careful one of those things doesn't fall out," Marjorie said as she put her bag on the table.

"They're not getting out," George replied. "No way. They're as bad off in there as you'd be if you went walkin' around in Crazy Glue . . . in a pair of high-heel shoes. I gotta set out a few more of these things around the walk-in refrigerator."

"Did you get started on the menu for the fashion show while I was gone?"

"No, I was out in the workshop," George replied. Marjorie propped her hands on her hips, which gesture always provided a framework for reading the riot act to her husband. George knew the signal well, and he responded to it now with the same look his son gave stewed prunes.

"Look, George, Mrs. Donahue and her friends on that committee were supposed to have a menu to look at yesterday. What are you trying to do, lose the job for us?"

"Who else are they going to get besides us?"

"Are you nuts? This is a catering business we're operating, in case you've forgotten. Which means you cater to people or else they find an outfit that will. Like that outfit in Stanleyville with the fancy panel truck that looks like an engraved invitation, the way they've painted it. If you'd get off your ass maybe we could get a new delivery van. With that wreck of ours, people probably think we're coming to sell them baskets, like the Gypsies."

"The Gypsies don't come around here anymore. What are you talkin' about?"

"Well, if they don't, it's probably because they're wholesaling baskets on the Cape and getting rich while you're out in that workshop building some Rube Goldberg birdhouse. Who cares whether we have any birds in the yard anyway? I think squirrels are better for us to have. They live exactly like we do. Running around like crazy just to accumulate a few crumbs." Sinking into one of the kitchen chairs, Marjorie heaved a sigh of exhaustion. She brushed her hair off her forehead indifferently, as if to say what the hell difference does it make how I look? She looked up at George, who was squinting at the roach trap again. Then she looked at the bag she'd brought home from Booth's market.

"I've got an idea, George," she said. "Why don't you see if you can't remodel that birdhouse of yours into a roach trap big enough to hold Evelyn Booth?"

"What's wrong with her?"

"What's wrong with her? She probably weighs a hundred and

114

fifty pounds more than I do. And every ounce of that weight is one more ounce of satisfaction."

"Why don't you put on some weight, then? Go ahead. Eat up, if it'll make you happy."

"You know, George, I've forgotten what makes me happy."

"Oh? I know what I like. I've never had any doubts about that." George was poking around inside the roach trap with a pencil. Marjorie watched him. It was remarkable, she thought, how he still had all his hair. And how it hadn't gone gray yet. Only his face showed his age; it had creases, sharp creases. But his eyes hadn't changed. They were just as they'd been when she'd met him: dark brown, deepset, and cagy. George's eyes were puppy eyes—that was what Marjorie had thought when she met him in high school—and they still were, only the puppy was a dog now, of the breed that can't wait for you to turn your back so it can get into the garbage.

"Are you through with the car?"

"Why?" Marjorie asked.

"I want to go . . . get some things."

"What things?"

"We can't very well plan the menu for the fashion show unless we know what the wholesalers are going to have available. . . . I'll take a run down to the wharf, I think, and then I'll stop off at the liquor store and talk to Henderson. We'll need probably eight or ten cases of Great Western."

"So go. I'd like to think we accomplished a couple of things today."

Leaving the roach trap on the counter, George took the car keys from his wife. He walked out to the driveway and opened up the car. Already it was heating in the sun; out of George's memory came an erotic snapshot that he had always treasured: the time he picked up Mary Scavone after school and she burned her ass on the hot car seat and jumped out again and danced around the parking lot with her little butt cupped in her hands like a honey-dipped dough-nut right out of the fryer. Christ.

The Oldsmobile station wagon that Marjorie and George used in their business was one of the last highway personnel carriers to come out of Detroit. It held the road pretty good, George often observed, but the road holding was more a matter of gravity than cleverly engineered suspension, and the wagon had to be almost floated in gasoline, like the big barge it was. Marjorie hated the Olds. George, however, liked the gadgets the car had, the power windows, the power seats, the climate control. Sometimes George would pull over to the side of the road and just sit for a while, fooling around with the power assists, running the antenna up and down, letting the stereo radio seek out a signal. It reminded him of high school, this fooling around in the car—it reminded him of the time right after he'd gotten his license, the time when the interior of a car was almost as intense a place to be as up a girl's dress. And when you were in the car, there were all these buttons and knobs and gauges—and the gas pedal, shit, the gas pedal, that you could stand on and lay rubber halfway down the block.

The way the girls used to sidle up to your car. They'd even put on their lipstick in your rearview mirror. And you'd be sitting behind the wheel, real cool like, looking at their boobs and asses out of the corner of your eye. What boobs they had back then. Like somebody had stacked up everything that sex amounts to and put a tight rubber band around it. But you get older, and the band becomes less elastic. It can even snap. That was what was happening to George lately. Something in his mind would snap, and he'd be running, all of a sudden, in neutral, unable to impel himself forward. It was as though the bands in an automatic transmission had worn out; George would stand idle for several moments and then lurch back into his daily routine.

The automatic transmission in George's head—the *drive* gear that was supposed to be taking him to the wholesale fish market and the liquor store—ran out of fluid on the shore road. He pulled the big blue Olds over to the side of the road and shut off the engine. Then he turned the key back a notch and rolled down all the power windows. He switched on the radio. But he didn't really hear the music. Or the surf hissing on the rocky beach below. The sky was a clean sweep of blue. Far out on the ocean, which was a darker blue than the sky, a lobsterman's boat rocked like the toy rocking chair in Jennifer's old dollhouse. George just sat there, idly watching the boat, for a long time.

George was gone for two and a half hours on his so-called errands. When he finally strolled into the kitchen and announced that maybe they could get oysters even though they weren't in season and maybe they'd have tomalley for dips if enough lobster bodies were available, Marjorie flew into a rage.

"Maybe? Maybe? All this time you were gone and you couldn't find out anything definite?"

George shrugged and examined the roach trap again.

Marjorie began to cut up the string beans with bitter, sharp-edged precision.

"Of course, we could just forget about doing the fashion show," she said. "Maybe I could get a job in the school cafeteria in the fall, passing out windmill cookies and little cartons of milk. How about that, George? Isn't that a good idea?"

"The way they wiggle around their feelers after they get stuck," George observed.

"Will you put down that disgusting thing? Do you want me to mix some of them up in your vegetable soup?"

George was sitting at the kitchen table, with the roach trap held up to his eyes. He looked to Marjorie like one of the kids playing with a Viewmaster. Marjorie threw a string bean at him. He caught it in his right hand with the fluid reflex of a big league pitcher and stuck it in his shirt pocket.

"You know what the trouble with you is, Marge?" he said. "The trouble with you is you don't take the long view. You gotta ask yourself this, you gotta ask yourself, 'What difference is it all going to make fifty years from now?'"

"Fifty years from now we'll still owe Master Charge, that's what difference it makes. Ooh. Honest to God. Sometimes I could crown you."

"Crown me what? The Duke of Earl? You'll still be my duchess, baby, even though you heed your mother's warnings every time we go to bed."

Marjorie picked up the colander with the cut-up string beans in it. Her lower lip puffed out like dough hit by a rolling pin. She charged at George. He didn't bother to duck. And Marjorie crowned him with the colander. Removing the colander as casually as he would if it were a cap, George reached inside the roach trap and removed a squirming insect. The bug was so big Marjorie could see its eyes. She screamed.

"Don't you dare come near me with that thing," she yelled.

George walked over to the sink, flicked the cockroach off, and turned on the water. The insect swirled in a circle and was gulped down the drain.

"You see, babe?" he said. "Down he goes. With his Master

117

Charge and his Visa and all the other insects' accounts receivable. And that's where you and me are gonna be in fifty years, the place where you get to if you take a right at Mrs. Ferguson's septic tank and a sharp left at the roots of that tree stump they got the World War II plaque bolted to. And if you don't know where that is, ask any worm."

"You're out of your mind, George. You're really going off the deep end."

"Maybe I am. Or maybe I'm one of those guys who's figured out that you can do any fuckin' thing you wanta do. 'Cause it ain't gonna matter—it ain't gonna matter *nohow*—in fifty years. Christ. Not only will it not matter what you did, there won't be a soul around who even remembers what you did."

"Why don't you just go back out in your workshop and whittle? Go on. Go. So I can get down on my knees and pick up these lousy string beans and wash them off and put them on the lousy, goddamn stove." Marjorie was forcing herself not to cry.

"Okay, call me when it's ready." George went out as casually as he had come in.

A little later, the kids came in, one by one. Marjorie sent Jennifer out to get her father.

They ate. Mark picked a scab on his knee. Jennifer saw him and made a gagging noise. Junior called his brother a "gross little asshole." George laughed. Marjorie spread butter on a piece of white bread. She ate it. Then she ate another slice. The bread and butter didn't make her feel any heavier—or one bit more satisfied.

Marjorie and George went to bed early. George turned over on his side, putting up the usual Sheetrock between them. Marjorie read the *Reader's Digest*. One thing she liked about the *Digest* was the "Drama in Real Life" section. Once, early in her marriage, she had liked to picture George in the various heroic roles: getting all the deaf kids out of the smashed-up school bus in the nick of time, ditching the crippled plane in the Pacific, pulling the old man out of the car a minute before the freight train from Vermont was due. When George was in his National Guard uniform Marjorie hadn't had to stretch her imagination very far. But now . . . there was an old picture of George in his National Guard uniform on top of her mother's television set. Also there was Marjorie's brother Ed in his navy uniform, and three cousins, two in the Army and one a WAC.

And in the middle of all the military pictures was an American flag stuck in a wooden base. Marjorie's mother had come down from Canada and been naturalized. So she was patriotic and proud of all the family who had been in uniform.

She should know, Marjorie thought, how many of us are still in foxholes. She frowned at George's blank back. *To think when he went away to that crazy two-week summer camp I'd get out that old Shirelles recording of "Soldier Boy" and cry listening to it.* What have I got to show for all of that? Marjorie asked herself. This house with its six little rooms that looks on the outside like something you can see riding along any interstate? Three kids who might not make me as unhappy as they possibly can so long as I wait on them morning, noon, and night? Of course, I do get to look at the pretty clothes of all these women with their diamonds so big you wonder how anybody could wear one without cracking her knuckles.

Resentment crossed Marjorie's mind. She turned to "It Pays to Increase Your Word Power," said to herself, "Bullshit it does," and flopped the magazine down on the spread. Just wait till tomorrow, she thought. Just you wait until I start talking on that show. They think they can get away with murder in this town. Finding a dead body at the Perry House and everything else, and that Evelyn Booth, sneaking around all the time like some kind of padded Mata Hari, always acting and talking like she's got the goods on everybody. I'll show her. I'm going to prove something to her and *him* (she scraped George's thick shoulder with her glance) and everybody else around here, including the crowd with the diamond jubilee on their fingers. There's going to be one hell of a town meeting over this killing—this whole Perry House business—and when they have that meeting *I* am going to be running it. I'm going to be running the whole show, just you wait and see.

Marjorie had gotten herself so keyed up thinking about what she was going to do that her shoulders were heaving. She put her hand over her heartbeat. There was a fervor in her, the same kind of fervor she had once felt reading her husband into "Drama in Real Life" situations. I'll make a difference, she promised herself. People are going to remember me for a long time. Maybe even in fifty years, I'll be remembered as having done something—you sunufabitch.

CHAPTER ELEVEN

Evelyn Booth was tying up the line on "Get It Off Your Chest" again. There had been three calls in a row from people who were afraid to go anywhere alone since they heard about the murdered girl. Now Evelyn Booth was saying that most people are murdered by people they know, and since nobody in town had known the dead girl, that meant she was probably killed by an out-of-towner.

"I don't know anybody who grew up around here that's capable of murder anyways," Mrs. Booth added. "Around here we learn to use plain common sense, and common sense will tell you that killing somebody is not the Christian thing to do, and it don't settle anything either. You may shut a person up by killing them but you won't keep them from coming back to haunt you. I for one think that this reincarnation business is something that actually goes on. And I've got common sense enough to know that if I was to kill somebody, that person might come back as a goldfish and watch me all the time right in my own living room. Might even come back as a lightbulb, and flash off and on to let me know that it ain't forgotten what I did to it. It makes you shudder to think about it. No, I don't think anybody from around here killed that girl. They got too much common sense. But anybody from outside, anybody who came here from somewheres else, them I can't speak for."

Hearing that, Marjorie glared at the radio. The nerve of her. She always was one of the ringleaders of that bunch who always had to let you know that if you weren't born and brought up here, you were automatically suspect. Marjorie noticed grease on the radio dial and wiped it off with Fantastik on a paper towel. She would have liked to wipe Evelyn Booth's face with Fantastik, the way they used to wash kids' faces in snow. That's what she needed, and have her mouth washed out with a good, strong detergent into the bargain.

When Evelyn finally finished speaking her piece—and some piece of work it was, the usual crazy quilt of patter—Marjorie picked up the telephone receiver with vengeance in her heart.

"My, but we have a lot of armchair detectives in this town, don't we?" she began. "Let's see. So far we've figured out that whoever killed that girl was not a native of the area. Also the murderer was not a Christian. And he doesn't believe in reincarnation and probably not UFO's either, because if he did he'd be afraid the goldfish or the little green men are watching him. Therefore the murderer is an out-of-towner who never looks at the *National Enquirer*. We certainly are making progress in this case, aren't we?"

"Whattaya think we oughtta do then, Margie?" the talk master asked jovially.

"The first thing we should do is call a special town meeting to find out what's going on with the Perry House. That's item number one, in my book. Item number two is to find out what happened to that girl. We don't even know who she was or where she was from. For all we know, she might have been from around here. Maybe she was bringing something home to roost—when somebody stopped her. Anyway, you notice I'm putting the Perry House first here, whereas most people would think the murder should get first priority. I have a reason for that. One thing usually leads to another, and I'm sure that once we start uncovering the truth about the Perry House a lot of other things are going to be exposed, too; the truth always snowballs. You can't stop it once it gets started."

Marjorie could almost see the talk master nodding his assent in the momentary silence that followed her pronouncements. Then, right on cue, old man Tucker called in.

"I'm gettin' up a petition, by Jesus," he announced. Flailing his false teeth with his tongue, he sputtered something about "them people gettin' away with . . . too much for too longa time," and then he nominated Marjorie for moderator of the special town meeting.

"A lot of people will probably want to second you on that one," the announcer concurred.

A damper in Marjorie's chest opened. She put down her sponge and clung to the edge of the sink with both hands. She felt as though she were being transported from the kitchen to the absolute center of things.

In Booth's market, Evelyn, who was listening to "Get It Off Your Chest," packed a quart bottle of Welch's tomato juice on top of a dozen eggs.

Another day passed, and the weather grew hotter. Old man Tucker went from door to door with his petition, and was joined in his effort by a Right to Life lady and an antinuclear carpenter, which, in Cable Harbor, represented a coalition more broadly based than any Marjorie could have imagined possible.

The weather in Cable Harbor now had a heavy gold weight in it. In the afternoon there was in the distance a thickening yellow; thunderstorms were brewing, as in the lives of the people of Cable Harbor shocks were about to be generated and carried, crackling, from one huddled household to another. Evelyn Booth had too much common sense to subscribe to any old-fashioned notions about tempests in the atmosphere paralleling turmoil in the lives of the people below. But conditions were now such that, superior technology not withstanding, anyone hovering over Cable Harbor in a UFO would be running to the window to watch.

CHAPTER TWELVE

Marie woke up with the birds. This was the third morning in a row that she had awakened with Herbert beside her in bed. Marie lay listening to the clatter of the birds outside; she looked at the clock— 6:00 A.M. And the birds were already bustling in the branches, scraping their beaks like spatulas, reestablishing their territory, turning over worms. The birds certainly set an example for the rest of the inhabitants of Cable Harbor. No sooner did the sun rise than they were up and at 'em. Marie thought how nice it would be to have that kind of primal urge to get you going in the morning; as it was, evolution seemed to have limited man's instinctive responses to the evening hours. So what would it matter if we all had wings? In the morning we'd still be flying blind, or fluttering helplessly in the backyard until the maid put coffee in the birdbath.

How long is this going to go on? Marie wondered. She rolled over and saw Herbert's shoes lying where he'd left them on the Portuguese needlepoint rug. If only we were on a train heading west, Marie thought, and those shoes were outside the door of our compartment, freshly shined. That's how an impulse becomes an affair: you've got to get on a train or a plane or a boat. You can't act on an impulse and stay put. Because then the impulse turns into an arrangement, a temporary arrangement. Marie pictured herself and Arthur and Herbert opening one door and closing another like the old vaudeville routine; that was how such arrangements were usually orchestrated. And who had the energy for that routine?

One thing Marie knew she had to find the energy for was a visit to Vivian in her hospital bed. That would have to be today. Marie dreaded the prospect. Seeing poor Vivian's suntanned face on a white hospital pillow would be like seeing a child with steel braces on its legs; the poor thing will never be able to play baseball like a normal child, you think with a pang. Just as Marie knew she would think when she saw Vivian, the poor thing can't sit and watch people at the Bath Club all day, like a normal divorcée. Hey, wait a minute, Marie told herself. You're exaggerating the degree of crippling there, aren't you? She reviewed in her mind the events of the past few days, pondered the significance of it all for a few moments, and then decided, no, I'm not exaggerating.

Still, Vivian couldn't be left alone in her hospital bed to think that nobody cared about her at all. Easing herself quietly out of bed so as not to disturb Herbert, Marie trundled into the bathroom. She felt like a walking fruit and vegetable stand—ready to cascade all over the place. She had had too much to drink—again—last night, and though she wasn't hung over, her right hand felt numb and she was light-headed. There wasn't much doubt where all this booze was going: right into the extra pockets around her eyes. The bathroom mirror made that clear enough to Marie. There was no sense in trying to stop, though, not until things got better. Meanwhile the liquor acted as a preservative for a positive outlook. Vodka was the best lens Marie knew for rose-colored glasses.

Gargling with Lavoris, Marie held her head back until she became slightly dizzy. She shook her head to straighten out the wall, and padded out of the bathroom. Then she put on her robe and went downstairs. Elsie was already in the kitchen.

"Mornin', Mrs. Cartey," Elsie said.

"Good morning," Marie said. "Oh, how wonderful. You've already put up the coffee." She smiled at Elsie as she poured herself a cup and Elsie opened the refrigerator and took out a basket of blueberries.

"How 'bout some nice fresh blueberries and cream?" Elsie offered.

Sitting down, Marie said, "Super. I'd love 'em." She watched while Elsie poured the berries into a bowl. Elsie was built a little like the Michelin tire man; she was all inner tubes and toy balloons stuffed into a pink maid's pantsuit. Her face looked like nothing so much as a sugarbowl, and her home-dyed hair might have been

124

snatched off the head of a clown. Yet Elsie was always brisk and energetic—and her face was almost entirely free of lines. That was more than could be said for the women in Flash Donahue's crowd, none of whom were much older than Elsie. Some of them looked like toby jugs, what with their jowls and bulging eyes. Better to look like a sugar bowl, Marie thought. Nobody ever got to look like a toby jug by boozing it up at church suppers.

"I've got to go and see Mrs. Black in the hospital today," Marie said as Elsie put the blueberries in front of her.

"Oh, that poor woman," Elsie said. "How's she doin'?"

"I guess as well as can be expected. I'd like to try and get in to see her early . . . so I can have the whole afternoon to recover from it. Hospitals always depress me so."

"My sister Maggie does volunteer work upta the hospital. Pushes aroun' a wagon with candy and magazines on it. She says it's good for you to see how other people are suffering. Then you don't go aroun' feelin' sorry for yourself."

"It's not that hospitals depress me because there are sick people in them. They depress me because every time I go in one of them I think about going to see some dying relative. Which is something I'd like to forget. I think it takes a very special kind of person to push around a cart in a hospital . . . or to attend the twenty-fifth reunion of your high school class, as far as that goes."

Marie spooned some sugar onto her blueberries.

"Is there anything else you'd like right now, Mrs. Cartey?" Elsie asked.

"No, nothing, thanks," Marie replied.

Elsie reached for her handbag, which had a straw daisy on it that could be wiped clean because the bag was coated like a plastic place mat. She pulled out of the bag a piece of paper.

"I got to read this over," Elsie said. "Tom Tyler, the carpenter, with the ponytail, gave it to me. They want to call a special town meeting or some fool thing. I guess that Hanson woman is going to be made the moderator. On account of Enoch Harding's on vacation in the Grand Canyon with his wife and two grandchildren. Cute as buttons they are, those grandchildren of Enoch's."

"What do they want to have a meeting for?" Marie asked.

"Oh, I hear it has to do with that girl who got herself killed, and where she got killed, and I don't know what all else."

"Where she got killed? She got killed at the Perry House. Are they going to bring up the Perry House at this meeting?"

"I honestly don't know, Mrs. Cartey."

"Can I read that when you're through with it?"

"Surely," said Elsie. Marie was wide awake all of a sudden. And she hadn't even finished her first cup of coffee.

She didn't finish it, either. After reading the petition, she poured the rest of her coffee in the sink and made herself a bloody mary. Obviously somebody was out to get Dan. He'd probably have to attend this town meeting, even. Either that or be dragged into court, along with his company. What a pleasant way to start the day; the petition might as well have been written in adrenaline.

Taking her bloody mary with her, Marie went back upstairs. Herbert was stirring. Marie told him that she wanted to go and visit Vivian Black today. Herbert said he had to get back to the house to see how the reconstruction was going. He asked Marie to spend the evening with him there.

"It doesn't hurt to move around a little when you're doing what we're doing," he said.

"I know," Marie replied. "It prevents calluses . . . and bed sores."

Marie had two more bloody marys before leaving for the hospital. She didn't know what condition Vivian was going to be in, so she adjusted her own condition as a preventative measure.

The hospital that served Cable Harbor was located in Munsonville, which was five miles inland. Munsonville was an academy town with one movie theater and two sporting goods stores that both sold green and gold sweat shirts, green and gold being the colors of Munson Academy. Nobody seemed to live in Munsonville in the summer except yard men and garage mechanics. So the town was a good place for a hospital to be located: there was little to disturb the peace other than young garage mechanics chirruping the rear tires of their cars when they pulled out of McDonald's at night. Munsonville seemed muffled even more than usual by the summer heat. As Marie drove past the bandstand, she felt the glare of the day hitting her directly in the face—it was as if the sun had gold-leafed the entire town.

Thank God the hospital was air-conditioned. It felt like a supermarket inside; walking along the corridor, Marie felt like a head of lettuce arrested in the middle of wilting: returned to crispness, but still feeling damp and unhealthy. Marie asked a wintergreen nurse where Mrs. Black was. The directions led her to an open door. Knocking on the heavy door, Marie walked into the room. Vivian was sitting up in bed. The first thing that Marie noticed about her was that she was wearing jewelry—three cocktail rings and two gold bangles on her arms. Her hair was nicely combed, too (it didn't even look as if the color was coming out, which was what usually happened first when you were sick).

"Oh, Marie, I'm so glad you came," Vivian said. She held out her arms and Marie went up to her and kissed her.

"You look wonderful," Marie said. "I'd never know that anything had happened to you."

"Well, I know that something happened to me," Vivian replied. "Sit down, Marie."

"Look at all your pretty flowers and cards," Marie said as she pulled up a chair. "You got mine, I hope."

"Yes thanks, I did," Vivian said. "I'm going to have a big job hauling everything out of here. They're releasing me tomorrow."

"So soon?"

"I have to come back for a few more treatments, but I don't have to stay here any longer. I was ready to leave yesterday, as far as that goes."

Vivian seemed remarkably animated. Her brown, triangle-shaped face, which normally seemed expressive of a sour aftertaste, was bright and burnished with fresh makeup. What gives here? Marie wondered. I expected her to look like death warmed over. But she actually looks *good*. What the hell are they giving her? Pot?

"You've certainly made a wonderfully fast recovery," Marie said. "Why, you look better now than you did the night of Arthur and Herbert's party . . . of course you looked great then, too."

"I did? Probably I looked rather wan. That's the way I usually appeared in public."

Marie was shaking her head no and opening her mouth to voice a protest, but Vivian wasn't about to listen to objections to the plain facts. She said, "There's no sense in denying it. Don't try to flatter me, Marie. I know the way I looked—an aging Mia Farrow, with the paleness showing right through the suntan."

"You didn't look like that at all," Marie protested.

"Oh yes I did. That's why the bat chose to come down my chim-

127

ney. When you're pale at heart you attract all kinds of trouble—bats, Rosemary's baby, bee stings."

"Bee stings?"

"Yes. Didn't I ever tell you? When I was a little girl I got a terrible bee sting and went into convulsions. It happened right here in Cable Harbor. Out in front of my parents' cottage. I was reaching out to touch a hydrangea blossom and a bee came out and stung me on the hand. That was the start of all my troubles."

"It was?"

"Yes, it was. I came to that conclusion while I was lying here. All my life I've been afraid. Terrified of reaching out . . . for anything. I think I was even afraid when Joe slipped the wedding ring on my finger."

"In that particular instance you had reason to be afraid," Marie said. "We should have been warned, all of us: if you get married you're liable to get stung."

"Yes, that's true. You are. But what are you supposed to do instead? Women have to reach out for things. We have to give our hands to somebody. Otherwise they'd make more dresses with pockets in them."

"My wedding gown didn't have any pockets in it," Marie said. "It was made of white organza and chantilly lace trimmed with silk Venice lace. My mother made it. She was at the sewing machine for a solid month—cross-eyed. And I wore this sweet little lace Juliet cap with a veil of illusion that had lace appliqués. Now that I think about it, the only part of my bridal outfit that was appropriate for the occasion was the veil of illusion."

"Nothing I wore was right," Vivian said. "If I'd been carrying a bouquet of hydrangea blossoms with a beehive in the center—that sure as hell would have been right for me. But I didn't know. I just didn't know."

"My bouquet was exactly right," Marie recalled. "I mean, for a bunch of flowers, it was amazingly accurate. Yellow roses, chrysanthemums, carnations—and babies' breath. It was the babies' breath that was right on target. When Dan and I got married, we had a baby breathing down our necks. So to speak."

"You had to get married, huh?"

"Everybody had to get married in those days. Pregnancy just expedited the process."

128

"Well, back then we all did what we had to do. Now we have to think about what there is left for us to do. I'm telling you, Marie, I'm going to be a very different person from now on. I've already told Dr. Wallace that I want to start easing up on the Valium. Eventually I'm going to give it up altogether. And then I'm going to open up that dress shop I was telling you about . . . and it's going to be so trendy it'll stop a pair of Geoffrey Beene shoes right in their tracks."

"I don't get it. You're attacked by a rabid bat and all of a sudden you're brimming with self-confidence. How's that possible?"

"I hardly know myself," Vivian replied. "But I think it's a little like learning about the birds and the bees. You never really understand what it's all about until you lose your virginity. I didn't understand about the bats and the bees until I got stung the second time."

"What's to understand?"

"Only that you have to keep reaching out—whether or not you get burned or bitten or stung. You just can't pull back and retreat all the time. You have to get back out in the world and do whatever you can do—and when the bees come, duck."

A nurse who smelled like rubbing alcohol walked into the room. She smiled and Marie saw that her teeth were crooked and broken. Probably she was a practical nurse. Registered nurses had nice even teeth and ruined the marriages of a lot of doctors' wives.

"Time to take your temperature," the nurse announced. She stuck an odd-looking thermometer in Vivian's mouth. The thermometer had a curly cord like a telephone's attached to it, and the cord fed into an electronic box that was hanging around the nurse's neck.

"What's that, Nurse," Marie asked, "a digital thermometer?"

"That's what it is all right," the nurse replied. "An' the darn thing ain't workin' right." The nurse banged on the electronic box.

"I have digital scales," Marie said. "But science still has a ways to go. Maybe when they have electronic Robert Redfords on the market we'll finally be able to say that technology satisfies our appetites."

"Darn thing," the nurse said. She took the thermometer out of Vivian's mouth and went back out into the corridor.

"What'll they think of next?" Marie said. "A digital thermometer yet. I'd like to stick one of those up my ex-husband's behind. Then maybe I could get a readout on a few things."

129

"You should be thinking less about Dan and more about yourself, Marie."

"Myself? Who's that? I'm a mother, Vivian. Once upon a time I was a wife, too. That was my identity: Marie Cartey, wife and mother. Now, except for the motherhood, I'm back at square one. I'm an adolescent girl again, and I like to whisper secrets over the telephone. My ex-husband's secrets, especially. I've even been calling up that silly talk show they have, that 'Get It Off Your Chest.' I whisper things about the Perry House. It's just like high school. Did you know I met Dan in high school?"

Vivian shook her head. Marie said, "Well, I did. After I'd been going out with him for a couple of months, he showed up in study hall one day with his fly unzipped. And a couple of the boys in the class said to him, 'Whatsa matter, Cartey? You run into Marie in the corridor?' And everybody in the room hooted and laughed. And Dan blushed. I heard about it the next day. My girl friend Beth told me about it. About how sheepish Dan acted. I turned red myself when I heard the story. But secretly I felt proud. So proud. To be Dan Cartey's girl friend."

"And now you're back to square one," Vivian said. "It's not as if I don't know the feeling. The terrible dependency. But I think now that dependency . . . on anything . . . a husband or therapy or Valium . . . or whatever, has to develop out of a given set of circumstances. It all has to do with where you are or think you are . . . in life . . . your environment . . . your real environment and the psychological environment that grows out of you, like a winding vine . . . it all becomes a mesh, with you in the middle of it. . . ."

"A mess?" Marie said.

"No, a mesh," Vivian said. "And once you start cutting loose, everything you've allowed to grow up around you just . . . pulls away, like a vine that's lost its grip."

"What are you suggesting, Vivian?" Marie said. "That I use a pair of garden shears to get out of my girdle?"

"No, I'm suggesting that you go in with me on my shop. Try to do a complete psychological turnabout, like I'm doing. You'll be amazed at the difference in yourself. You won't need the telephone nearly as much."

"I don't know," Marie said. "You had a bat to give you . . . whatever it was it gave you."

"A poisonous hickey," Vivian replied.

"That's not much worse than what Laura says she's gotten out of the dating bars on Third Avenue," Marie said. "Although what she's gotten hasn't motivated her particularly."

"You and Laura are enmeshed," Vivian said. "That's why you can't move. Summer itself is a mesh. All these squares of broad daylight. We don't see that the squares are forming chain links because the daylight is so broad, and the days are so long. Look at the calendar for the month of July. Such a pretty picture up above. But below, a grid of days, a mesh, each square numbered."

"Hospitalization has made you philosophical," Marie said. "But somehow I think you're making sense. Maybe, up here in the summer . . . you can get trapped in the treillage. And in the winter, in the city, in those high-rise apartment buildings on the Upper East Side, the ones like the building Laura lives in . . . the kind of building I was looking at last year . . . God. It's true. They're all laid out in grids, squares on top of squares. And I'm talking from the perspective of somebody who's been trapped in an elevator with a CPA from Great Neck."

"Once when my daughter came back from visiting her roommate in Marin County she was all full of talk about 'occupying your own space,' " Vivian said. "And all I could think of was her taking a pill like Alice in Wonderland and growing so large that she entirely filled that little room of hers at college. Which wasn't very far off the mark, as it turned out. Now I think 'occupying your own space' can mean something very different. It can mean breaking out of the pattern altogether. You can construct your own little world and panel it and . . ."

"Move in the racks of dresses," Marie filled in.

"You got it," Vivian replied. "If you're starting at square one, you might just as well make your little square a retail space. How about it, Marie? Want to be partners in a really trendy dress shop?"

"I'm not sure what you mean by 'trendy.' "

"I mean carrying a line of antique clothing, for one thing. You should see the twenties dresses they about give away at the auctions up here. And I want to have a bar and plants that are for sale."

"A bar?"

"That's right. With a woman bartender. Or maybe even a man, a Warren Beatty type."

"I think you may have something there, Vivian. All the dress shops I've been to I've always felt there was something missing. Maybe it's men that I miss."

"Could be. I know when I've stared at rack after rack of dresses for a couple of hours, I can come away with an acute sense of penis envy, and my therapy group always said that was one of my problems."

"True. All too true. Life is an empty dress, a flight of uncarpeted stairs. . . ."

"How's that again, Marie?"

"Nothing. Nothing. I was just paraphrasing a poem by Edna St. Vincent Millay. Right now I'm in a situation with somebody that involves a lot of paraphrasing of poetry, and sneaking around."

"Huh?"

"Don't say 'Huh,' Vivian. It sounds like you're slipping back into that old gangly adolescent-girl insecurity of yours, and I don't want any backsliding, not after what you've been saying."

"What are you up to, Marie?"

"I'll let you know when and if it comes to anything."

"How about the dress shop? When are you going to let me know about that? Or is whatever you're up to going to interfere with your making plans?"

"Did you know that Edna St. Vincent Millay got to go to Vassar because she was in Camden and recited a poem she'd written, and a rich woman heard her and decided to provide for her education? How's that for having your life turned around because you decided to spend your summer in Maine? I bet they don't whisper about men up at Vassar these days. I bet they put *wife and mother* under small *d*. Computer programming being small *c*. And birth control Roman numeral number one."

"Think about it, Marie. The two of us running a nifty new dress shop with a bar and twenties dresses and antique wicker furniture."

"What Vassar girl would be proud of the idea that a study hall class thought some guy's fly was open because of her?"

"We could open up in Soho. Maybe even on Madison Avenue."

"My life was ruined because I took an open fly too seriously. Did you know I was a candy-striper in high school? Once an eighty-year-old man wanted me to help him pee in the bedpan. But this older nurse popped in just in time and told him, 'Oh no you don't. None of that.' She knew the score. Like they know the score up at Vassar these days. Why was I so naïve?"

The nurse with the irregular teeth returned. This time she brought a conventional fever thermometer.

"This is one courageous lady you have here," Marie told the nurse. "She's going to defy all the odds. She's going into business for herself."

"Isn't that nice?" the nurse said, shaking down the mercury and putting the thermometer in Vivian's anxious-looking mouth.

"My sister has her own vegetable stand," the nurse added. "And she's doin' a darn good job with it. Helps to send my niece to college."

"She's a regular entrepreneur," Marie said. "It seems like half the people up here are . . . entrepreneurs. Or voyeurs. Me, I have a hard time getting out of bed in the morning. But then maybe my bed is my . . . square one."

"Marie, mutt are moo up to?" Vivian mumbled.

"I'm trying to put myself in the way of opportunity," Marie replied. "Like Edna St. Vincent Millay did. When she was alone in Maine for the summer."

"Marie." Vivian plucked the thermometer out of her mouth. "Marie, you can't start your life over in bed. Beds are the boxes within the boxes. When you take the lid off a high-rise apartment building, that's all you see. Beds. Beds on top of beds. And everybody tossing and turning. Until the day they wake up with a start and see the blank walls all around them."

"Here, here, here," the nurse said. "We have to keep that in. Under your tongue. Please cooperate with me or else I'll have to call the doctor."

Reluctantly Vivian allowed herself to be stopped up again.

"I better get going," Marie said. "I think I've caused enough excitement for one day."

Vivian shook her head no.

"Yes. It's best that I get going. Look, Vivian, I'll call you tomorrow at home. Okay?"

Vivian twirled the thermometer to the side of her mouth in order to get out a "No, stay here," but Marie was already up and waving good-bye.

Jerking the thermometer out again, Vivian shouted after Marie,

"I'm not kidding! It's my life and I'm going to start living it. For myself!"

Marie turned around and confronted Vivian.

"Me too," she said. "I'm telling myself a new story, too. And the beginning of it is 'Once upon a mattress.'"

"Men are the oldest story there is," Vivian said. "They're hard luck stories written for women."

The nurse whistled through her teeth.

Vivian stuck the thermometer back in her mouth and pulled the sheet up over her head.

"Wish me luck?" Marie said plaintively.

CHAPTER THIRTEEN

Jamie was awake before Laura. He heard the gulls out on the rocks, keening loudly over their shattered crabs. Jamie pushed off his sleeping bag and went outside the tent. The sun splayed out over the water, which was flat, as it usually was in the early morning and at twilight: you could count on calm seas at either end of the day—at cocktail hour, or just after daylight, when the insomniacs were finally asleep. Maybe it all had to do with the pull of the moon; Jamie's grandmother had a theory to that effect.

Since he'd been in Cable Harbor, Jamie had gotten into the habit of swimming in the morning before taking his shower. The cold ocean water gave sleep a clean shave. It cleaned off all the moss, the way it did with driftwood, so that you came out feeling hard and knobby, clean-limbed and ready to go.

Trotting down over the rocks, Jamie reached the water's edge and flipped himself in. He surfaced fifteen feet out. Reaching easily, he followed the wave-hammered shoreline for a quarter of a mile. As he swam, Jamie turned over in his mind what had been happening. Laura Damon was different from other women. Or she felt different; she responded differently. Or perhaps he was responding to her in a way that he hadn't responded—emotionally—to a woman . . . since his mother's death. What was it about Laura? Jamie couldn't quite explain to himself her appeal. But he was aware that she had awakened in him, somehow, an old memory. A memory of helplessness.

He was around six. He remembered that he was riding with his mother and father in the back of their black limousine. His head was in his mother's lap, and her hand was resting on his shoulder. She thought he was asleep, but he was only pretending.

"I know all about it," Jamie's mother had said to his father. And then she had begun to cry, very softly. Although his mother's crying frightened him, Jamie still pretended that he was sleeping.

"I'm glad you do know," Jamie's father said idly. His mother stroked Jamie's shoulder. And cried softly. Breathing shallowly, in her lap, Jamie kept his eyes tightly shut against the velvet of her dress, so that the fabric was all of a piece with the pulsating red field he saw with his closed eyes.

How many years ago had it happened? Twenty years? More? Jamie was not certain. But he was sure of this much: his mother had held him that way—gently, lovingly—only once, and in her self-pitying sorrow she had made him feel like a small, dead pet.

Trying to put the old memory out of his mind, Jamie concentrated on his swimming. He told himself that Laura Damon did not remind him of his mother. Probably it was just that in her sexuality she seemed motherly. Sometimes it seemed almost as though she might be asking, is my body keeping you warm enough at night? Being with Laura had speeded up the past few days; time passed more quickly, as it was inclined to do when sexual anticipation was urging it along, and the things Jamie did to pass the time had become more interesting. Eating. Swimming. Even changing a tire on the van could generate enthusiasm and interest. Driving Laura to her house to pick up clothes had been a low-key adventure. So had their two tennis games. Even the visits to the bat lady in the hospital and Mrs. Cartey's house (the maid had said she was out, and Laura had thought she'd seen a furtive face appear for a moment between the draperies in the bedroom upstairs). Everything had been suffused with mild excitement. Which was sexual excitement, Jamie knew—and he had no objections whatever to that.

Knifing through the water, on his way back to the inlet where he'd made his camp, Jamie was thinking that he'd have to persuade Laura to stay on—at least through the summer.

While Jamie was out enjoying his early-morning swim, Laura was lying in her sleeping bag trying to think, which at this early hour was as difficult for her as trying to talk underwater. One thing

136

was clear, though. The brief ache she'd felt when she'd come to and found that Jamie was not there beside her was a warning. Laura knew enough to beware of dream situations: one does not live like Peggy Guggenheim in Venice, encouraging young artists in their art and all of that—and one does not live in Big Sur on top of a cliff, making coffee for disillusioned directors—and one does not spend the summer living in a tent with a Lawrence. Realistically, the best one hopes for is a meal at the Café des Artistes provided by a guy in a middle-management position with an English accent. Of course, with the English accent usually came a receding hairline (even though the hair was blond and curly) and all kinds of class problems owing to the fact that no Englishman with any real class would ever be inclined to emigrate in the first place.

The trouble with a dream situation, in Laura's view, was that you couldn't set up housekeeping in one. You had to be practical. Nobody brings home champagne, night after night, in a grocery bag. Wisdom militates against signing a lease on an apartment in Paris. Or summer residences in tents. Reality is an apartment on East Eighty-first Street and a publishing job with the discipline and security of grammar school ("We expect *everyone* to be in at nine sharp") and a Dag bag with La Yogurt in it. That was what was needed, Laura decided, reliability—labels that told all the caloric and emotional content, spelled it all out for you in black and white.

Resolutely Laura put on a plain Lilly Pulitzer dress (one with sort of shrinking flower petals) and drew back the tent flap to face daylight once again. The ocean looked flung out on the horizon, as abandoned to the air as a child joyfully letting go on a carrousel. Gulls were drifting in the spotless sky like kites. Jamie was no doubt doing his morning lap of the shoreline. Without him in it, the landscape was incomplete in Laura's eyes. It lacked a certain dimension. It was like Sardinia or Capri in a Progresso can. The flavor was right, but the atmosphere was . . . lacking.

Wherever Jamie had swum off to, Laura was sure that he'd be back soon. She didn't mind being alone for a while, either. When he wasn't there to distract her she could think more clearly. And Laura felt she had some serious thinking to do. That was the trouble with summer and sex, especially when you had to deal with the two of them in combination. All you wanted to do was lie back and enjoy it. And not make any plans. Batting a puddle out of the seat of a canvas director's chair, Laura sat down to map a plan of action in spite of the terrain, which was about as conducive to the planning of long-term survival strategies as Omar Khayyam's picnic grove.

The first thing that came into Laura's mind was Jamie. That was only natural, she felt: Jamie Lawrence was very good-looking, very intelligent, very wealthy, and very good in bed. So why shouldn't he come to mind first? Any girl who thought in terms of who was a good catch and who wasn't would think, reel this one in; when you have the ring on your finger, you won't notice the blisters you got landing him. It was true. Most girls wouldn't think twice about it. They'd just go after him. Hammer and tongs.

Laura, however, was given to having second thoughts. She had told Marie that once, and Marie had told her that if that was the case she was ahead of the game, since when you were a woman marriage was usually your first thought—and divorce your second thought. For a long time—Marie was right—Laura's first thought had been marriage. Getting married and having a family and a home of your own. It all seemed so comfortable and cozy and easily arranged, like the tea parties you'd have in your room for your dollies when you were little. Cheryl, Laura's roommate at school, had left to get married at nineteen. She hadn't even outgrown propping a Raggedy Ann against her pillow. She was going directly from Raggedy Ann to motherhood—which, when you thought about it, was a painful transition when it came to the delivery room but psychologically no transition at all.

Cheryl was now a divorced mother of two who was selling real estate. Laura wondered if there was a Raggedy Ann in the backseat of the car Cheryl used to drive prospective buyers from property to property. Probably not. Had Cheryl looked more closely, she would have seen that Raggedy Ann had her eyes wide open all along. Raggedy Ann knew you couldn't depend on the Andys of this world to keep you and your little tea party going forever.

You couldn't blame men, really, Laura had decided. Sexual freedom had freed them from having any second thoughts at all—except that a few of them now wanted custody of the children and alimony payments from their working wives. So those who did have second thoughts about marriage—women like Laura—had to be entirely responsible for what happened to them.

Laura had decided that falling in love was irresponsible. She had loved before—and she had been hurt before. But she had never been deeply *in love* and so she had not suffered for long.

I've really got no choice but to find myself another job, Laura thought. She thought about what a job could mean to a woman in this, the age of sexual liberation. A job was something like a convent with an open-door policy. You could come and go. Every day at work you could be pure and holy. And then, if you felt like it, you could head for one of those professional hangouts around cocktail hour and maybe be asked to fly down to Puerto Rico for the weekend by the guy who does the evening news on Channel 7 (that had happened to Laura twice—once with a newscaster and once with a salesman from Potamkin Cadillac). Yes, with a job you could come and go as you pleased. And have no second thoughts about any of it. With a job your little tea table was always set. And there was order and security in the world.

It seemed to Laura that working was the true provider; having a job now meant what having a husband used to mean: it provided stability, security, and comfort. You could even love your work. And you could change jobs a lot more easily than you could husbands. There was always a job for a woman who was willing to work, but there was not always a man for every woman with a willing heart. So you have to put your heart in your work, Laura reasoned, unless you want to risk a depression worse than anything that deterioration of the economy might bring about.

Laura's thoughts were interrupted as a pair of wet hands clamped over her eyes. Jamie had sneaked up on her. Like an Indian brave. A young Indian brave with muscles that glinted in the forest.

"Guess who?" Jamie said.

"Are you the Cable Harbor strangler?"

"Guess again?"

"Hm. Well, you're certainly very aggressive, the way you've latched on to me like this. Are you somebody's husband?"

"Nope."

"This has really got me puzzled. Whoever you are, would you mind massaging the back of my neck? I've been sitting here thinking, and whenever I do that my neck gets stiff."

"Okay, sure."

"Mmmm-mmm."

"Better?"

"Yes. Much better. Jamie?"

"Yeah."

"I've been thinking."

"What about?"

"I've been thinking that it's about time I headed back home. This is basically our first date, you know. If that's what you want to call it. I know that's what my mother would like to call it. And for a first date it's turning into an awfully long dance marathon . . . without any dancing . . . although I'm sure my mother would like to think that dancing is what we've been doing."

"Why not call it that, then? Our first tango."

"I suppose we could. . . . Still, I don't feel right about borrowing your shampoo and your shirts. Of course, I would have had everything if I'd brought back that steamer trunk my mother had ready for me. All the same, I think three changes of underwear and three fresh dresses are enough to have along for the first date, don't you?"

"I want you to stay here," Jamie said.

"I did. I have. But . . ."

He lifted Laura out of the director's chair and turned her around so she was facing him. She tried to avoid his blue eyes.

"Move in with me," he said. "We'll go over to your parents' house today and pick up whatever else it is you need."

"Are you serious?"

"Of course."

"You want me to live with you out here in this tent . . . for the whole summer?"

"That's right."

"I feel like Jennifer Cavalieri getting here wool hat pulled down over her eyes. But somehow I think this is a better deal you're offering than the one she got. I couldn't believe that locker room scene in *Oliver's Story* when Ryan O'Neal turned around and there was a pimple on his ass. Hey, what are you doing there? Stop that! Oh no . . . oh no, don't . . . stop."

"You moving in?"

"Yes, yes, yes . . . oh-oooh, you feel so go-ood." But the deal may be off come September, Laura thought.

Herbert became depressed almost as soon as he walked through the door of the house he shared with Arthur; Last Resort was no different than any of the other houses Arthur had a hand in—it was beautiful, but it was unsympathetic. There was no room in any of the rooms for human frailty, no rumpled sofa with a shine of wear on the arms, where you could sink in and be comfortably gloomy. Every place Arthur occupied was a place where your head was turned toward beauty. Opening up the built-in bar in the living room, Herbert poured himself a glass of scotch. Across the room, on the Victorian mantel that always reminded him of an Austro-Hungarian army officer in oak epaulets, Herbert reacquainted himself with his friends, five Chinese Export vases.

The vases, which were among the few accumulated objects in the house that were friendly to Herbert, were a set—chimney garniture. On each of the vases flat goldfish swam. The fish looked out from their confinement in the glaze with wondering Mandarin eyes. They looked as though they might be about to be hooked, as Arthur so often was, by the dangling of some exotic bait. The fish were what Tadzio, the staring youth of *Death in Venice*, would have caught had he not been angling for Gustav Mahler. Herbert wondered what flesh-and-blood object had transfixed Arthur this time. Then he wondered what the point was in wondering.

Herbert had to wonder, though, about what was going to come of this brash interlude with Marie. She was so open and generous, and in return wanted only companionship and a little affection. Marie was the kind of woman Herbert would have liked to know in his youth. She was past the stage where she would want to get married to settle the ongoing when-are-you-ever-going-to-settle-down argument with her mother. She was past childbearing (Herbert had never wanted children; he had no desire to repeat his unhappy childhood, and he knew from knowing his relatives that the continuation of the family line would only prove the law of diminishing returns). And Marie was sharp and funny. There was no doubt about it. She represented a threat to Arthur. Insofar as Arthur was capable of being threatened. That was one thing that you could say for self-absorbed people like Arthur: they weren't jealous. Still, if this were indeed the final break, Arthur would have to feel some effects from it.

Arthur was not invulnerable, Herbert knew. That he insisted on living in showplaces, that he insisted on wearing outrageously expensive clothes—what were those determinations other than defenses? And what was his need for constant sex but a need to establish a sense of self-worth by accumulating around him the wants of others? Herbert was becoming resigned to the fact that Arthur was never going to get over being picked on in junior high. What a sad business to spend one's life flaunting money in order to get even with some poor seventh-grade bully who once twisted your arm and who now in all likelihood was working two jobs just to put starch on the table. Perhaps the saddest thing of all was that Arthur used young gay men to increase his stores of vainglory. The victim had become the victimizer. And that was not a necessary cycle.

Herbert knew that two people could still come together and provide for each other's happiness. There was still such a thing as curling up together in front of a fireplace, watching the flames. Which maybe represent in your unconscious all the hell in the world. Which is why you shouldn't build home fires for the unfaithful: it's a good way to wind up carrying a torch.

On his way out to LaGuardia, in a cab, Arthur was thinking about the three days he'd spent with the kid he'd picked up in the bar on Fifty-third. He had gone to the bar expecting nothing—looking, he felt, as if he were going to a routine performance at the Met, or worse yet, going to a performance at the Met on his mother's subscription. But, despite the odds . . .

It had been nice. It had been especially nice watching him walk around nude in the bedroom in the morning. The kid's smooth taut body was a vision, the kind of vision Arthur blinked to imagine when he told gay friends that he'd like to be a fly on the locker room wall when the Munson Academy lacrosse team came in from a practice. How poignant it had been when they'd finally gone through the ritual of exchanging telephone numbers, over their coffee, only a half hour ago. Depression or no depression, in New York there was always a dust bowl with little folded pieces of paper marked with telephone numbers. Blowin' in the wind.

Standing at the door on Sixty-seventh Street, Arthur had watched with a heavy heart as his three-day diversion turned the corner. He stood there, feeling emotionally numb, until he saw a young black bopping along the street. The black kid was carrying a cassette player as big as a suitcase. Oh brother, Arthur thought. The corn roll and the ankle sneakers and the rolled-up jeans and the whole bit.

Arthur backed inside and was about to close the door when an odd note struck his ear. The music blaring from the cassette player was familiar.

"Viiii-iiiss-si da-ah-arr-rtay!"

Good lord, Arthur thought. The kid was playing a cassette of Maria Callas singing *Tosca*. And as he sashayed by he leered licentiously at Arthur.

It's true, Arthur thought. The whole world *is* gay. His spirits lifted, he went back inside to pack for the trip back to Cable Harbor.

CHAPTER FOURTEEN

Marjorie was pulling into a parking space in front of the town hall when she spotted Evelyn Booth and her husband, Sanford. Marjorie's nickname for Sanford was Golly Gee. Golly Gee was always as wide-eyed as the *o* on a package of Oleo, and his wife let him go around with three or four different patterns on all the time. so that his clothes looked like three or four different layers of cheap wallpaper. Today he looked as crazy as ever. Checked flares, a loud striped shirt, a wide tie with feathers printed on it, and socks wrapped around his ankles that were like a "Star Trek" poster on a kid's wall; what were they supposed to be anyway? Rotating planets on a field of navy blue, evidently. Golly Gee was walking so quickly, it was hard for Marjorie to make out the design. Marjorie had figured out why Golly Gee married Evelyn in spite of her size: he must have been one of those goony kids with glasses who always got left behind, so he married Evelyn in order to be pulled along in her wake, like a dinghy tied to the stern of a trawler.

Where were they off to, the two of them, in the middle of the day? Marjorie wondered. They didn't see her getting out of her car, so she watched them getting into their car and driving off. They must have had something important to do, to leave the market in their kids' hands. (When those bratty kids of theirs were running the place, you wondered if you were going to be able to get your groceries past the rock music they were playing, and it wouldn't be a surprise if the girl were to stick her gum on the side of the register while she totaled up your order.) And Evelyn had had that look on her face that Marjorie had come to distrust: a look like a bag of potatoes that have sprouted in the dark. What was going on? Maybe Golly Gee had seen somebody shoplifting and Evelyn was going to their house to collect while he hid behind her. That was probably it. In any event, Marjorie couldn't spend time worrying about what those two were doing. She had her own business to attend to.

Marjorie's business was in the town hall. George had told her once that real estate transactions are matters of public record. So Marjorie had come to the town hall with the intention of looking into the records on the Perry House. The town clerk, a retired schoolteacher with white hair and a huge black typewriter that could have been made out of a steel rake and a wheelbarrow, was always accommodating to Marjorie. Now she was even more accommodating than usual. She, too, thought that there "ought to be one good long town meeting about this situation"—one in which, she confided in a whisper, her sister and she were sleeping with their late brother Lem's sawed-off shotgun under the bed.

Miss Pearson obligingly dug out every record of transactions and permits and variances involving the Perry House. Marjorie spread out the whole business on top of a pair of file cabinets. There was a ton of it: mimeographed maps and notarized agreements and letters from lawyers. It reminded Marjorie of the history notebook she'd kept in high school and then had to sort out in order to pass the final exam. It was all a blur of treaties and dates, so Marjorie picked out Napoleon because he was little and cute and Queen Victoria because she had a face like the bowl of Marjorie's grandmother's old-fashioned water closet. As luck would have it, the essay question had to do with Napoleon, and Marjorie had received a 91 on the test. Now Marjorie felt lucky in the same way. She picked out from the pile of papers a folder with variances in it, choosing that particular folder only because the pulp it was made of was especially creamy, as grass is sleeker over a septic tank. For an hour Marjorie read and reread. Miss Pearson made a pot of tea and worried about Marjorie's having enough light to read without tiring her eyes.

Then Marjorie spotted something. Something you wouldn't notice unless you squinted hard—like a navy blue sock matched with a black sock. Pulling two different pages out of the folder, Marjorie

145

placed them side by side and looked first at the fine print on one, and then at the other. This *date* was wrong—that was it. It had to do with the Perry House's power and telephone lines. According to the records, Homer Shute had been paid a sum of money by the Mid-Coast Development Company for an easement crossing his land. But the land was not his when he sold the right to cross it. Two months before, he had transferred title to Louise Patterson. That meant that the variance the Perry House's developers had obtained, which was contingent on buried power and telephone lines running through the Patterson land, was legally built on a sand foundation. Someone with no title to the land involved had sold an easement across it.

"Miss Pearson," Marjorie began, "could you please step over here a minute? There's something here I'd like you to see."

Miss Pearson reached for her eyeglasses, which were hanging around her neck on a black cord, and got up to look at the page where Marjorie had propped her index finger. Marjorie showed the date on one agreement, then turned the page and pointed out the date on a second agreement.

"My word!" Miss Pearson exclaimed. "Would you look at that? I may only be a justice of the peace and notary public, but I can tell you those dates look illegal to me. Darned illegal. The nerve of people. Why, this is worse than what that cousin of Mrs. Booth tried to do, getting one set of license plates for their two cars and swapping them."

Smiling with satisfaction, Marjorie asked if she could have copies of the two agreements. Miss Pearson produced them in two minutes ("I'll have them for you in two shakes," she promised, and then produced them in a shake and a half).

"I'll bet you're going to talk about those two pieces of paper at the town meeting, aren't you?" Miss Pearson asked. She was on tiptoe with excitement, and as fluttery as a bird casing a crust of bread.

"I sure am," Marjorie replied. "But I'd appreciate it if you'd keep mum about this until the night of the meeting. We want to surprise a few people."

"Oh, I will, I will," Miss Pearson promised. "I won't even tell my sister."

"One thing you could tell me, if you know anything about it,"

146

Marjorie added. "Is it true that Hopkins, the real estate man, is the agent for the people who put up the Perry house?"

"He certainly is," Miss Pearson replied. "Ooh, that Hopkins. He'd take the gold out of his mother's teeth, if he had the chance. Come to think of it, he did. The poor thing died last February. Living all alone, she was. I went to see her in the funeral parlor and I swear they were burying her without her dental plates. Why, she had no chin at all."

"Hopkins and the Perry House people and quite a few others around here are goin' to have some explaining to do before all this is over," Marjorie assured Miss Pearson. "They're going to find out you can't steal the eyeteeth out of people forever. Eventually they get wise to you. The date switchers and the license plate swappers and the lazy, idle rich, and the people who sell you the same meat for ground round as they do for plain old chopped beef. They just switch the labels, like others do with license plates and dates. They're all going to meet their Waterloo, you just wait and see." (The comparison—Waterloo for all the cheats in town and her high school triumph of Napoleon turning out to be the essay question—was an apt one in Marjorie's mind. History was repeating itself. Everything was falling into place. Only this time Marjorie was making the history.)

Walking out of the town clerk's office with the telltale records under her arms, Marjorie was fairly glowing. She felt as though she were at a big public party, with everyone playing pin the tail on the donkey. And she, Marjorie, was the only one playing without a blindfold. She imagined herself walking up behind Evelyn Booth and pinning a license plate to her big fat behind. She imagined Hopkins nervously checking the gold teeth in his safe deposit box. The only thing she couldn't imagine was George helping her in any way—or getting any shared satisfaction out of her efforts bearing fruit. Well, he could just stuff it. Hold up inside his crazy birdhouse —and have an eye-level view of all the heads going by at the top of pikes.

Evelyn and Sanford Booth had gone to pay a special visit to Lester, Evelyn's cousin, who had recovered from his bat bite and was home taking it easy for a couple of days before returning to work.

Lester was twenty-nine and portly and blond. He looked like the son of Heidi—a strong, sturdy, ruddy-cheeked outdoorsman who had grown up like a billygoat, the constant, good-natured butt of the other boys' fun. Lester had married Donna Paine at nineteen. They lived, with their three children, in a house trailer that sprouted a new plywood porch or bedroom every other year.

Evelyn was pleased to find that Donna had taken the kids shopping with her: she wanted to talk to Lester on the q.t. Lester was happy to see Evvy again, but he was not equally happy to see her husband—he always looked as though his mother were making him wear rubbers, and he was always talking about what went on at the Rotary Club, probably to make you feel inferior because you weren't a member.

"How you doin' today, Lester?" Evelyn asked as she compressed the sofa cushion.

Watching Evvy seat herself, Lester couldn't help but grin. She sure was a big one. Lester had observed once that you could put in a fairly good-sized foundation for a house in the amount of time it took Evvy to set herself down on a beach blanket. But that didn't mean he didn't like her well enough. He liked listening to her a lot. She was one of those women—like your grandmother—who you could really sit and listen to those times around Thanksgiving or Christmas when everyone was through eating and just sitting there kinda comfortable.

What Evvy said at the kitchen table was always the center of the talk, almost the way when you're in a kitchen, you pay attention to the stove because it's the most important thing. Course Evvy wasn't that much lighter than a gas range, so maybe it was just natural for her to be in command in the kitchen.

"I'm pretty good today," Lester said. "I'm feelin' pretty good."

"I see you're reading a *Playboy* there," Sanford said as he sat in the rocking chair and started rocking. "You know what I like about *Playboy*? What I like is those sports pictures painted by Leroy Neiman. The president of the Rotary, he has an original print by Leroy Neiman on his living room wall. Boy, it must be nice to be able to collect original art like that. But we haven't done so bad with our Hummels. We got a Hummel Christmas plate that's worth over a thousand dollars now." Sanford said *a thousand dollars* with a sense of reverend wonder in his voice, and looked at his wife for corroboration. Evelyn folded her arms and nodded comfortably. She looked to Lester as though she'd just piled two logs on the fire— her arms were that hefty. Lester hoped that he wasn't going to have to listen to Sanford brag about their Hummels again. Lester didn't like Hummels much. They all looked like Christmas angels, only they wore shorts and carried umbrellas. Sometimes he wished they were real and running around the floor—none of 'em more than three inches tall. It would be fun stepping on them.

"Them Hummels, they're a darn good investment," Evelyn said.

"They are. Yes, they certainly are," Sanford chimed in. "Everybody in the Rotary is doin' just what we're doin'—spendin' their money on somethin' solid 'fore it gets worth even less than it is now. We've all got *inflation psychology*." Sanford said *inflation psychology* in a flag-waving tone of voice; that was another thing about him that grated on Lester: he was always coming up with new expressions that showed he was in the know and parading them in front of your face.

"You got inflation psychology, Evvy?" Lester asked.

"No, I'm fully inflated now," Evelyn replied.

Her answer made Lester laugh. Good old Evvy, always making jokes on herself.

"But I think Sanford is right about people havin' to look out for inflation. Donna sure does have to buy a lot of groceries, don't she?"

Lester looked out at the kitchen glumly and said, "No denyin' that, Evvy. Donna's thinkin' about goin' to work in Andrews's lobster pound. I don't know if I like the idea of her doin' that. Workin' around boiled lobster an' melted butter, when you get home at night you 'bout have to bathe yourself with a bunch of those there Wet Naps."

"It sure would be a good thing if you could get yourself a promotion, wouldn't it?" Evelyn said.

"Not much chance a' that happenin'," Lester replied. He started turning the pages of *Playboy* to brighten his spirits a bit.

"Whoever was to put the finger on the one who killed that girl, he'd be in line for a promotion, now wouldn't he?"

"He sure would," Sanford said, answering his wife before Lester could. "The policeman who solves that case will be invited to speak at the Rotary. I can almost guarantee it."

"I don't think I'd want to speak to the Rotary unless I was chief of police," Lester said. "I'll probably never get that far, but I sure wouldn't mind a promotion to sergeant. Not one little bit."

"Then maybe you'd want to come in with us on a little private investigatin'."

"How do ya mean?"

Evelyn gave Lester a look that indicated her head was a pretty full cookie jar and said to him, "Look here, Lester. I think we got a good reason to be suspicious of a certain party. But it might be hard to prove anything if we went through normal channels."

"What other channel is there?"

"There's the way the CIA operates, for one."

"We made one big mistake when we *shackled* the CIA," Sanford pointed out. "We had a former FBI man to speak at our club and he said the CIA should never have been *shackled* the way it was. You don't pull the covers off somebody who's doin' somethin' *covertly*."

"What do ya wanna do, then?" Lester asked. "Put bedspreads over our heads and start spyin' on everybody?"

"No," Evelyn replied. "But I wouldn't be above obtaining some evidence outside the usual channels. Now, I already had a little talk with Midge down at the post office. She's worried an' I don't blame her. Got a daughter the exact same age as that girl who was killed. It was Midge told me about them strange packages George Hanson gets in the mail. She said to me that the next time another package like that comes for George Hanson she's gonna hold it out so's we can have a little look-see."

"You can't open somebody else's mail," Lester said. "It's illegal. You need a warrant."

"That's why we're planning this operation *covertly*," Sanford whispered.

"When he gets it he's gonna know somebody's been into it," Lester warned.

"How's he gonna know?" Evelyn shot back. "When was the last time you got anythin' in the mail that didn't look like a cat had sharpened its claws on it?"

"We want you to be present when we open up the package," Sanford said. "You'll make it official—or at least you can bring whatever we find out to the right officials. And then they can get a warrant to enter the Hansons' house."

"I dunno," Lester said. Just then they heard Donna pulling up in the car.

"Think it over," Evelyn advised. "It's your future."

Donna came in with the kids, who were clinging to her and asking for Coke. Donna put her bundles in the kitchen and got Cokes for everybody. She also squeezed some cheddar cheese spread that came in a shaving cream type of container onto a plate of Ritz crackers.

"This girl is truly a gifted hostess," Sanford said.

"Runs her house better than I do mine," Evelyn agreed.

"I get ideas out of *Family Circle*," Donna said. Lester insisted that she point out some of the things she'd made. So Donna started pointing. She'd made all the curtains in the window, and she'd made the coffee table by fitting window glass to the top of an old lobster trap, and she'd stripped and painted the dining room table and chairs.

While the two guests were eating their crackers and cheese, Lester proudly described his wife's accomplishments in entertaining.

"I know Donna'd never use George Hanson to do her work for her," he said. "Whenever we have people over, she goes down to your store and gets a few boxes of that frozen Banquet chicken. Then she heats it up and puts it all in this Colonel Sanders bucket that we saved. They think they're all gettin' Kentucky Fried Chicken and they're pretty impressed."

"That's the way to run a house," Evelyn agreed. "Use your head. You have to, with prices the way they are."

"We didn't even have a caterer for our weddin'," Lester said. "You remember. Everybody got together and mixed up the potato salad and coleslaw the night before. And at the reception Donna went right out in the kitchen and got her own beer. She wasn't havin' anybody waitin' on her hand and foot, wedding gown or no wedding gown."

"I like a girl like that," Evelyn said. "But a type of woman I can't stand is that Marjorie Hanson."

Sanford grimaced in approval of his wife's sound judgment. Donna bowed her head slightly to acknowledge the general praise she was receiving for her superior domestic arrangements. Lester was beaming. Although he was not altogether sure that Evelyn's plans were going to work out.

"She's a clever one all right," Evelyn said to her husband after they'd finished their snacks and were heading for their car. "But her and Lester'll never have anything much unless he gets a little more ambition."

"What we have with this situation here," Sanford pointed out, "is an opportunity to kill two birds with one stone. We may well wind up putting a homicidal maniac behind bars, and we'll be helping Lester to go places in the police department in spite of the fact that he isn't very ambitious."

And I'll be putting that Marjorie Hanson in her place once and for all, Evelyn thought. Evelyn's eyes narrowed to slits. Remembering things, Evelyn wore on her face the same grim expression she had worn the day Marjorie first crossed her path. It had been hot, like the weather was now, and it seemed as though the whole town was at the beach. Marjorie Hanson had only moved in recently then, but she was in a big hurry to attract attention. Going in the water up to her shoulders, she had taken off the top of her bathing suit and waved it at the group she was with—a group that was mostly male: friends of her husband probably. Evelyn had coolly appraised Marjorie right down to the last nickel of her worth, with just that waving halter to go on. That was all she needed to go on, because she knew the type. A show-off, wagging her tail at the men: that was what she was. Hard as nails and every bit as cheap and common.

Not long after the top-waving incident Evelyn had become personally acquainted with Marjorie. At first it was only a business acquaintance, on account of the market, but it very quickly got personal. Evelyn and her kids had been using the footpath that ran by the Hanson house and two other houses for years. It was a shortcut to the beach. And Evelyn needed to use shortcuts if she wanted to get where she was going without a lot of huffing and puffing. Shortly after the Hansons moved in, a sign appeared at the beginning of the path: PRIVATE WAY. That had been followed by a NO TRESPASSING sign. Evelyn had ignored both warnings. Then Marjorie herself appeared with an ultimatum. Evelyn remembered her nasty little speech word for word.

"I'm sorry, Mrs. Booth, but we just can't have people cutting through here all the time. It's eroding the whole hillside and we have to keep shoring it up with rocks from the beach. I'm afraid I'm going to have to ask you to use the public parking lot like everybody else."

Thinking about that line of hers made Evelyn boil even now.

152

I'm sorry. I'm afraid. If she was so sorry and so timid about it, why didn't she keep her mouth shut?

"We've been taking this little shortcut for years—long before you were aroun' here—and it never bothered the Fredericks or the Harpers any." That was what Evelyn had said to her. And what did she get back?

"I'm sorry, Mrs. Booth. I can't help what the Fredericks or the Harpers have allowed to go on in the past. *I'm* asking you to be more considerate."

Sorry, huh? Humph. The more nerve they have, the more apologetic they pretend to be about it—talking down to you like you were a child. Evelyn had not bothered to argue the point any further. She felt it was beneath her to quibble with the likes of Marjorie. So she had majestically hoisted her umbrella and beach chair and barged right on through to the beach. But she had never used that shortcut again. And she resented deeply the inconvenience. As far as Evelyn was concerned, Marjorie Hanson had violated an old common trust, like somebody who'd put in a septic tank right next door to your artesian well.

There had been one more encounter with Marjorie. A year ago she had called Evelyn to complain about what was going on in the woods. She seemed to think that Evelyn's son and his cousin had organized a teenage sex ring. To that accusation Evelyn had curtly replied, "I've always held that kids should fight their own battles. And if your daughter can't put up the little bit of a struggle that it takes to keep a boy's hands off her, there's not a whole lot I can do about it."

Marjorie had hung up with a bang at that. And so the bad blood between the two women had thickened. It was a feud a man could not possibly understand. Evelyn knew that; therefore she didn't even attempt to explain when Sanford said to her, "Boy, you really have it in for that Hanson woman, don't you?" It was enough for Sanford to think that Marjorie Hanson complained about the meat all the time simply because she liked to make a stink—and now for him to think that maybe the woman's husband was a sex killer. That much he could grasp ahold of.

For her own part Evelyn understood all she needed to understand too: she understood exactly the type of woman who would wave her top at her husband's men friends, the type of woman who blocked your way when she saw you crossing her property, the type of woman who couldn't control her own daughter but wanted to tell you how to raise your kids. Yes indeedy. Marjorie Hanson was the type of woman who had to be put in her place. Or one fine day— if your husband ever got tired of you being a little on the heavy side and started looking around—there'd be a woman of Marjorie Hanson's type right there waiting for him. And then where would you be? Yes, that type had to be put in their place. Constantly. If you wanted a place for yourself.

CHAPTER FIFTEEN

Herbert made dinner for Marie. After dinner they went out by the pool to drink their glasses of Sambuca and watch the moths and mosquitoes fly into the ultraviolet trap. Marie thought that was the thing to do after her visit with Vivian.

"She's emerged from her shell at last," Marie said. "The little white moth is determined she's going to look like a butterfly."

"More than one person has been brought out by a bite on the neck," Herbert observed.

"I don't believe it," Marie said. "The transformation is too sudden. Maybe she's still in shock. Maybe this is all just a prelude to a nervous breakdown. All these manic plans she's making. That is deeply unstable. I know. Stability is only achieved by living from day to day—it's getting yourself across that swinging rope bridge between the bloody marys in the morning and the martinis at night. . . . What a romantic glow that pool light is making. If only my makeup mirror cast the same light."

"You don't have to apologize in front of the makeup mirror, Marie," Herbert said. "I've been unstable myself—but I've always chosen the people I sleep with carefully."

"You men do have that choice," Marie replied. "But women haven't always had the same freedom to choose. There used to be a sort of Living Bible for Women, and one of the psalms was 'Be not picky, lest ye be not picked.' "

Toying with his cordial glass, Herbert said, "Marie, this decision . . . to be with each other these past few days . . . that was a conscious choice that both of us made . . . wasn't it?"

"On my part it was more instinctive than anything else—give the mare her head and she'll find her way to the hay. That's an old New England proverb. I think that's the way it goes. Or maybe it's supposed to be, 'You can lead a mare to the hay, but you can't make her give head.' "

"That sounds more like an old Long Island proverb," Herbert said.

"Do you think I should go in with Vivian on her dress shop?" Marie asked. "Maybe she really has got her act together."

"I think it's worth the risk," Herbert replied. "I won't mind getting back to the city this fall. Getting back to work . . . whether or not I'm still working with Arthur. We have too much money, you realize. This whole crowd up here is too wealthy for their own good. Everybody needs to have work to do. You need to have a reason to get out of bed in the morning. If you don't you lose years out of your life, because your attention gets starved, and you begin to feed on yourself."

"How true . . . how awfully true. You can only examine your fingernails just so long before you begin to nibble on them. You can only go to Georgette Klinger so many afternoons . . . until finally plastic surgery begins to look even better than a facial. Laura is right. So is Jackie Onassis. If you don't get into publishing or something you'll be caught in a steel trap made from your own coathangers. Either that or you'll become dependent on exercise, therapy, and sex and have to move to Beverly Hills . . . which is a fate worse than moving to Marin County . . . though of course it isn't quite death."

"No. Death is Dayton."

"I thought it was Dubuque."

"Actually it's summer stock."

"Oh, of course. You're right. It's one thing to be middle-aged and horny, but it's quite another thing to be a middle-aged actress doing *Same Time, Next Year* . . . in summer stock."

"What do you say, Marie? Are you going to go to work in Vivian's dress shop this fall? Are you going to stop thinking about yourself?"

"If I ever stop thinking about myself I'll probably also stop drinking. Think of that . . . a purpose in life . . . and Perrier."

"The two of them do go together."

"No, Perrier goes with dieting . . . which is most people's purpose in life. It's an indirect relationship . . . sort of like our relationship."

"How is that?"

"We sort of came together indirectly. You're a bisexual and I'm a divorcée. That's not exactly common ground. But here we are. Neither of us being very particular anymore. It's poignant how little we ask for in the end. When we start out asking for so much. Love everlasting. Someone to watch over us. Someone who'll be faithful and true forever. I even know a woman who won't go out with men who smoke. And gay men are even worse. They're even more demanding. They not only want love everlasting—they want a *variety* of it. But in the end . . . in the end I think all anybody wants is a little genuine human contact. It's so rare. And so precious."

"You've had a lot of human contact, Marie. And you're hardly near the end yet."

"Once upon a time. But I've felt out of touch now . . . for ages and ages."

"Why don't we go back inside? I'll put on a Frank Sinatra record if you like."

"How romantic, Herbert. Frank Sinatra and Sambuca. If only you were a plumbing contractor I could convince myself I've run away to Las Vegas with you."

Standing up, Herbert gallantly offered Marie his arm, and she accepted it as daintily as a prom girl. Strolling through the french doors, they crossed the living room, where at one end the stereo system had been built in. Herbert settled Marie in the cushions of one of the plush banquettes and pulled out a Sinatra album. Marie looked at the jacket and said, "Remember how in the forties it was sexy if a man pushed his hat back on his head? Then Jack Kennedy came along and made it sexy for a man not to wear hats at all. That was when I threw away the saddle shoes I'd kept since high school and hoped that Dan would never leave me."

"And now he has left you," Herbert said.

"Yes," Marie replied. "I think that's my cue to put my flighty hand next to my throat and wander over to a window, like Katharine Hepburn in *Long Day's Journey into Night*. They should have filmed that movie up here." Marie had a sip of Sambuca and accidentally got one of the floating coffee beans in her mouth.

"O'Neill understood the pain of being unable to reach the people who mean the most to you," Herbert said.

Pushing the coffee bean back into the cordial glass with the tip of her tongue, Marie said, "O'Neill understood the Irish. We're born without umbilical cords, you know. What connects us to each other is copper tubing, like you use to build a still."

"So you keep hammering away, huh? Trying to make the tubes bend."

"Something like that," Marie replied. "I admit I wouldn't mind throwing a monkey wrench into Dan's network of leaky plumbing. I'd like to find out what he's up to with the Perry House. Force his hand if I can." Marie lit a cigarette.

"What's the point, Marie?" Herbert said. "You're never going back to him. And you're smoking too much, you know."

"I know, I know," Marie said, exhaling. "A girl I know in New York once said to me, 'Cigarette smoke is the exhaust that comes from running love affairs.' Anyway, I realize I'm never going back to Dan. But there is a point to getting at him somehow. The point of it is . . . Let me put it this way, Herbert. My mother used to deny that I ever delivered newspapers to earn my school lunch money. But I *did* deliver newspapers—from a little rusty red wagon that I pulled along behind me. In the slush. I could never get my mother to admit that. If she had, it would have mattered to me . . . even now. It would have made a difference. It would sort of . . .validate a part of my past. And I need validation, Herbert. I need reassurance. I need to know my complaints are legitimate. If I could just catch Dan in the act. Expose him somehow. So that the whole town will know what he's planning to do with the Perry House. That would matter to me, too. Not as much as my paper route mattered. But it would make a difference. It would be a boost."

"I think what you're really saying, Marie—about your mother and about Dan, too—is that if you can't get them to say they love you, you're damn well going to know the reason why."

"I guess so," Marie said. "It's almost as though I have to say to myself, 'At least I'm satisfied on that score,' before I can . . . get on with my life."

Herbert got up and refilled their glasses. They sat for almost two hours, sipping and snuggling and listening to records. Frank Sinatra and Peggy Lee and the Beatles. Marie looked at the Peggy Lee album jacket and took comfort in it.

"It's amazing," she said. "She's managed to put all the information about halting the aging process that is known to southern California on a teensy-tinesy piece of microfilm, and she's hidden the microfilm under that beauty mark on her cheek. She makes me jealous."

"Do you realize Mick Jagger is close to middle age now?" Herbert said.

"Please don't remind me," Marie said. "Once when I visited my mother in the rest home she was all upset because my brother had been there first and he wasn't looking too well. You know what she said to me?"

Herbert shook his head and Marie added, "She said, 'My baby! My baby is so *old!*' I don't know why any of us should apologize for being horny . . . all things considered." Herbert squeezed Marie's leg reassuringly. Around eleven they went up to bed.

At eleven-thirty Arthur's chartered Beechcraft landed at the Cable Harbor airport. He hadn't called Herbert because he wanted to surprise him. Herbert's face always lit up when Arthur surprised him; Herbert was like a little boy in that respect—as obvious in his ups and downs as a carrousel horse. That was one thing Arthur had always loved about Herbert: his ingenuous way of showing his feelings. Arthur was glad he'd come back so soon. Monogamy when it's violated turns to sentimentality, Arthur well knew, but still he was anxious to be with Herbert again. He had had his lust lanced in the city. The inflammation was gone, the infatuation with it; now back to the everyday reality of Herbert, which was not such an impoverished reality—Herbert was attractive enough to have almost any queen he wanted, and of course he didn't want any of them, which made him doubly attractive, the one precious thing in Arthur's life that nobody could duplicate.

Arthur caught a ride to Last Resort in Smith's taxi, which was a rolling playpen with windshield wipers that Arthur had told people should be running constantly to keep the baby's drool cleaned off. The smell in Smith's cab always made Arthur blanch; it was onions fried in b.o., or worse—maybe they used diapers for seat covers. Smith had brought along his wife on the trip, which he often did when he answered late calls. She was sitting next to him in the front with a kid who looked hollowed out in the head.

"This 'un's all tired out," the wife announced. "But he's awful good. Don't make a sound."

The child stuck a dirty finger in his mouth and watched Arthur through half-closed eyes.

The only guarantee of security is stupidity, Arthur thought.

"Went along with his sister and me to the grocery today," Mrs. Smith continued. "The two of them went right up and down the aisles, pickin' out their jelly."

Myself, I'd find it hard living with two child prodigies, Arthur mused.

Smith, who was very fat, laughed with approval. Arthur couldn't stop looking at the wife's hair. Was it possible to do a wash and set with olive oil?

"It's nice of you to come out this late," Arthur said as Smith pulled up to the end of Last Resort's circular driveway. He handed the fat man a five to pay for the two-dollar ride.

"No trouble," Smith said. "The later I come out, the more I make." Where have I heard that observation before? Arthur wondered.

"My brother-in-law—you know him, Booth that runs the market? He says I'm settin' pretty bein' in a cash-only business. Beat the income tax that way."

"He's real big in the Rotary," the wife added. "Most of them that are in the Rotary, they're cash only. It's the best policy."

"I agree with you one hundred percent," Arthur said as he shut the door. "Unfortunately I'm in a business that caters to vain people. And vanity exists on credit."

"Makes sense," Smith said as Arthur walked up the driveway.

"Don't make no sense to me," his wife said. "What'd he jus' say?"

"What's it matter? These rich people, they all talk with their wallets anyways."

"I dunno what that means either. My uncle, the one who went to the track all the time, he always used to say that so-and-so 'talks through a paper asshole.' Is that anythin' like talkin' with your wallet?"

"Same thing exactly," said Smith. Hearing that, his wife was satisfied and turned to tying her child's shoe.

Arthur was surprised to find the house mostly dark. He glanced up at the third floor. There was still a black eye on the façade, but clearly the carpenters had already accomplished a lot. Letting himself in, Arthur checked the mail, which Herbert had left on the hall pier table. He brought a letter and two bills with him upstairs. Herbert was evidently in bed already. Arthur opened the door to their bedroom—and was aware of a sudden rustling and a gasp. He flicked on the light. Sitting up in bed, Herbert confronted him with his bare chest. The other person—my God, Arthur realized, *Marie*—screamed and pulled the covers over her head.

"My husband and my best friend," Arthur said coldly. "How predictable. But then everyone else's life is soap opera—why should ours be any different?"

"Yes," Herbert said. "Why should I live any differently than you do? With your cheap little tricks all the time."

"You're the one who's always preached about monogamy," Arthur replied. "And this is what I come home to. And with *Marie*."

Marie burrowed more deeply into the sheets.

"You've betrayed me, the two of you," Arthur went on. "Casual sex is one thing, but this . . . this kind of back-stabbing. It's ugly. It's mean. And meanness like this is only becoming to the very young . . . to adolescent girls. . . ."

The sheets rose up on the bed. Marie, hiding under them like a Halloween ghost, made for the door. Arthur grabbed the end of a sheet and tugged. Marie, who could hardly see where she was going, stumbled.

"Leave her alone," Herbert yelled.

"No, I won't," Arthur said. "These are my Porthault sheets. I want them." Arthur gave a yank and half unwound Marie. Marie shrieked and bolted through the door. Arthur was only one step behind her. He held on to the sheet, trying to unravel Marie as she fled.

Grabbing his bathrobe, Herbert followed the two of them as they bumped along the corridor.

"Homewrecker!" Arthur shouted at the reeling Marie. "Wench! Tart! Divorcée!" Screaming, Marie started down the stairs with sheet pulling off her by the yard.

"Stop it!" Herbert bellowed.

Arthur had the sheet off Marie's head and shoulders and wouldn't let go. Her breasts were exposed and bounced as she desperately fled down the stairs.

"D cup!" Arthur yelled. "Weight Watcher! Madam! Sneak!"

At the foot of the stairs Arthur gave a vicious yank and tore the sheet from Marie's waist. Naked, she ran across the foyer and into the living room.

Hot on her heels, Arthur waved the sheet over his head like a triumphant wild Indian.

"Doughnut hips!" he shouted. "Thunder thighs!"

Marie burst through the french doors and out into the terrace. Herbert, who was right behind Arthur, grabbed his waving arm but let go when he saw Marie running blindly for the pool. Knocking her knee against a green Fitzhugh garden seat, Marie spun around and fell backwards into the water. Without thinking, Herbert threw off his bathrobe and dove in after her.

Arthur watched them splashing for a moment. Then he calmly walked over to the garden hose, picked it up, and turned on the tap full blast. Marie had her mouth open, gasping for breath, and that was where Arthur aimed the jet spray from the hose. Next he splatted Herbert in the ear.

"Riot control should begin in the bedroom," Arthur muttered to himself as he twisted the nozzle to make the water pressure greater.

"Stop it, you bastard!" Herbert spluttered. "Stop it or I'll break your goddamn neck!"

"Is that so?" Arthur said. He threw down the hose, and it snaked about on the terrace, spraying water in wide whiplashes.

"I may have fucked around with people," he said. "But I never threatened you . . . *quite like that.*" Arthur touched his cheek with his fingertips as though it were bruised, turned his back, and went back into the house.

"Gha-ah-ack," was what came out of Marie as she spat water out of her mouth and tried to get a breath of dry air at the same time. Herbert had his arm around her in a lifesaving position; he let go so she could breathe more easily, and then he urged her over to the shallow end and the steps.

Arthur went upstairs and picked up his suitcase. He carried it back downstairs and into the kitchen with him, where he put it down and picked up the telephone. He called Smith's taxi service. A half-awake girl answered.

"Could you please tell your father to come back out to Last Resort?" he asked. "I left my address book in my other pants—and I left them in New York. So I have to go back right away."

Marie's teeth were chattering. Herbert wrapped her in his bathrobe and rubbed her arms to warm her up.

Arthur came back out onto the terrace with his suitcase in his hand. He saw Herbert huddling over Marie and had to swallow because jealousy was suddenly blocking his windpipe, his lungs, his heart.

"One more thing," Arthur said.

Marie and Herbert stared at him.

"If you people were trying to emasculate me, you're a little late. My mother beat you to it."

With that, Arthur turned around and walked across the living room and out the front door.

Marie could not stop trembling.

And now Herbert was shaking himself.

CHAPTER SIXTEEN

Flash Donahue's Cable Harbor house had not been substantially altered since it was built in 1908. The house was a pyramid with shutters. It was four stories tall, and it had a still-active dumb waiter running from the basement kitchen to the second floor butler's pantry. All six fireplaces were of Carrara marble. All five bathrooms had been finished with Italian and Portuguese tiles. When a tile loosened, Flash hired a tile man from Portland who knew how to work with foreign shapes and sizes to glue it back in. Thus the house and Flash herself were maintained: what dried out and loosened was smoothed back into shape by a specialist from the city.

Despite the maintenance it received, Flash's house was slowly fading inside and out. The oriental scatter rugs and the chintz-covered chairs in the living room had all gone predominantly pink; their original colors had been made anemic by summer after summer of sunlight. And the house's gray shingles and green shutters had a patina that suggested an old photograph. The absence of modern alterations contributed to this effect too; approaching Flash's house was like turning a page in an old album: suddenly it was years ago, and everything in the landscape was stiff and mute.

George Hanson approached Flash's house with resignation. He hated having to deal with old women; all he could think of when he was around them was a bunch of sick canaries chirping in a cage—with a purple dress thrown over it. Hollowness and warbling, feeble scampering, frail arms, birdshit. It aggravated George every time he saw one of them with her white head barely as high as the steering wheel of her Cadillac. But they had money and they spent it, even though their hands shook writing out the check. So George had to be nice to them; he had to put on his gray butler's coat and list canapés in a loud voice. He had to listen to their instructions and smell their cabbage breath.

It annoyed George that Marjorie hadn't come along. Here she'd been bitching about the fashion show coming up and now when he wanted to finalize things with the old bag she said she had to spend the morning following up on some bullshit she'd dug up at the town clerk's office yesterday. *Women.* It was no wonder men died younger. They either drove you nuts with their mouths . . . or they used their bodies. And their bodies could make you so crazy you blacked out . . . almost. At least this old bag Donahue couldn't give you a hard-on; old ladies had that much going for them—lift one of their purple dresses and what were you going to see: probably that the bottom of the bird's cage needed cleaning out.

George rang Flash's doorbell. The bell sounded castrated. A maid opened the door. She had a nasty expression on her face; she looked as though she had no intention of letting George get so much as a glimpse of the hallway unless she had no choice in the matter.

"Yes?" the maid said.

"I'm Mr. Hanson, the caterer. I'm here to see Mrs. Donahue about the plans for the fashion show."

"Oh. Yes, I guess she's expecting you. Come in. Actually you should come in through the service entrance, but I suppose it doesn't make any difference, the way things are done today."

"Thank you," said George, stepping inside, and fuck you, he thought.

George was shown out to the sun porch, where Flash was sitting with her aged poodle. The dog was losing its hair in patches, especially around its rump, which looked to George like a pink moon crater, and the dog's eyes were even more disgusting to look at: glazed marbles set in burnt pie crust. Then there was Flash herself, with her skin that could have passed for dough in various stages of kneading.

"Oh, Mr. Hanson," Flash said when George was announced, "don't you look elegant today?"

George surveyed his butler's coat with a smile, picked off a thread, and waited to be asked to sit down. The maid departed, probably to stuff a damp dishcloth up herself, if George's speculation was right.

"Do sit down, Mr. Hanson," Flash said, gesturing at a wicker chair. George sat down, and the poodle, using its right front paw like a blind man's cane, came over and sniffed his pant leg.

"She wants to play," Flash said.

What could this thing play besides dead? George wondered.

Flash watched her dog fondly. After sniffing both of George's cuffs, sticking its tongue out at one of his shoes, and then rolling it back in again, the animal found a circle of sunlight and curled up in it.

"What a playful girl she is today," Flash said.

Probably that way every day that she's not on dialysis, George thought. He wished he were Hugh Hefner. He wished he were Hugh Hefner sitting by the pool out at the Playboy Mansion West while a bunch of starlets roller-skated around. With just bikini bottoms on. No tops. The old bag looked like a bunch of dried cornstalks. All you'd have to do would be give her one little push, and she'd topple over as easily as a long-stemmed flower arrangement in a short vase.

"You can't have a fashion show without those elegant little tea sandwiches," Flash said. "We are going to have tea sandwiches, aren't we, Mr. Hanson?"

"Of course," George replied. "We can do pretty much anything you ladies want. I thought, for the tea sandwiches, we'd have crab meat, tuna, cream cheese and olive—"

"I worry about cutting the crusts off the bread to make the tea sandwiches," Flash said, frowning. "It seems like such a waste. It's a pity we can't send the bread crusts to somebody over in Asia."

"That wouldn't do much good," George said. "My wife and I, we're in with that Foster Parents' Plan. We send a little each month to a little girl in Thailand."

"You do?" Flash exclaimed. "Aren't you elegant to be doing something like that?"

George wished he hadn't said anything about the little girl in Thailand. Almost as soon as the words were out of his mouth, he felt a pang of regret that he had spoken them. The little girl over in Thailand was sacred. George had kept every one of the letters she'd sent, letters telling about how much she was able to do for her family and herself with the money her foster parents sent. The poor kid.

George imagined himself picking up old Mrs. Donahue by her fragile teapot-handle hips, turning her upside down, and shaking her until all the loose change fell out. These old bags could stand to be emptied out—as George felt emptied. Emptied and living at the bottom of a barrel that had already been scraped. George sometimes wondered if your immortal soul grows bigger in you when you're hungry. Was emptiness food for the spirit? His emptiness? His private, physical hunger for the bodies of women? The absence of fulfillment did leave him light-headed at times, and full of airy dreams, so that he felt a spiritual closeness to the little girl from Thailand who could eat because of him. And who was an unspoiled little woman who sent him her love. Which was pure love, the emotional equivalent of the pure sex that George, in his troubled mind, so often turned to.

"We can give the crusts to the birds if we can't give them to the poor children, can't we?" Flash asked her dog. "Can't we, Coco darling? Mm?" The dog lifted its head like a disturbed invalid.

"The Foster Parents' Plan wouldn't want our old bread crusts, would they, Mr. Hanson?"

"No, they couldn't use them," George said quickly. He wanted to get on with it and get out.

"I'm a little hungry, talking about all this eating," Flash said. "I think I'll have Mabel bring us some tea and brownies. Wouldn't you like a brownie, Mr. Hanson?"

"Yes, thanks," George said. Flash stepped on a button that was concealed under the rug. In a moment, Mabel appeared and Flash asked her to bring out the snack. George wished he were Bob Guccione. He wished he were Bob Guccione shooting a center spread of a model with her legs spread. He wished he had a ton of money, like Guccione. He wished he had about fifty silk shirts to wear open to his navel, just about, and a bunch of gold chains to wear around his neck. And one day the little girl from Thailand would be all grown up and come and visit him in his penthouse. She'd be wearing one of those dresses slit up the side, and she'd come over to him and give him a peck on the cheek. She'd be innocent and girlish and beautiful.

167

The disagreeable Mabel returned with a silver tray that had a silver teapot and a plate of brownies on it. She put a cup and saucer by the side of her mistress and a cup and saucer on the table near George. The dog lifted its head to watch, and Flash fed it a few brownie crumbs. The maid retreated to the kitchen again, looking more indignant that ever. While Flash fiddled with the tea things George idly began to scratch his chest. He reached inside his gray butler's coat and undid a couple of his shirt buttons. He wished he could undo all of them, like Guccione. He wondered what would happen to the old lady if she turned around and saw him standing in front of her stark naked. He wondered if she'd have a heart attack. He wondered if he could get undressed, give her the heart attack, and get dressed again without the maid catching on. George wound a little batch of chest hairs around and around in his fingertips. Giving a sharp tug, he felt a couple of the hairs pull out. In his fingers, they seemed as significant a secret as his penis was when he was in second grade and unsure if the girl who sat next to him knew about it.

"The fashion show," Flash said. "I don't know why people make so much of it . . . but they do." Her voice was fluctuating in timbre so that it suggested, alternately, resignation and exhilaration. "And why they keep asking me to model . . . year after year. But I suppose it's my civic duty. How foolish, though . . . to be looking at fall clothes in the middle of the summer. Do you think people look forward to the fashion show, Mr. Hanson, because it makes the fall . . . makes the fall, which we all know is coming, don't we? Do you think people look forward to the fashion show . . . because it makes the fall seem like . . . it's going to be promising? You need the fall season when you get to be my age, Mr. Hanson. And you need the spring, too. They become one and the same, after a certain point in your life, spring and fall do . . . they're either end of . . . the lovely summertime. And we don't even think about the wintertime until we get to Palm Beach, do we, Coco, darling?"

Flash leaned over to feed the dog again. George looked at the black hairs he had in his fingers. He looked at the plate of brownies. He reached for a brownie, and planted his chest hairs on another brownie. He did it in an instant. Even if Flash had been a card sharp, she wouldn't have noticed.

When it was clear that the dog was not going to die in the act of chewing, Flash said, "I forget what you told me, Mr. Hanson, do you like one lump of sugar in your tea, or two?"

"Just a lemon slice, please," George replied.

"That's what I like, too," Flash said. "Lemon slices are ever so much more elegant than sugar."

She selected a brownie.

The doctored brownie.

George watched her.

Flash chewed thoughtfully. Then she appeared to be in consultation with her dental plates. Her tongue made a circuit of her lower gum.

"Um-uck, ah," Flash muttered.

George puffed himself up to appear solicitous.

Flash reached between her lips and dug around. Then she slowly withdrew a hair. She examined the evidence through her other glasses and then looked scandalized. She stepped on the maid's button hard.

George felt very light-headed. He thought, she'd look real natural toppled over like a bunch of plastic flowers in the cemetery.

Mabel showed up again, with the "What is it?" expression on her face.

Flash had retrieved a second hair.

George wanted to say, Hey, the old lady's havin' trouble—she's never sucked a guy off before. He actually was on the verge of saying it. But then there was a terrible outcry. From the floor. The maid had stepped on the dog.

Laura's mother was determined to have Laura and Jamie over for dinner. Now that it was clear Laura would not be moving back into her room—at least for a while—Mrs. Damon wanted to give this new young man in her daughter's life the acknowledgment of a place setting at her table. Not that such an acknowledgment would make the relationship last any great length of time, but it would hint at a kind of old-fashioned order and stability, like the table settings one saw on Tiffany's second floor: believe those glittering, immaculate arrangements, and you could believe that there were still young people around who paired off appropriately and neatly and dined and lunched with other young people who were equally well matched.

169

"It will be just the four of us," Mrs. Damon had told Laura. "You, Jamie, your father, and me. Maybe the two men will play billiards afterward—and smoke cigars, while we girls chat. Wouldn't that be wonderfully Victorian? Do you have that romantic *Finnegans Wake* dress to wear?"

"You mean my *Ryan's Daughter* dress, Mother," Laura replied. "I have it but I'm not wearing it. And I don't think Jamie will want to smoke a cigar with Daddy. He might smoke a joint with him, maybe."

"I'm sure your father would be agreeable to that. Do they have Havana marijuana?"

Seeing that her mother was going to have her little dinner party no matter what, Laura had given in to most of her mother's wishes and promised to come with Jamie the following evening. She was about to break the news to him when the camp telephone rang again. It was Marie. Laura was amazed at how quickly she had been traced to Jamie Lawrence's tent; everybody had been calling—they were like a pack of St. Bernards sniffing you out in the wilderness and approaching with their hearts tied under their chins.

"Laura?" Marie said. "Is this Laura?"

"Yes, it's me, Marie," Laura replied. "What's the matter? You sound funny."

Once she was sure she was speaking to Laura, Marie began to cry. She cried for five minutes solid. Laura could almost see the poor thing's shoulders heaving, she was crying so hard. Laura could not get past the wailing wall no matter how she tried. Every plea, every solicitous question was met with the same waves of sobbing and swept aside. It seemed that a bird could not stand on the telephone wire without being rocked by Marie's grief.

Finally the emotional storm abated a bit, and Marie was able to shout through her anguish, "Laura, I was almost drowned last night —by Arthur!"

"What?"

"Herbert and Arthur had a terrible fight. And I—I was the cause of it all. I was right in the middle of it."

"How is that possible?"

"Ah-a-arthur went to New York . . . and I . . . I slept . . . with Herbert. Arthur came home unexpectedly last night and caught us, caught us together . . . in bed. He chased me down the stairs and pulled off my sheet."

170

Laura held the telephone receiver away from her ear a little, in order to allow comprehension to sink in. Her knees felt weak. She might as well have been looking at a hundred human bodies all tangled up together in an orgy—tangled up in knots and jammed into a trunk, one of the old trunk houses that were lined up in Cable Harbor. Good God, was this actually the way it was? Did they teach us all sex in order to lock us up together and throw away the key and leave us groping for one another with our blind knowledge?

"Marie, you've got to calm down," Laura insisted. "Where are you now?"

"I'm s-still at Ar-arthur and Herbert's. Oh, Laura, Herbert's just sitting out by the pool with a drink and s-staring into spa-ace. Uh-hoo. He doesn't *say-ay* anything. And Arthur disappeared last night. Who knows where to? What if he's killed himself? He almost drowned Herbert and me, with that garden hose."

"Arthur would never commit suicide," Laura said. "He's much too vain to let anybody see him . . . that way." (Laura had meant to say *with his head in an oven*, but thought better of it.)

"What am I going to do with Her-her . . . poor Herbert?" Marie wailed.

"Sit with him, Marie," Laura advised. "Look, I'll come right over."

"Oh, Laura . . . oh . . . could you?"

"Just sit tight," Laura said.

Laura hung up and looked around for Jamie. She found him out on the rocks. He was listening to a baseball game on the shortwave radio that Laura loved—in the tent at night they listened to the BBC and even Radio Moscow.

"Jamie, I've got to go see Marie right away," Laura said. "She's in trouble. Where are the keys to the van?"

"Have you called the fire department?" Jamie asked as he fished in the pocket of his jogging shorts.

"It's not that kind of trouble. Marie got herself into a ménage à trois—and now she can't manage it."

Jamie handed Laura the keys.

"You want me to come along?" he asked.

"No," Laura said. "This will have to be something I handle alone. You'd only remind her of . . . that other indiscretion."

"Marie should keep a record of her indiscretions. She might be able to get something off on her income tax."

"Oh, you keep quiet," Laura said, snatching the keys. "By the way, my mother has invited us to dinner. Candlelight and probably quite a few courses. Could you endure an evening of my mother in a formal setting?"

"Why not? I endured—days—with my own mother in a Florentine setting."

"Okay, I should be back late this afternoon. What would you like for dinner tonight? I'll shop on the way back."

"Anything. I don't care." Jamie hooked a hand around Laura's leg and began massaging.

"Here. None of that, now. I've got to get going. Marie was hysterical on the phone."

"Do I get a kiss good-bye?"

"All right. All right." Laura knelt and touched Jamie's lips. He made the peck into a real kiss, a prolonged one, and Laura's heart fluttered involuntarily. She was aware, as she wound up the Volks, that she was moving out of a security zone. That was what this camp had come to feel like—in these few days—it was a refuge from all these nets that were constantly tangled and broken, broken and tangled.

Marie met Laura at the door. Marie's face was tear-streaked and pale, and she talked in broken whispers, as if she were going to take Laura to where Herbert was resting in his coffin. But Herbert was not dead; he was just uncommunicative.

"Talk to him . . . Laura . . . please," Marie pleaded.

Laura went out to the pool and slowly approached Herbert's chair. Marie followed her timidly. She seemed terrified that a glass was going to be smashed . . . or worse.

"How are you, Herbert?" Laura asked. Herbert looked up.

"Laura," he said. He thought for a moment and then he said, "How am I? To tell you the truth, I'm depressed. I'm also ashamed . . . of myself."

Laura sat by the coping of the pool. Marie stood near her, wringing her hands.

"I'm ashamed, too . . ." Marie whispered. "I hate myself."

Herbert looked at her.

"No, Marie, don't say that," he said. "I'm to blame for all of this. I had no right to drag you into . . . the swamp that Arthur and I live in."

172

Laura had a vision of Arthur slogging through the swamp after a Tarzan who looked like Jamie.

"You two did what your feelings told you to . . . whenever you did whatever you did," Laura said. "Acting according to the way you feel . . . in your heart, that's nothing to be ashamed of. You can't keep feelings in your pocket. They have a way of falling out."

"Falling out into the street in my case," Marie said bitterly. "Every time I feel something slipping out I . . . I should attach one of those hotel tags to it that says 'Please deposit in the nearest mailbox.' That way all . . . all the consequences would arrive on my doorstep that much sooner . . . a-hoo."

Laura handed Marie a Kleenex.

Marie blew her nose loudly.

Herbert sighed.

"Look at those summer clouds . . . just drifting along," he said. "Around five it'll be clear, I suppose. I've always thought of death as being like clear blue sky. Without any horizon line. Do you think we answer to anybody when we die . . . do you, Marie? Do you, Laura?"

"I don't think St. Peter is waiting up there for us, if that's what you mean," Laura said.

"I'm going to have to answer to Sister Don Bosco," Marie said. "I can hear her now—'Ahah, it's the Mulligan girl. And your life was every bit as miserable as I thought it would be, wasn't it?'"

"I think we do answer to somebody," Herbert said, almost to himself. "I think those of us who were lucky enough to fall in love— just *once*—I think when we're facing that empty blue sky, we can face it peacefully if we can say to the memory of whoever that one person was, if we can say, *Yes, I loved you more than life itself*."

Marie began to cry again.

"Don't, Marie," Herbert said. "Don't. We just have to face the truth. I do, anyway. As much as I may regret it. And the truth is that the only person I have ever loved is Arthur Conrad."

Laura had to take hold of Marie.

"Please, Marie," Herbert said. "Don't make it any worse. I'm miserable enough about this whole thing already. I know now that I was using you in a way . . . and God knows I never planned to, or wanted to. . . . It was all unconscious . . . some way to try to *get at* Arthur that my . . . mind . . . cooked up. . . . Oh, Christ."

173

Herbert got out of his chair and put his arms around Marie.

She tried to push him away. She tried to push Laura away.

She looked up at the sky in a panic and said, "Oh, God. Isn't there anybody kind and gentle . . . anywhere . . . to love me?"

That ought to do it nicely, Marjorie thought as she finished typing her letter to Hopkins, the realtor. She pulled the letter out of her daughter's Royal portable and read it back to herself.

Dear Mr. Hopkins:

I am writing to inform you of my intention to raise certain questions about the status of the Perry House. I understand that you represent the owners of the Perry House, and I hope you will ask them these questions too. It's only fair that they should have a chance to answer.

The questions are as follows:

1. Why does the easement which allows the Perry House to run power and telephone lines across the Patterson land show a transfer of right of way from Homer Shute, who had no title to the land at the time?

2. In light of the death of a teenage girl on the property belonging to the Perry House, can the owners of the Perry House show cause why this property should not come under the "attractive nuisance" statutes of the township and be fenced and guarded to protect the safety of local children?

3. Since the Perry House's developers were granted their variance to construct a hotel, doesn't the Board of Adjustment have the right to call a hearing to find out why a hotel has not been built on the site and to hear what the present intentions of the developers in fact are?

I look forward to hearing from you and your associates before the upcoming town meeting on this matter.

Sincerely,

Marjorie Hanson (Ms.)

Could have been written by a lawyer, Marjorie thought. She folded the letter and stuffed it in an envelope. She'd finished just in time for "Get It Off Your Chest." The show opened with surprising

174

news. The county coroner's report had come in; it showed that the girl found at the Perry House had died of a broken neck that she had apparently suffered in a fall. There was no sign of sexual abuse. The police department was saying that she had fallen—or had been pushed—from the third floor balcony of one of the Perry House's unfinished suites, where, it seemed, she had spent the night. Traces of marijuana had been found in the room, as well as personal effects.

An attractive nuisance if I ever heard of one, Marjorie said to herself. It's a wonder kids haven't been in there playing with matches. Naturally Evelyn Booth was the first caller.

"Secrets," Evelyn said in her usual ain't-much-that-I'm-not-wise-to voice. "That girl probably had some kinda secret that she was hidin' up in that room. Plenty of people aroun' here got secrets hidden away—an' maybe that girl knew somebody's secret. Maybe somebody was payin' her to keep quiet. Wouldn't surprise me any. I wonder if the county coroner checked to see if she was pregnant. Gettin' pregnant and that marijuana usually go hand in hand."

You should know, the way your kids smoke it, Marjorie thought. And get other people's kids started on it into the bargain.

"I hope this here town meetin' isn't just gonna be a lotta gabbin'," Evelyn said. "There's plenty of people'd just as soon be at the Legion playin' bingo rather than listen to a whole lotta talk that ain't gonna be worth a darn."

Like your husband's idea for a Rotary Memorial Park that we had to listen to at the last town meeting, Marjorie muttered.

Old man Tucker got on the line right after Evelyn Booth. He said the effects of marijuana were the same as the gas they used during World War I. You could be up walking around and the next thing you know you'd fallen over choking.

"Never knew no harm come to nobody from chewin' tobacco, though," he added. "I recommend it. Baseball pitchers chew it, and they're settin' a good example for the young people."

Then there was a call from a woman in the middle of a recipe who'd spilled water on her file card and wanted to know if anyone knew how many eggs a regular pie-sized quiche would call for.

Somebody else called with free kittens. Probably that old tomcat of Evelyn's, Marjorie thought. And I swear it's sprayed the Gold Medal flour in that dump of a grocery of theirs, too.

Marjorie picked up the phone after the announcer had taken the kittens' address down.

"Howya doin' today, Margie?" the announcer said.

"I'm pretty good," Marjorie said. "Just finished a little letter which I'm going to send off—certified—to some people who have a little explaining to do."

"Could those people have anything to do with the Perry House?" the announcer teased.

"They know who they are. That's all I'm saying."

Hopkins, the realtor, who was listening to the show in his office, frowned.

Next thing she'll be stickin' her nose in the Rockefellers' affairs, thought Evelyn, who was tuned in at the cash register. It'd serve her right if the CIA left her by the side of the road in Montana or someplace. An' I bet the FBI knows what her husband sends for a the mail. Holier than thou—that's what she is. Well, she's gonna get taken down a peg or two.

"Looks like you're going to be in charge of this town meeting we got coming up," the announcer said, coaching Marjorie.

"I don't want to run things," Marjorie said. "All I want is to clear a few things up."

Hell you don't want to run things, Evelyn thought. You oughtta be clearin' up the dishes in your own sink.

"I just feel we've been a little too gullible around here for too long now," Marjorie was saying. "Why, there are people who are probably ready to believe that poor girl died trying to board a flying saucer that was hovering by her balcony. And they'd be just as ready to let the Perry House sit until whatever scheme that's being tried there works out."

I know who you're talkin' about with that flyin' saucer crack, Evelyn thought angrily. She snatched a Three Musketeers bar out of the candy rack, unwrapped it, and stuffed it in her mouth defiantly.

Hopkins decided he'd better place another call to New York.

Arthur had spent the night in Boston after flying down with a kid who owned a Piper Cub and was only too happy to be awakened in the middle of the night for an unexpected charter—Arthur had paid him triple the going rate. From his room in the Ritz-Carlton Arthur had a view of the Public Garden. He ordered brunch from room service and pulled a chair up to the window to eat. The Public

176

Garden looked like a landscape by Seurat: beds of flowers and strollers made grainy by the moisture-laden atmosphere of summer. The students were still around, carrying their book bags, even in July. Boston sure was a student town—all corduroy and brick walls with posters on them. Arthur wondered if he would want to be back in college. When he was at RISD, the Rhode Island School of Design, the future had seemed vast as the universe, the coming months as promising as a window thrown open on a spring day. Was it that he had been satisfied with so much less in that era of his life? Or was he dissatisfied now that the future was arrayed like packages with predictable things inside: like an adult Christmas? Christmas in July; that was Arthur's mood exactly. As he sat mulling over his scrambled eggs, Arthur thought it might be a good idea to walk over to Shreve's and buy himself something in gold—some ornament to celebrate the season, the winter about the temples.

As he left the hotel, Arthur was struck by a vision of life without Herbert. The vision appeared in the shape of an adolescent boy in a black satin sport jacket. The kid, who was coming into the hotel with his mother, sounded English and looked it. The rep silk tie, the round glasses. The white jogging shoes and the satin jacket—a public school outfit with latterday hippie alterations. Arthur imagined himself sitting at Uncle Charlie's restaurant with such a child. He imagined himself arriving at the Pines for a weekend with such a child. The child would look like what he was: a youth with an open mouth and a limited variety of thoughts in his head. And Arthur would look like—what? At best he'd look like the headmaster of a prep school, somebody trying to pull youth on over his head like a pink Shetland sweater. He'd be one more laughing stock trying to do that ballet with youth—in Bass loafers and this year's waiter's haircut. The look of loss that suddenly came over Arthur was such that the doorman asked him if he was all right.

A suspicious-looking package addressed to George Hanson had arrived at the Cable Harbor post office. The return address on the plain brown wrapper did not name a firm or an individual, only a post office box in California. When Midge saw George Hanson's name on the package, she looked about quickly to be sure nobody was watching her, and then, holding her breath, she nipped it out of the pile and put it in with her lunch, in the tote bag she brought along to work every day. Right up until five-thirty Midge was nervous about having George Hanson's queer-looking package in her tote bag. She kept looking at it as though it were ticking. Midge drove straight home after the post office closed. And as soon as she got into her kitchen she picked up the phone and called Evelyn Booth.

"Another one of em's come for 'im," Midge said before she even said who she was. Evelyn recognized Midge's voice and figured out what had happened almost in the same instant.

"Can you bring it over tonight?" Evelyn hissed.

"Are you kidden'? I've been scared to death holding on to it this long."

"Okay, okay, honey. Don't panic, whatever you do. I gotta get in touch with Lester. He's not that many days out of the hospital and I don't know whether he'll want to . . . ah, what am I sayin'— I'll get him to come out; I'll say it's a matter of life and death."

"Should I bring it over right away?"

"No, not now. Wait until tonight. After nine the kids'll all be out. The fewer that know about this little meetin' we're gonna have, the better."

"I'm afraid to be alone with it."

"Put it in your refrigerator. That's the best place to hide things. I keep my jewelry in a Peter Pan peanut butter jar and I keep the key to the cabinet where we got the Hummels in a plastic container a' cranberry."

"What if something happens to me on the road gettin' to your place? What if I have an accident and they find me with somebody's mail on me? I could get five years in jail."

"What's more important? You takin' a little bit of a risk or your daughter's life and limb?"

Midge put her hand on the back of a kitchen chair and felt the cool strength of the chrome flowing up her arm into her backbone.

"My daughter," Midge said. "I'll do anything to protect my baby."

"That's how I thought you'd feel about it," Evelyn said. "Try and get here a little past nine. And drive careful."

"I will," Midge said. "I'll be prayin' to God the whole way, though."

Evelyn called Lester then.

"Man I know's got a chance to turn his whole life aroun' tonight," she said to him.

CHAPTER SEVENTEEN

When Lester arrived at Evelyn and Sanford's house he saw that they had drawn all the shades. The chinks of light showing made Lester think of a scene his father had described to him: a World War II blackout—those times when a soldier would come banging on a person's door with a gun butt if so much as a pinhole of light was visible on the beach, and cars would snake through the darkness with half their headlights painted out. Lester knocked on the front door with three heavy-handed thuds (the same code he had used to enter his best friend's tree house when he was a kid). Evelyn answered.

"Come on in, Lester," she said.

In the living room Midge from the post office and Sanford were sitting stiffly, like people keeping watch in folding chairs at a viewing.

There was a package on the coffee table that Midge was watching as if she were afraid it might contain spiders.

"I got the teakettle goin' out in the kitchen," Evelyn said. "You want a cup a' coffee, Lester?"

"Yes, let's all have coffee," Sanford said. He rubbed the legs of his pants anxiously.

"I'll come out and help you get it," Midge volunteered. She seemed to welcome the chance to get away from the parcel she'd delivered.

"Have a seat, Lester," Sanford said. "I want to show you the new Hummels we've got." Lester sat down and began drumming his

179

fingertips on the arm of the chair, which was wide and flat, sort of a stuffed version of the hood of an old Hudson, in Lester's eyes. Sanford unlocked the broad-chested glass display cabinet that was crowded with the Hummel figurines; the collection and its cabinet reminded Lester of a picture he'd seen in a schoolbook—Gulliver tied up on the ground with a mob of teeny-tiny people running all over him.

Sanford picked out a figurine and held it under the lamplight. It was a little girl with rosy cheeks and chubby knees. She had a basket of fruit. Sanford turned her every which way under the light so Lester could see the details: the polka dots on her scarf, the eyelash painted with a single brushstroke. Sanford nodded sagely at the figurine and then gave Lester a meaningful look and said, "Three hundred and twenty-five dollars. That's what this one is worth now."

"How 'bout that," Lester replied.

The women returned with the coffee and Sanford replaced the figurine in the display case.

"I'd be afraid living with such a valuable collection as that one," Midge said. "My sister had her whole coin collection stolen out of their basement. It was worth over five thousand dollars and they didn't have a penny of insurance on it."

"Insurance premiums just eat up the gains you make when an item goes up in value," Sanford said. "Our insurance is to always have somebody around, either us or one of the kids, and never leave the doors unlocked."

"Still, I'd be worried," Midge replied. She set a plate of cookies on the coffee table and sat down on the sofa and looked worried. To Lester, Midge looked like one of those women in a World War II movie who sit in front of a mirror brushing their hair—and then they see in the mirror somebody sneaking up on them and turn around startled. Midge looked like that, like a World War II girl. She combed her hair the same way and her mouth was always tight like a rosebud.

Evelyn put coffee cups in front of Sanford and Lester and then landed herself on the sofa like a crate dropped by parachute.

She took a cookie and said, "Well, there it is in front of us. The question now is what're we gonna do with it."

"We could try to steam it open," Sanford suggested.

"Steam'd never penetrate that masking tape they got around it." Evelyn said.

"Before you do anything, I think we all oughtta be clear on what this is here," Lester said. "This here little party we're havin' is a conspiracy. Even the four of us gettin' together and plannin' ta do this would be a conspiracy. Now, that's what the law says."

Midge appeared frightened by that information; she was about to make some sort of protest when Evelyn cut her off with, "The law's got a darn sight too much to say about what decent people do to protect their lives and property while common criminals get off scot-free."

"A-men," Sanford said.

"Just thought you should know what the facts are," Lester said.

"If we're going to go through with this," Midge said, "the best thing to do is rip the package open at one end. Make it look like it got hacked up on a conveyer belt. Plenty of mail comes through that way, I can tell you."

"Why don't we hang on to whatever it is?" Sanford suggested. "There's no reason to deliver it to him at all, once we examine it. You say he gets these funny packages in the mail all the time, Midge. Who's to say that one of 'em might not get lost?"

"No need to make this a bigger conspiracy than it already is by addin' mail theft to interference with the mail," was Lester's official advice.

"Okay, okay," Evelyn said. "We'll just open it up, have a look at it, and see that it's in Hanson's post office box tomorrow." There was agreement on that.

"Shall I do the honors?" Sanford asked.

"Might as well," his wife replied. "You're the one carves the roasts."

"You better wear rubber gloves unless you want to leave fingerprints," Midge said. She was clinging to her seat like a lonely clothespin on a line.

"Good idea," Sanford agreed. He went into the kitchen to get his garden gloves.

Wearing his thick garden gloves, Sanford looked to Lester even more like a clown than he usually did. What with his wide eyes that somebody might have mounted whitewalls around and his hair shining with pomade, Sanford could have been going out in the morning to distract rodeo bulls; now, tearing at the package with toenail scissors, he was certainly having the same effect—the three co-conspirators were transfixed in their chairs.

When Sanford had shredded one end of the package, he reached into it and pulled out a thin white box. Inside the white box was a reel of film.

"What's that—a Mickey Mouse cartoon?" Lester said.

"I bet it's something a lot more serious than that," Evelyn answered.

"It's eight millimeter," Sanford said. "You want to show it?"

"Of course," Evelyn replied. "Get the projector."

Evelyn struggled up and took down a painting of waves breaking over rocks that she had done herself. Lester had never thought much of that particular painting; the waves were too much like cotton.

"We'll show it on this wall," Evelyn said.

"I'm afraid," Midge said. "What if somebody comes while this is on?"

"We'll just shut off the projector and pull out the movie we got of Stevie in his bassinet, that's all," Evelyn replied.

"Wouldn't surprise me if there was a bathtub in this movie of Hanson's," Lester said. "Maybe it's a movie of that wife of his in the tub. That's one home movie you couldn't get the Kodak people to develop for you."

"Oh, don't say it," Midge said. "I hope and pray it isn't anything embarrassing. If it is I'll close my eyes."

"You can't close your eyes to what's goin' on," Evelyn warned. "We're all here tonight to get our eyes opened up to whatever George Hanson is tryin' to hide from all of us."

Sanford set up the projector and threaded the film. He asked Lester to get the lights. There was a flicker on the wall of different-colored slashes like a child's crayon scrawling, and then a title appeared.

BEST FRIENDS

"Them are usually diamonds," Evelyn commented in the dark. "A girl's best friend is diamonds. That's what they say."

"If you want friends to keep you in your old age, you're better off collectin' Hummels," Sanford said.

182

The hell with them Hummels of yours, Lester thought. If you want to know my opinion of 'em, I think they're dumber than animal crackers.

A girl appeared in the film. She was walking along a sidewalk. Walking behind her was a telephone repair man with tools in his belt.

"Shorts and high heels she's wearin'," Evelyn noted. "And her bare belly stickin' out. Looks to me like she means business."

"Monkey business," Sanford speculated.

"Loretta Lynn does her hair like that," Evelyn said. "A big pile of it on top and a whole lot hanging down to her shoulders besides."

"She's probably a singer," Lester put in.

"Yeah, a singer with no piano and no music," Evelyn commented. "I know that type. No talent but dyin' to get up in front of people and show off. Like that Marjorie Hanson."

The girl in the movie had turned into what seemed to be a motel parking lot. She seemed pleasantly surprised to learn her phone was dead. The repairman followed her into her room, which was number seven. The telephone man went to work. The girl put on the radio. She snapped her fingers and bounced around with her eyes half closed. The repairman grinned at her.

"That must be bebop music she's got on," Midge said

Bebop? What the hell is that? Lester wondered. Some music from World War II?

The repairman stopped fixing the telephone and started dancing like John Travolta. He dropped his tool belt.

She's gonna get more 'n her phone fixed if she don't watch out, Lester thought.

The girl reached behind her back and began to unsnap her halter.

"Uh-oh, I don't like the looks of this," Sanford said.

"Let's just see what's gonna happen," Evelyn advised.

What happened was another girl came into the room. This one was blond and had faint acne scars on her face that her makeup didn't quite cover. When she saw the repairman her lips formed an *ooh.*

"She looks like somethin' from outer space with that black eyeliner she's wearin'," Evelyn said.

"You should know, Evvy," Lester said. "You're the one's been to Mars."

183

"I've never been. But I'm willin' to bet there's people who have. The Air Force covers it all up so there won't be panic—nationwide."

The blonde with the heavy makeup raised the repairman's T-shirt. The first girl—a brunette—calmly removed her halter and stuck out her bare breasts the way a child sticks out its tongue.

"Oh no, it's dirty, it's dirty," Midge wailed. "I was afraid of this."

"Ha," Evelyn said smugly. "I'm sure this is only the beginning. Only the beginning. Of the dirt we're going to be digging up. On the Hanson family."

The bare-breasted brunette hopped up on the bed and patted her thighs. The bare-chested repairman joined her.

The blonde took off her top, too.

"Those two seem to have this down to a routine," Lester said.

Sanford's face, which Lester could make out in the flickering white light of the projector, was starting to *spell concern*, which was the Rotary catch phrase for heavy snow or impending tax audits.

"I hope they're not going to make a group effort out of this project," Sanford said.

"Oh, don't say it," Midge pleaded. "Don't even think it."

"I always wondered if this is what 'Three's Company' is really about," Lester said.

The brunette wriggled out of her baby-blue hot pants.

"How can a decent girl expose herself like that?" Midge said.

"Not much decent about them two," Evelyn replied.

"I think we should stop this movie right now," Sanford said. "I think we've seen enough to have a pretty good idea what George Hanson's been up to."

"No way," Evelyn said. "We're seein' this thing through to the end. We might recognize a pattern in it."

"An m.o., huh?" Lester added. "They didn't find any telephone man's tools by that dead girl's body, ya know."

The brunette was unzipping the repairman's fly. He put his finger in the waistband of her panties and began tugging. The blonde skinned off her jeans and hopped up on the bed too.

"Oh, lordy," Midge said.

"What a pair of hussies," Evelyn said.

Then the camera focused on the repairman's fly. The girl's hand gave a yank, and out popped his penis.

Midge screamed.

The girl opened wide.

So did the other girl, but not her mouth.

The groping and slurping began in earnest.

Midge leaped up from the sofa.

"I think I'm going to be sick," she yelled.

"Help her," Sanford shouted.

Evelyn rocked back and forth urgently, trying to get up enough momentum to reach her feet and help Midge to the bathroom.

Lester hit the lights. Midge was reeling, clinging to her stomach and making gulping sounds. Evelyn lumbered after her. She didn't see the cord of the projector. It snared her ankle. For an instant it seemed to Lester that he was witnessing a miracle of flight, something like a 747 becoming airborne, but then gravity took over and Evelyn collided head on with the display case full of Hummels. An oak knee of the cabinet buckled, and it sagged. There was roar of sliding porcelain and breaking glass. And Evelyn lay in a heap on top of the bits and pieces.

Sanford's mouth opened wider than Lester had ever seen it open. Then it snapped shut again and began opening and closing wildly, though Sanford wasn't making any noise. A moan came from Evelyn, who was waving her arms and legs amid the rubble like a helpless, overturned turtle. Midge was behind the sofa on her knees, gagging and spitting into her embroidered handkerchief.

The movie was still running, although a climax had already been reached.

Sanford fainted. He folded up on the floor as neatly as he hung up his white coat when his day behind the market's meat counter was done.

Lester tried to help Evelyn. He took hold of one of her groping hands, and was pulled downward as if by a heavy anchor. He wound up on the floor beside her. Hummels crunched beneath their bodies.

Lester saw that Evelyn was wild-eyed. Her dress was hiked up almost to her hips, but she didn't seem to care.

"I'll get her for this," Evelyn hissed.

"What?" Lester said. He had managed to pull himself up again.

"That Marjorie Hanson. That *slut*. She's the cause of this."

The film finished and snapped off the reel. The loose end flailed at the housing of the camera like a whip in the hands of a lunatic.

185

"Was she all right when you left her yesterday?" Vivian said.

"I think it depends on what you mean by all right," Laura replied. "She wasn't hysterical or anything, but do you know what she told me she was going to do tonight?"

"No, what?"

"She said she was going to go to a church supper . . . with her maid."

Vivian removed her sunglasses and stared down the stretch of gray beach that the Bath Club's deck overlooked. She looked as though she was trying to decide whether or not the phenomenon dancing before her eyes was a mirage.

"*Marie* . . . is going to a *church supper* . . . with her *maid?*"

"That's what she says," Laura replied.

"And I can't even get her to go to an auction with me . . . what on earth does she think she's doing? Is she going to convert to Congregationalism and spend her old age in a sewing circle?"

"This thing she had with Herbert . . . and Arthur . . . it really threw her for a loop, on top of that fire she started, too."

"I've been thrown for a loop myself in the past few days," Vivian pointed out. "But I'm doing my best to come back from it . . . positively. What's Marie going to do when she finds out they don't serve cocktails at church suppers?"

"Your guess is as good as mine," Laura replied.

"You know what I think could be happening to Marie?" Vivian said. "I think she could be riding the crest of a wave. Like I was up until a few days ago. . . . It's hard to explain. But it's like a dream I had once. . . . You know my daughter Samantha, don't you?"

Laura nodded.

"Last year she came home from school with a peasant dress on and all she could talk about was natural foods—organic this and herbal that. She gave me a natural tranquilizer to try. And at that point I was up to forty or fifty milligrams of Valium a day, so I said to myself, why not? And that night, when I was on this organic tranquilizer, I dreamed I was riding the crest of a huge, gigantic tidal wave—backwards. And everywhere around me there was nothing but blue ocean, and this enormous wall of water with me balancing on top of, it just racing along, backwards. I could hear the wave roaring in my ears even. It was terribly vivid, the whole thing. It was like a hallucination."

186

"You must have been awfully frightened when you woke up," Laura said.

"That's putting it mildly. I was in a cold sweat. I never tried natural tranquilizers again, I'll tell you that much. I think they must make them out of morning glories. Anyway, what I was trying to say about Marie is that she's probably up on the crest of a tidal wave, the way I was. She's just being swept along—backwards, so that she can only see where she's been, not where she's going. With me the wall of water was Valium; with her it's a wall of vodka."

"You're probably right," Laura said. "Still, I never heard of booze floating a person up to the door of a church supper."

"What are you doing for supper tonight, Laura?"

"Me? I'm going to my parents' . . . with Jamie. My mother is absolutely dying to have him over."

"Oh. That'll be nice. I'm packing a picnic myself, which I'm going to eat at this very promising evening auction I'm going to. I thought you might like to come along."

"I would, but obviously I can't. I might go with you another time, though."

"That'd be nice. I don't mind admitting that I'm recruiting for my new shop. I've been asking and asking Marie . . . of course I know you're in publishing . . . and now you have your new young beau—"

"Beau Copyright," Laura said.

"Huh?"

"Beau Copyright. He's a fictional character I just made up. He's another Rhett Butler. I'm combining in Beau Copyright all the characteristics of the nice-looking young guys you meet in dating bars and all the characteristics of the New York publishing jobs that are offered to young women. My heroine will go to bed with Beau Copyright and the next morning he'll be gone and there'll be a pink slip on the pillow next to her."

Vivian had a sip of lemonade. Then she said, "Does that mean you might be able to work with me in the shop next fall?"

"It's a possibility," Laura replied.

"Ooh, now I'm even more optimistic than before."

"Optimism . . ." said Laura, mulling over the word. "I've always tried hard to be optimistic, but it gets to be like living in a foreign country; all the currency has to be converted. You have to convert every uncertainty to a possibility. And life can drive a hard bargain that way. The exchange rate can be . . . unfavorable."

"You're starting to sound like Marie, Laura. And there's no earthly reason to. . . . Why, you've never even been married . . . and divorced." A faraway look came into Vivian's eyes.

"No, you're right," Laura replied. "I never have been married. But I've been relationshiped. Which is sort of like the way the old joke about the woman in the doctor's office goes: she tells him, 'No, I've never been X-rayed, but I've been ultraviolated.' "

There was a long pause after Hopkins, the realtor, finished reading Marjorie's letter over the telephone. During the pause Dan Cartey was looking out his office window at the Pan Am building; he was remembering the helicopter crash on the roof—how the rotor had fallen to the street, where it struck down a woman who was walking home after work. And he was remembering, too, the executive who had taken a nose dive from an upper story of the same building. Maybe it was bad luck to have a view of the Pan Am building. Maybe lawyers from other conglomerates watched you from its windows, and made paper planes with claims written on them to sail into your eye. Maybe some lawyer had made this sharp little paper missile for this dame up in Maine.

"What the hell does she want?" Dan asked. "Money?"

"Beats me," Hopkins replied. "But I wouldn't put it past her. When you been in the real estate business long as I have, you find out two things: everything comes on the market eventually and everybody's got a price tag."

"How long before they call that bloody goddamn town meeeting?"

"Three weeks . . . a month, I'd say, at the outside."

"That gives us a little time. Look, the last thing I want now is to have the Perry House mucked up in legal proceedings. Our options with the place will evaporate before we can get any benefit out of them. I'm going to handle this myself. Book me a suite in that inn in Munsonville. And then see if you can get this dame to meet me privately for dinner. Say, six-thirty, this coming Tuesday. I'll fly up Monday night late. I don't want anyone else in Cable Harbor knowing I'm around. So see if you can get her to keep her mouth buttoned up."

"Even a woman can keep a secret if she knows it's in her own interest to," Hopkins said. "My wife says that. She says, 'One of the reasons talk is so cheap is that nobody gets a commission on it.'"

"That may be true up where you are," Dan replied. "But down here there are plenty of people who get their cut on the basis of what people are saying. They're called publicists. I'd hire one to improve the Perry House's image—only things have gone too far."

"No reason to throw in the towel yet, Mr. Cartey," Hopkins said. "I'll just do like you want me to and follow through on that reservation and that appointment. I'll take care of those two things directly. You try to have a good day, now."

"I'll have a couple of martinis with lunch is what I'll do."

"I'd like ten center-cut pork chops cut nice and thick," Marjorie said. She was mildly surprised to see how pale Booth looked today. He was standing behind the meat counter staring at her as if she'd asked for spare ribs out of his own rib cage. He seemed to come to, though, and went into the walk-in. Marjorie heard the knife thunking . . . and then—she thought she heard—a *sob*.

CHAPTER EIGHTEEN

Before leaving with Elsie for the church supper, Marie had three drinks.

"They got a good program tonight," Elsie said. She was sitting in the passenger's seat of the Porsche, with a tin of fresh cookies in her ample lap.

"Oh, what is it?" Marie asked.

"Color slides," Elsie replied. "Luella Freemont's givin' a talk about her trip to China."

"That sounds fascinating," Marie said. She wondered what she had let herself in for—but if color slides of China and a three-dollar supper were all it took to book passage to the land of innocence, so be it. It was what Marie wanted now: the simple life. She wanted to see for herself the other side of Cable Harbor; she wanted to be convinced that life could be simple if you didn't allow desire to complicate it.

The supper was being held in the hall of the First Congregational Church. The hall had the scale of the great hall of a castle, only it had been built in the fifties, of wood, with vaguely Danish modern beams in the ceiling, kitchen linoleum on the floor, and sliding partitions, which had been put in, Elsie said, so the Boy Scouts and the couples' club could meet at the same time. As she walked into the hall from the coatroom, Marie took a deep breath of the pure air, which smelled faintly like cooked carrots. She insisted on paying for Elsie's supper, and handed six dollars to the man at the card table with the cigar box full of wrinkled bills. The man, whose shirt was buttoned up to his neck despite the heat, looked like a retired Disney character—Horace Horsecollar, Marie thought, Horace Horsecollar living on a fixed income.

The mean age in the hall must have been eighty. Elsie introduced Marie to a woman younger than the others who apparently was serving as a church social director. Marie pegged her as one of those smiling widows who are always having a grandchild delivered via UPS or something. Marie didn't quite get her name right with all the babble going on, but it sounded like April May, which, if it really was her name, certainly suited her.

Elsie wanted to sit with the Kents, so she reserved two of the folding steel chairs by propping them against the table. Mrs. Kent looked to be in her mid-eighties. One of her hands shook when she showed Marie the bracelet Mr. Kent had made for her by wiring together seashells. Mr. Kent was a retired engineer. He was a little hard of hearing, but very animated. He had brought along a working model of a windmill he hoped to get patented. He'd built the model in his basement. The model had hinged blades that seemed to whip up their own energy with even the slightest breeze. The old people were taking turns huffing and puffing on the blades, which were whipping around at an ever-increasing velocity. Marie watched for a couple of minutes and then had to pull out her folding chair and sit down because she was getting dizzy.

Mrs. Kent whispered in Marie's ear. She said her hobby was walking down to the harbor and picking up the papers and trash that people left. Every morning starting at five-thirty she did this. She asked Marie if she had any hobbies.

"Nothing as civic-minded as what you do," Marie said. Mrs. Kent revealed the fact that she was a graduate of Vassar and so felt a duty to pick up the candy wrappers of thoughtless people.

"If you're that sensitive about eyesores, you must not like that half-finished Perry House very much," Marie prompted. She noted with pleasure that Mrs. Kent's face was assuming an expression much like the one Marie's mother used to put on her face every time she came in from the yard to announce that another dog had "left his calling card."

"Oh, *that* place," Mrs. Kent said. "It's so modernistic, what there is of it. It doesn't fit in with the houses around here at all."

191

"It does look like a Holiday Inn, doesn't it?" Marie said. "Can't you picture it? With one of those big, splashy signs, with flashing lightblubs marching around the rim?"

Mrs. Kent raised her hand as if to ward off the details of a terrible operation. Marie was torn between delight in her own deviltry and sympathy for the sensitive old lady. What an unmitigated bastard Dan was that he couldn't leave these harmless people alone in their unspoiled little haven.

"Don't even think such things," Mrs. Kent said. "I couldn't bear to see the town all commercialized . . . and cheapened."

"If only we could all get together on it," Marie said.

Mrs. Kent's voice fell to a whisper.

"They're already doing things," she confided. "I've heard that somebody's been looking into the real estate deals that . . . that . . . Well, I've heard some pretty shady things were done around the time that Perry House place was begun."

"You don't say," Marie replied. I wish I knew what they've found out, she thought. Marie was about to ask Mrs. Kent if she knew who had been snooping around in the real estate records when the minister called for quiet by tinkling his glass with a spoon. Then he said grace, and right after the mumbled *amens* the food came on. The crowd at Marie and Elsie's table looked up from their milky crockery as if they were crouched at a starting line. First came the dinner rolls. Then the carrots and the string beans and the mashed potato and the ham loaf. Everyone was passing plates and piling up food. Marie almost lost her grip on a platter of ham loaf as she tried to pass it over the blades of Mr. Kent's model windmill.

"Good food and plenty of it," Elsie said proudly.

Marie thought the vegetables were overboiled and bland—but then again, seasonings and sauces and crunchy string beans and sexual disappointments were what Marie had had her fill of.

By the time people were starting on their second helpings Marie wouldn't have minded a glass of wine. But the high school girls were making the rounds with pitchers of coffee and tea instead. All the wholesome food had absorbed the vodka more completely than Marie had anticipated. A familiar nervous tension began buzzing in her. The vague fear that without a drink she was going to faint—or somehow make a fool of herself again.

Marie reached in her bag for a cigarette, but then she realized

192

that nobody was smoking. These old church people would frown on smoking, of course. Mrs. Kent would spot her for one of the people who leave cigarette packs scattered around the harbor. And stare with that expression of sadness in the face of abuse that the advertising council gives Smokey the Bear.

Irrationally, Marie took her Dupont lighter out of her bag and put it next to her plate for a feeling of security. At least the lighter was related to cigarettes, and therefore a small comfort.

There were three desserts: vanilla ice cream with chocolate sauce, chocolate cake with chocolate frosting, and a large variety of homemade cookies. Marie ate the ice cream and a couple of bites of cake. She asked for tea and rattled her cup trying to drink it. The table was cleared quickly, so quickly that Marie didn't notice them starting to roll up the paper tablecloth. Pushed along the length of the table, with each person helping to roll it up, the paper snowball was upon Marie before she had a chance to pick up her Dupont lighter. Realizing what was happening, Marie grabbed for the lighter and got her arm caught in the moving roll of paper.

For an instant, Marie thought she was going to be turned upside down. She jerked her arm back and the roll of paper ripped. Everybody looked aghast. Marie felt her face heating up to a bright red.

"I left my little—compact—on the table," she mumbled. "Wasn't that dumb of me?" Mr. Kent, who was holding his model windmill safely up in the air, appeared to agree. So did everybody else at the table. Except Elsie, of course. Elsie reached into her own pocketbook and said to Marie, very quietly, "Isn't it time for you to take your prescription now, Mrs. Cartey?"

"What prescription?"

"Your cough medicine. I remembered to bring it along."

Elsie pulled a bottle with a pharmacist's label out of her bag and handed it to Marie. Then she deftly shifted Marie's teacup to her lap while everyone else was concentrating on the renewed tablecloth gathering. Taking the bottle from Marie, she opened it and poured its contents into the teacup and put the cup back on the bare table.

"It's nice you held on to your teacup," Elsie said. "You can finish what's left together with that little bit of medicine while they're setting up for the program."

Marie took a sip from the cup. It was vodka. Faintly flavored with tea.

"Elsie, you're a godsend," Marie whispered.

"Oh, I just happened to think of it before we left. Mrs. Kent brings her special medicine to the suppers, too."

Marie looked at Mrs. Kent. She was blowing on her husband's windmill as if it were a birthday cake. And her hands weren't shaking anymore.

"I should have known," Marie whispered. "An old Vassar girl like her."

Announcing that it was time for the program to start, April May folded her chair and brought it to the front of the room, where the slide projector was set up. The rest of the crowd followed suit, carrying their chairs more or less the way a crutch is used. April May distributed hymnals and asked for a volunteer to accompany the singing on the piano. But there was no volunteer. So April May tried to establish the key by poking out a few notes, and there followed an a cappella chorus of the first verses of three different hymns. Mouthing the words, Marie looked about her and tried to decide if Protestants move into cedar closets when they get old—everywhere there was that odor that is more common to disused bureau drawers than it is to the body.

After the hymn singing, April May introduced Mrs. Freemont, who looked very much like a world traveler: she was wearing a pantsuit with a lot of pockets and a canvas hat that she kept firmly planted on her head. Mrs. Freemont stood to one side of the screen with a remote control in her hand. She started flicking and talking. Mrs. Freemont's lecture was remarkably detailed. Before she even got into the slides of Hong Kong, she showed a succession of maps evidently photographed where they appeared in the pages of high school geography books. She followed the courses of rivers and tapped major cities with a yardstick.

Marie had forgotten what a comfort true boredom can be. Mrs. Freemont's monotonous voice was almost as soothing as a massage on the temples. Marie closed her eyes the better to enjoy the relaxing action of Mrs. Freemont's steady drone. Herbert seemed further away than the Forbidden City. The fire might have happened in an anteroom belonging to the Dowager Empress. This was bliss; Marie felt utterly disengaged from life and more particularly life's thorns—love and sex. Elsie did not notice Marie nodding off. Neither did anyone else, until Marie began to snore. She woke herself up with the noise she was making. She opened her eyes and realized that people were looking at her. Worse yet, Mrs. Freemont had stopped the show and was waiting with her arms folded.

"I gather you've been on a trip to China yourself," Mrs. Freemont said icily.

"Er, no," Marie mumbled.

"Oh," said Mrs. Freemont. "I thought you might want to take over the podium from me. But if you don't, I'll continue."

There was considerable throat clearing in the audience. And then Mrs. Freemont resumed her lecture. Though she was humiliated, Marie was also moved—by Mrs. Freemont's passionate defense of her little slide show. Obviously she was one of those displaced women who take traveling to heart. There was no escaping desire, Marie realized. Even at a church supper. It was unmistakable, desire, and Marie could see it clearly now in the lonely figure Mrs. Freemont was pointing out—herself—high atop the Great Wall.

Arthur was sitting in a blue funk in the living room of his house on East Sixty-seventh Street. He felt as if he were sitting in a roofless villa in Pompeii. The frescoes on the walls were still fresh and everything was swept clean, but still you couldn't help but feel them falling on your shoulders like thick snow: ashes, ashes, ashes. Arthur had set the Chinese low table in front of him for an appropriately desolate repast: vodka from the freezer and bare Ritz crackers. While he was in the kitchen getting the Finlandia out of the freezer, Arthur had removed a butcher knife from a drawer and contemplated it for a minute. He tested various points on his body with the blade, gently touching his Adam's apple with the point, drawing the sharp edge delicately across his wrist. Suicide was a tantalizing proposition.

Arthur considered committing hara-kiri right then and there. On the Italian tiles that he and Herbert had picked out for the kitchen at Country Floors. But no . . . the look wasn't right. To commit hara-kiri you had to have on a black wig done up in a bun with a long pin stuck in it. And a silk Sulka bathrobe. Besides, even when Arthur was drawing the knife lightly across his wrist he could not actually conceive of his own death. It seemed too faraway a prospect, too unlikely altogether. Without himself in it, Arthur had difficulty imagining the world's continued existence.

But then again, life without Herbert was unimaginable. Except in terms of barrenness. Camping with no audience to truly appreciate it. Camping—out on the Jersey meadows. With amyl nitrite lingering in your lungs like sulfur from the refineries.

Arthur was afraid that Herbert's return to women was irreversible. Perhaps it had been inevitable all along. These years with Herbert had been a freak of love, and if that love was gone . . . Herbert would naturally look for a different kind of love where he could most readily find it . . . with women. But with Marie? Yes. It could happen. With her as well as with any other woman; women were always ready to fall in love just as men were always ready to have sex.

Drinking his cold vodka, Arthur wondered if he should go after sex tonight. It was out of the question to go to the bars—not with a face that showed you were walking through the valley of the shadow of rejection. What else was there? A hustler? Perhaps a call boy? Arthur thought about that possibility and then dialed a number that he knew.

"I want somebody young, cute, and blond," he told the party who answered. "A California surfer type. The best one you've got . . . and I'd like him for the whole weekend. . . . Do I want what? No, that's not necessary. I'd like him to look like a lifeguard, but he doesn't have to be wearing a whistle around his neck. . . . Okay . . . fine, terrific. . . .

"Yeah, that's right. . . . I want to put him on my American Express."

"What do you think you might be doing when the summer's over, Jamie? Do you have any . . . specific plans?"

Laura knew that that question from her mother was going to be asked in the course of the evening no matter what, but she wished it hadn't had to accompany the shrimp cocktail. Jamie was less bothered by the inquiry than Laura; he had his reply pulled out as adeptly as he had held Mrs. Damon's chair for her while she sat down.

"I'm thinking about starting an alternative foundation," Jamie said. "In New York. We've always been involved in philanthropy. Most of the people in my family have—although my mother used to say, 'Charity begins at home.' Until she got to Italy and decided it begins in Rome. Anyway, for my own part, I'm considering going

196

to New York and getting into what you might call philanthropic activism."

"Philanthropic activism?" Mrs. Damon said. She looked puzzled. She leaned forward and her diamond earrings appeared to tremble. Laura was wondering why Jamie always had to bring his mother into the conversation. At times he sounded like everyone else in Cable Harbor: my mother did this to me and my mother did that to me. Which Laura knew was only blaming somebody else for your own inadequacies. But Jamie wasn't inadequate. Was he?

"I suppose philanthropic activism is something like giving to the Philharmonic . . . and then going to it," Mr. Damon volunteered. Laura couldn't help but smile. Her father was such a dear, like a teddy bear in pinstripes. If she hadn't loved him anyway she would have loved him for going out gardening in a business suit and a tie.

"It's not quite like that," Jamie replied. "Philanthropic activism means giving to people who don't usually get funds very easily. Like tenant organizations in the cities. Or women's rights groups. Antinuclear groups get money from activist foundations, for example. So do gay rights groups."

Mrs. Damon removed a black entrail from one of her shrimp and placed it on the side of her Royal Worcester plate with discreet distaste.

"Antinuclear groups?" she echoed. "And gay rights groups? Can't you cover the gay rights groups by giving to the New York City Ballet?"

"Not really," Jamie replied. "The basic idea behind alternative foundations is social change: using money to work for a more equitable society. And frankly it's fun to do things with money that the Ford Foundation wouldn't do."

"Who works for Equitable?" Mr. Damon asked.

"No, Daddy, we're not talking about insurance," Laura said.

"Oh," said Mr. Damon. He adjusted his tortoiseshell bifocals on his nose and returned to his shrimp. Mrs. Damon patted her lips with her batiste napkin, which was one of the exquisitely made set she had had the maid dig out for the occasion.

"Goodness," she said. "It sounds as if you want to be running a very different kind of foundation indeed."

"There's a book about the kind of foundation I have in mind," Jamie said. "It's called *Robin Hood Was Right*."

"About stealing from the rich to give to the poor," Laura added.

"I don't think we need go that far, need we?" Mrs. Damon said. "Perhaps we could all give to the City Opera instead of the Met. That would be the same thing, wouldn't it?"

"That'd be close enough," Jamie said. "It'd be a little like my mother's involvement with La Scala. She used to provide bed and board for promising tenors."

Laura put down her fork so carefully that she seemed to be marking a boundary on the tablecloth. Imperceptibly and almost involuntarily, she drew her shoulders together, as though closing herself off from something.

"How satisfying it must have been for your mother," Mrs. Damon was saying, "to be able to sit at a sidewalk café with an Italian tenor. My lunches back in the city . . . in New York. Even during the season, they're certainly nothing like that. No tenors at the table. I eat with a group of middle-aged women, like myself, and our lunches are what you might call . . . mezzo-mezzo."

Laura looked at her mother as if she were uncertain who this woman was. Mrs. Damon returned Laura's glance matter-of-factly, and then looked at Laura's father, evidently in a kind of summation. Laura nearly put her elbow in the bowl of lobster bisque that the maid was placing in front of her.

"Do you know Stewart Mott, by any chance?" Mrs. Damon asked Jamie.

"No, I don't," Jamie replied. "But I wouldn't be surprised if I run into him when I move to New York."

"Yes," Mrs. Damon agreed. "I suspect you'll be running into him or people who know him—what with your ideas about, er . . . progressive philanthropy. Your mother certainly showed you the way . . . with her progressive ideas."

Laura wished her mother would leave the subject of Jamie's mother alone. For that matter, she wished Jamie would leave the subject of his mother alone. But it seemed that something had taken hold of Laura's mother, some impulse that Laura hadn't known was in her. It was as if Laura's mother and Jamie were exchanging innuendos that gave each of them, in a different way, some personal satisfaction. Laura felt isolated. Her pleasure, in sitting at this dining table at all, was supposed to have come from showing off her new boyfriend, her new relationship. But the conversation was turning to Jamie's first relationship, his relationship with his mother, which was sounding to Laura more and more like the pivotal one in his life.

"My mother's philanthropy was democratic in its outreach," Jamie said. "But it wasn't as progressive as my grandmother's has been. My mother liked the idea of tax shelters. So she moved into one—emotionally. She gave away enough so that she could keep . . . more than life ordinarily allows people to keep . . . for herself."

"Who was your mother's accountant?" Mrs. Damon asked.

"Now, who did I know at Equitable who was getting Havana cigars out of London?" Laura's father wondered aloud.

"There comes a time in everyone's life when there should be some sort of emotional accounting," Mrs. Damon said. "One day last April, when I was having lunch with Louise Wilson, she pulled out a bill from Bergdorf's and showed it to me and said, 'This is how much I spent, and you see how it looks on me, and I absolutely insist on paying for lunch, which with the tip will be eighty dollars, rounded off. Can you please tell me from these figures if my life amounts to anything?' "

"Louise Wilson has always had problems," Laura said.

"Yes . . . well, enough about her," Laura's mother replied. "My, it seems as though we're all going to be heading for New York in the fall. And more lunches. At least you'll be busy setting up your new foundation, Jamie. And you, Laura, will be doing something equally interesting when you get back into . . . publishing."

"I hope something interesting," Laura said. "But I certainly won't be doing anything exciting." Feeling relieved that Jamie's mother and Louise Wilson and company, emotional accountants, had been left to their historical devices, Laura added, "Back when I was working I used to try to think of ways publishing could be exciting. . . . Maybe it could be if you could read lips and know what all the editors and agents are saying about each other when they're eating lunch at The Four Seasons." Yes, it can be exciting, Laura thought . . . in its way.

"Oh, they probably just talk about the mid-life crisis, like all my friends at Le Cirque," Mrs. Damon said.

"Maybe. Anyway it would be interesting to find out, if not all that exciting. What would be exciting would be to go to lunch at the Four Seasons in a Swifty Lazar mask."

"It would be healthy if everyone would drop all those things they do at lunch," Mrs. Damon reflected. "With the exception of eating."

"Occasionally they do," Laura replied. "That's why when I was working I sometimes ate in this little lower-level cafeteria I found in Rockefeller Center. With all the secretaries. Every lunch I had there sat very well with me. I never felt any of the eye movements that you feel when you're eating in a room full of editors." *But I kind of miss the tension now.*

"Well, dear," Mrs. Damon said. "If you want to eat like that you'll have to go to work for an alternative-publishing house. Someplace progressive, such as Jamie's foundation is going to be."

"The only alternative-publishing houses are small presses in the Berkshires and Vermont," Laura replied. "When you're working for one of them you can skip lunch altogether, which might not be a bad idea . . . good for the waistline."

"Your waistline is fine," Jamie said.

"Nobody in this family has ever gotten fat," Mrs. Damon said with the confidence of a horse trader who knows the bloodline. "Of course, I've had to be careful myself. . . ." She put down her soup spoon thoughtfully even though she still had some bisque left. And glanced at her husband, who was slurping away regardless.

The lobster bisque was followed by poached salmon, a salad, and dessert and coffee. At Mrs. Damon's suggestion, they retired to the billiard room with glasses of brandy. Mrs. Damon wanted to sit down with her daughter and watch the men play, but Jamie insisted that the women play too. Mrs. Damon pleaded to be excused. Laura pulled her up out of her chair, though, and fitted a cue into her waving hands.

They played three games.

Mrs. Damon won two of them, and Jamie won one.

"I bet you didn't know my mother was a pool hustler," Laura said to Jamie after they'd finished the final game. "These ladies who lunch . . . at Le Cirque and Côte Basque—they can take care of themselves."

"Oh, nonsense," said Mrs. Damon. "Beginner's luck."

Mr. Damon had a good laugh at that. And when he stopped laughing he offered Jamie a cigar, which Jamie took, and lit one for himself. Then he started laughing again, apparently at some private joke connected with his wife's surprising skill at billiards. Mr. Damon poured more brandy, and Jamie offered him a joint when he offered a cigar for the second time.

"Is it true this stuff helps prevent glaucoma?" Mr. Damon asked.

"Yes, that is true, Daddy," Laura said.

"Don't mind if I do, then," Mr. Damon said.

What with the brandy and the marijuana, the little party did not break up until one-thirty in the morning. Laura's mother held her back at the front door just long enough to whisper in her ear, "He's a younger version of Stewart Mott. If I were you I'd take the chance on him. It's obvious he adored his poor mother. And where there was an attachment like that, there's bound to be a strong need for the love of a woman. He might not even stray."

Since Jamie was getting into the van—and was well out of earshot, Laura lingered a moment longer to ask her mother what she had decided was an important question.

"Mother," Laura said, "back when you and Daddy had that problem between the two of you—years ago—it was probably a relief for him to go to the office, don't you think?"

"Why, what a funny question to ask, Laura."

"I think it's important," Laura said. "An office can be a second home. It can even be your one solid roof, the only place where you're . . . sheltered."

"Sheltered? Who'd want to be sheltered like that boy's mother was?"

"Look, Mother, no man is ever really turned out of doors when the marriage breaks up, because he has his work to go to. And whatever the work might be, it goes on *inside*. That's what I want to be sure of, Mother, I want to be sure I can always be inside somewhere. Not alone in an empty house. . . . No place is more exposed to the elements than the inside of an empty house."

"I know one place more exposed," Mrs. Damon said. "Fifth Avenue. Fifth Avenue in midwinter after you've just eaten lunch with the girls and you have that little walk home . . . and then the rest of the afternoon . . . ahead of you. Look, Laura, he's starting up the car. Don't keep him waiting—*don't*."

CHAPTER NINETEEN

The exhibition was from seven to eight, with the auction beginning promptly at eight. Vivian arrived at seven on the dot. She chose for herself a chair near the front of the tent and put her picnic basket on it to hold it. Dealers had already taped their names to most of the chairs—women dealers—Vivian was well aware that most of the men in the antiques trade elected to stand in the back, where they could quickly consult on pool bids and monitor the retail buyers and the women dealers in the front rows. Vivian felt she would have no reason to watch anyone: she trusted her own eye and always established for each item a limit that she never exceeded—except, of course, when she was taking a calcuated risk on a Heriz in order to provoke the rug pool.

Vivian would be bidding with an edge on most of the dealers here anyway; few of them ever went over 50 percent of the retail value (the ruggies never went over 20 percent), and since Vivian was planning on opening shop on Madison or in Soho, she could automatically plan on charging double retail. So for her retail was wholesale, a fact of New York life that could occasionally prove advantageous.

At first Vivian was disappointed by the accumulation that was going on the block. There was Sears, Roebuck oak everywhere. And fifties household junk—nothing from the thirties or forties, no Fiestaware, not even one of those Deco radios. But here and there . . . The more Vivian poked around, the more she began to see.

Opening an old box that looked as if it might contain sparklers—it was covered with Hong Kong calligraphy—Vivian found a fan. And what a fan. It had been fashioned from ivory, and the fabric that connected the ribs was hand-painted silk. Vivian picked up a second, similar box and opened it. Another fan, this one made of peacock feathers, not one of which was even ruffled. Perhaps the old lady whose estate this was had a rich, fashionable relative who sent her things she wearied of. What else might there be?

Rolling up her sleeves, Vivian dug into the pile. In a box of junk jewelry she found a sterling-silver Art Nouveau pin that was nothing less than miraculous. The pin was similar to a cameo, but the woman's face was looking straight at you instead of assuming the usual profile. And the face was fabulous. It could have been Sarah Bernhardt or Isadora Duncan. The silver hair piled on top of the head cascaded down and ended at the throat in a glorious swirl: that final Art Nouveau flourish. Maybe three hundred dollars on Madison, Vivian thought.

She was still burrowing into the pile when the auctioneer clamped the microphone to his lapel and asked everyone to be seated. Cramming her notepad and pencil into her pocketbook, Vivian hurried to the chair she'd reserved for herself. Sitting next to her was a matronly woman, obviously a dealer, who was talking to the woman beside her about flying up from Virginia to Boston and then renting a U-Haul and a car there. To the right of Vivian was a young woman who might have been a doctor's wife; she had the look of somebody out to educate herself in antiques—and she was dressed well enough so that there could be no doubt that she could pay for any lessons she learned by bidding.

The first item up for bids was a silver fruit bowl about as thin as a tin can, with minor dents in it. The auctioneer asked for ten dollars to start it off, didn't get it, and sailed it across the tent to one of his assistants, who caught it neatly.

There was a ripple of applause and a five-dollar bid. Vivian was already on the edge of her seat. She was, as her mother had liked to say, "all atwitter"—but this was not the old nervousness; this was different. It was anticipation now, whereas before it had been dread. Maybe they were the same emotion, like love and hate. And like love and hate, maybe the one that you felt depended on the way you felt about yourself.

When the peacock fan came up for bids Vivian was ready for it. She let somebody in the back start it off for ten dollars. There was a flurry of bidding that took it up to thirty-five, where it stalled. The auctioneer opened it up and fanned himself. Forty. Forty-five. The bidders were down to two and tiring. Vivian raised her hand. Fifty.

"Fresh blood," the auctioneer said with a smile. The two bidders resisted until sixty-five. And then Vivian had won.

"I like your taste," the woman who was obviously a dealer said to Vivian.

"Thank you," Vivian replied.

When the ivory fan came up three pressed-back oak chairs and a meat grinder later, Vivian opened the bidding. The auctioneer asked for fifty to start and Vivian said distinctly but not loudly, "A hundred."

"Whew," said the auctioneer. "Guess the lady means business." Heads turned to look at Vivian.

"Any advance?" asked the auctioneer. There were no other bids. Vivian's strategy of intimidation had worked. She had the second fan.

"Are you in the business?" the lady dealer from Virginia with the U-Haul asked sweetly.

"I'm just starting," Vivian said. And in saying so she felt as much pride and anticipation as she had the day her engagement was announced.

"Where's your shop?" the lady dealer asked.

"New York," Vivian replied. "Soho . . . I think. The location isn't definite yet."

The lady nodded knowingly and said, "New York. Yes. In New York you'll be able to get those prices—and then some."

Vivian felt justified to hear that. Justified and vindicated and . . . joyful. She opened up her picnic basket and offered the lady from Virginia a cherry tomato.

"The boys in the back are going to be getting together on those five or six pieces of furniture," the lady said quietly as she graciously accepted the tomato. "Would you be interested in forming an association of two to give them a little run for their money on, say, the spade-foot candle stand, that little bird's-eye-maple three-drawer stand, and perhaps those two windsors in old red?"

"I'd love to," Vivian replied, "but I'm not after the furniture.

I'm opening a boutique, and I only want to carry smalls. Little accessories to go with antique clothing."

"Oh, Christie's is doing that," said the lady. "The Worth gowns. I'm sure you'll be a big success if that's what you're planning to do."

"I hope so," Vivian said. And for the first time in her life, her hope was brightly colored with confidence.

George was in the post office at nine-thirty in the morning; he had established a routine and liked to keep to it; pick up the paper, go to the post office, see the wholesalers if a party was coming up. George had found that sticking to a routine like this lessened the effects of boredom and frustration: the more efficient you were, the more mechanical in your daily operations, the less you were aware of what you were doing. It was like the effect of a plane on wood— the rhythmic back and forth smoothed out the roughness so that the doors in your head with a tendency to be sticky quietly closed, and everything clicked into place. This morning, as George pulled the wad of mail from his post office box, and saw the torn package, one of the doors that routine was supposed to keep closed suddenly banged open. And a cold draft blew from the pit of George's stomach to his head.

Somebody had been looking at his mail. Who? Postal inspectors? Did they have the right to do that? With first-class mail? George saw that the film was there. But it had been seen. His private life had been discovered, viewed by persons unknown, who now knew about him. George stood frozen in the middle of the post office. He noticed that the floor had just been mopped. There was a sign that said: DAMP FLOOR. WATCH YOUR STEP. George read the sign twice, three times: he was trying to steady himself with an everyday notice; he was clinging to a commonplace as if it were a rope railing in a storm. Folding Marjorie's *Ladies' Home Journal* around the torn package to conceal it, to stanch the escape of his privacy, George slapped shut the door of his box. Through the little windows in the boxes above he saw the face of the woman who worked in the back— Midge, or whatever her name was. He thought he saw her mouth twitch. He thought he saw her quickly look the other way.

With his head down, George hurried out to the Olds. He put the mail on the seat next to him, burying the torn package under bills and magazines. Then he thought better of it and pulled out the

205

package and ducked it under the seat. He started the car and rolled down his window. Then he realized he had the air conditioning on and rolled the window up again. He backed up without looking and a horn blared at him. George slammed on the brakes and the car lurched and stalled. He tried to start it and flooded it. On and on the starter whirred. The sun seemed to be everywhere: a thousand spotlights you couldn't see the source of, and behind the spotlights were eyes, eyes that were lowered, looking down, examining.

In a spasm of effort, George brought his foot down on the accelerator with crushing weight and held it there, at the same time holding the key rigidly in *start*. The car yielded and turned over.

In the window of Booth's market Evelyn stood watching. She watched until George Hanson had driven off. Then she went back to unpacking a case of Sacramento tomato juice. Near the bottom of the box she found a badly dented can. It looked as if it had been savagely kicked, or cruelly squeezed by machinery. Evelyn imagined an assembly line in California, with can after can of Sacramento tomato juice coasting along it. And then this one can. This one can rocked a little as it rode along the belt, and the machinery got ahold of it—and bit into it. Hard. The metal gears, the steel rollers, bit, bit into the flimsy tin. Bent it inward. Mangled it. Evelyn held the dented can in her hand, and looked out on the sunlit street where George Hanson had just been. And she ground her teeth. And smiled.

Marjorie was surprised to hear from Hopkins so soon after she'd sent her little letter of inquiry. And by telephone yet. Still more surprising was the invitation he extended—to meet, privately, with Mr. Cartey himself, at the beginning of the week. What were they up to? The only way Marjorie could find out for sure would be to accept the invitation. She knew she could handle herself. Whether Mr. Cartey was a big New York executive or whether he wasn't, it made no difference. All men were the same. They were little boys with their eyes on things. And you could manage them exactly the way you managed a child when you were out shopping with it—you let them stand there with their eyes on the counter until you'd finished, and then you took them by the hand and tugged. Perhaps it wasn't exactly that way when they got older, but it was close. You didn't exactly tug them along—but you did sort of take them by the hand, and let them think they could *touch*, let them think their hands could go where they had their eyes. And then they trailed along after you while you led them where all along you had intended to go.

The surfer type Arthur had ordered over the telephone proved to be the genuine article. He arrived wearing a T-shirt that commemorated the national surfing championships in Hawaii, and he had long blond hair and blue eyes that regarded you like the eyes of a snake sunning itself on a rock—in Malibu. As Arthur let the kid in he noticed the comb sticking out of his back pocket. Why did all hustlers have big combs sticking out of their back pockets? Why did they always wear cheap belts? What had made them gay when they looked so straight? Pollution from the Metropolitan Opera blowing over into Jersey?

The kid's name was Chad. Arthur offered him a drink and he said he'd like a beer. Naturally, Arthur thought. Chad sat on the Marlborough sofa, and its satin upholstery seemed to creep up on him, until he said to Arthur the inevitable "This is some place you got here."

"You think so?" Arthur replied. "It's homey, anyway."

A grand fatigue, which felt as gray and grainy and immense as the twilight outside the windows, settled upon Arthur. He examined his Gucci loafers, which were shined beyond the point of polish—to a mellow, rich patina—and decided they were irrelevant. He looked at his Corum watch, at the twenty-dollar gold piece that was the dial, and decided it was irrelevant. As was the hour of the day. So, too, was this room irrelevant, with its great furnishings, the museum pieces that came as close to being dowagers as fretted-over wood can—which was quite close, Arthur realized—but also essentially irrelevant. So what was relevant? What did matter? Arthur raised his eyelids to look at the stunning youth who was sitting opposite him. The youth, Chad, who was casting about the room, trying to take in all the riches, sensed that his host's eyes were on him and returned the look—tried to parry it, almost, Arthur thought. Defensive, but trying not to show it.

"This really is some place," Chad said.

"I hope you'll be comfortable in it," Arthur replied. "Seeing as you're going to be my guest for the weekend."

Chad smiled and crossed his sneakers, like a self-conscious little boy. He needs clothes, Arthur thought. He recalled a friend in San Francisco who had picked up a kid in the street and taught him opera, table manners, and grammar. Then the kid had gone on to develop an interest in books, of all things, and gardening. They had been together ten years now, the friend and the foundling who was to thrive with cultivation. But it had been a long process, the cultivating. And Herbert and Arthur had been cultivating each other —yes, even nurturing each other—for how long? As long as the twilight extended its mantle. Arthur sighed.

"I must tell you something about myself," he said to Chad. "I am not a new person, like you are. I'm damaged goods. I can't possibly be as refreshing to you as you are to me. But still I would like you to have a good time this weekend. So what we will do together will not be routine. It probably won't be what you've come to expect."

Chad appeared to draw back a bit. He said, "You into S 'n M? Is that what you mean?"

"S and M?" Arthur laughed. "Good Lord, no. Gratuitous cruelty? Me? Never. I'd never try to duplicate artificially what already occurs naturally in human nature. No. What I have in mind is something quite different . . . a *Pygmalion* scene, if you will."

"What's that? I once went with a guy who put mustard on me and licked it off. Is that what you mean by a *Pygmalion* scene?"

"No, that's a piggy scene. What I mean by a *Pygmalion* scene is that I'm going to take you places. I'm going to take you shopping, for one thing."

"Oh yeah," said Chad, brightening. "Where?"

"We'll talk about that over dinner. Which I guess will have to be in the Village or Soho. You're not exactly dressed for Lutèce."

Chad looked down at his jeans and his Hawaiian shirt with the band of flowers printed on it—the surfer's racing stripe. Nobody had objected to this outfit before. Usually it was what they wanted. Chad saw that he was shaking his foot and stopped doing it. He would have to stay cool, even though this guy was pretty weird.

Marie began going to the Bath Club again, but she never took off her sunglasses while she was there, which made her look like a refugee or a recent face-lift. When Vivian and Laura pointed out that fact of life to her, Marie told them, "After what's happened to me, I'm lucky to be able to go outdoors with nothing more than sunglasses to hide behind. I should have a scarf tied over my head and I should wear a trench coat with the collar turned up."

"I know that look," Vivian said. "That's the look of a Hollywood actress who has a boyfriend in the Mafia who gives her black eyes."

Both Marie and Laura looked at Vivian with mild surprise. Lately she had started saying things that made you hold the tuna salad in your mouth when you were about to swallow it. Not only was her new self-confidence apparently unshakable, but she seemed to have become, almost overnight, more worldly, sharper. She had even gained a smidgen of weight, which gain was becoming to her; she no longer looked as if she had just crawled out from under the ropes of that arena of diet and exercise that was as rigorous, in its way, as bare-knuckle boxing.

"Vivian, you've stopped going to that therapy group altogether, haven't you?" Marie asked her.

Vivian nodded.

"And I never see you doing your yoga exercises anymore," Laura said.

"That's because I've stopped doing them—except for that rapid snorting that I use to clear my nasal passages." Vivian gazed out at the calm blue sea with much the same serenity as was playing over the water, which picked up the sun in its millions of tiny ripples the way the facets of a sapphire or an emerald refract light.

"I don't see how you could dump everything all at once," Marie said as she reached for her vodka and lemonade. "No more therapy. No yoga. Hardly any Valium. Why, all you have now to hold you together is that shop that you haven't even opened yet."

"Yes . . . my shop," Vivian replied. "You girls just don't seem to realize how satisfying goal-striving can be."

"What do you expect?" Marie replied. "How many women do you think there are in the Lions Club?"

"Maybe it isn't goal-striving that matters," Laura speculated, "as much as just having something to do every day. What difference does it make if you get to the top or not?"

"Getting to the top only matters in the movies," Marie said. Then, thinking for a moment, she added, "And in the fashion industry too, I suppose. Like Diana Vreeland. Now there's a woman who's had a life for herself."

"Diana Vreeland's life has been a triumph of rouge over rough edges," Vivian remarked as she rubbed some aloe lotion on her brown arm. "But I like to think of fashion as artistry, not just high gloss."

"Do clothes really matter that much?" Laura wondered.

"Diana Vreeland has organized fashion retrospectives for the Metropolitan Museum," Marie pointed out.

"Certain clothes do matter," Vivian said. "They're . . . the trappings of the times."

"I don't know about you, Vivian," Marie replied, "but when I go to the fashion show I don't expect to get a sense of history in the making out of it."

"You'll be looking at a tapestry of our era," Vivian said.

"I've already seen the tapestry of our era," Laura said. "*Guernica*."

"You don't have to worry about clothes anymore, Laura," Marie said. "You have Jamie. And he doesn't care about how you dress, does he?"

"Yesterday he told me about his mother's black dresses," Laura replied, from a slight distance. "She owned over a hundred of them— all black."

"Let me get one thing straight," Vivian said. "You're both going to the fashion show, aren't you?"

Laura nodded.

"Of course we're going," Marie said. "Philosophical discussions like this have nothing whatever to do with the real world. And the fashion show is the real world. That we have to live in, every day."

"So for you fashion is reality," Vivian coaxed.

"Of course it is," Laura said. "The first decision you make, every day, is what you're going to wear. When I had my job, it was also the most important decision I made, as a rule."

"I'm not surprised to hear that," Vivian said. "Every day we make a fresh debut, before the world, and the impression we make depends largely on what we're wearing."

"Oh, debut-schmoo," Marie said. "I never made a debut myself. Growing up in Boston, I wouldn't have made a debut even if my parents had the money. I would have been part of a cotillion and I would have been presented to Cardinal Cushing. Whose outfit was always better than anyone else's anyway." Marie picked up her glass of lemonade and vodka and took a drink.

"Flash Donahue once told me that the fashion show is really the debut of the fall season and that's why everyone is quivering and trying not to show it," Vivian said.

"Flash Donahue said *that?*" Marie replied. "That was a rare lucid moment."

"Clothes bring out the best in us, don't they?" said Vivian as she screwed the cap back on her bottle of aloe lotion.

Arthur took Chad to Berry's in Soho and saw to it that he had a good, nourishing continental-*chinoise* meal. After eating, the two of them walked over to Steve's of Soho and looked in the window. Arthur looked first at the figure of Chad and then at the expensive clothes in the window. Sizing everything up, he said, "We'll come back here tomorrow."

"Okay with me," Chad said.

They took a cab back up to East Sixty-seventh Street. In the cab Chad casually rubbed Arthur's leg with his hand. Arthur smiled but did not respond otherwise. Professional courtesy, he thought. How enthusiastic they can appear to be.

The house was evenly cool inside, with the silent air conditioning wafting down from the concealed outlets in the ceiling.

"That was really great food," Chad said. "Thanks."

"Glad you enjoyed it," Arthur said. "After-dinner drink?"

"Sure," said Chad.

Arthur got two glasses of Cointreau. Then he sat down next to Chad and got him to talk about himself. Chad did not have too much to say. His childhood evidently had been a series of shifts from dingy city to dingy city, a shuffling via Greyhound.

Looking at the luxurious surroundings, Chad asked Arthur how he had gotten so rich.

"It was mostly timing," Arthur said. "I was heavily into the stock market in the sixties. But I pulled out of it before what they call the go-go years ended. And then I moved into real estate. And used the experience I'd gained playing Monopoly with my mother. That's what realtors are, you know, mean mothers who want to get out of the house."

Chad yawned.

"Ready for bed?" Arthur inquired.

"Sure," Chad replied. Arthur realized that Chad thought "Ready for bed?" was a hint. But it wasn't. The temptation was there . . . but, somehow . . .

"I'll show you your room," Arthur said.

He led Chad to a third floor bedroom with a bath.

"You'll find anything you might want in the medicine chest in the bathroom," Arthur said. "Toothpaste, marijuana, shaving cream, Aramis, cocaine."

"You have cocaine?" Chad said.

"There are two jars of Vicks VapoRub," Arthur replied. "One of them does not contain Vicks. The pot's in the Dr. Scholl's foot powder can. And if you want any other entertainment—here." Arthur pushed a button on the wall by the bed and a panel in the woodwork glided up, revealing a television screen and a complex of hi-fi equipment.

"Where's your room?" Chad asked.

"Beneath you, on the second floor," Arthur replied.

"When do you want me to come down?"

"Come down? All I want is for you to be comfortable . . . here."

"You mean you don't want to . . . ?"

"I just want you to get a good night's sleep," Arthur said.

Chad looked disappointed. Genuinely disappointed. The house turned him on, Arthur thought. Ah, the simple, uncomplicated materialism of American youth. If only I could be that uncomplicated again.

"Can you think of anything else you might need?" Arthur asked.

"No . . . thanks," Chad replied. "This room has . . . everything. You're sure you don't want to . . ."

"Sleep well, then," Arthur said. And then he went down to the master bedroom. He locked the door behind him. Then he lay on the bed. Thinking. One thought made him feel cold, so he pulled the bedspread over himself. The thought was, sex is irrelevant.

The Lawrences' house seemed to be a demonstration of attention to detail despite size; the gardens alone made Laura blink—how big an army did it take to disallow every tiny shoot of clover, every failing blossom? How many windows were there? And how many of those unflappable yellow canvas awnings (had they been ironed?)? So this is what they call the old school, Laura thought. Mrs. Lawrence's 1948 Ford Woodie was parked near the house. As Laura walked by it she noticed that on the rear door some craftsman with an uncannily steady hand had rendered the Lawrences' coat of arms on a shield little more than an inch square. The shield, small as it was, only added to the impression Laura had from the banners waving on the roof that this was a place where people gathered for cocktails before the Crusades. It was Camelot unmussed by touch football games.

Unlike their estate, the Lawrences proved to be slightly rumpled. Mrs. Lawrence did nothing to her hair except comb it, and one lock of gray was askew on her forehead. She was one of those women who, in their day, would have been called handsome. A perfect sitter for a portrait by John Singer Sargent—not a sitter really, Laura thought, she would have stood to be painted, to show off that long neck and that ruler-backed posture, which even now, in her late seventies, she maintained.

Mr. Lawrence looked like one of those yachtsmen who are ever ready to take over the helm. He was wearing a blue blazer and a pair of Topsiders almost whitened with salt water. He had Jamie's gemstone eyes, Laura noticed. And all his hair, which was white and fluffy.

After the introductions at the front door, the four of them went out to the terrace that overlooked the ocean. A black butler with the unimpeachable air of aristocracy that comes from years of domestic service served drinks, and Laura began gradually to relax. The Lawrences seemed to want her to relax; there was nothing stuffy about them. If anything Mrs. Lawrence was sprightly—her eyes sparkled with mischief or memories of it, and Laura pegged her for one of those girls who learn about the age of seven that with their looks and their position they can do as they please. You wouldn't want to be Mrs. Lawrence's roommate at school—when? In the twenties probably, Laura thought. If anybody could upstage you with or without a raccoon coat, it would be a young Mrs. Lawrence. That kind of girl always got what she wanted—but sometimes their daughters didn't do so well. How could you follow an Alice Roosevelt?

Laura thanked God that her mother wasn't a Mrs. Lawrence or an Alice Roosevelt, but decided that she liked Mrs. Lawrence even though she had probably upstaged a lot of girls like herself in the course of her social career. It was unlikely, Laura realized, that Mrs.

Lawrence and Jamie's mother could ever have had much to say to each other.

"How do you like roughing it?" Mrs. Lawrence asked.

Laura wasn't sure whether Mrs. Lawrence meant that in the sense of rustication or cohabitation, so she replied, neutrally, "There certainly isn't any lack of conveniences."

"Yes, I hope I saw to that," Mrs. Lawrence replied. "I don't see why camping should be uncomfortable. I still get backaches from that time I slept on the ground in Mississippi."

Laura looked at Jamie quizzically.

"Gram used to go on freedom rides in the early sixties," Jamie explained.

"Really?" said Laura.

"And she got arrested in Washington during a peace demonstration," Jamie added.

"Some of the nicest people I know have records," Mrs. Lawrence said. "But I don't particularly like to be reminded of mine. Those were difficult times. Sometimes I thought the only person in the social register you could have an intelligent conversation with was Robert Lowell."

"Gram met Dr. Spock on a bus," Jamie said.

"The longshoremen wouldn't take his boat off a freighter because of his ideas about the war," Mr. Lawrence said. "Damned unsporting is what I call that."

Now I know where Jamie gets his ideas about progressive philanthropy, Laura thought. I wonder who the biggest influence on him was, though. I bet it was his mother. That's always the way it is: the crueler the neglect, the more helpless the love.

Dinner was served on the terrace. The conversation got around to the murder at the Perry House. One thing led to another, until Mrs. Lawrence offered her view of capital punishment: that it was the form of birth control most favored by Right to Life groups. Laura had the feeling that Mrs. Lawrence had been stopping conversations all her life with such remarks; it was the sort of thing Isadora Duncan probably had right on the tip of her tongue when the scarf cut her off—only death would dare interrupt.

Picking up the scarf of the conversation after Mrs. Lawrence had given it that abandoned fling, Laura said, "I wonder what they really are planning to do with the Perry House."

214

"Maybe it's going to be the site of a nuclear reactor," Jamie suggested.

"I was not arrested at Seabrook, Jamie," Mrs. Lawrence pointed out. "Only detained for an hour."

"Right, Gram," Jamie said, smiling.

"Anybody with stock in utilities is a damn fool," Mr. Lawrence added.

"Are you all going to that town meeting they want to call?" Laura asked.

"I'm sure Gram is going," Jamie said. "Remember, when she gives the signal, we all go limp."

"He picks on me because I've been like a mother to him," Mrs. Lawrence said. "I suppose it's only natural."

Jamie got up and walked over and kissed his grandmother on the cheek.

"Ooh, he's so sexy," Mrs. Lawrence said, "even if he is my own flesh and blood."

Laura felt herself blushing.

The dignified butler who was standing by with his arms folded suppressed a chuckle. A liberated grand dame, Laura thought. No wonder these two live in their own little world; they're not *social*. They're not inhibited by their money—they're not afraid of losing it all. And they don't seem to be afraid all the other rich people are going to rat on them, the way they did with Tolstoy. They must have loved having a playboy for a son. And a daughter-in-law with a stable of Italian tenors.

After-dinner drinks—three of them—did not mellow Mrs. Lawrence at all. Even when it was 1:00 A.M. and time to go (Laura insisted that it was time to go, as Mrs. Lawrence clearly had no intention of hinting by consulting her watch; perhaps she had never lived her life according to the clock—she seemed to synchronize her movements with the leaps and bounds of her mind). Laura promised to have the Lawrences for dinner at the camp next week, if they didn't mind the inconvenience of not having a table to dine on, or a dining room, for that matter. And that invitation launched Mrs. Lawrence into recollections of an African safari she had been on in 1951 (she shot the animals with her camera and made nasty faces at hunters carrying guns).

When they were finally alone in the van, heading back, Laura said to Jamie, "Your grandmother is something else."

"She is an original, isn't she?" Jamie replied. He seemed to think for a moment. His smile faded.

"Is something the matter?" Laura asked.

"No. . . . I was just thinking about my mother. She and my grandmother were very different. My mother never quite forgave my grandmother for getting into the papers . . . in London . . . the *Daily Mirror*."

"How did your grandmother get her picture in the *Daily Mirror*?"

"She was helping Bertrand Russell get to his feet. They'd been squatting in a public square all day, as part of a demonstration, and Russell had gotten stiff. He was in his nineties at the time."

"Oh, and your mother didn't approve of your grandmother being involved in demonstrations?"

"No. About the only thing that had her full approval was the way the crowd dressed for the races at Ascot—and only a certain part of the crowd even then."

"I wish I had known your mother."

"So do I," said Jamie. Laura saw that his eyes were sparkling—with tears. Something in her heart was released.

"Were your parents really all that bad?" Laura asked. "Maybe they were just selfish. There's an innocence in selfishness; it's basically so childish. Tell me more about them."

"There isn't much to tell. My father was a terrific sailor . . . with a girl in every port, as they say. Palm Beach. Fishers Island. Nantucket. Bermuda. Let's see, what other ports are there? Besides the Port of New York, that is, which was where my father had two girls . . . according to my mother. Oh yeah. I forgot. The Bahamas. He didn't have one specific girl in the Bahamas. That was where he went sport-fishing with a bunch of other guys. Which means you tie up the Bertram at a different island every night and see who's standing outside the bar."

"Your mother must have been bitter about that."

"No, I think she was relieved when the divorce became final. Like she was relieved when she gave me to the nursemaid every day and every night . . . and relieved when I could be sent off to school. You see, my mother was an English aristocrat from a family who'd managed to keep their money in spite of the tax structure. The worst kind of aristocracy that lot is—Christ, I sound like I'm back in school again, talking like my Australian roommate. In their hearts, *that lot* still finds work and working people offensive, and next to work they despise sex—sex that isn't kinky—and children. I think my mother thought that my father was in some way . . . Irish."

"But your family isn't Irish."

"You've met my grandmother. She's a socialist and a poet. She might as well be Irish."

"Did you ever see your mother and father . . . very much?"

"How much is very much? Sometimes, during the school holidays. Sometimes they softened up, like Ebenezer Scrooge's father, and saw me at Christmas. Otherwise I saw the maids and the houses . . . and my grandparents. Who are kind people."

"I could tell." Laura reached over and took Jamie's hand, which he had been rubbing, nervously, on the leg of his jeans. Tonight she knew she would have to try to give him more than sex, she would have to try to give him comfort. His eyes were still shining with tears. Laura thought, if I feel his tears on my breast—falling right over my heart—I don't know . . . It's possible I could . . . really fall in love with him.

With his eyes trained on the road ahead, Jamie said quietly, "My mother . . . and my father. Ashes to ashes, dust to dust. One night my father was playing poker with Adam Clayton Powell, on the island of Bimini . . . in the Bahamas. And the next night he was floating in the Caribbean . . . drowned. They say the propeller on the tender must have gotten snagged, and he went over the side to try and fix it. And he never came up again. And my mother, she was dissatisfied with something the maid had done, the maid she had in her suite at the Gritti Palace . . . she was complaining to me about it, and I went to get a drink because my mouth was dry . . . and when I came back . . . there she was. The whole staff of the Gritti Palace sent flowers. Because they knew her so well . . . better than I ever did."

"Jamie . . ." Laura said.

"What?" he replied. He looked at her almost coldly, as if he were impatient with her. He seemed to think she should know what it was he needed.

CHAPTER TWENTY

Saturday, Arthur took Chad shopping, as he had said he would. They went to Steve's of Soho and Andre Oliver and Tiffany's. Arthur had rented a limousine for the day. It was a Lincoln with dark windows and a television antenna. The limousine was so long the chauffeur all but had to fold it in the middle to get around the street corners of Soho. At first Chad watched television, but after leaving Andre Oliver, he couldn't, because there were so many clothing boxes piled in the back with him and Arthur. Arthur took his young friend to the watch counter at Tiffany's and said to the immaculate clerk, whose appearance and manner suggested that he had just been freshly brushed from head to toe, "This young man needs a watch. He's athletic, so he needs something sturdy. See if you can fit him with a Rolex Submariner. A gold one."

The immaculate clerk glided along the counter for a distance of six feet or so, and then dipped into the showcase. He brought out a watch with a band as heavy as a tractor tread and a blue face that looked watertight as a porthole. He snapped the watch onto Chad's wrist and it fit.

"It's beautiful," Chad said.

"And practical," Arthur added, "which most beautiful things are not."

"Will you be taking it, then?" the clerk asked.

"Yes," Arthur said. "Clean it up a little, though, will you? Some Arab may have left fingerprints on it."

"Certainly, sir," the clerk said. "Will this be cash or charge?"

"Charge," Arthur replied. The clerk went to get his salesbook. And Arthur added, "The last time I paid cash for something in this place, the clerk said to me, 'And you are Dr. . . . ?' I said, 'I'm not in the medical profession,' and he fell all over himself apologizing."

"Every two weeks I see this dentist who always gives me cash," Chad said.

"I'm sure he does," said Arthur. "Interesting, isn't it? That even with the Bill of Rights and all those other constitutional guarantees there are in this country, the only real freedom we have comes from unreported income."

"Hey, you know you're spending a fuckin' fortune on me," Chad said in an effort to restrain Arthur a little.

"So?" Arthur said. "What's money? I'm not in the fashion industry, so I can't try to seduce you by promising you modeling jobs."

"But you don't have to seduce me," Chad protested. "What am I with you for? Last night, if you'd wanted to, you could have . . ."

"I know, I know," Arthur said. "I know I could have. But that's not what I meant. When I said, or implied, perhaps, that I was trying to seduce you. Let's just say I'm trying to get you to like me."

"I like you already. You're unbelievably generous. You don't have to spend money to get people to like you—at least not this much money. Maybe a dinner or two. A couple of shirts. But you're spending thousands and thousands of dollars. . . . I'm not worth all this."

"Are you a hustler or aren't you?" Arthur asked.

"Yes," Chad said quietly. "But . . ."

"No *buts*," Arthur said. "If you're going to hustle, hustle for every last shred of cashmere, every dime you can get. Then maybe you'll eventually be ready to get into show business."

"I tried that already," Chad said. "I can't act . . . or sing . . . or dance."

"Neither can a lot of people in show business," Arthur said. "It's all done with publicity, the way magic acts used to be done with mirrors. But nobody's going to start publicizing you until you prove you're worth the publicity. And you prove that by doing your grasping exercises every single day."

As Chad and Arthur left Tiffany's, Arthur said, "If you don't believe what I'm saying about show business I'll prove my point by taking you to a show tonight . . . and afterward we'll go backstage."

The show Arthur and Chad were seeing had in its cast a number of notable Broadway actors and one actress who was more notable than the rest because of movies and television. Chad recognized her name from a TV series.

"I've heard of this one, this Helene Kimball," he said.

"She's the one you're going to meet afterward," Arthur said.

Chad blinked.

Sure enough, as soon as the final curtain was rung down, Arthur got up and led Chad up the stairs to the stage and then into the wings. When Arthur found the right dressing room he barged right in and was met by a startled girl with two small dogs and a makeup kit.

"Where's that old bag?" Arthur asked.

There came a shriek from the bathroom, and then a flush, and then Helene Kimball came running out in her slip and grabbed Arthur and kissed him on the face and ears a dozen times. The girl with the makeup kit and the squirming dogs fluttered a bit, then put down one of the dogs and modestly began picking up clothes from the floor, where Helene Kimball had dropped them. While she was picking up she smiled subtly at Chad, who was not looking at her.

"Arthur, Arthur, Arthur," Helene raved. "Arthur *darling*." She rocked from side to side, clinging to Arthur's neck, and throwing endearments at him. After almost five minutes of this, Helene saw Chad and screamed, "Look at him! He's gorgeous." She let go of Arthur then and fell upon Chad. She put her hand inside his shirt and felt around and gasped.

"What a chest," she said. "Oh, Arthur, where did you get him, where did you get him, where did you *ever* get him?"

"*Dans la rue*," Arthur replied.

"Oh, that's where I come from," Helene said in what seemed to be delighted surprise.

"His name is Chad," Arthur said.

"Oh, hello, Chad," Helene said, removing her hand from his shirt. "Dear, dear. Fuck. I'm being terribly impolite. Arthur and Chad, this is Melanie, who is hoping to be another Eve Harrington."

"Hi, guys," said Melanie, from the floor.

"Everybody sit down," said Helene, "and we'll talk. Melanie, if we could possibly have some Bourbon?"

"Coming right up," Melanie said, and then she went behind a curtain and came out again with a bottle, glasses, and ice.

Once they had drinks in their hands, Helene and Arthur started reminiscing. They talked to each other in the filthiest language Chad had ever heard, anywhere, out of anybody's mouth.

The pleasant conversation went on for a half hour. Toward the end of it, Arthur said, "Helene, there's something I'd like to settle— for the benefit of my young friend here—before we leave. Tell us, does breaking into show business require any special talent?"

Helene tapped the rim of her cocktail glass with a red rocket of a fingernail.

"Wigs count," she said slowly. "But they're not everything. Hmm. Does it take any talent to get into show business? Maybe not to get in . . . but to stay in . . ." Turning her eyelashes to Chad, she added, "Darling, have you ever made a sex partner believe you were enjoying it when you really weren't?"

"Yes, I think I have," Chad replied, without any evident pride in the accomplishment.

"Then you can act," Helene concluded, "and therefore you can get into show business."

"You mean you guys think acting is just pretending to enjoy sex when you really don't?" Chad asked. He looked crestfallen.

"Of course," Arthur replied. "The wellspring of all art is sexual frustration. Or sexual idealism, as in the case of Michelangelo's *David* or the Brontë sisters' books. Sex has given us the stage just as death has given us religion."

"Only flowers are showy . . . and content," the famous actress added, gazing at a bouquet of roses that had been sent to her by the Trenton chapter of her fan club.

"Angela is happy," Melanie offered modestly. She was referring to the fatter of the two white dogs, which was sprawled on the floor, displaying its round, pink belly.

"I think it's time for us to be going," Arthur said to Chad. "If we don't get going she's going to start talking about the press, and then we'll be here forever."

"Horseshit, Arthur, they reviewed this show pretty decently," Helene protested.

"Well, that was just an excuse anyway," Arthur replied. "I want to go home and fuck." Seizing Arthur and clinging to him like

221

Desdemona in her innocence, Helene said, "Oh, I know the feeling, I know it, I know it so *well*. It's my first thought every time the curtain falls. The hell with fame, I want to fuck!"

"There's a nice doggy," said Melanie as she rubbed Angela's pink stomach.

Promising to see each other soon, and kissing several times, as though they weren't satisfied with the imprint of their lips, the famous actress and Arthur managed finally to part. Melanie and Chad took their leave of each other more simply—with incomplete smiles. Once outside the dressing room, Arthur paused by a flat that looked like a front porch and rested his head, momentarily, against the canvas clapboards.

"Oh dear. Oh dear," he muttered. He blinked three or four times, giving Chad the idea that he couldn't see straight and was trying to focus.

"Are you okay?" Chad asked.

"Me? Oh, of course, I'm all right. I'm always all right. But that poor woman. My poor friend. Poor dear. Oh dear me. Oh shit."

"What about her? What is it?"

"She's slipping."

"Huh?"

"I said *she's slipping*. Declining. Getting old."

"How do you mean?"

"Remember what she said about Alexander H. Cohen?"

"Yeah. Man, the stuff she said about him. What'd he ever do to her?"

"My dear, what she said about Alexander H. Cohen was almost complimentary. She was so gentle. So forgiving."

"What? I never heard anybody bad mouthed like that ever—"

"She was passing out bouquets, believe me. Oh dear. She's mellowing. She's grown charitable, merciful. And mercy is an acknowledgment of mortality. I never thought I'd live to see her reach this stage. I thought maybe she'd play under dimmer lights as she got older, but I never expected mellowness, not from her."

"How long have you known her, anyway?" Chad asked as Arthur headed dejectedly toward the stage door.

"We were living in the same apartment building in the Village," Arthur replied. "One night she started banging on doors because two buttons were off her dress and she had to be onstage wearing it in an hour. She couldn't sew. So I let her in and sewed the buttons on for her. And we've been friends ever since. Androcles and the lion. That was twenty odd years ago . . . our meeting."

As Arthur and Chad climbed into the back of the blacked-out Lincoln, a passerby said to her companion, "Are they anybody famous or are they just rich?"

"Just plain rich," Arthur said, shocking the two onlookers. "You wouldn't want to be famous, girls, take it from me—when you get old it only makes the distances between you and other people seem greater."

When they arrivd back on East Sixty-seventh Street, Arthur made two gin and tonic nightcaps and took Chad out to the garden. The garden, which was enclosed by a brick wall, was so removed from the city that the horns and sirens of the streets beyond sounded as though they were part of the sound track of a television movie that had been turned way down. The garden was Japanese, with dwarf conifers and a softly lit cherry tree. Smooth stones were artfully interspersed with mossy mounds and still pools. The garden might have been a fertile valley belonging to a landed China doll. Though it was past midnight, the garden was warm; it was a true summer night in New York—humidity and ash were in the air.

Chad took off his shirt.

"It's hot," he said.

"Fearful symmetry," Arthur muttered into his glass.

"What'd you say?"

"Not a single pimple mars thy fearful symmetry . . . I see," Arthur said.

Chad tossed Arthur his shirt playfully. It caught on a cherry branch.

"Once my lover and I had a party out here," Arthur said. "To benefit the City Ballet. We put up several clotheslines and hung tutus and leotards on them. Before I die I'd like to hire some avant-garde artist to string a clothesline all along the length of Fifth Avenue. Art should be brought to the people, don't you think?"

"I dunno," Chad replied. "They'd probably rather have the sex than the art."

"Oh, you remembered what I said about sex and art, huh?"

"I listen to what you say. You're interesting."

"I am? I wouldn't know. I don't think I'm very different from a

223

lot of people, actually. I talk too much, I'm sure. So do most of my friends—who are mostly women. I think we try to talk our way out of reality, the way you try to talk your way out of a traffic ticket—when you get stopped. But things are getting more and more like they are in Boston, where they don't just give out parking tickets, they put these iron 'boots' on the wheels of your car, so you can't move it . . . you're hobbled . . . and that's when all the talk starts to seem . . . pointless."

"I've been to Boston," Chad said. "Up there even the gays think of sex as something you do in the freezing compartment of the refrigerator."

"That's their Puritan heritage," Arthur explained, "combined with their Irish Catholic heritage. Nobody up there has known what to do with their hands since the textile mills moved south."

"If you don't mind my saying so," Chad said, "you don't seem to know what you want to do . . . with me."

"Oh, I thought we've been having a rather busy weekend. All sorts of activities."

"Except when it's time to go to bed."

"Yes . . . you're right about that. I admit it. Listen, Chad, I'm not an easy person to understand. My lover has always said—and I'm sure he's right—that I'm so fucked up I don't know what I want. Neurosis is so much more fun when you make a guessing game of it, don't you think?"

Chad was watching a column of ants climbing up the trunk of the cherry tree. He did not want to look straight at Arthur. He wasn't even sure if he could say what he was thinking.

"I like you," he said after a moment. "How do you feel about me?"

"Do you want an honest answer?"

"If you wouldn't mind."

"All right," Arthur replied. "I hesitate to give you an honest answer, since honesty is basically antisocial and we're having such a nice time together—but, all right. If you must know, I think you have the beauty of an angel with Swedish blood, and your beauty is only enhanced by your innocence . . . which is . . . almost *liquid*, but I'm afraid that if you keep on hustling you'll probably either contract hepatitis-B or wind up dead in a river somewhere. Which is a tragedy I am unable to prevent, unfortunately."

Chad stood up. He walked over to Arthur. Standing in front of him, he looked as though he were pleading with his eyes, offering up his physical attractiveness in the hope of some kind of salvation.

Finally he said, "Don't you want me?"

"No, I think what I want is Herbert, my lover. All my life I've wanted everything, and everybody—as reparations, I suppose, for my unhappy childhood—but now I think I would prefer to have peace and quiet, in the few years that are left to me—with Herbert, who is sympathetic and understanding and will scatter my ashes out at the Pines, as I've requested, to help prevent further erosion of the dunes."

Chad sat down again. He seemed taller in his slouch, as if his body were being lengthened by depression, his arms and his legs mere shadows.

"I would have liked to live with you," he said. "I envy this guy Herbert. I'd like to be him. I'd like to be your lover."

"Don't feel you have to flatter me," Arthur said.

"I'm not," Chad replied. "It'd be easy for me to love you."

A pang of guilt went through Arthur. He had remembered something about hustlers that he had forgotten: with every lease you took out on their bodies came a human heart with all its unpredictable options.

"If I were alone in life, Chad, it would be different," Arthur said. "But the fact is I'm not."

"You're one of the lucky ones," Chad said. "I'm not lucky. I never have been. I'm the cat out in the rain."

"The cat?"

"Yeah. The cat. You see, once when I was a kid I heard this alley cat meowing outside our house. It was meowing real loud. It was raining, so I let it in. I dried it off with a paper towel and gave it a dish of milk. I saw it had a patch of mange on its side. It drank up all the milk and then it hopped up on the bed beside me and purred. It sounded like a truck. Loudest purring I ever heard from a cat. It thought it had found a home. That was why it was purring so loud. But I had to put it outside again before my mother got home. When she got in, it was by the door meowing louder than ever. She chased it away with a broom. I didn't know it then, but I know now. Letting that cat in when I knew I couldn't keep it was the meanest thing I ever did."

225

Arthur's lips had become a little dry. He moistened them with his tongue.

"What is the implication of that parable?" he asked. "That I am a nasty person?"

"No. You're unbelievably generous. But you're one of those people who are the most selfish when they're giving stuff away."

"Spoken like a true hustler. The arrogance comes in at the end."

"You know, if I wanted to, I could smash your face in," Chad said.

He stood again. He made fists of his hands. Arthur swallowed. Chad was in front of him in three strides. He grabbed Arthur's lapels and pulled him up. Then he put his arms around him and hugged him. Hugged him tightly, like a frightened child. Arthur felt the tremor in his body and his fear gave way to remorse.

"I didn't mean to hurt you," Arthur said faintly. "I've never been out to hurt anyone. . . . I didn't realize you could . . ."

Chad let go.

"I'm sorry," he said. "I wanted to feel protected . . . for a minute."

"It's all right," Arthur said.

"You know guys who hire hustlers, they sometimes get hepatitis too," Chad said. "And sometimes they wind up dead. It's a two-way street, just like the rest of life is."

"If you're trying to caution me you needn't worry," Arthur replied. "You, Chad, are the last. . . . I'm not paying anymore, I'm not paying these prices . . . or exacting them, whatever I've been doing."

"Then you want me to go?" Chad asked.

"No," said Arthur decisively. "Stick around until Monday. I want to have one additional transaction with you."

"I don't understand," Chad said.

"Look," Arthur said. "If there's one thing I've always been, it's a conventional queen. And since I'm that, I've always liked gold. Two kinds of people hoarded gold before it got ridiculously expensive: queens and French peasants. Neither of those groups is ever going to be much liked by the rest of the world, but what does that matter when you have your table wine and your security?"

"I don't see what this has to do with me," Chad said.

"It has everything to do with you. I'm going to give you some gold. Or the profits I made from gold. You see, a few years ago I

226

bought a lot of Winnebago stock as a joke. I thought, those campers are such *appliances* that I just know middle America is going to buy thousands of them and use them to flatten chipmunks in Yellowstone Park. Well, they did. And I made two million dollars. But then I decided to sell and plow the profits into gold. That's what any responsible French peasant would do if he won a Winnebago on 'The Price Is Right,' he'd sell it and buy gold. As soon as I did that, the energy crunch came and Winnebago went down and gold went up, up, up. The two million turned into . . . well, let's just say enough to allow me to indulge a whim like this. How would you like to move to Los Angeles?"

"Los Angeles?"

"Of course. You might like to have a beach house in Malibu. And a Porsche to pick up your groceries. The more I think about it, the more I like the idea. Somebody with your youth and beauty arriving in L.A. *with* money instead of going there to hustle for it. What an intriguing proposition. You'll short-circuit the whole system; the lights will go dim in Beverly Hills."

"I don't understand," Chad said. "Why? Why do you want to do all this for me, for somebody . . . you haven't even slept with?"

"You're the last in a long line," Arthur replied. "You've lucked out. I'm going to see to it that you'll never have to sell your body, and you're not going to wind up floating in a river. Which is one definition of successful parenthood. You're the one beautiful child I've managed to keep my hands off—which is another definition of successful parenthood. So you see the comfort I'll derive from you in my old age. If you can ever find the time to call your poor auntie and tell her how you're doing, that is."

"I don't believe this," Chad said.

"Why do people always believe implicity in bad luck and doubt they they can ever have any good luck? What a positively French attitude. You'll believe all this on Monday, when we go down to United States Trust and make the arrangements. Meanwhile, can you suggest a way for me to get my lover back? I think he may have gone straight."

Chad shook his head. He was trying to clear it of astonishment. He said to Arthur without thinking, "Tell him you love him."

"Thanks a lot," said Arthur. "I make things easy for you—and you make them difficult for me."

CHAPTER TWENTY ONE

Marjorie told George that she was going to a meeting to map strategy for the showdown over the Perry House. She did not tell him that there would be only one other person at the meeting, nor did she mention that she would be having dinner with that person. It didn't seem to make any difference what she reported or withheld, however; George was acting more and more like a sick person whose sole concern was concealing from himself and the world the symptoms. Whatever Marjorie said was either ignored by her husband or barely acknowledged with a grunt.

The day of her meeting with Cartey, Marjorie had supper on the table at five-thirty, and she had the dishes in the sink by six. Nobody—not one of the kids and certainly not George—noticed that Marjorie had hardly touched anything on her plate. For once she was happy to have a family that ate like cars filling up in a gas station: pulling up, idly chewing, and then pulling out again, into the traffic outside the house that occupied them. With the kids headed for the beach parking lot where they'd sit on the hoods of cars and stare at other kids all evening, and with George sealed up in his workshop, Marjorie had plenty of leisure to prepare herself for her eight o'clock appointment with Cartey.

And prepare herself she did. To a fare thee well, as her mother would have said. First Marjorie took a long bath, filling the bathroom with steam and relaxing her facial muscles in it, so that the few lines she had, which were mostly from tension, would uncross.

Crosspatch, draw the latch,
Sit by the fire and spin.

That old nursery rhyme came back to Marjorie as she was soothing herself in the tub. That was how you got old all right: shutting yourself up in the house and sewing while the world went on outside. You slowly turned into a crosspatch with your hair, futilely colored, sitting on top of your lined face like grandma's dustcap. No, thank you, Marjorie told herself as she sat soaking. I'm going to be political—and I'm going to keep myself up, too.

Once she was out of the tub and dried off, Marjorie sat down at her vanity table, which had a ruffled pink skirt, like the outfits girls wore to dances in the fifties, and carefully put on her makeup. She was pleased, when she had finished, with what she saw in the mirror. Marjorie was aware that she looked younger than her age; when everything came together just right, as it had now, she could pass for early thirties. Putting on one of her best dresses, which she had bought on sale at Lord & Taylor in Boston the summer before, Marjorie slowly turned around in front of the full-length mirror on the bedroom door. I'm ready for anything, she thought.

Dan Cartey, who had checked into his room at the Munsonville Inn at six-thirty, was all set to deal with this Hanson dame. He'd feed her dinner and as much of a line as was needed to entangle her. Women were easy to outmaneuver, Dan thought; you simply let them talk and talk, dribble along, and then at the right moment you grabbed the ball away from them and dunked it. Plop. Not only would they be surprised by the display of skill, they'd probably also be attracted to you. Unless, of course, they were beyond being attracted to men, but usually that was true only of women executives who knew too much (the ones who had started out as secretaries). This Marjorie Hanson obviously wasn't playing in that league. Cable Harbor was bush league, nothing but bushes with mosquitoes in them. The one danger was some dame starting the bushes burning with her nervous cigarettes and her poking around in the undergrowth. That could start a blaze that would cost money to control.

At ten to eight Dan went down to the lobby and sat in one of the leather armchairs to wait for his dinner guest. The inn amused Dan. With its murky mahogany paneling and English hunting prints, it looked like the old-maid aunt of a Red Coach Grill. What would this Marjorie Hanson look like? Probably like Louise Day Hicks. Another Louise Day Hicks—without the lace-curtain Irish cunning or the cement hairdo. This Marjorie Hanson was most likely a bitch with limited instincts; she wouldn't be aware that you can only run with it just so far before you're at the end of your clothesline.

To his surprise, the Hanson dame kept Dan waiting for twenty minutes. He thought she'd be right on the dot, if not early, but she didn't arrive at the inn until well after eight. Marjorie and Dan recognized each other immediately, even though neither of them was ready for this first impression: Marjorie had expected a warthog with a clean shave, a gold tie bar, and a thick gold watch; Dan had expected a woman contoured along the lines of a telephone receiver. What greeted Marjorie, in the place of the lumpish conniver she had expected, was a man who looked as briskly whisked off as one of the Kennedys. He was really quite dashing—in a gray businesslike way. Dan, for his part, was surprised that the person who had come in place of Louise Day Hicks was actually attractive: there was no mistaking that involuntary stir of the swizzle stick, the sudden scattering of bubbles in the bloodstream. True, this Hanson dame had a sort of country and western hairdo—with the pile on top and the ringlets cascading down—but she also had a bareback rider's body, and maybe as much passion in her as there is in a country and western song. (Dan had always liked country and western songs; they always seemed to him to be sung by the kind of simple, decent girl his mother had hoped he would marry.)

As Dan took Marjorie's hand, he noticed her perfume, and he liked it. What was it? Half Arpège, half the freshly sawed chip on her shoulder? Whatever it was, it caused in Dan another momentary swirl.

"So you're Mrs. Hanson," Dan began. "It was nice of you to agree to see me." He held on to Marjorie's hand two beats too long. For her that was time enough to read the first message of this meeting: the long bath had done the trick.

"It's nice of you to meet with me," Marjorie said. "There's not many big, important businessmen who will take time out to listen to the concerns of a bunch of people in a small town. Especially when their spokesperson is an ordinary housewife."

"An extraordinary housewife, I'd say," Dan replied.

230

"Thanks," Marjorie said. "Really I'm not the least bit extraordinary. I'm outspoken, I suppose, but I've only been that way since I started helping my husband out with his business. If you don't talk up when you're involved in a business, you finish last, right?"

"Let's just say if you're running a corner grocery, it's never going to become a supermarket chain," Dan replied. "Shall we go into the dining room?"

The dining room of the Munsonville Inn suggested the dining room of a steamship, with the attendant creaking and soft moaning of wind from beyond the black windows. Marjorie and Dan were shown to a table with a white cloth that looked as if it had been laundered a hundred times and darned once or twice. The table was set with silverware for more courses than anyone ate anymore, and there was a single rose in a nickel-plated vase in the center. The dining room made Marjorie think of trains no longer running; the inn had become a destination with a dust cover over it. Munsonville was what Cable Harbor would have been had it not been directly on the ocean. The lesson in the economics of geography had not been lost on Marjorie: if you wanted to survive you had to be right on the edge, out on the tip. Even ten miles into the great middle of things was nowhere.

After Marjorie and Dan were seated, a busboy whose face was in a panic of acne poured water into their goblets. Then a waitress in a pink uniform made from the kind of cotton that is closest to paper came over and asked Marjorie and Dan if they would like drinks. Marjorie thought first of having a whiskey sour, but changed her mind and ordered a vodka martini, straight up, with a lemon twist, instead.

The waitress had to ask what "straight up" meant.

"I'm sorry," she said. "I'm new. I just started today." Marjorie explained that "straight up" meant without ice. Dan asked if there was Absolut vodka in the bar. The waitress had to check. Returning, she said, "I'm really sorry. All he has is Smirnoff. But that's a very good brand, isn't it?"

"It's good enough," Dan replied. "I'll have a vodka martini myself, straight up, with an olive."

"Yes, sir," said the waitress. She didn't seem to be abbreviating any of the words she was writing down on her pad. Biting her lip, she hurried back to the bar.

"Cute girl," Dan said.

"Isn't she sweet, though?" Marjorie replied. "I think I know her. I think she's married to one of the policemen in town. In Cable Harbor. Not Munsonville. But I could be wrong."

Marjorie was right. Lester's wife, Donna, had grabbed the job at the Munsonville Inn as soon as she heard about it. She had told her husband that it wouldn't be nearly as messy as working in the lobster pound, and the hours would be short because the dining room at the inn catered to people who went to bed early. Lester had said okay partly because at the time Donna came up with the job he was caught up in the whirlwind Evelyn was trying to generate over George Hanson and the murder at the Perry House. By the time the whirlwind had sputtered out (exactly one day later) Donna had the job. And Lester had in fact come close to losing his own job, if he could believe what the desk sergeant said about interfering with the mail on the advice of some amateur detective who ought to stick to stacking up boxes of detergent. All Donna knew of this ruckus was that it somehow involved Evelyn and the Hanson family. So when she saw Marjorie Hanson sitting in the dining room of the Munsonville Inn with a strange man, something told her to let Evelyn know about it. Maybe in the long run the information might help Lester.

While the bartender was mixing the martinis, Donna slipped into the lounge and called Evelyn. She felt a little foolish doing it, but there had been such a fuss, and Lester had been so upset. And now here was Mrs. Hanson eating at the inn with a strange man. Donna felt that Evelyn just had to know about it; no matter how old you got, life stayed the same in some ways—there always seemed to be a teacher in the front of the room who would know what to do when you told on someone. Not that Donna had ever been a tattletale, but in grammar school, as now, when you knew about something that was probably nasty, you did tell. That was what separated the girls from the boys, or part of it anyway.

Evelyn answered the telephone and Donna whispered her information to her as quickly as she could. She half thought that the phone was going to fizzle and smoke before she could get it all out, the way the cassette decks in the pay phones always used to do on "Mission Impossible." And the drinks were ready, too. But Evelyn had heard enough when Donna said, "Mrs. Hanson and a man who looks like he's real big in something." She said to Donna, "Thanks, honey, you've been a real big help. More than you know." When she hung up, she had to pause for a moment to retrieve her breath, such was her excitement.

Panting, she yelled out, "Sanford! Sanford, get the camera! Get the car out of the garage. Somethin' is up. Somethin's goin' on!"

"What?" her husband said. He was in the kitchen. Still in mourning for the Hummels, he was sitting at the table trying to mend some of the fractures with Elmer's Glue. In front of him were an "Angel Serenade with Lamb" (the lamb had been sheared off) and an "Out of Danger" that had been decapitated. In his hand Sanford held a little girl with a fissure in her creamy knee; when Evelyn yelled to him he had been searching in the porcelain jigsaw puzzle for the missing kneecap. Her voice exasperated him so that he swept the bits and pieces away and took a napkin out of the holder to wipe the sweat off his forehead.

"What is it now?" Sanford said as his wife appeared in the doorway. "What are you all heated up about now?" A lump came into his throat and he gently set the little girl with the broken leg on the table.

"What am I going to do with this one, with her knee all shattered?" he whimpered. "Make her a leg brace out of paper clips? What's so important, with a tragedy like this that's happened to us, that you got to be yellin' from upstairs?"

"The one that's responsible for this is eatin' her supper right this very minute, at the Munsonville Inn, with a man Donna's never seen before. An' she says that he looks like a pretty big cheese. We are gonna go out there and have ourselves a look-see."

"Haven't you had enough of the Hanson family?" Sanford said. "Look at all this . . . mess. All the glue in the world isn't going to replace the equity we had in this collection. Could have paid for a place in Florida. Two weeks ago I could have gone down there and bought a place right on top of Walt Disney World, if I'd wanted to, and had money left over. Now what's this collection worth? Nothin'. None of these figurines will ever have any market value ever again."

"If you don't get out the camera and the car, I'll do it myself," Evelyn said. "This may be our big chance—to get revenge."

"I don't want revenge, I want security in my old age," Sanford replied.

Evelyn grabbed the car keys off the pegboard that was next to the sink.

"Where's the camera?" she demanded to know.

When Evelyn moved as fast as she was moving now, Sanford feared for her heart. A double tragedy was more than he could bear, so, capitulating, he got up from the kitchen table.

"All right," he said. "I'll go along with you . . . this time." In an emotional falsetto, he added, "What have I got to lose anyway?" Bent over like a weary old man, with the camera slung over his shoulder, Sanford followed Evelyn out to the garage.

"I hope this isn't just another wild-goose chase," he said. "Like gettin' ahold of that dirty movie that didn't prove a damn thing."

When she got into the car Evelyn had to concentrate on quieting her heart, which was making her ears tingle. This time she had to get the best of Marjorie Hanson. She knew instinctively that she was in a war of personality in which the Hummels had been casualties. Now she had to strike back decisively, or be for the rest of her life fat and humbled.

"Despite whatever you may think you uncovered in the town clerk's office," Dan was saying, "I'm not a corporate villain, and my company doesn't want to destroy Cable Harbor."

Marjorie set straight her cup of vichyssoise, which had arrived cockeyed in its bed of cracked ice. Then she said to Dan, "I might be willing to believe that, and maybe you'll be willing to believe that I'm not just another small-town busybody, but it seems to me that both of those maybes depend upon whether or not we're honest with each other, right from the beginning. First of all, I was right about that easement, wasn't I?"

"Frankly, yes," Dan replied. "It's common knowledge that the phone and power companies have strung their lines across empty land for years without asking anybody's permission. And after enough time has passed they don't have to ask permission. 'Notorious abuse' is the legal phrase for it; you see if you trespass long enough without being challenged you can establish a right of way, *de facto*."

"I'm sure the phone and power companies have done very well being notorious," Marjorie said, "but do you want your company to have a reputation like that?"

234

"I admit our image is important to us," Dan said, stroking his necktie.

"Step on it, will you?" Evelyn urged.

"I'm doin' sixty now," her husband replied. "You want me to run us off the road?"

"You sure the film in this camera is still good?" Evelyn was clutching the Minolta like a prayer book, and on her face was a look of missionary pallor. She knew where the savage was now—parading naked on the beach—and now she was going to corner her in her brazen toplessness: having a nice little dinner date with a married man.

"Mr. Cartey," Marjorie was saying, "I'm sure you realize that with the death of that girl, the Perry House can't just sit there anymore. It's become a hazard to the safety of our children."

"I agree that we're going to have to post a guard on the property," Dan said.

"But what are you going to *do* with it?" Marjorie persisted. Dan smiled at her in such an obvious attempt to charm her that Marjorie felt sugar pouring into the serious cup of black coffee she had intended this dinner to end with; she decided not to have another sip of the expensive white wine Dan had ordered until the conversation moved off dead center. There had been enough wavering and wobbling. The talk was like the table, with one leg shorter than the others and the defect compensated for with a matchbook underpinning. It was time, Marjorie decided, to turn the whole business upside down and find out where the screws were missing.

"Mr. Cartey, you don't mean to sit there with that grin on your face and try to get me to believe that the Perry House was put up only to be a landmark. I know that you're playing some kind of waiting game, and everybody else in town knows it too. There's been a death out there now—a *death*—and the townspeople are going to demand you tell them exactly what you're holding out for. And if they aren't given satisfaction on that score, I for one can show them that it's doubtful that building has any legal right to be stuck where it is at all."

"Okay, you've got your cards on the table," Dan said. "You want me to cut them?"

235

"I didn't come here for a polite bridge party, Mr. Cartey," Marjorie replied angrily. "Don't underestimate me. There's a new movement in this country, and a lot of you businessmen don't see it coming."

"What movement is that?"

"Housewives waking up."

A familiar disorientation began to affect Dan. He was suddenly aware of his shirt collar clamped to his throat, and the awareness made him uncomfortably conscious of the process of swallowing. Dan was aware of Marjorie's sexual presence in the same discomfited way; the automatic ease of interaction was no longer there. What had gotten into women? Dan wondered. They were no longer the way they had been when Dan was coming of age, in the early fifties. It seemed to him that many of the privileges of being male had been taken away. Women seemed to want to take over, sexually, the role of an authoritarian schoolteacher, and send men back to being little boys again.

"If you're waiting for condominiums to come of age up here, you're wasting your time," Marjorie went on. "The wealthy people want flower gardens and people like me want vegetable gardens. Nobody wants to live attached to the next guy, with no land around them."

"All right," said Dan as he crossed his silver on his plate. "Okay. There's no sense in beating around the bush any longer. You, Mrs. Hanson, have certain information about the Perry House that you can use at the town meeting, for whatever advantage you think you'll gain, if that's your choice. And I have certain information which I'm going to confide in you now . . . and then I'm going to leave it up to you whether or not you'll want to exercise the option that you've so cleverly developed for yourself."

"What are you going to do, run into that dining room with that camera like a private detective?" Sanford said as he pulled up in front of the inn.

"I got it all figured out," puffed Evelyn as she lumbered out of the car, holding on to the roof to hoist herself. "It's Donna's first day on the job. She'll get the busboy to take a picture of her in her new uniform—but we'll get her to stand so's that the picture takes

236

in that Marjorie Hanson and whoever it is she's with. We won't even have to be sneaky about it."

"I wouldn't call that exactly subtle," Sanford said. "I highly doubt that the CIA operates that way."

"The hell they don't," Evelyn said. "My cousin in Washington whose husband's with the FBI says that it's all like in that movie *The French Connection*. The crooks get away. This time, though, it's gonna be a different story. We'll have the evidence right on Kodak color film."

Trooping into the inn's lobby, with Sanford lagging behind, in his uncertainty, Evelyn announced to the clerk behind the desk that she had come to see her favorite cousin-in-law on her first day at work—and would he mind if they took a couple of pictures of her in her new uniform for Grammy, who has nothing to do all day but sit and clap her hands and sing "Roll Out the Barrel"?

The clerk, who had an aging grandparent himself, readily went along with the idea. He went into the dining room to fetch Donna, who appeared after a minute or two with a water pitcher in her hand and a sheepish look on her face.

Directing Donna not to say anything by staring at her, Evelyn said in a stage whisper, "We wouldn't want to intrude in the dining room or anything, but maybe the busboy could snap a couple of pictures of you out there . . . *standing by one of your tables.*"

"Oh, sure, sure," Donna said.

"We just wanna get a couple of pictures for Grammy."

Smiling benevolently, the clerk returned to the desk.

"You know where to stand," Evelyn whispered fiercely. "Try to look natural, and *stand a little to one side.*"

"I know what to do . . . I think," Donna replied. She handed her water pitcher to Sanford and took the camera from Evelyn. Then she hurried back into the dining room."

"I got to see who she's with," Evelyn said.

"If she sees you, we're finished," Sanford warned.

"She won't," Evelyn said. Creeping across the carpet, she approached the entrance to the dining room with the tentativeness of a ten-gallon hat held up to test for Indian arrows. She peeked. And pulled back again all in one heartbeat. She put her hand on her chest. To Sanford, Evelyn appeared to be bulging all over, as if she had just swallowed something that sank immediately to the tips of her toes. He was afraid that his wife was having a heart attack. But then she seemed to recover herself, and she smiled at the desk clerk, who said, "They taken it yet?"

"It'll all be over in two shakes," Evelyn replied.

The busboy was focusing the camera on Donna, who was posing in front of Marjorie and Dan with the relish tray. Dan was chuckling.

"This must be a big deal for her," he said. "Her first day."

Pressing the shutter release, the busboy captured Donna and the relish tray, all of Marjorie, and enough of Dan's profile to identify him and see that he had been caught in a moment of amusement. The second shot did more or less the same thing—only in that composition it was clear that Marjorie was not amused, and Donna's smile was uneven because of her apprehension.

"It's him," Evelyn whispered to her husband. "I recognize him from when they used to come into the store before they got divorced."

"Who?"

"*Cartey*, that's who. The one that's behind the Perry House."

"Good Lord."

"Pictures going to come out all right?" the desk clerk inquired.

"Oh, I'm sure they're going to come out perfect," Evelyn said. "We'll be able to show them to Grammy—and everybody else—next week. Why, I'll probably even bring them along to the town meeting, I'll be so proud of them!"

Donna came back into the lobby. She handed the Minolta to Sanford.

"I was so nervous," she said.

"You did fine, honey," Evelyn assured her. "I'm sure them pictures are going to be just perfect, yes, everything's going to come out real sharp and clear. This is one time people are going to see things in black and white from a couple of color snapshots, yessireebob!"

Thanking the desk clerk again, Evelyn headed for the door. Sanford, who didn't seem to know what to do with his hands and finally straitjacketed them in his pants pockets, followed. The desk clerk felt sorry for Evelyn, with her feet slopping out of her shoes. He hoped the pictures would brighten up her life a little, and her

238

poor Grammy's life—singing "Roll Out the Barrel" the way she did, in her old age. The desk clerk was a sympathetic and helpful person; he had been an Eagle Scout in his youth, and now he was a scoutmaster. He was one of the people whose resentment Evelyn was counting on, one of the people who do not move very far in life, and who are fooled every time. Even when they're just trying to be helpful.

In the dining room Dan was saying to Marjorie, "So there you have it. If we don't unload the Perry House fairly soon, we're going to hold on to it and try to turn it into a casino."

Marjorie looked as though a cupful of quarters were spilling onto her lap.

"You can't be serious," she said.

"I'm very serious. But I'm not talking about Las Vegas or Atlantic City here. I'm talking about old-fashioned elegance. One casino in town only. And that one as exclusive and high-tone as it can be made. What we want to establish in Cable Harbor is a casino like the one they had in Saratoga a hundred years ago. No neon. Nobody in white shoes and white belts coming to be entertained by Wayne Newton. The Perry House would be all hand-carved moldings and blue chips. . . ."

"You'll never get it through the state legislature," Marjorie said. "Much less the town meeting."

"Really? Don't forget that New Hampshire was the first state to introduce a lottery—and New Hampshire's more conservative than Maine; it's an Orange County where they raise crab apples. Look, Mrs. Hanson, in the most conservative state in the union the public would approve of teenage prostitution if they thought it would lower their taxes."

"But if the Perry House becomes a gambling place, it's bound to change the town—drastically. People would be moving in all over the place. . . ."

"You're right about that, Mrs. Hanson. Think what all those people moving in would do to property values. How much land do you have, if you don't mind telling me?"

"About three acres."

"Let's see, at about a hundred thousand for each quarter of an acre, that would be . . ."

"One million two hundred thousand . . . dollars."

"With that much money, you wouldn't have to worry about canning your own vegetables anymore, would you, Mrs. Hanson?"

"The summer crowd will never allow it. They'll say a casino would cheapen the place."

"Not necessarily. Most of them know Saratoga. A couple of them even have houses there. The idea of this becoming Saratoga-by-the-Sea will probably suit them just fine. All their friends will fly over from Deauville."

"They'll think the Mafia is behind it."

"No they won't. They're insiders, all of them. They know that the Mafia doesn't own half the stuff people think it owns. Half the stuff the Mafia is supposed to control actually belongs to General Mills. Like Lacoste shirts."

"You mean General Mills makes them? The shirts with the alligators on them? I never knew. . . ."

Dan shrugged, as if he had proven the point. Then he added, "You see, Mrs. Hanson, if there's a big row at the town meeting, if you make a big issue of . . . the information you've turned up . . . my company might be forced to show its hand. And then it'll be too late for you . . . to pick up any odd parcels of land . . . that you think might be likely to appreciate in value." Dan pulled a cigar out of his pocket.

"Mind if I smoke?" he asked.

"No," Marjorie replied. "No, go ahead."

The busboy came over to clear the dishes. Donna appeared and recited the dessert menu like a child who has memorized all the state capitals. She lost her place and had to repeat "with chocolate sauce" twice until she remembered the next item.

All Marjorie wanted was tea. Dan asked for Irish coffee.

Finally Marjorie said to him, "You know what I was going to suggest to you? I was going to suggest that you make a community center out of the Perry House, so our kids would have a place to go and your company would have a write-off. But if the Perry House does become a casino our kids could go anywhere they please—in their own cars—couldn't they?"

Dan blew a smoke ring.

"Very likely they could," he said. "Anybody who picked up a few vacant lots in southern California twenty years ago—you see the

240

kids of anybody who was that smart tooling along Rodeo Drive, in Porsches, Mercedes, their mothers' Cadillacs. . . . "

"Oh shit," said Marjorie. "I feel like I've got something boiling on the stove and the heat is out of my hands. I can't control it . . . but I can keep the lid on for a while yet . . . can't I?"

"That, as I say, is entirely up to you, Mrs. Hanson."

"Hopkins . . . Hopkins, does he know what's in the works?"

"Hopkins is nothing more than a watchdog. And he doesn't have the best sense of smell in the world, either."

"Then he won't pose any problem," Marjorie concluded. "The only one, other than myself, who knows anything, is the town clerk, Miss Pearson. . . . I suppose I could think of some way to keep her quiet about the easement until . . ."

"Until you've completed any real estate transactions you might want to make. Hopkins has so much land that's going begging. . . ."

"I'm going to have to think about this," Marjorie said. "I can't tell you right now what I'm going to say at the town meeting . . . or what I won't say. I need to think things over."

"I would think about it, if I were you," Dan said. "I'd think long and hard. I agree with you that a lot of women—housewives like yourself—have been waking up. But a lot of them are sleepwalkers. They've gotten out of the house, but they're not exactly wide awake."

"Yes," Marjorie said. "Yes, I know who you mean. The women who go out and work against the ERA . . . the small-town cheerleaders. Who can't get past the idea that their job is to jump up and down, on the sidelines . . . in order to keep the men running around out there. I was a cheerleader myself, so I know. But I quit cheerleading when my best girl friend had a miscarriage. From jumping up and down. She was three and a half months pregnant and nobody knew. So she didn't stop cheerleading . . . until it was too late." Picking up her wineglass, Marjorie finished what was in it in three gulps.

"I don't know," she said. "I just don't know. There's this noontime talk show up here, on the radio, that I call up a lot. To talk."

Remembering Marie's debut on that radio show, Dan began to drum his fingertips on the tablecloth.

Donna brought the tea and Irish coffee and Marjorie stopped talking until she was again out of earshot.

"I thought I was getting a real feel for politics," Marjorie said. "But I see now that there's more to it than persuading people that you have the right ideas. When you get into politics even when you're a beginner at it, like I am, you start to become an insider, you start to see how things actually work . . . operate, whatever it is that goes on."

"No sense being political if you're not going to get the inside track on things," Dan said. "You started with a daytime talk show and wound up running a town meeting. Lyndon Johnson started in the Senate and Lady Bird wound up with a television station. Same principle."

"I suppose so," Marjorie said. "And here I thought I'd be influencing things. You can't really, can you? It's like the time—I remember it so well—like the time my father said to my mother, 'If God is so good and so all-powerful, how come He allows all these terrible things to happen?' My father was always wondering about things like that—after he retired. So he asked my mother that question, for the umpteenth time, and she was only half listening to him, because she was busy cooking his dinner, so she said to him, 'Look, Joe, you can't tell them how to run the government.' She got the question about God mixed up with the question about the Massachusetts General Court and how they could be so corrupt, taking the money working people had struggled to earn. But it doesn't make any difference, does it? The mysterious ways in which God acts and political corruption, they're both the same thing; and we're powerless to do anything to change any of it."

"There is a way," Dan said.

"What way?"

"Get into real estate," he said simply.

"How are you, Mrs. Hanson?" the voice asked. "The last time I saw you was in the kitchen the night they had the fire at Mr. Conrad's house."

"Mrs. Cartey?" Marjorie said in wonderment. She was standing before her kitchen sink, into which she had been pouring Drano when the telephone rang. The sink was filled with gray water, which was forming fat bubbles from the digestive process now going on in the pipes below. This unexpected telephone call immediately took

242

on, in Marjorie's mind, the characteristics of the blockage in the sink: the fat that she'd put on the fire had chilled, encountered a turning point, and thickened. Exactly how much did Mrs. Cartey know? Even if she knew about Marjorie's meeting with her ex-husband, what reason did she have to call? They were divorced, weren't they?

And wasn't this voice—Mrs. Cartey's telephone voice—the same one that had been condemning the Perry House lately on "Get It Off Your Chest"? Was Mrs. Cartey the party who had said the Perry House was only the tip of a mercury-contaminated iceberg that was being floated to Cable Harbor from Japan?

Swallowing, hesitantly, the natural guilt she felt about talking with a woman with whose husband she had secretly dined, Marjorie said, "Mrs. Cartey, this is a surprise."

"Call me Marie," the voice said, in a tone that sounded friendly but at the same time calculating. "I'm Mrs. Cartey in name only."

Marjorie realized that Mrs. Cartey was calling because of that; she was out to get him.

"I understand you're the one who got this town meeting organized," Marie said. "I'm very much interested in that. In that town meeting. I have a personal stake in the outcome of that meeting. I feel. The fall of the Perry House would be 'The Fall of the House of Usher' for me, personally. It would be like the ending of *Jane Eyre*. All those hotel rooms . . . of my husband's going up in smoke. So to speak. Do you ever read any of those romantic paperbacks, Mrs. Hanson?"

"I've read *The Flame and the Flower*," Marjorie said.

"That's not exactly what I mean," Marie said. "I mean one of those Gothic books like my friend Laura used to work on. The ones that always have a cover . . . with the heroine running away from this castle on the coast . . . that has one yellow light on in an upstairs window. The heroine is fleeing and pulling her cloak around her and looking back . . . nervously. The book ends when the castle burns. That's what I'd like to see happen with the Perry House. I'd like to see the castle burn."

"Mrs. Cartey, I'm not about to burn any buildings, if that's what you have in mind. I'm a concerned citizen. And that's all I am."

"Oh, I don't want to burn any buildings either. I already tried

243

that once this summer. But I would like to burn a few bridges. Behind me. I don't think I can do that alone, though."

"Mrs. Cartey, I'm not sure how I could . . . be of any help to you."

The sink burbled.

"What do you know?" Marie asked. "What have you found out?"

"Nothing too terribly important," Marjorie replied. "Only enough to make me want to look further . . . perhaps."

"Can I look at what you've got?" Marie asked.

"I don't have enough to make it worth your while, Mrs. Cartey."

"Oh . . . then I assume it's really good, sensitive stuff, huh? And you're not going to leak any of it until . . . you're sure it's the right moment, huh?"

"Mrs. Cartey, are you trying to suggest that I . . . ?" Marjorie paused to let Marie step in with whatever it was she had to drop.

"No, no, I'm not trying to suggest anything . . . of the kind," Marie replied. "I just wonder why a public-spirited person like yourself has to be so secretive. Whenever you have civic-mindedness and secrecy going hand in hand . . . there's usually a power play in the offing, isn't there? But don't go by me. I don't know my civics very well."

"I wish I could be of some help to you, Mrs. Cartey," Marjorie said. "But I can't. I only know the little bit that I know—and that's really nothing."

"Thanks anyway," Marie said. "I just wanted to be sure . . . that you have something on him. You have what you have . . . and I have my little plans. That makes two of us. You need at least two. You couldn't have a gunfight at the O-K Corral without . . . a decent cross fire. Have you ever read any paperback Westerns, Mrs. Hanson?"

"No, I'm sorry, I haven't," Marjorie said.

"I liked *The Ox Bow Incident*," Marie said. "It was supposed to be about a lynching but it was really about Nazi Germany . . . and mob psychology. And *Jane Eyre* was really about Sister Don Bosco. I know she must be locked up in an upstairs room in a convent somewhere. With a single yellow light burning in her window."

"Mrs. Cartey, I'm sorry I—"

"Yeah. I know. You're sorry you couldn't be of more help. Don't worry. You will be."

244

There was a click. Marjorie stood there, listening to the buzz from the receiver, and trying to think what to do next. It was as if she could feel the telephone wires in the town tightening and taking shape, as string used to do between her father's fingers when he would manipulate it to form a coffee cup.

CHAPTER
TWENTY TWO

Marie had not yet been able to decide for herself what it was about the fashion show that made your hand tremble when you were trying to put on your lipstick. She couldn't quite accept Vivian's philosophy that life was so slight, people could have a visceral reaction to clothes. Nor was she completely convinced by the wisdom of Flash Donahue: that the new clothes suggested the new season and the possibility of new beginnings. No, there had to be more to it.

Maybe, Marie thought, it was the presence of the professional models up there on the ramp, the mannequins that Saks mixed in with the locals, to imply that, with the right outfit, anybody could look good. Yes, maybe it was the models who did it, walking way up there on that ramp in glassy-eyed serenity. To Marie they always seemed like a breath of the West Coast—the wave of the West Coast. The way they smiled, as if to say *We represent the life of the body*. See how healthy we are? See how we shine? And you down there, you represent the life of the mind, you with your anxieties. Your neuroses that curl up in your heads like tapeworms and gnaw.

You thought you were smart once, didn't you? Marie said to herself, echoing in her mind the voices of the mythical models. But we're smarter than you ever were. We know that thinking is insidious. We jog. We play tennis. We fuck when we feel like it. And whoever we want. And what we have on, love, you could never, ever, in a million years, wear.

Maybe that was the basic appeal of the fashion show, Marie thought as she sat at her dressing table the morning of the event: narcissism and self-loathing, the two components of middle age. Neatly separated, for the occasion, by the ramp, as the white of egg is separated from the yolk.

As usual, the fashion show was being staged on a lawn, with the ramp and the rows of folding chairs set up under a tent. Each year a few more women showed up, so that inevitably a few spectators were pushed out into the sun, where they would fan themselves with their programs and gasp in sympathy when a model came out in a woolen outfit. The spillover was in the minds of many an indication that the show had become a circus, but still it was for charity, so people merely threatened not to come—and absolutely everybody came. Since it was traditional for members of the committee and their daughters to model along with the professionals, that tradition, and the location, on a friend's front lawn, made the show seem like a large private affair rather than an increasingly unwieldy public promotion. And the show was intimate, in spite of itself, in this way, too: no Cable Harbor model could walk the ramp without inspiring comments of a personal nature from her friends—observations of the sort that finally had made Laura resolve to get the wedding dresses off her back.

Too often, in Laura's view, the comments that went around at the fashion show sounded as if they were coming from people with unsweetened iced tea in their veins.

> She certainly has courage getting up there
> —with her thighs.

> Or:
> Poor Judith, she kept herself looking like
> a model for twenty years so Hubbard wouldn't
> start fooling around—and then he up and dies
> of a heart attack at fifty-five.

The day of the fashion show was yet another in the succession of universally blue days that had made this July shimmer so. Flash Donahue's house looked like a cityscape of shingles; the house and the puffed-up tent on the lawn were made surrealistically three-dimensional by the clear air. Laura felt high just looking at them.

247

She had smoked a joint with Jamie before leaving for the show. She told him he should be stoned if he was going to be ushering the Cable Harbor models off the ramp: it was a matter of adjusting his coordination to that of a bunch of nervous women with two or three screwdrivers in them, Flash Donahue especially, whose promenades under normal circumstances were a sort of ballet vertigo.

"You won't be just ushering them on and off that ramp," Laura said to Jamie as they were driving to the show, "you'll be the Catcher in the Rye, hooking them by the waist a second before they go over the edge."

"That's how I used to observe Mother's Day," Jamie said unemotionally.

Oh, not her again, Laura thought. In her own mind anyway, she quickly changed the subject.

She began to wonder what effect Jamie's presence would have on the crowd at large; this was the first major event of the season that she would be attending with him. With everybody knowing exactly what was going on. And commenting about it. The prospect conjured up a mixed emotion in Laura: pride and fear, which, if not exactly the pity and fear of Greek tragedy, was akin to them, as living with somebody is akin to marriage.

Jamie looked wonderful. He was wearing his blue blazer and white ducks and a blue Brooks Brothers tie printed with little rams for his zodiac sign, Aries. Aries the ram. The ram who was going to make people butt their heads together whispering about him. Jamie had parked the van at the end of the fourth row of cars that had been directed by the detail cop onto the broad lawn that adjoined Flash's cutting beds.

Walking toward the tent, Laura and Jamie were met by Vivian and Marie.

"Hi, kids," Vivian called out. Vivian was wearing a dress that she could have worn for a tennis match circa 1905, and she was twirling on her shoulder a frilly confection of a parasol.

"Vivian, you look fantastic," Laura said.

"Don't you love it?" Vivian replied. "Believe it or not, it came out of a box lot in an auction in Belfast."

"Shop, shop, shop," said Marie. "That's all she talks about, is what she's picked up for her shop. Jamie, you look beautiful. If you weren't with Laura, Barbra Streisand would probably want you for

248

her leading man." Turning on Vivian, Marie added, "See? What you wear doesn't make a damn bit of difference. If you want to look good, sit opposite a good-looking man."

"Nonsense," Vivian said. "Looks are not transferable. They don't rub off on you."

"Says you," Marie replied. "Streisand knows what she's doing. A kiss from Robert Redford you can slap all over your face like a night cream with Candice Bergen's complexion in it. When you've got two people paired off, like matching salt and pepper shakers, nobody bothers to look at the individual grains, nobody sees that the salt may be caked, as it is in my case. . . ."

Laura felt as though she were the object of a dispassionate inquiry, like the ones doctors have over unconscious patients, probing and poking and speculating, internally. She decided she had to put a stop to this uncomfortable consultation, so she interrupted Marie.

"Jamie has to get up to the ramp, girls, so if we could continue this discussion when we find seats. . . ."

"Oh, that's right," Marie remembered, "Jamie is the ringmaster this year. Just keep in mind, sweetie, that when each girl comes off the ramp you hit her right on the head with that sledgehammer—hard. I know it's unpleasant work, but we all like our bacon in the morning, don't we?"

"Marie used to be irrespressible," Vivian observed. "Now she's incorrigible."

"I'm more experienced now," Marie replied. "And—uh! Oh, my God! Look over there!"

Marie had spotted Herbert. He was sitting at a card table, selling tickets to people who hadn't come with them in hand.

"So he's finally left the house," Vivian said.

"Isn't that one of the guys who threw the party that ended with . . ." Jamie hesitated.

"The fire," Marie filled in. "My campfire, which is as good a way as any, I guess, of talking about a blaze ignited with amyl nitrite. God, he's finally left the house. I thought he was going to sneak out at night and fly to their house in Majorca, or else barricade himself in there until September."

"Do you suppose he's heard from Arthur?" Laura wondered.

"He couldn't have," Marie replied. "He looks so depressed. I'm sure he's only here out of a sense of civic duty."

"That's why I'm here, isn't it?" Jamie asked Laura.

"No, you're here so that all these women will be able to believe, at least for an hour or so, that clothes actually have some meaning." By way of reply, Jamie gave Laura an affectionate little hug.

Vivian and Marie responded to the display of natural affection like very young schoolgirls whose bickering had been brought up short by a kiss at the far end of the playground. Both of them were momentarily disoriented.

"Yes," Marie said, recovering from the shock, "yes, Herbert's here out of a sense of civic duty. And you, Jamie, you're here to give us all a sense of civic pride." Confronting Vivian again, she said, "You know when I have a sense of real civic pride? Not on the Fourth of July. But any weekday when I see some half-naked construction worker digging up the street, with his chest all shiny with sweat and—"

Vivian had muffled Marie by clamping a hand over her mouth. Sticking the parasol in her back, she marched her off to the tent, pausing only to throw over her shoulder to Laura and Jamie a remark about incorrigible children and how they had to be handled.

"Marie's on the sauce again, huh?" Jamie said.

"I'm afraid she is," Laura replied. "If only Vivian could get her interested in that shop."

"Everybody needs to have some basic interest in life," Jamie said. "That's just the way it is." The comment sounded to Laura like something meant to be significant, but she felt too nervous and too high to deal with it, so she told Jamie he ought to report for duty, and the two of them started walking toward the tent.

Mrs. Lee greeted Jamie with an enthusiasm that was familiar to Laura; it was the same enthusiasm her mother had for physicians who had successfully brought her through minor surgery (the typical case history: a scalpel as a penis substitute). And Jamie wasn't even a doctor.

"You certainly are the handsomest man we've ever had for this little job," Mrs. Lee was saying. "Why, nobody will want to look at the clothes."

Already Laura was aware of all the eyes on Jamie, the comments being covered up with programs. Suddenly she felt possessive; she wanted to wrap herself around him, cling to him, knit her fingers in his.

250

Jamie was being drilled, sweetly, by Mrs. Lee, in the ceremonies he would be performing; all he had to do was lend a hand as the models mounted the ramp and descended from it. He would be a courtly masculine presence, an escort whose role Laura envisioned as similar to that of the guy in the dinner jacket who wades with you in the Central Park fountain at 6:00 A.M., in the pink and grainy dawn. Laura tried to remember which ingredient you have to have to manufacture such evenings that memories are made of—was it Drambuie or Chanel No. 5? Actually the only ingredient that was essential was the courtly masculine presence. How many little editorial assistants were there in the world who put on Chanel No. 5 and drank Drambuie and were told by their analysts to tell themselves they were intelligent and pretty and then fell flat on their faces in the fountain anyway?

And who among those who would walk the ramp today or sit under this tent making remarks wouldn't wade through the Love Canal with Jamie Lawrence? Laura felt very fortunate and very threatened. To be the object of envy was, in her mind, to invite bad luck. For a long time now she had been telling herself that all she really wanted was enough job security so that her New York apartment did not become a floor to pace off a day's idle shopping the night before you did it. That was enough, or should be enough for anyone in this day and age: an apartment to come home to after a day of satisfying work. To want more was to stick your neck out.

Sticking your neck out like this, in public, was double jeopardy. How tempting to fate, to show up at the fashion show, of all events, with Jamie Lawrence. What a terrible mistake this might prove to be, to come with him to this eagle-eyed hen party, with everybody ready to really dig in there under the feathers, where the white skin was. How many of these women, Laura wondered, would look at Jamie, and then look at her, and hope secretly that in due time she, Laura, would get her neck wrung by the farmer's wife? The same farmer's wife who cut off the tails of the three blind mice with a carving knife so that you never saw such a sight in your life . . . as the three of them running around tailless, starting fires with poppers, opening dress shops, looking for a job at a small publishing house only to find it's absorbed by a bigger one and there are no jobs. God, that was powerful grass, Laura thought. The three blind mice.

251

Jesus. If there's one thing worse than being an editorial assistant who falls on her face in the fountain it's being an editorial assistant who has to work on children's books.

On and on Mrs. Lee droned with her instructions and compliments. Laura shook her head to clear it, but the grass kept slipping in slides and Laura couldn't help projecting. Into her mind flashed an image of Vivian the blind mouse being bitten by a flying mouse and then becoming rabid for antique clothes. Was Marie a blind mouse too? No, she was one of the three little pigs. No doubt that was what she'd say about herself. Only the story was screwed up and Marie was huffing and puffing on her own front door—from the inside.

One minute things made sense and the next minute Laura was all mixed up, what with the eagle-eyed hens and the blind mice and divorcées who wanted everyone to think they liked piggy sex. There was a squeal from the amplifying system in the tent. Realizing that the fashion show was about to begin, Laura broke in on Mrs. Lee's pep talk long enough to tell Jamie she had to find a seat. He looked at her as though he wanted to kiss her—but Laura didn't dare let him, not here; she feared a blast of envy so strong it would bowl her over. Jamie gallantly took up his station by the ramp as Laura hurried to look for a chair.

Vivian was waving her parasol in the air to attract Laura's attention. Spotting the parasol, Laura made her way along the aisle uneasily; she couldn't shake off a vague intuition that she had left something behind—the same intuition she had experienced the time she left a ring on the basin in a powder room: it was a sense of something missing that could not quite be confirmed until you felt for a familiar thing and got the shock of an empty space. It was an odd sensation to be having, Laura thought. She had not misplaced anything, but . . . but she had left Jamie's side, left him to do his little chore, while she looked on, at a distance. Distanced from him, for the first time in . . . days. My God, Laura thought, has he already become as much a part of me as the ring on my finger?

Removing her picture hat from the chair she'd been saving for Laura, Vivian said, "I sure am looking forward to this. I'd like to see Saks come up with one outfit that's a match for the linen sailor dress I picked up last week. Think of it, a seaman's rating appliquéd on the sleeve, just like one I remember selling at PB 84."

"Big deal," pooh-poohed Marie. "My son's girl friend at school has a tattoo on her right boob."

"Listen here, Marie," Vivian said, "you shouldn't go knocking things you haven't even tried. The auction world is fascinating, endlessly fascinating, why—"

"Run a slave auction for me at the New York Athletic Club and I might get interested," Marie countered.

"Oh yeah?" Vivian replied. "Only a sucker would go to an auction and bid on a man. No matter how much you paid you'd still wind up the underbidder in the long run."

"Shshshsh," Laura hissed. "Here comes Saks."

A managerial woman with a pair of glasses hanging from her neck was tapping the microphone. Behind her on the ramp were two professional models with bodies that appeared to be adapted best to a young boy's T-shirt.

"I think the model with the black hair has on a Calvin Klein," Marie said.

"How do you know that?" Vivian replied.

"Because she looks like something out of Brooks Brothers ladies' department," Marie said. "So does Calvin Klein, if you stop to think about it."

Laura shushed them again.

The managerial woman welcomed everyone to the show.

"I think the other one is wearing a Perry Ellis," Vivian whispered. "It has to be. Look at the shoulders. Everything he does is constructed like a Turkish towel. Give me a 1932 Fortuny crepe any day."

"Give me a creep born in 1952," Marie suggested. "Where are the Geoffrey Beenes? I only feel comfortable in a Geoffrey Beene. Maybe I should start carrying around that koala bear I've had since I was a little girl. It sort of looks like Geoffrey Beene."

"Just once I wish that flunky from Saks would preface her remarks with an announcement that all dress designers hate women," Vivian said.

"That's not true," Marie said. "Gloria Vanderbilt is a woman."

"She hated her mother," Vivian pointed out.

"Really?" said Marie. "I'll have to try on a pair of her jeans and see if they fit me. They say misery loves company. And when you're miserable you usually do put it on in your hips."

"Shshshsshsh, for heaven's sake," Laura said. "I think she's about to introduce Jamie."

A moment later Jamie was introduced. He smiled and nodded. And drew applause that sounded to Laura thunderous.

"They're registering their approval," Marie said.

"And dreaming of the bridal register at Tiffany's," Vivian added.

The Saks representative raised her eyebrows, which were as black and businesslike as typewriter ribbon, and began describing the dress that Marie had thought was a Calvin Klein.

Marjorie and George had set up tables by Flash's rhododendron bushes. George was having difficulty with one of the coffee makers, which was spitting out a rusty fluid that looked more like radiator coolant than Maxwell House. Marjorie had taken the Saran wrap off several large bowls of sandwich spread and was about to make the tea sandwiches. She uncovered a large plate of bread slices that had been trimmed of their crusts. Noticing something odd about the bread, Marjorie reached for a slice and realized the second she touched it that it was stale. It was as stiff and brittle to the touch as whiskers.

"George!" she said. "Do you realize this bread is stale?"

"Huh?" George said.

"The bread is stale, I said. What the hell are we going to do?"

"There's a garden hose over there," George said. "Why don't you wet it?"

"Wet it!" Marjorie couldn't believe her ears.

"Yes, wet it. Put the nozzle on sprinkle. That'll moisten it up real good."

Is this my punishment? Marjorie wondered. Am I being punished for calling up "Get It Off Your Chest" all those times? Did what I had to say somehow reach Mars, and now they're beaming back their reply through my husband's mouth?

"George, what are we going to do about this goddamn stale bread?" Marjorie shouted. Several women on the fringe of the fashion show turned their heads.

"Let them eat cake," George said.

Marjorie picked up a piece of the stale bread and rolled it between her palms until it turned into a doughball. Then she threw it at her husband. George ignored her. Marjorie made a snowball out of a

254

handful of tuna salad. The women who were seated just outside the tent began to stare and talk anxiously among themselves. Marjorie threw the tuna salad ball. It hit George on the side of his head and splattered.

There was a gasp from the women who were watching.

"Here comes Flash Donahue," Marie said. "God, what have they got her up in? Those ruffles. A rose is a rose is a rose. Except when it's Lycra spandex and nylon."

"I used to believe those rumors about her," Laura said. "That she was Anastasia."

"The Czar's daughter?" Marie said. "No way. Rasputin's daughter, maybe."

"It isn't Lycra spandex and nylon at all, it's silk," Vivian said. "Take off those sunglasses, Marie. You're like a horse with blinders on."

"At least I put one foot in front of the other," Marie replied. "I avoid stepping in the horse shit . . . and the bat guano."

"What's going on?" Laura said. There seemed to be a ruckus on the other side of the tent. Everybody was turning to look at the same time. Including Flash Donahue, who was at the end of her tour of the ramp and about to execute a turn.

As she was turning, Flash tried to get a glimpse of what was going on. She lost her balance and began to reel. The people in the front rows looked up at the ramp in horror. Somebody screamed.

Flash was falling.

But Jamie Lawrence was under her. He had moved quickly, and when the old woman stepped into the air he reached for her and seized her arms and brought her safely to the ground in a movement so fluid that it seemed he had only lifted her up and put her down. The crowd rose from their seats and pressed forward. There was pandemonium for a minute, with people moaning and craning their necks and shouting.

Herbert had risen from his seat at the ticket table. He did not see Arthur approaching him from behind.

"That's what happens when you try to adjust to soft contact lenses at eighty-three," Arthur said.

Herbert wheeled around.

Marie managed to work her way up to the front of the tent. They had Flash stretched out flat, and she was covered with someone's shawl. A lady doctor was checking her vital signs, but Flash appeared to be all right. Her eyes were flicking around like canaries in a cage, and Marie thought she heard her ask the lady doctor for bourbon. Laura and Vivian were trying to fight their way past people's shoulders. Marie called out to them, "I think she's okay." But Laura persisted in pushing through. Marie looked at Jamie. She looked at one of the professional models, who couldn't take her eyes off him. Neither could most of the other women who had worked their way into a position where they could see him. Not only was he beautiful, he was heroic. You better get your ass up here fast, Laura, Marie thought.

Needing air, Marie found an opening and walked out onto the grass. The sun blinded her for a moment. She heard the rattle of an engine. She opened her eyes and saw Herbert's diesel Mercedes heading toward the gate. And behind it, running and waving his arms, was . . . Arthur. Marie blinked. Then she saw George Hanson, the caterer. He was throwing cherry tomatoes at his wife, peppering her. She was deflecting the tomato barrage with a serving tray, and pelting him with what looked like cookies. Marie sat down on the grass. She thought she might as well be comfortable while she watched the world go mad.

The day after the fashion show it rained for the first time in two weeks. There was a massive thunderstorm followed by a steady sifting of water from the gray overcast. Marie wandered around her house with a bloody mary, pausing every now and then to press her nose against a windowpane or do an obscene finger painting in the condensation on the glass. Vivian set up a dress dummy in her bedroom and backdropped it with a roll of grass cloth left over from last summer's papering. Then she began taking flash photographs of the dresses and hats and outlandish accessories she had acquired. Before her store opened, she would fill the windows with these pictures to tease passersby. Some of them she might even use for illustrated ads in *Women's Wear Daily*. The clouds and the rain prompted Vivian to take a couple of Valium, though—and to marvel at her progress even as she was swallowing them. Before, when the weather was this gloomy, she would have been popping them like cashews (that was around the time that Marie told her she

256

should stop keeping cashews on the coffee table for her guests and put out bowls of Valium instead).

Laura was zipped up inside the tent with Jamie. The rain spattering on the canvas was so soothing to her that she could have believed the moisture outside was amniotic fluid. They had done a few lines of coke, and the sex they were having was for Laura orgasm made elastic: she absolutely could not stand it, but then it stretched yet a little farther, and she was ready to die all over again.

Herbert was sitting in a bar in Munsonville. He had stayed in a motel overnight and had decided to lie low for the day in a place where Arthur would never look for him: a highway tavern surrounded by pickup trucks.

Marjorie had not bothered to put on a rainhat. Her hair was pasted to her cheeks and her neck, and she had to keep blinking the rainwater out of her eyes. She was struggling with one of the benches that went with the redwood picnic table. It was hard for her to keep her balance, but even so she had worked up a certain momentum, and the door to George's workshop was gradually yielding to the battering.

Evelyn was reading an account of an interplanetary excursion to Sanford.

"When they take off straight up like that their ears must close up for days," she said.

"What makes you think they have any ears?" Sanford said.

"They have to," Evelyn replied. "They came here in the first place 'cause they picked up the BBC. I've been sayin' for years that they can hear every word that we say on 'Get It Off Your Chest.' Only one to contradict me on that score was that Marjorie Hanson. Hah. She won't be contradictin' anybody after that town meetin.'"

George was parked by the side of the road. The rain was cascading down the windshield in fat rivulets. The gray ocean was being scrubbed by the wind. George pushed the lighter in and waited for it to pop out. When it popped out, he used it to burn a hole in the center of a wad of Master Card and Visa receipts. Then he threw them out the window. Closing the window, George chanced to look into the rearview mirror. Someone was walking along the side of the road. George could tell from the hood the person was wearing, and the contour of the body, that this was a woman approaching. He switched on the radio and lowered the window again.

CHAPTER TWENTY THREE

Marjorie wanted to reduce George's birdhouse to splinters. She wanted to make toothpicks out of it; in her mind it stood for the apartment building in Lowell that they might have owned if George hadn't blown the down payment at the track; it stood also for the very house they lived in, with its partitions and its separated lives. And worst of all, the birdhouse and the workshop where it was always being built represented to Marjorie the aerie George had chosen for his sullen roost, the state of mind he so often was in now: Who cares? So what? *You* do it. And when she tried to do it he made a fool of her; the fashion show was the payoff. Marjorie was determined to smash the birdhouse to bits and then take every last dime out of their savings and buy up every scrap of land Hopkins had to offer. And then when that casino went in she'd move to Palm Beach with the profits and build a tree house in one of the palm trees for George—if he ever wanted to visit.

When the door to the workshop finally cracked under the blows Marjorie was giving it with the picnic bench, she let go of that blunt instrument and pushed through into the dimly lit room. On George's workbench she quickly located another blunt instrument: a mallet with a heavy rubber head, which she thought would take care of the birdhouse nicely. Turning on a light, Marjorie pushed her wet hair back from her eyes and looked around for the birdhouse. It wasn't there. Or was it? Near the workbench, on the floor, were a few pieces of plywood, one of which had a round hole in the middle of it. Marjorie picked up that piece of wood and looked through the hole. She stuck her finger in it. It was about the right size to accommodate a sparrow. This had to be the birdhouse. And this was as far as George had gotten with it, in all these months.

Marjorie had to sit down. She felt she had slipped through the hole in the piece of plywood—into Wonderland, or a black hole somewhere out in space. Maybe he has some Seagram's Seven in that bar, she thought. Marjorie got up and went to the bar and tried to slide it open. Finding it was locked she gave it a swipe with the rubber mallet. The door slid back with a bang. Marjorie looked on the first shelf. She found a stack of white boxes. Opening one, she discovered a reel of film. She took the film over to the lamp, lifted off the shade, and held the strip up to it. Her eyes widened. She went back to the bar and dug out more boxes. Unwinding reel after reel, holding footage from each up to the light to see what was on it, Marjorie finally gave in to the shock of it all and sat on the floor in a damp heap. Tangled film lay all around her.

So George was running his own little porno palace out here. So this was why he was always shutting himself up in here to "work." Marjorie sneezed so hard she saw stars. Then she began to feel queasy; probably she was going to get double pneumonia out of this. What now? Maybe I should go pick up a few copies of *Playgirl* and cut out the penises and paste them all over the refrigerator door, she thought. No, that wouldn't work; the kids always went for the refrigerator and they'd be around again—when?—Marjorie consulted her steamed-up watch—in a couple of hours. At least he wasn't having an affair, Marjorie told herself.

And then she began to wonder why he wasn't. And for that matter, why she wasn't. Maybe Mrs. Cartey knew more than she was letting on. Maybe she knew about the secret meeting at the Munsonville Inn, and suspected that Marjorie was having an affair with her ex-husband. And why shouldn't she? Why *not*? If people suspected you were carrying on, then you might just as well be carrying on. Life in Cable Harbor was like that; if you had any moral obligation at all, it was to justify the suspicions of your neighbors.

"Kinda wet out there, ain't it?" George yelled through the window of the Oldsmobile. The hooded figure trotted over and looked in at him. She was young. And she was smiling. She said, "Man, it sure is pissin' down, isn't it?"

"Where you trying to get to?" George asked.

"No place special," the girl said.

"You're almost there," George replied. "You want to go the rest of the way, I'll be glad ta take ya."

"Great," said the girl. Looping around the car, she opened the passenger door and said, "My pack's all wet. Should I throw it on the floor in the back?"

"Sure, sure," George said. "Don't worry about it." The girl slung her pack into the back and slid in next to George. She pulled back her hood and shook her hair out.

"Raining cats and dogs, huh?" George said.

"Raining cat piss," said the girl. George saw that the girl had small features that were finely made but not delicate; they had the hardness of wood worked by hand. And this was especially noticeable in the girl's nostrils, which were dovetailed, and in her eyes, which looked as if their sockets had been formed by the pressure of a thumb. The girl unzipped her pullover and stretched, arching her body and extending her fists to the roof.

"Oh, shit," she said with weariness in her voice.

"Shitty day," George said. He wondered if this was how his oldest son talked to a girl this age—everything piss and shit.

An inquiring look appeared on the girl's face.

"What's that on the radio?" she asked. "Is that what they call 'easy listening'?"

"I don't know," George replied. "You want to listen to a rock station? If you do, I'll try to find one." He turned the dial.

"Man, you are eager to please," the girl said. "What's your name?"

"George. What's your name?"

"My name's Sandy, George. Hey, George, tell me something. What were you doing parked here all by yourself in the rain? You get your wires wet or what?"

"No, no, I was just sitting here," George replied. "Just enjoying being by myself."

"You like being alone, huh?"

"Sometimes. Sometimes I think. Sometimes I don't think. Either way it relaxes me."

"You sound like you're talking about sex."

George laughed and said, "No, no, I wasn't even thinking about that."

"Bullshit," Sandy said. "How old are you, George?"

"I'm . . . forty . . . forty-five."

"That's old enough to admit it when you're thinking about sex—or at least not to deny it, especially when you've got a chick sitting next to you in your car and you're checking out her tits."

"Where . . . where do you want to go?" George asked.

"You're married, right?"

"Yes."

"Then let's go to a motel."

"What are you? Some kind of a . . . ?"

"Don't look a gift horse in the mouth, Georgie-Porgie."

George reached for the ignition key. His hand was trembling.

There's the car, Arthur thought. I knew if I just drove around long enough . . . He must be in there drinking Miller Lites one after the other and playing "Stand by Your Man" over and over again on the jukebox. Reading the sign on the irregular clapboards of the building as he got out of his car, Arthur said to himself, "Flanagan's Corner"—hm, last year I think it was "The Four Leaf Clover"—but it still looks like a geodesic outhouse.

Locking the door of the 450SL, Arthur crept up to the roadhouse's black picture window and peaked in. At the bar were two men with their sleeves rolled up and a woman who was turning her head as though she were checking the cap on a jar for tightness. Herbert was sitting in a corner booth with several Miller Lite bottles in front of him.

He looks like a monk separated from the Canterbury tour group, Arthur thought. Just sitting there with his little tale to tell, and nobody to listen. Arthur straightened his shoulders and walked in.

It was ten o'clock and George was still not home. Marjorie was sitting alone in her living room with a copy of *Reader's Digest* open on her lap. The printed words kept backtracking. Marjorie had one false tooth in her head, and tonight she couldn't get her tongue to leave it alone. Where was George? She knew where he had been the night that girl died—she had looked up the date on the calendar. He had been home in bed. There was about an hour in that day

261

when he was not around; supposedly he was at the fish wholesaler's. There was no reason now to suspect he hadn't been there, other than those movies. But what did they prove? A bunch of home movies, that was all they were, only they were based on the kind of home life men wanted, at heart: no barbecues, no babies, no birthday cakes, no grandma and grandpa smiling and waving at the camera, none of that. Just the wife filmed fifteen years younger than any wife ever looks, just the wife. Filmed vacuuming in her panties.

Marjorie wondered if the town would suspect George of murdering that girl if they knew about his dirty movies, if they knew about the missing hour in that day. Probably they would suspect him. And probably Mrs. Cartey knew about the meeting at the Munsonville Inn. What could you hope to hide in a small town? Nothing. Eventually everybody's dirty laundry was run up the flagpole to flap in the four winds.

It occurred to Marjorie that her marriage might actually be ending. Now. This summer. She and George had at last come to the end of their rope. In this town. In this house. For some reason she recalled an incident in her childhood, something that happened when she was around eight. A brash boy who lived in the neighborhood dared her to follow him along a log that lay across a small stream. She had been very frightened, but she had done it. Because he was waiting for her on the other side. Once, in Marjorie's mind, being divorced had seemed like being out on that log, with nobody waiting on the other side. But now Marjorie no longer thought of divorce in those terms. She had come to think of it as the partial plate in your mouth that you removed at night and put in a glass of water—and stared at, with your tongue moving into the empty space in your row of back teeth, the gap where the years had been. The problem, in divorce, Marjorie now realized, wasn't that it stranded you out on a limb; it was that it left you with an opening for the tongue, and in a state of mind where you might even welcome your dentist's fingers in there, whether they were pudgy or not.

From a distance, George was aware of what he was doing, and of the consequences, but his libido had suspended guilt, and he was allowing the dream to happen, and numbing himself to the knowledge that in the dark outside was the possibility of nightmare. He had driven the girl to a flat-roofed motel that catered to truckers.

The clerk, whose movements seemed to start from a friction drive linked to gum chewing, had been so indifferent that George was reassured. However, he had trouble getting the room key in the lock. Sandy finally opened it with her hairpin. She told George it would have been easier with a credit card, and that all that really counted for a lock in a motel was the chain once you got inside.

Flinging her pack onto one of the twin beds, Sandy went into the bathroom. George sat down on the other bed and folded his hands. This was real, he knew, this was actually happening; yet it seemed like a movie, one of his movies. Was this what happened when you finally got what you wanted? That you somehow could not feel the reality, that you could only act out, in the flesh, the want.

"Want to fuck, man?" Sandy said. She had come out of the bathroom naked, except for a white T-shirt with Donny Osmond's face on it. The T-shirt was soaking wet. George could see the dark circles of her nipples. Sandy walked over to him and sat on his lap.

"Giddy up," she said. "You're cute. You're like my daddy. He used to tuck me in at night. And then reach under the covers. And play with me."

George took hold of her thin shoulders and kissed her. She ran her tongue all over the inside of his mouth. She squeezed the front of his pants. George put his hand under her wet T-shirt. He located one of her breasts, and he closed his hand on it. Everything in his life left him, all memory, all responsibility, even his breath: there was nothing in the universe but his grip on her, and the feel of her hand gripping him.

"I'm sorry, I'm so sorry to bother you," Marjorie was saying, "but I didn't know who else to call. And you'd given me this number . . . in case anything happened."

"I said you should feel free to call me anytime, and I meant what I said," Dan Cartey replied. "You sound upset. What is it? Is that woman—the town clerk—has she threatened to blow the whistle? Or . . . has my ex-wife been calling you again?"

"Oh no, it's nothing like that," Marjorie said. "It's me. Me and my husband. We had a terrible fight yesterday, right in front of half the town, and he . . . he's taken off. It's eleven, and I have no idea where he is."

"Maybe one of your kids would have some idea where . . . " Dan suggested.

"I don't know where any of them are either," Marjorie said. "But that's normal . . . for this house." Marjorie was beginning to fill up.

"You live in New York," she said. "You must have seen those ads that come on at ten and some famous person says, 'It's ten o'clock, do you know where your children are?' "

"Yes, I've seen them, but—"

"George and I saw one last fall, when we were in New York on our annual weekend vacation, and I had to say to myself, 'No, I don't know where my children are, but I hope to God my only daughter is doing it in the back of a van instead of getting more poison ivy on her bottom." Marjorie burst into tears.

"Mrs. Hanson—"

"I'm Mrs. Hanson in name only," Marjorie blurted out. "This after . . . afternew—hoon I . . . I discovered my husband has been looking at dirty movies rather than building a birdhouse."

Dan held the telephone receiver away from his ear a little and looked at it as if it were a curiosity.

"Oh, Mr. Cartey, my life is coming apart . . . how can I possibly be thinking about real estate . . . or town meetings. I'd like to call up 'Get It Off Your Chest' and tell them . . . tell them . . ." Marjorie reached inside her blouse, unhooked her strapless bra in back, worked it loose, pulled it out, bunched it up, and threw it across the room.

"Mrs. Hanson, are you all right? Are you still there? Hello?"

"I don't know what I'd tell them," Marjorie said quietly. Her breath was coming in little pants.

"Mrs. Hanson, you've got to try to calm down. . . ."

"Life is such a ton of bricks," Marjorie said despondently.

"Why, is your husband a Mason?"

"What did you say?"

"I said, is your husband a Mason?"

Marjorie laughed. She couldn't stop laughing. She almost became hysterical.

Dan chuckled. To himself. He was holding the phone at a slight distance again. But his tongue was moving tentatively along his upper lip. Listening to Marjorie's uncontrollable laughter, Dan felt an old lilt in his heart again: women, women, women. You couldn't live with them or without them. Women, women. Women and men: they were like the Kilkenny cats who fought until only their tails were left. All that was ever needed, though, was tail. And the merest wag, to start the grand scrap all over again.

When Marjorie was too out of breath to laugh anymore, Dan said to her, "Look, Mrs. Hanson—Marjorie—there's no sense in your working yourself up over what'll most likely turn out to be nothing. Why don't you take a couple of sleeping pills and go to bed, and if your husband isn't back when you wake up in the morning, give me another call? Okay? How does that sound?"

"I guess that's what I should do," Marjorie replied. "Go to bed." A fresh awareness had come into Marjorie's mind, a clearing, after the storm of tears and laughter. She said to Dan, "I probably should have gone straight to bed instead of bothering you, Mr. Cartey—Daniel. . . ."

"Dan." What is it about this woman that I like? he was thinking. Is it everything she doesn't have in common with Lee Radziwill?

"Dan. It feels funny calling you by your first name—I feel like you're my doctor—but I think you're right. I should go to bed. We sleep through so many of the things that happen to us anyway. I mean, what could we do about it if we were awake?"

"Probably nothing," Dan replied.

"Yes, that's the truth of it—nothing. There's nothing you can do. I suppose if there's such a thing as life after death it operates something like that: things keep happening but you sleep through them all. Maybe you're aware of your former life the way you're aware of a TV show when you're dozing off."

"Could be," Dan said. "But one thing I am sure of is that as long as you're still alive and kicking, things always look better in the morning."

Reminding Marjorie to call if anything went seriously wrong, Dan said "Sleep well" and, when Marjorie said, "Good night," answered her with another "Good night" instead of hanging up. There was a hesitation on both ends, and then the decisive click. It was Marjorie who had hung up.

Now, there's a spirited woman, Dan thought. Or was she? Thinking about it, Dan recollected that spirited women were usually only redheaded actresses who used to be typecast opposite John Wayne. This gal amounted to more than that. What Marjorie Hanson had,

Dan reasoned, was a kind of down-home appeal. An appeal that Dan couldn't explain to himself, except emotionally. Thinking about Marjorie led his mind back to those private occasions when he would allow a lump to come into his throat as he listened to a female country and western singer on the quadraphonic stereo system in his Seville. They always sounded so plaintive, those singers, and yet so strong. And when one of the big rigs, a Peterbilt or a Marmon, barreled by the Seville, bound for home and a woman like that, Dan longed for what he had missed in his marriage and his affairs: a roll in the hay *where you could actually smell the hay's sweetness.*

Now Marjorie had walked into Dan's life. And he didn't want her to walk away. When he was talking to her on the telephone, he could see her face clearly. Because the focus of his familiar longing, which now had shifted to her, a woman he had actually met, was so very sharp.

After hanging up, Marjorie went over to the fireplace and fished out her crumpled bra. One of the kids could come home at any minute; it wouldn't do for them to know that their mother had been flinging around her undergarments. Marjorie wondered what had got into her. And she wondered if she should call Daniel Cartey— Dan—again if George didn't show up, or if he *did* show up. It dawned on Marjorie that she was going to call Dan no matter what. And part of the same realization, which felt as breathtaking as sky swept clean by the wind, was that divorce didn't have to leave a gap. It could mean freedom. It could mean an awakening from the big sleep of marriage. More than that, it be a broad avenue to that man on the other end of the telephone line. I should burn this bra, Marjorie thought, like the hippies said to do back when I was changing diapers. I'll burn this bra, I'll burn that rotten log across the brook, yes, that's what I'll do, I'll burn all the bridges behind me. And in her mind Marjorie saw a glorious new span that stretched from Cable Harbor to New York.

Marjorie took her bra out back to the charcoal grill. She poured lighter fluid on it and lit it with a wooden kitchen match. The bra quickly turned brown in the flames, and it began to curl up. Bring out your hot dog, George, Marjorie thought.

Sandy was curled up naked, next to George, in a pose so shamelessly exhibitionistic that her body seemed as hard to hide as a large

266

brown stain. Picking at George's chest, with her fingernail, Sandy was saying, "That was nice, man. It was real nice of you to take me here. To give me a lift . . . and all." George smiled at her. He wanted to get out of bed and get dressed and go home. To try to outrun the guilt.

"How would you like to take me a little farther?"

"Huh?" said George.

"I got other places to go, man. Want to take me? I'll share the driving."

"I don't understand what—"

"It's simple, Georgie. This is as far north as I feel like going. It's time to head west. You want to take me or not?"

"I can't," George said. "I have a wife and kids. I've got a business."

"What the fuck difference does any of that make, man? You're fuckin' miserable. I thought you were going to cry after you came."

George felt as though his body were shrinking. He took Sandy's wrists in his hands and squeezed them hard.

"What are you doing?" she demanded.

"I got to know you're real," he said. "I got to know you're not a picture somebody took."

Sandy laughed and jerked her arms free of George.

"I'm real and I fuck," she said. "What more do you want?"

"I want . . ." George could not think what he wanted.

"I want," he said again. "I want; I want . . . I want." He began to cry. Sandy watched him crying for a couple of minutes. And then, with genuine tenderness, she wiped the tears off his cheeks with the sheet.

"Take me west," she whispered. "You've been waiting a long time for someone like me. Am I right or wrong? Tell me."

"Yes," said George. "Yes. Yes."

CHAPTER TWENTY FOUR

"Give up," Marie said. "For God's sake, Vivian, you're as persistent as a Moonie."

"But it would be so much more fun if the two of us were running the shop," Vivian persevered.

"Carter could have put an end to the Iranian crisis in a week," Marie declared, "if he'd used Moonie paratroopers—without parachutes."

"Stop trying to change the subject, Marie, will you please?"

Marie got up and went to the bar. She tossed the melted ice in her glass into the stainless-steel sink, opened a fresh bottle of Finlandia, and poured. And kept on pouring, until her glass overflowed.

"Just like an old-fashioned soda fountain sundae," she said with satisfaction.

"Or a typical Sunday afternoon in Cable Harbor," Vivian replied. "If you're trying to appall me with the amount of liquor you're consuming, you're not going to succeed. It's an old device and it doesn't work. I know. I once tried it on my mother."

"Whatever are you talking about?" Marie replied breezily.

"Look," said Vivian. "A friend of mine from college used to tell me that the only way she could control her mother when she went to visit her was to go to the bar and start pouring scotch and keep pouring it until the nagging stopped. She said I should try it on my mother. So I did."

"So you did. And what happened?"

"I filled a sixteen-ounce glass up to the brim. My mother stood there watching, and finally she said, 'Oh. You make yourself a drink. But you don't bother to ask me if I might like one.'"

Marie stared into space for a moment as if she were stupefied.

Then, taking a drink, she said, "I wonder how much Valium is consumed in this country on Mother's Day."

"About as much as on Father's Day," Vivian replied. "I remember the first Father's Day after Joe and I got the divorce. I was wandering around in the attic and I found the baseball glove he'd given to Stan when he was six years old. It was such a tiny little baseball glove. I picked it up and held it against my cheek and then I cried. For about an hour."

"The national pastime," Marie said.

"Baseball? It *was* the national pastime back then."

"I meant crying."

"Oh."

Marie sighed and had another sip of her drink. Outside, an owl was hooting.

"Instead of mannequins, why don't you use stuffed animals?" Marie said.

"What?"

"In your dress shop, I mean. It would be sort of amusing to see a moose head with a mink stole or an owl with a velvet turban on its head."

"That sounds like something Arthur might come up with."

"Huh?"

"Don't you remember the time he made you drive down from Maine with him, during the hunting season, and he had nude mannequins with catsup on them tied to the roof of the car?"

"Oh, that's right. I forgot. He was wearing a bear suit. He said he got the idea from a Charles Addams cartoon. Arthur is the only person I've ever known who wanted to translate Charles Addams's cartoons into meaningful social action. He said it was Marxism according to *The New Yorker*."

"I wonder where he and Herbert are right now."

"Who knows? I try not to think about it. It depresses me."

"Marie, did you ever stop to think that all this depression might come from having nothing to do?"

269

"Yes, I've thought about that. But ansher—shit—*answer* me this, Vivian. What are you supposed to *do* when you're one of those people whose heart tells her that anything she *does* is just a shadow moving on a blank white wall . . . when she knows that she's going to be alone in her bed that night?"

"You know what you've done, Marie?"

"No, what've I done?"

"You've filled a hope chest . . . in your mind . . . with things like my son's baseball glove."

By morning the sun had returned; when Laura looked out of the tent, she saw cobwebs effervescent with moisture in the grass, and when the breeze stirred the blue spruce nearby, she heard a remnant of the rain coming down. Jamie was still asleep, as it was only seven-thirty. Digging a shift out of the cottage bureau she had somehow fitted into the tent, Laura put it on and went outside. She made coffee and then consulted the refrigerator. She decided she would have to do some shopping today. Perhaps it would be a good idea to do it early; it seemed as though the heat was going to return along with the sunshine. When she finished her coffee Laura went back into the tent, wrote a brief note to tell Jamie where she was, and kissed him gently on his cheek. She went back outside, washed, and brushed her hair. Turning the key delicately, in the hope that the car would start quietly, Laura pulled away from the campsite and headed down the dirt road.

Out on the shore road, Laura lowered the window all the way. It was nearing the end of July now, and summer was at its fullest. Even this far north in Maine, where usually everything was so sparse, there was a thickness in the wild rose bushes, the pines, the maples. And from the unusual heat there was a shade of yellow here and there, a spot of desert amid the green. The wild grass simply couldn't take the sun all day without the relief of shade. It parched. Grass grew best with a roof of leaves over it; perhaps the same was true of people. Laura thought of Marie—and Vivian before she discovered antique clothing—baking all day on the deck of the Bath Club. *Unaccommodated man is no more but such a poor, bare, forked animal* . . . Wasn't that from *King Lear*? Laura couldn't remember, though she did recall she'd heard it from Herbert, who liked to quote Shakespeare, and who had said it when their group came upon a raccoon foraging in a restaurant trash barrel. My table at the Four Seasons, Laura thought sourly, as she rounded a sharp corner with a squeal from the Mustang's tires.

If unaccommodated man was a raccoon who couldn't get a good table at the Four Seasons, what was unaccommodated woman? A patch of dry skin on the beach? Laura chose not to think about it any longer. Instead she thought about buying some nectarines for Jamie and feeding him one so the juice from it made his mouth and her hand sticky and sweet.

"I can't do it," George said, "I can't go with you. My wife will call the police. They'll put out an all-points bulletin."

"For what? Are they going to arrest you for stealing your own car, man?"

Sandy was leaning against the Oldsmobile casually. She was wearing cut-off denim shorts that were so tight, so nearly absorbed by her body, that they seemed shortened by biting, like fingernails.

"No, I don't know. I just don't know. But I know I can't do this. It's crazy."

"Crazier than what you've been doing?"

George wiped the sweat off his forehead with his hand. He saw stars, the way he sometimes did when he sneezed, little points of white light floating in his field of vision. Maybe it was his blood pressure that caused it; he hadn't cared enough to find out. Trying to clear his head, George blinked, and into his mind came flashes of the craziness that had become his life: jerking off in front of a crude movie, slinking away from the post office in a terror that the small world of Cable Harbor had some hidden access to his emotional interior, being sneered at by the kids who only wanted the car, and money for this and money for that, going to bed at night to escape from the day. The day, and Marjorie, to whom he'd been married so many, many hours.

"What difference does it make?" George said. There was no longer any tension in his voice.

Sandy sprang at him. She put her arms around him and talked into his chest.

"Does that mean you'll go away with me?" she said.

"Yes," George replied. There was a surge of feeling in him, an enormous uplift in his spirit; he felt utterly impoverished, stripped of all he had ever worked for, all he had managed to put together over the years, and he felt young again, and free.

"I haven't even got any clothes," George said. He could feel Sandy's breasts sticking into his chest and he was flooding with fresh desire.

"So what?" Sandy murmured. "We'll buy you some."

"What are we going to use for money?"

Sandy laughed and reached through the open window of the Oldsmobile for her pack. Pulling out her billfold, she unsnapped it and a long string of credit cards fanned open.

"My parents are divorced," she said. "They hate each other. I was their only daughter. They hate me, too. So they keep sending me a ton of money. In order to keep me away from them. My mother sends me a little more money than my father because three years ago I had a kid and gave it to her to raise. She *really* wants me out of the way."

George felt a little weak. He opened the car door and sat behind the wheel for a few minutes. Sandy squeezed in with him. She played with the steering wheel like a happy child, making growling noises with pauses between, the way a child does when he's imitating shifting gears.

"Let's go, Georgie-Porgie," she said, sliding over.

"What about the police? They may be out looking for me right now."

"What about 'em? Tell 'em you and your old lady had a fight. And that I'm your therapist. Come on, man, get it together. Let's move on out. I hate hanging around motel parking lots. It makes me feel cheap."

George drove in a daze. He had to keep telling himself that none of this mattered. Even if this crazy girl decided to dump him in the middle of Ohio, what difference would it make? He could stop in the next town down the road and get a job as a night janitor and live in a single room with a hot plate and a television set. That was all he needed. It was all any man needed—after a certain point in his life.

"I got your note," Jamie said as he opened the door of Laura's Mustang.

"Good," Laura said. "I didn't want to disturb you, but I wanted you to know where I was, so you wouldn't be wondering."

Jamie laughed and said, "My mother was always sending me notes with her location mapped out on them. I had the boot shape of Italy memorized when I was eight years old."

With one foot on the ground and one foot on the floor mat, Laura paused.

"Jamie, I have to be honest with you about something," she said. "The truth is I'm just a little bit tired of hearing about your mother all the time."

Jamie blinked.

"I mean, you make her memory such a presence," Laura said, rushing through her speech though she didn't want to. "Sometimes I can almost feel her . . . between us."

"She's dead," Jamie said. "The memory is all I have of her. What are you—jealous?"

"Should I be?"

"Come on, Laura. What is this? Some kind of pop psychology you picked up from your divorced girl friends? I'm not hung up on my mother, if that's what you're implying."

"Then what would you call it?" Laura said. "Sometimes I think you have a checklist in your head. The only thing I can't figure out is how it works. Do you put down a checkmark when I remind you of your mother—or when I make you forget her for five minutes?"

"If I were testing you against her—right now—you'd fail. Badly." Jamie turned his back.

"Why are you turning away from me?" Laura asked.

"Because I think this conversation sucks," Jamie replied.

"You're condescending to me. But it's true, isn't it? I'm just a substitute for her, aren't I? When you're in bed with me, do you think of her?"

Jamie turned to face Laura again. His expression was a straight line that bore down so hard his mouth seemed like a rip across his face.

"Yes, if you must know," he said. "I do think about her. I think about her touching me. In my head I compare your touch to hers."

A tiny droplet from the words Jamie was spitting at her glanced off Laura's hot cheek. She pulled the door shut and started the Mustang.

"That's it, take off," Jamie yelled at her.

Numbly Laura searched for the gearshift lever. For a moment she thought, this isn't happening. But she knew she was awake. She had just been shopping. In the market, she had noticed the radiant chill from the dairy case, the smudged purple date on the carton of Hood's milk. But the chill was now in her soul. She had said what she had said and he had said what he had said and she was leaving. Slapping the shift lever into reverse, Laura stepped on the gas hard and churned up a cloud of dust. She found first and roared back up the dirt road, hitting bumps with slams to the car's springs that hurt her teeth. And she could hardly see, could hardly breathe, for the tears.

"Wake me up when we're there," she said.

"All right," George replied. "I will."

A half hour later Sandy woke up and said to George, in a baby's voice, "Are we there yet?"

Stroking her hair, George said, "No, we got a ways to go."

"How far?" said Sandy crankily.

"A few hours yet," George said.

Sandy smacked her lips contentedly and resumed her nap.

George imagined himself in some darkened motel in Vermont. With her. He put everything else out of his mind. And he developed an erection that lasted eighty miles.

Laura drove as far as she could, which was about six miles, and then she gave in and parked at the edge of a scenic overlook. Getting out, she half ran and half stumbled to the end of the narrow path that wound around the rocks. A hundred feet below her was the surf. Laura stood there, inches from the edge. She wanted to reach out and embrace the blue air. Her heart felt drawn to the rocks below. She had only to step forward, to let go. A warm wind was blowing her hair back, and Laura could taste salt spray on her lips. It tasted like blood, her own. Laura closed her eyes and pressed her arms to her sides.

It wasn't working. Anna Karenina I am not, Laura thought. She backed off. She sat down in a heap. She found she was too full of despair even to cry. But the pain was too intense just to sit and suffer it. Struggling back up the packed path, Laura picked up her car keys where she had left them on the ground. She noticed in the backseat of the Mustang the two grocery bags. Pushing the seat forward, she reached in and got a grip on one of them. She hoisted it out, and then she reached for the other one. With the two heavy bags under her arms, she struggled down to the cliff again. She set the groceries on a flat boulder, and she pulled the bag of nectarines out. Tearing the plastic with her teeth, she flung the bag like a sling, and the nectarines sailed in graceful arches to the rocks below, where they splattered and splashed. Laura took a large Perrier bottle by the neck and swung it against the flat boulder. Princess Margaret christening an Irish rowboat, she thought with bitter amusement. Ah, now the yogurt, she said to herself, snatching up four cones of Yoplait. She fired them at the rocks as if they were grenades.

Two sea gulls were soaring overhead, watching Laura's activities with increasing interest. Laura ripped open a bag of natural potato chips and tossed it. The potato chips fluttered, and the sea gulls dove. Next was a box of After Eight mints. Laura crammed five of them in her mouth and threw the rest over. Then she started to cry. She collapsed and dug her fingers into the dry grass. She tore up a dandelion and jammed it in her mouth with the mints. It was bitter, so she spit it out.

I'm not Scarlett O'Hara either, she thought. This isn't working. I should go back to New York and look for a job. That's all. That's all there is to it. Suddenly Laura was struck in the face by the meanness of what had been done to her. If he'd been looking for his mother all along, why hadn't he gone after Marie? But what difference did it make? No man ever wanted you for yourself, no matter who you were. You were never more than a body that happened to suit a fantasy.

"Oh, Jamie," Laura wailed aloud. "I loved you so. I even loved the sound of your name." Laura was struck again. Yes, it was true. She had. She had loved him, loved him, loved him so.

For a long time Laura sat still and quiet and numb. Then she got up, leaving the rest of the groceries for the raccoons. When she reached the car, she realized that she had no idea where to go. Then she thought, I'll go to Marie's. And she got in and drove blindly, with her eyes wide open and dry and aching.

Herbert did not see Arthur approaching until it was too late. He almost got up, but decided it was futile to run anymore. They'd been together too many years; Arthur would pick up his scent no matter where he went. It was best just to get it over with now.

"You again," Herbert said.

"May I join you?" Arthur asked. "Or are you waiting for the rest of the N.R.A. convention to arrive?"

"Sit down. I'm tired of running."

"Good. So am I. It's exhausting to have to follow the tracks of Michelin tires for thirty miles."

"I feel for you."

"Still, I can pick out Michelin tire tracks in the dirt the way Indian braves used to be able to spot hoofprints."

"You always did have arcane talents."

Arthur was eyeing the threesome at the bar.

"Why is it that whenever middle America goes out for a drink they have one and right away they look like they're five hours into the wedding reception?" he wondered aloud.

"I wouldn't know," Herbert said.

"You used to care deeply about such things," Arthur reflected. "Remember when we were young and didn't have very much money? How we'd go to Jones Beach and walk along it and have a contest to see who could spot the most hair curlers?"

"Yes, I do remember," Herbert replied. "I remember a lot more than you do from the early days."

"Yes. I know. You always were the romantic. You've always had a sentimental streak. I suppose that was what drew you to Marie, wasn't it? A certain nostalgia for . . . women. In my way, I'm capable of the same thing, though I express it differently. Remember last November when we flew up to Cable Harbor for a weekend and went to the church fair and I bought all those aprons and pot holders and preserves from the old ladies? Of course, I wouldn't have dreamed of going to bed with any of them, though."

"And they never dreamed that you would have their aprons and pot holders polyurethaned to make wall coverings for some faggy restaurant on Columbus Avenue."

"They have their handiwork; I have mine. How can anyone dance to country and western music? Will you answer me that? I'd also like to know if it's all over between us."

The bartender, whose thighs were almost as thick as Arthur's waist, came over and asked Arthur if he would like a drink. Arthur said he would like one of the Miller Lites that his friend was drinking.

"Yes, it is all over between us," Herbert said when the bartender went to get Arthur's beer.

"Why?" Arthur asked.

"Because I'm sick of your fooling around."

"You mean my tricking out."

"Of course."

"What about your tricking out with Marie?"

"That was different."

"How so?"

"She's a woman."

"Let me get this straight. It's all right for you to sleep with a woman when you feel like it. But it's not all right for me to sleep with men. Would you mind explaining that?"

"No. I don't mind. Marie and I were sleeping together out of need. Most women who sleep with men—or other women for that matter—do it out of need. You trick out because of greed. It's a fundamental difference. Between us."

"Would you like to know how I knew you'd be here?" Arthur asked.

"Not especially."

"I'll tell you anyway. When we drove by this place last summer you said it looked like a chicken coop and I said, 'It is a chicken coop . . . for the poor working stiffs who start drinking at eleven in the morning because they can't understand how they came to cross the road.' "

"Maybe you were right," Herbert allowed. "The other side of the road is a bar. So is the end of the road. And also the road not taken, which in my case—too bad for me—was Marie."

"Another thing I wanted to mention," Arthur put in. "I've become a father."

"What?" Herbert appeared to be genuinely surprised. The bartender returned with Arthur's beer. Arthur took out his wallet and showed him a picture.

"That's my foster son," Arthur said.

"Nice-looking kid," the bartender said.

"Isn't he, though?" Arthur replied. "He wanted to be a U.S. marine, but now he's in southern California stymying Rona Barrett, which is a lot rougher than getting through Parris Island, let me tell you."

"Once a marine, always a marine," the bartender said.

"Hey, Mike, gimme another rye high," sang out the disjointed woman at the bar.

The bartender said to Herbert and Arthur, "Let me know if you want a couple more," and then went back to his post.

"Where'd you pick up this one?" Herbert asked coldly.

"He really is my foster son," Arthur said, showing Herbert the picture. "His name is Chad. I really have set him up out there. He'll be moving into the house tomorrow. I've already spent half of this month's egg money on a Porsche 928. It's probably sitting in his driveway now. I told them to put a ribbon around it, but I don't know whether they'll follow through or not."

"You're all set, then, aren't you?"

"How do you mean?"

"Did you chase me down just to show me my replacement?"

"Replacement? I don't think you understand. Chad is my son. When I had him sent over I didn't know I was going to adopt him, but it worked out that way. Because I didn't want to sleep with him. What I wanted, I found out, was to provide for him. The way I've always been provided for. Chiefly by you—"

"I never provided for you. You were the one with the Midas touch."

"Yes, but you were the one who provided the love. That's what you're all about. That's what you've always been all about. You loved me. And I thrived on it. And now I've grown enough to love you back."

"Yes," said Herbert. "You're right about me. About me and loving. It's always been my great strength. And my greatest weakness."

"Leave it to Marie to pick up on that," Arthur said. "She has a

278

gift for stepping into a vacuum. Or coming on like a hopped-up vacuum cleaner. Whichever."

"What are you going to do now, adopt all your tricks?"

"No, just this one. The last one. One child is enough of a responsibility on top of being responsible for myself."

"Do you mean to say you're through trying to trick out?"

"Something like that."

"And didn't you just say that you love me?"

"It just slipped out."

Herbert allowed himself to smile.

"It's funny," he said. "In a way you always were a father figure to me. Because my real father died before we ever came to understand each other. And now you . . . you're actually able to tell me you love me. At least I've lived to see the other father in my life grow up. And that's something. It's a hell of a lot, in fact."

"Let's shake on that," Arthur said manfully. "No . . . on second thought, let's get up and dance."

They got up from their table. The jukebox was playing a Hank Williams song. Arthur and Herbert began dancing to it slowly.

"Faggots," said one of the men who was sitting at the bar.

The woman who was drinking rye highs and who looked as though she had washed her face with a dishcloth said, rather drunkenly, "Now, now, Jake, you shud-unt say things like tha'. After all, Jesus was a Jew."

The bartender and the men at the bar laughed at her.

"Oh no," said the woman. "I got it mixed up . . . didn' I?"

CHAPTER TWENTY FIVE

"My husband is gone," Marjorie said. "He never came home. And now he's gone. I know it."

"He may yet come in," Dan said. He was trying to be reassuring, but something in Marjorie's voice, something that was more collusion than confidence, together with his growing interest in her, persuaded him to start thinking along different lines.

"Let's say he does make himself scarce for a while," Dan said. "Is that going to materially affect your participation in the town meeting?"

"What do you think?" Marjorie replied. "This is a small town. People are going to say he's running away from something. From me. They might even say he's running away from something he did."

"Such as?"

"That girl who was murdered."

"Wait a minute," Dan said. "Wait just a minute now. Hasn't anybody in that town seen the coroner's report? There was no evidence of foul play whatsoever. That girl died of a broken neck that was sustained when she fell—or jumped—from the balcony of the room she was in in the Perry House. That's what happened. Nobody raped her or bludgeoned her or anything else."

"That's only a coroner's report. That's not what people think. They think everything's a cover-up. And if I go to bat for your company—with my husband missing—they're going to think I'm part of the cover-up."

Dan tried to think. He looked out his window at the buildings one on top of the other. He found them encouraging, in situations like this, when he felt pressured: one solid brick at a time and pretty soon you had solid rows where even the weather didn't have a look-in. All right. First, how was she? How was she really?

"Are you afraid for your husband's safety?" Dan asked. "Or your own?"

"My husband?" Marjorie replied. "No, I think he's just . . . up and left. I've seen it coming. But now it's happened. He's actually gone. And right now I'm at a loss. Dan . . . I don't know what to do."

"Did he leave you any money? Have you checked your bank account?"

"Money? We're middle-class people. We consider ourselves ahead anytime the Master Charge isn't filled right up to the five-hundred-dollar limit. God, I haven't even thought about money. As soon as the kids find out that their father has taken off they're going to be asking me who's going to pay for their college. What am I going to tell them?"

"Let's worry about first things first," Dan said. "Let's say you were to act as if your husband had never left when that town meeting comes up. Do you think anybody is going to have the nerve to make an issue of his disappearance?"

"I can think of one person in particular," Marjorie replied. "Of course, there's your ex-wife, too. I don't know what she has in mind. And I don't know if I can fend off these attacks if I have doubts myself."

"What doubts? I told you there was no evidence of foul play in that girl's death."

"If I could only be sure. If I could just convince myself. Maybe if I went out to the Perry House and saw for myself. Maybe I could sense from the surroundings whether or not George . . ."

Dan looked at the telephone receiver quizzically; then he said, "I don't think I understand."

"It's hard to explain. It's just that if I went there . . . to where it happened . . . I'd *know*. Call it woman's intuition if you want to. I just need, for my own peace of mind, to settle this once and for all. All I need is to account for that missing hour."

"I didn't know women had intuition anymore."

"Maybe in New York they don't. But around here some of them have so much of it they make radio contact with the flying saucers."

"What?"

"That's not worth talking about. I'm sorry I mentioned it. But I do mean what I said about going out to the Perry House . . . to convince myself that . . . George isn't guilty of anything other than desertion."

"How long have we got before the town meeting?"

"A week. Maybe ten days if Caleb who takes care of the town hall doesn't get over his annual attack of allergies before then."

"All right. What if I fly up there in the next couple of days and take you out to the Perry House to look around? Would that help to rebuild your self-confidence?"

"Oh, I don't want to put you to all that trouble."

"It's no trouble. Will it help? Yes or no?"

"Yes, I think so."

"Then it's settled. I'll book a room in Munsonville again. I'll call you back as soon as my secretary's got everything set up. Okay?"

"O-okay."

"Do you have enough money?"

"Yes, there's some in the bank. Not a lot. I wasn't kidding about most of our savings being in what we don't owe Master Charge."

"Then you won't have to be worrying about money right away. That's all I wanted to know. When I see you we'll talk about putting you on my company's payroll—temporarily."

"Mr. Cartey, I don't need charity. And I wouldn't accept it even if I did."

"I'm not talking about charity either. Being on the payroll is part of being in politics."

"I never said I was in politics. I was just a concerned citizen."

"But now you've got to be a little concerned with your own welfare. Trust me, Marjorie. I'll talk to you later."

"I don't have much choice, do I? I've got to trust someone."

After she hung up, Marjorie sat in the profound silence that follows a long-distance telephone call. It was true, she decided. She had to trust someone. It was always the same, whether you were putting yourself in the hands of a doctor or a dentist or a lawyer or—twenty years ago—a young man whose chin was shining with perspiration in the June humidity. You had to trust someone. And

282

anytime you had to have a working relationship with a man, you had to expect a series of meetings that would be like little marriages. With all the give and take. The question about this next meeting with Dan Cartey was whether or not there was going to be a consummation; Marjorie had been aware, during that first dinner at the Munsonville Inn, that she could have scratched the table linen and found underneath a made-up bed (and you could call that woman's intuition or whatever you liked). Would she take advantage of it this time?

She wasn't sure. She would have to cross that bridge when she came to it. But the only thing that stood out clearly in the haze was that bridge; and Marjorie had learned one thing in her life if she had learned nothing else: when you're sure of your footing, start walking.

When Marie answered the dull knock on her door she found Laura. Who looked as though she had anemia or was using gray pancake base. She collapsed in Marie's arms.

"My God, what's happened?" Marie said.

"He . . ." was all Laura could manage.

"Oh, no. You weren't attacked, were you?"

"Worse," Laura moaned.

"Oh lord. We've got to get you to a hospital."

"No hospital," Laura said, sagging to the floor and supporting herself there, with her arms, like a worn-out scrubwoman. "No hospital . . . please, no hospital . . . just a drink."

"A drink?" Something seemed to dawn on Marie. "Jamie. Where is he?"

"With his mother," Laura said. Her face was gray and desolate. She looked as if every tear had been squeezed out of her soul and there was nothing left but dry pain.

"Oh shit," said Marie. She gently helped Laura to her feet and walked her out to the pool and got her into a chair. Then she hurried in to the bar, poured a glass of vodka, and telephoned Vivian.

"Laura's having some terrible problem with Jamie," Marie said. "She's here and she's a wreck. I don't know what he said to her, but it must have been terrible."

Vivian groaned. After the fact sank in, she said to Marie, "Stay with her. I'll be right over."

Vivian hung up and began looking for her car keys. A sense of duty was running in her like cold tap water; that was what you did in these situations: washed the dishes, baked cakes, found rooms for people coming in for the funeral. (Vivian's mother had always been skilled at such organizing—funerals made her come alive, and Vivian had inherited at least the efficiency if not the morbid satisfaction. She knew what had to be done for Laura and she was ready to do it.) Putting a bottle of Valium in her purse, Vivian rushed outside. The sun was shining brightly even though it was late afternoon. It certainly was spiteful, the sun, Vivian thought. Right through any sadness, it went on shining. It reminded Vivian of her mother and reminded her of what she must not become: a functional widow, a guardian angel of the death notices. Yes, she would try to help Laura, but she would not, must not, allow herself to feel even the smallest satisfaction in Laura's tragedy—her winding up, so soon, like everybody else.

Marie's front door was wide open. Vivian walked in, looked around, and saw Marie and Laura through the living room windows. Laura was prostrate in a chair by the pool, and Marie was spoon-feeding her something. Vivian went outside.

"The poor kid," she said.

Marie was holding a teaspoon up to Laura's lips, trying to get her to take some nourishment.

Looking around when she heard Vivian, Marie said, "I'm trying to get a little of this booze into her, but it's dribbling all over her chin." Laura appeared to be close to comatose.

Vivian fumbled with her pocketbook. Realizing what she had brought, Marie picked up a candy dish that was full of mixed nuts and tossed them into the pool. Then she grabbed Vivian's pocketbook away from her, opened it, and pulled out the bottle of Valium. She emptied the bottle into the candy dish, wolfed down three of the pills, and then tried to get Laura to take some too. Laura merely shook her head, without opening her eyes.

"You shouldn't be trying to feed her vodka," Vivian said. "She needs to have some food in her. What have you got in the refrigerator?"

"How should I know?" Marie replied. "I leave that to Elsie, and she's off today. Maybe there's some leftover carrot soup."

"She needs chicken soup and some mothering," Vivian said, feeling Laura's forehead for fever.

"No, not that," Laura muttered.

"Of course not that," Marie said. And she hissed at Vivian, "Chicken soup and mothering indeed. This girl is heartsick, that's all. Do you want to make her dependent on top of it?"

"I just want her to have something in her stomach, if you don't mind," Vivian persisted. "When you don't have anything in your stomach it all turns to acid. Your feelings, I mean. Grief is bad enough without letting it corrode you inside."

Marie seemed to experience a momentary indigestion. She said to Vivian, "All right, if you insist. You know where the refrigerator is. Go. Go."

Vivian went to the kitchen while Marie rubbed Laura's hand to stimulate the circulation. In the refrigerator Vivian found some celery. She stuffed it with cottage cheese, adding spices at random in the vague hope that they might have some herbal property that would waft into Laura's blocked psyche.

The stuffed celery did seem to take hold of Laura at least enough so that she could munch a little, even though she did take a terribly long time swallowing. Gradually Marie and Vivian were able to get her to sit up and take a swallow of vodka, and then a Valium, and with it another swallow of vodka. All Vivian could think of was the time she tried to feed a family of baby birds through an eye dropper. (They all died, and it had taken Vivian forever to get over the idea that once the nest falls out of the tree, you're doomed.)

Bit by bit, Laura got out the story of what had happened to her. She was just so tired of hearing about Jamie's mother all the time that she finally said something to him. And one thing led to another. And he got mad and admitted that it was his mother he really wanted, that he was only fantasizing when he was with her, Laura.

Laura said she couldn't stand hearing, from him, what she had suspected all along, in her worst moments. She told how she had driven to the edge of a cliff but hadn't had the courage to throw herself over because she wasn't Anna Karenina, just a little nobody who had gone into publishing because she thought it would be like the movies, only more dignified, but then it turned out to be like television, only less dignified, and a lot like life. The way it all worked out.

Vivian and Marie both had blank looks on their faces. Vivian stuck two Valiums in her stuffed celery and began to nibble on it.

"Laura," Marie began, "I don't know any gentle way to put this. . . . You're a little idiot. Don't you know anything about men at all? Don't you realize that they all want to be taken care of? That they're just looking for their mothers?"

"For once she's right, Laura," Vivian agreed. "They're a bunch of little boys who want to be taken care of. And that's what good little girls are supposed to do. Take care of all the nasty little boys. And the kids, too. Until they grow up, the good little girls, and become women who are capable to taking care of themselves. Like I'm doing. Oh, Laura, why don't you come work with me in my shop?"

Marie stared at Vivian.

"Don't you have any shame?" she said. "The dress shop! How can you even mention it at a time like this? Why, you're like one of those Los Angeles funeral homes that put their ads on the benches where the old people sit waiting for buses!"

A twinge of guilt made Vivian's fingers twitch. No, I am *not* like my mother, she reassured herself, quickly. If Laura ever needed an interest in life, she needs one now. What's Marie's interest, besides men and booze?

"Look, Marie," Vivian replied, "I don't know how much of this celery and Valium I'm going to consume before this evening is over"—one pill was already gone—"but at least I know that when September rolls around I'll have more to look forward to than *that*." She stabbed at the vodka bottle with her celery, making it teeter. Marie threw out her hand to stop it from pitching forward, like a mother restraining a child when a car stops suddenly.

"I don't want to be anybody's mother without even being pregnant first," Laura said wearily. "It's double jeopardy. I want to be me."

"You have to fight to get to be yourself," Vivian shot back. "That's the biggest part of the problem. We haven't fought hard enough." Without thinking, Vivian snatched the vodka bottle off the table.

286

"Give me that!" Marie shouted.

"Back off, lady!" Vivian shrieked. Reaching inside her pocketbook, she pulled out her handkerchief and soaked it with vodka. Then she crammed it into the neck of the bottle.

"What are you doing?" Marie yelled.

Vivian took out her cigarette lighter and flicked it. She lit the handkerchief.

"That's going to explode!" Marie screamed.

Laura closed her eyes because she was feeling dizzy.

With the vodka bottle flaming in her hand, Vivian rotated her arm in clumsy circles. She let go, and the bottle arced into the air like a flare. Smashing on the rocks in front of the house, the bottle lit up the twilight with flames.

"What are you trying to do, you lunatic, burn my house down?"

Vivian watched with pleasure as the flames danced against the lowering sky; without responding to Marie with a look, she said, "It's just one more bonfire out on the rocks. Your house isn't threatened, Marie. You are. That bonfire is being fed by your breakfast drink."

"Everybody's going nuts this summer," Marie muttered. "It must be the heat."

"I'm not crazy," Vivian said. "But I am out of patience. I admit it. I'm sick of this system; I'm sick and tired of men always being on top. I'm fed up with men. I resent their penises and their prerogatives."

"Penises and prerogatives," Laura said dully. "That sounds like a book by Jane Austen."

Vivian knelt in front of Laura and began pleading with her.

"Don't give in to it," she begged. "Don't let the system beat you."

"She doesn't want to sell dresses, Vivian," Marie said.

"Maybe I do," Laura said. "At least when you've picked out a nice dress for yourself, you know that . . . that there really doesn't have to be a reason for prettiness. It's enough sometimes . . . just to be you and pretty, like a morning glory by the side of the road."

" 'Full many a flower is born to blush unseen,' " said Marie. " 'And waste its sweetness on the desert air.' That's from 'Gray's Elegy.' The poem I memorized for Sister Don Bosco when I was in junior high. It's really a wonderful poem. It has a warning in it, to the rich, not to mock the 'useful toil' and 'homely joys' of poor people. I took that advice to heart. I've always been extra nice to those older

287

women you see behind the counters in Bonwit's, because, in a way, I know I'm one of them. . . ."

"Oh, you're worse than Herbert with his Shakespeare," Vivian said. "God, it's stifling here. Let's go somewhere. Let's get some fresh air. This swimming pool is stagnant. It's not refreshing. Nothing is refreshing that alimony pays for."

"Vodka is . . ." Marie began, but Vivian had grabbed her by the hand. Pushing Marie along, she also scooped up Laura.

"What are you doing?" Marie protested. "With that fire burning out there, and Laura in a state of shock. Laura has to sit and rest."

"No way," Vivian said. "We're going for a ride—the three of us— *on my son's motorcycle*. We're going to tear up this town, just like Marlon Brando in *The Wild One*." Taking Laura by the hand, Vivian headed for her car. Reluctantly, Marie followed them.

Marie didn't believe that any of this was actually happening until Vivian bundled her and Laura out of her car and led them into the murky garage that stood beside her house. When Vivian pulled away the tarpaulin, sure enough, there it was, a huge motorcycle with a sidecar.

"We'll be killed on that thing," Marie said. "I want to go home, right now."

"The only way you'll get there is on this bike," Vivian said.

"It sort of looks like fun," said Laura. Her voice was as detached as that of an idle patient in a mental institution. She ran her finger along the motorcycle's bulbous gas tank.

Vivian went to a shelf and opened a long, narrow box. Inside was a bunch of old fireworks: Roman candles and rockets and cherry bombs. Vivian filled the pockets of her dress with cherry bombs and piled rockets and Roman candles in the crook of her arm as though she were gathering flowers for a bouquet.

"I'll drive," Vivian announced. "Marie, you can ride behind me, and, Laura, you can get in the sidecar—and be my gunner."

Laura climbed into the sidecar and sat there with her feet pushed out to the nose cone and a comfy, almost infantile look on her face. She might as well have been in a stroller was what Marie thought, watching her and growing increasingly alarmed. Vivian handed the clump of fireworks to Laura and, hiking up her dress, mounted the motorcycle.

"It'll run away with you and probably crash through one end of the garage," Marie said desperately.

"Nyah," said Vivian. "I watched my son run this thing enough times. It's just like a car only it's more macho. You run it by fucking with it." So saying, Vivian rose in the air and came down with a thrust, punching a rod with her foot. The motorcycle chuffed and vibrated. Vivian stomped on it again. There was a burble from the exhaust pipes, and then a roar.

"Climb on in back of me, Marie," Vivian said.

"I don't want to die," Marie whined.

"Chicken," said Laura.

Marie realized that she couldn't let Laura ride off alone with Vivian, what with Vivian having some sort of nervous breakdown and Laura acting like a sullen child, so she climbed on, and closed her eyes tightly. Vivian pulled a pair of goggles off the handlebar and put them on. She handed another pair to Marie, and pointed out a third pair, which was on the fuselage of the sidecar, to Laura.

"Here we go," said Vivian as she twisted the throttle.

"Whee," said Laura.

"Oh shit," said Marie.

The big black BMW surged backward out of the garage. Vivian changed gears and roared around the semicircle of her driveway and onto the road. Marie didn't know if the wind was yanking her hair or if it was standing on end because of her terror.

"Slow down," she shouted to Vivian.

"Are you kidding," Vivian shouted back. "I'm not even in second gear yet."

The motorcycle reacted to second gear as if it were born again.

"Where are we going?" Marie yelled.

"To Linda Keller's house," Vivian said.

Marie was not sure whether she had heard rightly or not, but she had a vague sense that some area had been targeted. Laura was gulping air like some kind of natural drunk.

They charged into the Keller driveway with all the motorcycle's lights on and its horn beeping and Laura's hands in the air as if she were grasping at salt spray. Spurting in tight circles around Linda Keller's lead vase with its geraniums spilling out, Vivian threw a handful of cherry bombs at Laura and said, "Shoot these off!" Laura fumbled with the short fuse and Vivian's cigarette lighter, finally produced sparks, and threw the first cherry bomb. It went off not ten feet away from the circling motorcycle, with an echoing report like a pistol shot.

"Fire at will!" Vivian screamed. Systematically, Laura lit three cherry bombs and launched them. Each bang seemed louder than the one before.

"Linda-aah," Vivian shouted. "Come out. Come out, come out, wherever you are!"

A figure that appeared to be trying to shelter itself in the quilting of a housecoat appeared in the doorway.

"Yea-ay-ay," Vivian hollered.

"Watch out, Linda," Marie yelled. "They're out of their minds."

"Bullshit," said Vivian. She brought the motorcycle to a stone-whipping halt and leaped off it. Grabbing a Roman candle from Laura, she stuck it in the ground and lit it. There was a hiss followed by a steady pumping of sparks that rose and flickered and died.

"Tell me honestly, Linda," Vivian yelled, "did you ever realize what was happening to you in dancing school when you learned to follow the boy's lead?"

"No . . . I didn't," Linda said. She was standing in her doorway, apparently unable to decide what to do with her hands.

"I didn't have any inkling either," Marie confessed.

Vivian turned on her as if she had heard the profession of the converted.

"Then get *mad*, you dolt," she shouted.

"I am . . . *mad*," Marie responded.

Vivian rubbed her hands together with wild glee and leaped back onto the motorcycle.

Out of the Keller driveway they roared.

"That's it, peel rubber," Marie shouted. "Onward! On to . . . the Perry House!"

Streaking along the shore road, they reached the darkened Perry House in minutes.

"Where's the guard?" Vivian said.

"Probably inside," Marie whispered. "Let's rocket the place and get him outside."

"Let's try one of these plastic things with wings on it," Vivian said. She selected from Laura's lap a stubby missile that bubbled when it was shaken, as though it were a species of torpedo.

"Let's see, it says 'Set on a flat surface,'" Vivian said. She placed the device on the hotel's tiled walk and lit it. Just as it whooshed into the air with a shower of yellow sparks, a face appeared in an upstairs window. It was the guard.

"Hey, you," he yelled.

"Get bent, buster," Marie yelled back.

The face disappeared.

"He's coming to get us," Laura warned.

"Give me that string of firecrackers," Vivian said. Laura handed Vivian what looked like a belt of machine gun bullets. Vivian lit it and tossed it at the building's main entrance. Then she jumped back onto the motorcycle just as the guard came through the door. The firecrackers went off. Hopping as if he had been given a hot foot, the guard was trying to avoid the explosions all around him.

"Who's next?" Marie asked Vivian as they accelerated away from the frantic watchman.

"Let's get his *tent*," Laura said.

"Go after Jamie?" Marie said in disbelief.

"She might as well if she's not going to be his mother," Vivian replied.

For four miles nobody could talk because of the rushing wind.

As they turned up the dirt road that led to Jamie's camp, Marie said, "Be careful you don't land us in these woods."

"What are you going to do to him?" Vivian asked Laura.

"I don't know," Laura shouted above the roar, "I don't know."

Then they were in the clearing.

"Circle the tent," Laura shouted.

Vivian nodded. Reaching out as far as she could, Laura snagged one of the ropes that was supporting the tent. Marie got the idea and grabbed another rope.

"Hold on," Laura yelled.

"It's pulling me off," Marie shrieked. There was a moment of sharp tension—Marie thought her arm was going to be pulled out of its socket—and then the tent collapsed.

"Bravo!" Vivian shouted.

Twisting the motorcycle's throttle, she headed for the dirt road.

"He wasn't even around," Laura said.

They were a half mile down the shore road when Vivian heard the siren behind them.

"Hold on, girls," Vivian said. "We're going to make a run for it."

She turned the throttle and the motorcycle flashed around a bend, lifting Laura's sidecar into the air.

Marie clung to Vivian and prayed that she could go back to being a simple Catholic schoolgirl with plaid knee socks and a simple blue frock uniform exactly like everybody else's. She would draw pictures of nuns in art class and then she would become a nun and walk by the sea on retreats for inspiration and her life would not be anything like this.

Laura was dropping cherry bombs in the path of the pursuing police car.

There was no stopping Vivian, Marie realized. She had hunkered down on the motorcycle and her body was rigid with madness or maniacal glee.

"He's going to start shooting at us," Marie whimpered.

"Really?" Vivian yelled. The motorcycle screamed across the road, shooting sparks, and barreled up a dirt fire road. Lester, who was responding to a disturbance-of-the-peace call about somebody shooting off fireworks, had spotted the speeding motorcycle and pursued it. But in the first quarter mile he had decided it must be Hell's Angels who were touring Maine after the races in Loudon. He was about to radio for help when the bike veered off the road and he had to put down the mike in order to keep his grip on the wheel.

Deeper and deeper into the woods the motorcycle roared. Marie had to duck to keep from being slashed by low-hanging branches. Laura burrowed into the sidecar.

Lester's police cruiser was wallowing in the ruts of the road. The headlights could not keep up with the multiplying darkness. The solid black ahead that Lester thought was the road's clearing kept shifting. Ten feet ahead of the cruiser's hood the black suddenly became the trunk of a huge spruce. There was no time to stop. The cruiser thudded into the tree and its sheet metal folded up stiffly like a milk carton. Lester banged his forehead against the steering wheel and was knocked out and immediately began to dream that his wife was being kidnapped by a flying saucer. The flying saucer was full of little men who looked like glowing Hummels, and at the controls was a creature with Darth Vader's helmet and Evelyn's body. Lester couldn't do anything to help. He couldn't even move.

"Where does this come out?" Marie wailed. "If that cop doesn't catch up with us, we'll be lost in these woods forever."

Vivian didn't hear Marie. She was concentrating on walloping the dirt road with the motorcycle's front wheel. Ahead she thought she saw a brightness; maybe they were near the shore road. It wasn't the shore road, though. Ahead was a grassy pocket in the woods where an abandoned 1955 Ford, peppered with buckshot, was rusting away. Near the rusting Ford was a moped, and on the ground were two very young teenagers with a beach blanket over them. They were fucking.

That was what Marie said as soon as she saw them hopping up, naked, in the glare of the BMW's unforgiving headlight.

"Shame on you!" Marie yelled at the kids as they made for the bushes.

"Another one being suckered into single-parenthood," Vivian said. She bounced them across the meadow and back into the blackness of the road.

"Maybe even worse than *that*," Vivian muttered, bearing down on her words as if to defy the thumping of the motorcycle's wheels. "Maybe she'll wind *up* . . . like my daughter's *friend Debbie* . . . who started out like *that* . . . and wound up taking the *Pill* . . . so many *years* . . . that she grew a *moustache* . . . and had to have . . . *electrolysis*."

"What?" Marie yelled.

"Shut up and lean when I lean or we'll wind up in a brook!" Vivian shouted back.

The fire road suddenly inclined sharply and the motorcycle burst out onto the shore road.

"Head for home quick," Marie urged.

"I am, I am," Vivian said.

They sped through the night, the wind drying the perspiration that had moistened their lips in the tight abrasive woods.

When Vivian at last eased the motorcycle into the private envelope of blackness that was her garage, Marie allowed herself the grand luxury of a deep breath. The three women sat there, in the dark, doing nothing but breathing, for what seemed a long time. Then Laura said faintly, "I feel like we're still moving."

Vivian rubbed her hands together to try to get rid of the numbness and the tingling in her fingers that the motorcycle's vibration had brought on.

Marie felt the impulses of the engine all through her body.

All three of them felt pulled forward; it was as though the momentum had to be drained away by sitting there, in the darkness of the garage.

Marie wanted to say, "Where do we go from here?"

But she was afraid even Vivian would have no answer.

CHAPTER TWENTY SIX

"So all that's happened is that you've been stared at?" Dan asked Marjorie.

"Yes, that's all," Marjorie replied. "The police have him listed as a missing person, but they haven't put out an all-points bulletin or anything like that. It's like I told you when we were eating. He's never going to make the wall of the post office."

"And your kids are taking it all right?"

"It's hard for me to be sure how they really feel. It's only been a few days. But sometimes I get this strange sensation: that they think of their father as a plumber who came for a few years and then left. They may be wondering if he's going to come back for his tools . . . beyond that, I just don't know."

"Not every father who works for a living is appreciated by his children," Dan said. "If there's such a thing as a perfect father he's probably a family dog who brings home a paycheck."

"Yes," said Marjorie. "Like Nana in *Peter Pan.*"

"Are you sure you want to go in there?" They were walking across the lawn of the Perry House when Dan asked Marjorie that question for the second time. At dinner she had said yes. And she said she was absolutely sure now, even though the bare lightbulbs burning in the building's empty rooms seemed eerie, almost like the red lights she used to see in the fun house when she was a child, the red lights that always prompted her mother to say in a spooky voice, "There's a red light. That means danger ahead." There was no danger in poking around the Perry House, Marjorie was sure, but it wouldn't be any barrel of fun either. After all, a girl had died here, and she was alone with Dan, since he had arranged for the guard to be gone this particular night. So far nobody in town was aware that they had met—twice now—and the Munsonville Inn had been tonight, as it was the first night, as quiet as a 2:00 A.M. train station. With the exception of that dizzy waitress who had to have her picture taken by the busboy *again*, this time because it was her birthday and somebody had given her a corsage (which looked homemade to Marjorie). So Marjorie felt fairly secure. Nobody had seen them driving through town, and nobody knew they were here.

The heat and humidity had returned, and the night was dripping like a wet towel. Dan walked up to one of the building's glass doors and tried a couple of keys. The second one fit. Pushing the door open, Dan waved Marjorie on inside, and then closed and locked it again behind them. Inside, the building was steel skin and bones. The floors that rested on the steel beams were just dusty plywood, and the stairs were little more than ladders.

"They speculate that the girl was using the room on the third floor that's right above us," Dan said. "You want to go up there?"

"Yes, I'd like to at least see it," Marjorie said.

"Okay, I don't know what good it'll do, but if it'll reassure you at all, it's fine with me."

"Let me just satisfy myself, that's all I ask," said Marjorie as she tested the plywood stair step with her foot.

"Don't worry, I'll be right behind you," Dan said.

Slowly they picked their way up to the third floor. There was no door on the room where the girl had supposedly stayed, and when Marjorie looked in she was almost startled by the view. Beyond the sliding glass doors was the ocean, with a broad ribbon of moonlight glistening on it.

"What a view from up here," Marjorie said.

"Nice, isn't it?" Dan replied.

"I can see how a young girl might want to camp out up here," Marjorie said. "It's certainly a romantic setting, whether it's unfinished or not." Marjorie went into the room and looked around.

"There must have been a lot of people up here doing the same thing we're doing," she said. "Look at all the footprints. They're everywhere."

"You're right about that," Dan said. "A lot of people did come up here to poke around—and they found no evidence of foul play whatsoever."

Marjorie walked up to the window. At one end of the hotel property was a stand of spruce trees. A man could approach the place through those trees and never be seen. Marjorie tried to imagine George slithering over the spruce needles. No way. Why was she here, anyway, on this fool's errand? Was it just an excuse to be with Dan?

"That railing out there was there when it happened, wasn't it?" she asked.

"Yes, it was."

"Then I don't see how she could have fallen . . . if she did fall."

Marjorie tried to push open the sliding door. It was stuck. Dan took hold of the door's handle and pulled hard. It opened with a sound of suction.

Dan stepped out on the tiled terrace. He put his hand on the railing and tugged to show Marjorie how solid it was. As he turned to come back into the room, his right leg shot out from under him as if it were on a ski.

Marjorie screamed.

She thought he was gone. He had gone over the edge. But then she saw his gold watch and his fingers grasping one of the railing's iron balusters.

He was dangling in thin air.

Marjorie rushed forward. She slid and turned her ankle. The tiles were as slick as a pan rubbed with Crisco. Crawling forward, on her knees, Marjorie reached desperately for Dan's hand.

"Hold on, hold on," she pleaded.

She grabbed the sleeve of his jacket with one hand, and got a grip on the baluster with the other.

"Pull," Dan said.

Marjorie yanked with all her might. Dan was able to grab the baluster with both hands and, with a tremendous effort born of panic, raised his leg in the air until his shoe hooked on the balcony.

Panting, he slowly hoisted himself up and rolled over on the tiles, exhausted. Marjorie felt as though she had run ten miles.

"God almighty," said Marjorie when she could breathe again.

Dan was still panting. He wiped the sweat out of his eyes and shook his head at Marjorie in disbelief.

"It's these tiles," Marjorie said. "The dampness. The dampness makes them as slippery as a greased skillet."

Dan shook his head again and muttered, "Oh, Jesus."

"What kind of tiles are these? I've never seen any like them."

"Mexican," Dan said slowly. "Maybe Colombian. I don't know. I think I remember the architect saying they weren't as expensive as they looked."

"That could be because they're made out of molded candle wax instead of clay," Marjorie replied. "Oh brother. To think that you nearly got killed because of . . . " Marjorie did not finish her thought; she suddenly remembered why they had come here, and she realized that she had found what she was looking for: final proof of her husband's innocence—as if there had ever been any real doubt. It was clear what had happened to the girl. All it had taken was one false step.

"Let's just go," Marjorie said. "I've seen enough."

Dan was loosening his tie with the relief of someone who'd stepped down from a scaffold after standing on the trap.

"You and me both," said Dan.

They closed the sliding door and carefully descended the make-shift stairs, trying out every other one as if it were a thin branch.

Outside, in the moonlight, Marjorie appeared to be brought up short.

"What is it?" Dan asked her.

Marjorie put her hand over her eyes. She said, "I was just thinking. That poor girl. She probably went out on that balcony to watch the sunrise. That's the sort of thing a girl that age would do. She went out on the balcony to drink it all in—and the tiles were damp with the dew—so she slipped and broke her neck."

Marjorie snapped her fingers.

"Life seems so complicated," she said. "And death is so simple. So quick. It can happen in the wink of an eye. I can't help but wonder . . . What is life, anyway? Do we just keep banging on doors and rattling doorknobs until a certain door opens unexpectedly and we push through into . . . emptiness?"

"No, there's more to it all than that," Dan said.

"What is there, then?" Marjorie asked. "Real estate? Casino gambling? Small-town politics? Childbirth? My mother told me, 'When you have a baby it's really something.' It was really something. But what comes after it? What do you have besides the memory of pain and one parting after another?"

"You have the will to hang on if you don't have anything else," Dan replied. "I know. I was hanging on for dear life a few minutes ago. And if you're lucky you'll find somebody who'll hold on to you when you're losing your grip. Like you just did for me, Marjorie."

"But I only . . ."

He was putting his arms around her.

"There are two ways to live," Dan said. "You can live alone. And when you die it's just a matter of moving from one empty room to another. Or you can live with someone, live *for* someone, and then when you die you die knowing that in the next room there's somebody waiting for you."

Marjorie felt weak in his arms. He kissed her, and she knew then where all her strength had gone. She had saved it to respond to him.

They drove back to the Munsonville Inn. Marjorie wasn't concerned about walking by the desk clerk with Dan. She didn't even feel concerned about the upcoming town meeting. Nor did she care about George's disappearance; her marriage to him was now officially over. Their partnership—in owing money—was dissolved.

And Marjorie was filling the gap in her life as soon as it opened up.

Laura moved in with Marie. She didn't even go back to Jamie for her clothes. Instead she called up her mother and asked her to send over the maid to pick them up. (The maid was Peruvian and was wonderful at doing errands because she knew only enough English to repeat what she had been told, and stood there repeating it until whoever it was came up with the required items.) Mrs. Damon was heartbroken to hear that Laura had broken up with Jamie. She said that he had been calling constantly. Why didn't Laura at least listen to what he had to say? Or let him see her? Laura would not say why. And she was adamant about not speaking to him or seeing him. Ever again. Mrs. Damon went into mourning for her hopes. When she arrived at Marie's with Laura's clothes, she was wearing the darkest pair of sunglasses she owned and daubing under the lenses with her handkerchief. The Peruvian maid helped Laura with her things. Mrs. Damon stuck her head out of the car window to kiss Laura and to say, "I don't know what happened between you two, but I do know that when I talk to him on the telephone he sounds terribly unhappy. Won't you at least give me permission to let him know where you are?"

"No, I won't," said Laura. "It's very simple. I'm not going to allow myself to be hurt that badly ever again."

"Well, what are you going to do?" Mrs. Damon asked, daubing again.

"Learn the dress business," Laura said. "Or go back to publishing. I may even start writing Regency romances. All I know is that any fervor I have left is going to be channeled into a business."

"Oh, Laura, what do you know about Regency romances?"

"That they're just typing done in a long dress. Please, Mother, don't ask me so many questions. I'll survive. I always have."

The Peruvian maid got back into the car. Laura experienced an irrational moment during which she pictured a group of Peruvian women with odd black hats reading Regency romances in the subway. Laura herself was on the back of each book jacket, photographed in a long dress in the middle of an open field, with her hair blowing in the wind. Maybe it wouldn't be such a bad life at that.

Dejectedly Mrs. Damon started the car.

"Laura, you're *sure* now," she said.

Laura nodded.

Mrs. Damon shook her head. And drove away.

Marie was sitting by the pool with a vodka and grapefruit juice.

"Is your wardrobe intact?" she asked Laura.

"I don't know," Laura replied. "I just plunked it all down upstairs."

"Was your mother at all sympathetic or did she just act like a mother?"

"She acted like a mother," Laura said, picking up her own glass of vodka and grapefruit juice.

"Maybe you should see him, Laura. It seems that every single time your mother calls it's to tell you that Jamie is desperately trying to get in touch with you. And I don't think you should have thrown away his letter without opening it. You never know what—"

"I don't want to know," Laura said flatly. "Anything further would only interfere with my rehabilitation."

"Reconciliation is a great rehabilitator," Marie said. "Who would

300

have thought Arthur and Herbert would patch things up so soon? And then be so nice to me? Inviting me over the way they did. Believe me, Laura, it was every bit as hard for me to face them as it would be for you to see Jamie again."

"It's different with you and them," Laura said.

"How is it different? Herbert and Jamie are very much alike, emotionally, if you ask me. They're both capable of love. But their love . . . is based on a prototype."

"Yes, and Jamie's prototype is his mother."

"Herbert's prototype was his father. Now Arthur is his father . . . his father figure. I don't know for sure, Laura. But I think what happens to some of us, when we go looking for love, is that we carry in our minds an image of one—or both—of our parents. Still, it isn't the parent we really want. What we want is to satisfy a memory of need that the parent represents, somehow, in our minds."

"Jamie told me outright that when he's with me he's thinking of his mother," Laura replied.

"Or his need," Marie said. "Take me, for instance. I have this need to top my ex-husband, just once. To one-up him. And I think I might just be able to do it. Arthur said he feels Herbert and he owe me something—after all that's happened. I said, 'You don't owe me a thing. But we might be able to do something for each other if we can come up with a way of keeping busy up here. Renting rooms, for example.' "

"Renting rooms?"

"Yes. I think I may be able to persuade Arthur and Herbert to buy the Perry House and let me manage it. Wouldn't that be something? Me taking over my husband's pet project? What would his company think? His ex-wife pulling the rug out from under him. Arthur and Herbert have the money. And Arthur would love decorating a whole hotel."

"Would you really want to be stuck up here in the winter, Marie? Just to prove a point?"

"We'd probably only keep the place open through December," Marie said.

"Would that make you happy, though? Running a hotel?"

"It would straighten out a lot of things," Marie replied. "It's funny about having been married, and living in a small town for so many summers. It's as though nothing you do outside that frame of reference . . . really *counts*. It's impossible to *move*, almost, until you've evened up the score. Otherwise you're running away . . . from failure. But it's always there . . . living in the town you can't really escape from."

"I understand, I guess," Laura said. "You run away, with your suitcase, but the failure comes along. It's what's left in your bag when you've taken the last item of clothing out. Failure. And a few grains of sand that you picked up in your shoes from some beach somewhere."

"Spoken like a true romantic, Laura," Marie said. "I wonder if Vivian would like to open a dress shop in the Perry House?"

"Maybe she would," Laura said. "For my own part, I can't wait to get back to New York. And unpack my suitcase. Whether I find sand in it or not.

"When I get back to New York I'm going to have an apartment full of plants," Laura added. "And I'm going to have shelves full of books. And I'll probably get a dog, too. I'm not sure which breed yet except I'm sure it won't be a French poodle."

"I'm glad of that," Marie allowed. "Having a French poodle is like confiding too much in your hairdresser. It marks you as a certain type."

"I am going to be a certain type," Laura said. "I'm going to be comfortable living with myself. I'm going to be contented with solitude."

"You'll probably have a portable TV in your breakfast nook," Marie said. "Sometimes I pour cream on the table when I'm looking at 'Good Morning America.' If only they'd let David Hartman do that show in his pajamas."

"I may even consider celibacy," Laura said. "But even if something does happen, I'll see to it that it doesn't last longer than a year."

"Including vacations?"

"Including vacations. The truth is, Marie, I really don't want any more involvements. I want to be alone. Garbo had the right idea."

"Good grief. If every single girl thought that way New York would be a sea of trench coats and dark glasses."

"That's no worse than what you see now. An army of secretaries who get up at six in order to have an hour to put on their makeup so that when they're out on their lunch hour they'll be whistled at by the sanitation men."

"Maybe it isn't," said Marie. "Still . . . celibacy? What was that story I heard years ago about some girl who was a really ravishing beauty? How did it go? I think it was that she made a debut, and there were so many young men after her that she just couldn't make up her mind about any of them . . . so she decided to become a nun. She could have had any of them, but she chose celibacy. And I think it probably worked for her, because she chose to deny herself, not out of bitterness . . . but out of *joy*."

Laura looked away from Marie.

"Laura?" Marie said. "Somehow I can't believe he's all that hung up on his mother—or more hung up than any of the rest of them. Why don't you let him see you if he wants to? What harm can it do?"

"More harm than I'm willing to risk," Laura replied.

"Well, you can't just water the goddamn geraniums until September rolls around. You haven't left this house for a week, Laura. You've got to go out again eventually."

"I will, I will," Laura said. "I don't want to take a chance on running into *him*, that's all."

"That's a chance you'll have to take, Laura. It's not that I don't know the feeling. But this is a small town and the earth is a small planet. There are no permanent hiding places except graveyards, and even there you haven't got any more privacy than you have in a studio apartment in a high-rise. I know. My aunt is buried in Forest Lawn."

"What do you want me to do, then?" Laura said.

"Go on as if nothing had happened. You can start by going out tonight with me and Vivian . . . and Arthur and Herbert."

"Where?"

"Oh, we're going to go to that town meeting they're having about the Perry House. Arthur wants to see if the place really is such a headache that Dan's company might be willing to unload it for reasonable money. I've been trying off and on to pry information out of the woman who's going to be the moderator. I know she's on to something, and she'll have to show her hand at this meeting."

"Weren't you making calls to that talk show they have about the Perry House, too?"

"Yes, I was. For a while. The announcer started calling me the

Dragon Lady because I kept issuing warnings about the Japanese invasion. But I gave up because people weren't buying the idea that Dan is in league with Mitsubishi Heavy Industries. I think the town'll be ready to listen to whatever that Marjorie Hanson has to say tonight, though."

"Marjorie Hanson, the caterer's wife?"

"That's right. Her. Her husband recently blew town, I heard. Right after that fight the two of them had at the fashion show. They're all saying he must have left because of a guilty conscience. They think he's the one who killed that girl. Which is a joke, because nobody killed her. The coroner's report said so, but nobody wants to believe it. They want a murderer. I guess so they can tell their relatives that something big finally happened in Cable Harbor."

"I can understand," Laura said. "They can't get the *New York Post* up here."

"Anyway, I'm sure it'll be fun," Marie said, finishing her drink.

"All right," said Laura. "I'll go if you want me to. I don't think Jamie is going to show up at that."

"I don't think so either," Marie agreed. "Did you know we can't vote because we're just summer people?"

"What difference does that make?" Laura said. "I remember my father telling me a long time ago that who votes has nothing whatever to do with who decides."

An hour before the town meeting, Marjorie received an urgent telephone call from Dan. What he said to her left her disoriented. After she hung up the telephone receiver, she glanced at the papers she had prepared for the meeting; they almost seemed to be written in a foreign language.

"I figure I'll let her rap that gavel just so many times," Evelyn was saying to her husband. "And then I'll lower the boom on her."

"These pictures could be an invasion of privacy, ya know," Sanford said.

"That might be so," Evelyn allowed. "If she was the kinda woman who keeps her privates to herself. But she ain't."

CHAPTER TWENTY SEVEN

Cable Harbor's town hall looked like a stark Congregational church on the outside. Inside, it looked like the dining hall of a summer camp. The varnished pine ceiling was supported by dark beams carved like newels, and the polished oak floor was crowded with folding metal chairs. Mimeographed announcements and bulletins handwritten on index cards covered the cork board on one wall of the foyer. On the small stage at the front of the hall were a lectern and an American flag.

Since the town hall was only a stone's throw from the harbor, it was damp inside. Though it was open all winter, with heat from a wood stove and an oil burner, it was one of those wooden buildings that seem more suited for dust and silence than for human activity and human voices. Meetings held in the town hall seemed to disturb it, and the rafters turned a cold shoulder on those crowding in.

"Oh no," said Marie, when she walked into the town hall with her entourage, "steel chairs. Those things grate on my hipbones something awful."

"I go to enough auctions so I'm used to them," Vivian said.

"Folding chairs are part of the political process in Maine," Arthur observed.

"I feel like I'm part of the political process when I'm standing in a dating bar on Third Avenue with a glass of white wine in my hand," Laura said.

"Otherwise she's politically apathetic," Marie put in.

"I'm apolitical," Vivian said.

"I was that years ago and now I'm working toward being asexual," Marie said.

"Hey, you said you weren't going to put yourself down anymore," Herbert reminded her.

"Relax, my hour may be at hand," Marie said.

"Let's sit here near the back," Laura said. "Then we can watch the action."

"Elsie told me that Marjorie Hanson built up quite a reputation for herself talking on the radio," Marie whispered. "But she also said she may have ruined it by not being able to hold on to her husband. There's Elsie over there. She's with that older woman who's chewing her false teeth. The funny part of it is Elsie doesn't even know I've been in touch with Marjorie Hanson."

Marjorie walked out on the stage. She was wearing her glasses. And she had a vinyl attaché case in her hand.

"She looks pretty close-mouthed," Marie said. "She wasn't close-mouthed in the kitchen the night I nearly burned down your house, Arthur."

"I wonder what happened to her husband," Vivian said.

"What happens to any of them?" Marie replied. "The population of other women has remained pretty constant; there's somebody for everybody."

"Let's see, I should be taking notes on this, shouldn't I?" Arthur said. "We'll drop the price a hundred thousand whenever there's a boo."

"We'd better sit down," Laura said.

Marie made a cushion for herself with her shawl, and they sat. Vivian refused to sit on her shawl because it was antique. Marie told her to sit on her hat. Laura and Herbert shushed them.

Evelyn walked in, followed by Sanford. With Sanford were Lester and Donna. Lester had a bandage around his head.

Vivian pulled a pair of sunglasses out of her bag and put them on.

"What are you worried about?" Marie whispered. "They never even got our license, and you've got that motorcycle buried under a ton of newspapers and lawn furniture."

"I can't help but feel a little guilty," Vivian said. "He was the cop who saved me from that bat."

"So remember him when you're out buying everyone .356 magnums for Christmas," Marie said.

"I'm not into guns anymore," Vivian replied.

"Then send him a Fortuny dress," Marie suggested.

"That fat woman is the one who runs the market, isn't she?" Laura asked Marie.

"I wonder what her dress size is," Arthur said. "What comes after size forty-two? Canned hams?"

"That's right," Marie said. "Brother. She looks even bigger here than she does when she's behind the counter. I wonder if she even bothers to set the table when she's at home. She probably just puts a full grocery bag at each one's place. And a whole shopping cart in front of herself."

"They didn't make tent dresses like that during the twenties and thirties," Vivian pointed out. "People prided themselves on being svelte."

"And dreamed of dancing with Fred Astaire," Marie replied. "Doesn't Ginger Rogers live with her mother on a ranch somewhere? My mother envied Ginger Rogers. Once my mother got to dance with Lawrence Welk, though."

"Skinny isn't everything," Herbert said. "You don't have to stand on the scales to be admitted to Saks."

"Let's just concentrate on the proceedings, shall we?" Laura counseled. "Oh. Oh, my God!"

"What? What?" said Marie.

"The Lawrences are here. His grandparents." Laura tried to make herself small while the old lady and the old gentleman found seats.

"But he isn't," Marie said, after looking around quickly.

"Want a Valium, Laura?" Vivian offered.

Arthur said, "You should take zinc with your vitamins. It's calming. I'm having our silver martini glasses zinc-plated."

Marjorie rapped her gavel. The town hall was filled. People were standing in the back and at the sides.

Clearing her throat, Marjorie said, "I guess we all know why we're here."

"Some of us do," Evelyn muttered.

Old man Tucker was on his feet already.

"Who's that?" Marie whispered. "He looks like Don Quixote in suspenders."

307

"A lot of, uh, people think the Rockefellers ain't as powerful as they used to be," old man Tucker declared, "but they are."

"It's true you still see pictures of Happy in W," Arthur said.

After handing down an indictment of the Rockefeller family, old man Tucker lit into Henry Kissinger, Betty Ford, and the Kennedys.

"They're all in W, too," Vivian pointed out.

"I'll take off a hundred thousand because Happy was mentioned," Arthur said. "And another quarter of a million for Kissinger."

Old man Tucker verified his facts by reiterating that he was a veteran of World War I, and then as he was sitting down he called for the impeachment of Earl Warren.

"He's dead, Henry," somebody said.

"Whoever he is, then," old man Tucker bellowed.

A number of people had trouble straightening their faces.

Marjorie adjusted her glasses.

Evelyn's lip curled.

"There's only one item on the agenda tonight," Marjorie said. "The Perry House."

There were several boos, and a few people applauded and stamped. Arthur wrote more figures in his notebook. Under the commotion, Evelyn said, "Must've tried to cover up the other items."

"I have a brief history of the Perry House project here," Marjorie said, opening her attaché case. Miss Pearson, the town clerk, nodded knowingly.

"We don't want any history," somebody shouted. "We wanta know what's gonna happen with that place."

There was a roar of approval.

"I hope you all realize that the development corporation that owns the Perry House isn't under any legal obligation to tell us anything about their plans," Marjorie said.

"What about their moral obligation?" one of the lobstermen yelled.

"Morality ain't anythin' she'd know about," Evelyn said.

"We had a death upta that place," Franklin, the house painter, said. "Mighty suspicious it was, too!"

"I mighta left town myself if I was some people," Evelyn mumbled.

"She'll hear you," Sanford cautioned.

"Fat lot I care even if she does," Evelyn replied haughtily.

Donna reached over to hold Lester's hand.

"Vinegary bunch, aren't they?" Marie whispered.

"Fifty thousand off for mentioning Betty Ford?" Arthur asked.

"They have too little to occupy their minds," Vivian said.

"What do you want them to do?" Marie replied. "Open up a cooperative and sell depression housedresses?"

"Shshsh," said Laura and Herbert together.

"The fact is there's been a complete investigation of that girl's death," Marjorie said. "And it hasn't turned up anything. No evidence of foul play." Marjorie had decided not to mention the treacherous tiles. For all she knew, that could result in a lawsuit being filed by the family of the dead girl. And that would not be in Dan's best interests. Or hers.

"Hey, are you with us or against us?" Albert, the plumber, asked.

"I'd say she's out for herself. And nobody else." Evelyn was on her feet. There was a sudden hush in the hall. Marjorie aimed her eyes at Evelyn. Evelyn avoided her look, and calmly cast her smug expression to all four corners of the room, each in its turn.

"There's been a little monkey business going on, in case anybody's interested in knowing about it. A little of what they call 'conflict of interest,' although you might want to call it something else too, anytime you happen to hear that the moderator of the town meetin' has been havin' herself some nice dinners with the head of the company she's supposed to be lookin' into."

Marjorie's face went white.

"What the hell are you talkin' about, Evelyn?" Franklin, the house painter, demanded to know.

"Sanford, may I have the envelope, please," Evelyn announced grandly.

Sheepishly, Sanford handed a nine-by-twelve envelope to his wife.

"Here goes nothin'," Lester breathed.

Donna was holding his hand tightly.

"The head of the company she's supposed to be looking into?" Marie said. "Good God, you don't suppose she means . . . ?"

Arthur's pencil was poised.

Vivian and Laura and Herbert were looking at Marie with alarm. Her face appeared to be passing through a pale color spectrum.

Evelyn calmly extracted from the envelope four enlarged prints. She held them up for all to see.

"There you are," she said. "The two of them together. Just as snug as two bugs in a rug. Mrs. Hanson and Mr. Cartey, the man behind the Perry House. And I know a chambermaid over at the Munsonville Inn who's willin' to testify that they did more than just have their supper together."

Arthur broke his pencil. Marie appeared to swoon. Herbert caught Marie, and Vivian began fanning her frantically with a nineteenth-century French fan painted with a courtier in a ballgown.

There was a terrific uproar in the room. Old man Tucker shook his fist at Marjorie and shouted, "Communist! Subversive!"

"You better get down from that podium, lady!" Albert, the plumber, warned.

"Order! This meeting will come to order!" Marjorie shouted. She banged the gavel again and again.

"Better go home and straighten your bedsheets," Evelyn yelled.

"Shut up, all of you," Marjorie shrieked. She banged the gavel so hard that the head flew off and narrowly missed old man Tucker.

"You tryin' to kill somebody?" Franklin, the house painter, shouted.

"Sit down and shut up," Marjorie said. "You want to know about the Perry house? Okay, I'll tell you about it. I'll tell you every last goddamn detail."

People began to sit again, but Evelyn remained standing.

"Siddown, you fat tub of lard," Marjorie hissed at her.

"Town pump!" Evelyn yelled.

Sanford tugged her back into her seat.

"Chorus girls, caterers' wives, waitresses in Howard Johnson's," Marie murmured.

Herbert held her and Vivian popped a Valium into her mouth and tickled her throat as one does to make a cat swallow.

"All right, you want to know the story on the Perry House, then you're going to hear it," Marjorie sputtered. "This is the story: they were planning to turn it into a gambling casino. Which would probably have made your property worth a hell of a lot more than it is now."

"Did she say *money?*" old man Tucker said.

There was another uproar. Several people cornered Hopkins, the realtor, either wanting to know what he had for sale or demanding that he take their property off his listings. One of the rich Texans who had been spending summers in Cable Harbor since he married a Philadelphian let out an ear-piercing rebel yell, batted his ten-gallon hat on his knee, and said to his wife, "The Hunt brothers sure were asleep at the switch on this one."

Everyone seemed to have forgotten about Marjorie. Evelyn rose from her chair with a look of bewilderment on her face; she had an awful, hollow sense of victory slipping away from her.

"He'll have his lawyers try to take the house away from me so they can turn it into a Harrah's," Marie whimpered. Herbert rubbed her hands and Vivian fanned faster.

"Excuse me," came a voice.

"Excuse me!" A gold-headed cane was brought down on the back of one of the steel chairs with an almighty bang.

Everybody looked around. It was old Mrs. Lawrence.

"Pardon me for interrupting this demonstration," she said, "But I would like to be heard for a few moments."

Something in Mrs. Lawrence's regal manner hushed people. They began to sit down.

"Thank you all very much," Mrs. Lawrence said. "I'll be brief."

Laura began to tremble slightly.

"A couple of days ago an old friend of my husband—a Japanese gentleman—telephoned to say that an American corporation was trying to interest one of his subsidiaries in a piece of property in Cable Harbor, Maine. Of all places. He thought we should know about it. He's been very kind to us over the years because we helped him out after the Second World War when he was just getting started—manufacturing motorbikes."

There was a ripple of voices in the hall. Mrs. Lawrence went on with her story calmly.

"It seems Mr. Cartey's company has done a number of feasibility studies since beginning the Perry House project. Making a casino out of the place was not one of the most feasible ideas, but it was a way of attracting foreign investors—who might be persuaded to take the Perry House off their hands."

Marjorie blinked several times.

"Some of you may be aware that there is an ospreys' nest right out on the rocks in front of the Perry House. My husband and I often watch the ospreys through our binoculars when we're out sailing. It occurred to us that if there is any further development of the Perry House the ospreys might become endangered. So we decided we

311

really ought to do something about it. Last night my husband telephoned our friend in Tokyo. And this morning his associates in
New York were kind enough to buy the Perry House for us. It worked
out very nicely. Mr. Cartey's company was so anxious to sell to our
friend that the necessary papers were all drawn up."

There was a great intake of breath in the hall.

"As soon as the funds are transferred the Perry House will be in
our name," Mrs. Lawrence continued. "We're planning to have the
structure bulldozed next week, or as soon as the contractors can
start. Anyone who wants the stones for a patio or the sliding doors
for a family room can go out there and help himself. The land we
are going to donate to the Maine chapter of the Nature Conservancy,
which is a lovely organization that's dedicated to keeping as much
land as possible forever wild. I'm sure many of you have heard of it."

"It must have cost them three million dollars," Hopkins, the
realtor, said aloud, to himself. "Three million dollars they spent. To
protect an ospreys' nest!" He looked as though his blood pressure
were rising like mercury in a thermometer. He had to loosen his tie,
and beads of sweat popped out on his forehead.

Marjorie scooped up her briefcase and dashed out the side door.
Then she dashed back in again, apparently having forgotten something, and went straight up to Evelyn.

"Thanks for the pictures," she said. "If you could spare four
copies, I'd love to have them. I'm going to marry him, and I'll stick
your photos in the back of our wedding album."

Evelyn's eyes became glazed. Marjorie turned on her heel and
was out the door again.

Everyone was talking at once.

"Let's get Marie out of here," Laura said. "She needs air."

Herbert took one of Marie's arms and Arthur took the other.
Laura and Vivian followed. Pushing through the crowd, they managed to get to the front door. Right by the door, Laura chanced to
look back. And she saw Mrs. Lawrence staring. At her. The noble
old lady's eyes were very sad.

CHAPTER TWENTY EIGHT

It took Marjorie only a day to clear out of the house. She was leaving all the furniture; Dan said they'd hire a decorator. The kids complained about leaving their friends, but shut up when Marjorie told them they'd have new stereos and new skis and go to boarding schools in Vermont if they wanted to.

When Hopkins, the realtor, came in to look things over, shortly after Marjorie and her kids had left, he found a tangle of film in the fireplace. And two pairs of men's shoes. In one of the shoes was half a postcard. Hopkins found the other half on the floor in front of the fireplace. He put the two halves together. It was a picture of Pikes Peak. On the back of the postcard Hopkins read: "I am happy now with my little girl. I wish you all the best of luck. Dad." Hopkins lit the postcard with a match, and threw it in with the film.

As August wore on, Laura began asking friends in New York to look around for a publishing job. Vivian kept trying to persuade her to come in with her in the dress shop, but Laura said she'd have to wait and see. She did go along with Vivian to one auction, and so did Marie, though she had to be dragged. There was some confusion in the bidding on an antique oriental that Vivian wanted for her shop. Marie accidentally began bidding against Vivian, and while Vivian tried to stop her a swarthy rug dealer in Bermuda shorts stepped into the breach. The auctioneer's hammer came down just as Vivian got her hand in the air again. The rug pool immediately claimed that they owned the carpet. There was a three-way dispute among Vivian, the auctioneer, and the rug dealer in the Bermudas. The rug dealer started shouting in Vivian's face and she grabbed the gold chain around his neck and gave it a terrific yank. The auctioneer said either the rug would go on the block again or he would call the police. The rug went up again.

And Laura, who had been stationed by Vivian strategically in the back of the tent against just such an outcome as this, outbid the rug pool. They did not give Laura very much competition, because they saw Vivian was not bidding, and it was Vivian to whom they wanted to teach a lesson.

"That was a nice day's work," said Vivian as the three of them drove off with the rug in their trunk.

"It was a little exhausting . . . but fun," Laura admitted.

"What are you going to call this shop with the blood you've already drawn setting it up? Saturday's Aggression? Karate Frocks?"

Vivian fixed on Marie, who was sitting in the back, by looking in the rearview mirror.

"Listen, wisenheimer," Vivian replied. "There's nothing wrong with asserting yourself a little."

"I do," Marie said. "But since that town meeting debacle I try to limit myself to parties. Then I can blame the booze."

"I'm looking forward to that cocktail party for the horse tonight," Laura said. "I have been all season."

"Leave it to the Williams's," Marie said. "They're having the first houseguest anybody has had this summer who's actually worth meeting."

"Kentucky born and bred," Vivian added.

"Yes. The few times I've heard that said about men I usually find out they went to Sewanee or North Carolina and they talk so slowly you fall asleep before you can find out whether what they're saying is actually as boring as it sounds."

Turning to face Marie, Laura said, "At least the horse isn't going to start telling you about his alfalfa acreage."

"No, and I imagine he'll come to the party nude, which is something else you don't expect from the average houseguest around here."

"It's hard to believe that this is the last big party of the season," Marie said wistfully. "Where does the time go?"

"Especially the summertime," Laura said.

"Labor Day is the only national holiday that's *guaranteed* to be a letdown," Marie said.

"Are you girls going to a party or a funeral?" Vivian asked.

"We're going to the last party of the season," Marie replied. "It's bound to be a little like a wake. We've come to the end. There's nothing more to look forward to."

"Nothing more here to look forward to, you mean," Vivian said.

"Yes," Marie agreed. "There's nothing more . . . here. I wonder how that can be? There's nothing much left. But nothing is settled either."

"It was a mistake for you to try to get at Dan in the first place," Vivian said. "You might as well have been trying to get back at that Sister Don Bosco you're always talking about. What would she be like now, if she were still alive? A feeble old woman whose glasses make little red dents in her nose. And Dan, what will he be a few years from now? An old man who gets up in the night to go to the toilet and forgets to flush it."

"Why is this conversation beginning to depress me?" Laura wondered.

"Why be bitter?" Vivian asked. "Nobody has more than a very short time on this earth. And when we're old we won't even be able to remember our bitterness. When you get old everything turns sickishly sweet, including your own body. So I say forget the past and get as much as you can out of today."

"Sister Don Bosco was around fifty when I had her," Marie replied. "She didn't need glasses then. She probably doesn't now."

"I'm kind of looking forward to this party," Laura admitted. "Even though it is coming at the tail end. Maybe I've grown more serene in my solitude. If solitude is what I have to look forward to in my old age, maybe it won't be so bad."

"I don't know about you two," Marie said. "But I'm going to this party with a little clutchpurse of hope in my hand. Summer isn't over just yet. Who knows, I might even line up something. Someone might find me . . . interesting."

"That's the spirit," Vivian said.

"Yes," Laura said. "It may not be the senior prom, but it's something."

Nobody had heard from Jamie Lawrence in some time, so Laura assumed he had left. Probably to look for an older woman. Good luck to him, Laura thought. She wasn't going to harbor any bitterness. He among you who is without sexual hang-ups, let him throw the first stone. Besides, freedom was beginning to feel good to Laura. Even promising. That was, no doubt, Vivian's positive influence.

Laura and Vivian and Marie had decided that they would go together to the Williamses' party. Laura and Vivian said that they would meet at Vivian's and then pick up Marie. En route to Marie's house, Laura and Vivian agreed that they would cooperate in monitering Marie's visits to the bar. But it was obvious as soon as she got into the car that Marie was not going to submit to friendly governance. Her excuse was that there had been a notice in *The New York Times* of Marjorie Hanson's engagement to Dan.

"They even listed her high school," Marie sputtered.

"So? What difference does it make?" Vivian wanted to know.

"What's she got that I haven't got?" Marie asked.

"If we knew the answer to that question," Laura said, "we'd also have a pretty good understanding of human sexuality." And then she added, "But you know what Arthur says about that: 'Human sexual response is the ultimate *New York Times* crossword puzzle.' "

When they arrived at the Williams's the party was already crowded. Instant Replay, the guest of honor, was standing in a silk stall, calmly munching oats.

"Isn't he a doll?" Marie said. "As soon as I get a drink I'm going right over and start talking to him."

"Want a gin and tonic, Laura?" Vivian asked. "I'm going to walk over with Marie."

"Yes, thanks," Laura said.

Laura experienced a moment of cocktail party trepidation: that odd feeling of being onstage and waiting for someone to feed you a line. Since there was nobody close by to give her a cue, Laura decided to wander around a little. The party was spread all over the Williams's lawn, and people were gathering in pastel clumps, like the flowers. Laura approached a group of familiar women. Janet Miller was recalling, ruefully, her Virginia childhood.

"The chauffeur would drive us around," Janet was saying, "and Phil and I would be in the back, making out. Then he came down with a mild case of hepatitis, and I had to go to my father and admit that I'd been . . . kissing him. That was pretty hard to do, with a Charlottesville upbringing."

No wonder we're all so helpless, Laura thought. If you want to make out in the back of a car, you should at least be able to drive yourself. Meandering over to the next group, Laura listened in on Susannah Hastings's conversation. She was telling about the troubles the Willoughby family was having. Two sisters and a brother shared the same summer house, and one sister had put in a swimming pool on her own initiative. The other two were refusing to contribute a dime to the pool's maintenance, though they didn't hesitate to use it. Laura felt like breaking in and telling about her friend from New York who shared a damp cottage bedroom in Kismet, on a biweekly weekend basis, but thought better of it. Why bother? Nobody in the group hearing Susannah's tale had what could be called a sympathetic imagination. They were oblivious to everything but sex and the little, occasional remissions of privilege that were nicely summed up, in Laura's mind, by your brother and sister welshing on the swimming pool.

What does matter, in the end? Laura wondered. One minute Marie was saying you shouldn't take yourself—or anything else— seriously, and nothing in life was more meaningful than a cocktail party. And the next minute she was telling Vivian that fashion is superficial. And a minute later she was agonizing over her ex-husband's indulgence of his middle-aged libido. Yet, despite her inconsistencies, Marie had a degree of self-knowledge that nearly everyone else at this party lacked. She had said to Laura only yesterday, "I'm still trying to find out what makes people tick. Whereas Vivian has developed a self-winding mechanism."

Deciding to eavesdrop some more to see if she could figure out what makes people tick, Laura sidled up to yet another group. Kay Parker was complaining loudly about a houseguest she had entertained at her place in Bermuda. Evidently the houseguest had decided to experiment with her hair while on vacation; she had tried out a new bleach formula, and the result was a platinum-blond explosion—or what looked like one. Even with a scarf on her head, the woman drew stares. In addition, this houseguest painted her toes a

317

red with lavender overtones, and to show off her little tootsies wore sandals everywhere she went. Because of this colorful person, Kay became the talk of Tuckerstown, much to her annoyance.

"But it is a *small* island," she said, lamenting the fact.

Finished with her account of her travails in Bermuda, Kay began a fresh narrative. This time her subject was a lopsided brother and sister who had been sent by their thoughtless parents to the same prep school. They were two years apart, and the brother was five foot two and the sister, five nine and a half.

"Think of the psychological consequences of that," Kay said. Laura closed her eyes for a moment to try to picture the unhappy siblings: what would they look like? Mutt and Jeff in Topsiders? Feeling light-headed, Laura moved slowly away from Kay's group. On the heels of the brother and sister who did not make a pair had come to Laura an image out of an old Fellini movie. Which one was it? *Satyricon?* Yes, that was it. Laura remembered the scene well. A tiny cripple whose body was a collection of right angles was picking his way across an unbearably bright, sandy landscape. Laura blinked. She saw in her mind's eye the front ranks of a parade. First the little cripple. Then the short brother followed by his tall sister. Next the Bermuda houseguest with the shell-shocked hair. And then Marie . . . who would be pulling behind her a long caravan of little red wagons like the one she used to deliver newspapers from and also like the ones they use on Fire Island to carry groceries to the houses. In the first wagon would be Herbert. And in the second one, Arthur, with a silver Tiffany rattle in his hand. The third wagon in the train would have Dan Cartey in it, along with that Marjorie Hanson . . . and right after them the fat woman who ran the supermarket, in her own separate wheelbarrow. The wheelbarrow would be connected by a tow chain to a Cadillac limousine, which would have in the backseat Janet Miller, whose dress would be up over her head. And then, walking by herself, under her own steam, would come Vivian. Followed by a bat built as bonily as the little cripple leading the procession.

Laura thought she might be drowning somehow, because the parade was now her own life flashing before her eyes. Hans, her German lover, still in his baby-blue pajamas. The lonely girl in her building who was always making mint tea. Four editors carrying a table from the Four Seasons. Jamie. Jamie's grandmother. Jamie's mother. No, Laura thought. No. wait. I can't see her. I don't even know what she looked like.

I have to sit down, Laura thought. She found an empty iron settee. How could I have been jealous of a dead woman? Laura asked herself. I wasn't really. It was just an excuse. I didn't want it to go on. Because I was afraid that this would be it for me. I'd fall in love with him. And if I ever lost him . . . what more would there be in life for me? All this time, all these years, what have I been doing? I've been saving myself, that's what I've been doing. It's like the fifties, only it's not our virginity we worry about losing, it's our hearts. God. What am I? I thought I was a feminist, but I'm not. I'm an uptight little girl out of the fifties who doesn't want anybody to think she's "easy." So I've kept my heart . . . intact. My soul is as pure as . . . Sister Don Bosco's, for Christ's sake.

Laura wanted to cry but couldn't. She felt dried out. In a desert. Across which she and all her foolish friends were marching. They made a column that stretched for miles. Laura felt worn out from the distance she'd traveled—to wind up here, at a cocktail party for a horse, alone in an iron chair, bitterly aware of what her life had been all about, a small, hardly noticeable tableau amid the panorama of absurdity that was life. The frivolity was not going to stop for Laura, either. Maybe Vivian would find her and give her her drink. And Marie would return, too. And the three of them would talk as usual of frivolous things, and, as usual, one of them would mistake a matter of frivolity for a matter of gravity—when the bearing of all the frivolity became, for a few moments, too heavy a burden.

I have to find a job, Laura thought.

"Laura."

It was Jamie's voice.

Laura froze. She felt his hand on her shoulder.

"How have you been?" he said.

Forcing herself not to tremble, Laura turned around.

"Oh, I'm all right," she said. She felt as though little hands were rising in her chest to fend him off. But there was no strength in them.

"It's . . . nice to see you," Laura added. "I thought you'd left."

"I did, for a few days," Jamie replied. "I went to New York, to do some preliminary work on the foundation."

"Did it go well? Your work?" It seemed to Laura that she had to catch her breath with every word she said.

"It went okay. Laura, could we possibly go somewhere and talk . . . privately . . . for a few minutes?"

"All right," Laura said. "Where?"

"Over there," Jamie replied. He pointed to a gray teakwood bench that surrounded the trunk of a maple tree. Getting up, Laura let him guide her through the crowd. When they were alone, Jamie said, "If I tell you I'd like to talk about my mother, will you listen?"

"Yes," Laura said. She remembered what Marie had said about a parent sometimes being the focus of a need. It seemed irrelevant now.

"I admit I talk about her too much," Jamie was saying. "I talked about her to you . . . too much. In a way I was aware of that."

"You were?"

"Yes. I was testing you, I suppose . . . in a way. I wanted you to see the worst side of me."

"Which is your bitterness . . . about the way you were treated," Laura filled in.

Recalling what Vivian had been saying, Laura added, "It's not a terrible thing to be bitter. Bitterness is something we can grow out of. . . ." Smiling for the first time since she'd arrived at the party, she added, "The passage of time is not an artificial sweetener. It's natural . . . and healthy."

"It's not easy to forget a childhood that was lonely," Jamie said. "But I'm not a child anymore. The memories do move further away . . . with every year. It's just that when I start to feel close to somebody . . . the closeness . . . calls the memory up again."

"You're afraid of feeling close to someone, and then being left alone," Laura said. "I know the feeling. All too well. Nobody wants to feel used . . . exploited. Women especially. We want so badly to avoid exploitation that we're entering a new era of . . . chastity. We don't want to be . . . ruined—I think that was the word they used for it in the fifties—by emotional commitments."

"So you keep it physical, huh?" Jamie said.

He reached over and touched Laura's wrist with his fingertips. His touch sent a pleasant shock through her and wetted, a little, the rims of her eyes.

"Yes, you keep it physical," Laura said. She shivered.

"Speaking of physical," Jamie said.

"Yes," Laura replied. "It's obvious, isn't it? My body still responds to your body."

"But emotionally . . . ?"

"Emotionally . . . I'm not the woman I was," Laura said. "I'm . . . in love with you."

"There they go, they're in the clinch," Arthur said. He had spotted Laura and Jamie together, and corralled Herbert and Vivian and Marie so they could all watch at a safe distance.

"That's the trouble with the female friendships that form in this town," Marie said. "The first man that comes along, they drop you like a hot potato."

"Oh, pipe down," Vivian said. She was wiping her eyes with an antique handkerchief that had on it the initial of some poor soul who was either in a rest home or deceased.

"Young love is beautiful," Arthur said. "Although I've come to prefer middle-aged love myself. The seasoning is more to my taste these days."

"I was young and in love once," Marie said. "In high school. I was in love with Dan. We broke up once, for a month, my junior year. And I threw up. The night we broke up. I've swallowed a lot since then, trying to get my fill of love, and my stomach has never been right. So I guess whatever seasoning I have doesn't agree with the male population."

"Marie, you promised you were going to stop belittling yourself," Herbert said.

"Oh, promises, promises," Marie replied, drinking her drink.

As soon as they were able to let go of each other, Laura turned away from Jamie just long enough to look around for Marie and Vivian and wave to them. Vivian waved back energetically and Marie nodded and muttered, in a sarcastic voice, "Yeah, yeah. We know. We know."

And then Laura left with Jamie.

After Laura's departure, Marie became increasingly difficult for her friends to handle. She ordered drink after drink, went up to talk to people and started looking elsewhere a minute into the conversation, or else she just sat—abruptly—in mid-sentence. Finally Vivian and Herbert ran out of patience and, instead of minding Marie, let a financial consultant from New Jersey tell them how small businesses ("forty million a year gross, say") went about getting loans.

Vivian and Herbert did not see Marie approaching the horse. They did not see her reach into the gilded stall and caress the animal's long, glistening neck. They did not hear her calling it "horsie" over and over, gently, soothingly. Arthur did witness these things, though, and he was hurrying to get Vivian and Herbert when the two of them noticed the sudden change in the pitch of the cocktail party conversation. They turned around. And they saw Marie walking away from the horse's elegant stall. With the horse right behind her. It took a couple of seconds to dawn on people that Instant Replay was loose. And it took half a second more to notice that he had an erection, which was protruding from his belly like a two-foot leather telescope. Laughter broke out. A few of the women screamed. Marie appeared to be confused. She looked back. And found she was looking Instant Replay in the face. He whinnied at her.

CHAPTER TWENTY NINE

A week passed before Marie would show her face in public again. By the fourth week of August she had enough courage to return to her corner of the Bath Club. It was there that Laura found her the day before she was to leave for New York with Jamie.

"Well, Marie," Laura said, "I guess this is it. I'll write you as soon as we have a permanent address. You'll have to come over and have dinner with us as soon as you're back in town."

"I'll be looking forward to that," Marie replied. "What am I supposed to say, Laura? Good luck?"

"I'm giving it a year," Laura said without conviction.

"A year. Fifty years. Who's counting?"

"Have you thought any more about helping Vivian with the dress shop?"

"It used to be they tried to fix me up with a man. Now they try to fix me up with a job. Times certainly have changed. Or I've changed. With the passage of time."

Marie lifted her lemonade cup and made a vague toast to the state of things before drinking.

"Try and take care of yourself, Marie," Laura said. She bent over and kissed her friend on the cheek.

"Can I be matron of honor?" Marie asked.

"Oh, shush," Laura said.

With the coming of Labor Day more and more people left for the season. Marie got a letter from Arthur and Herbert with a Los Angeles postmark. Inside was a Polaroid: Arthur and Chad smiling in the sunshine. On the back Arthur had written: "Chad and myself the day he was cast in the new Bob Evans movie." Marie shrugged. The workings of the West Coast were beyond her.

By the middle of September the Bath Club was nearly empty. Walking over to her usual corner, Marie saw a solitary Styrofoam cup being pushed along by the breeze. It was so quiet she could hear the cup tapping the boards. Somehow the cup made her think of sagebrush blowing through a ghost town. She wondered if there were any ghost towns left now. Hadn't most of them become ski resorts? There might not be any ghost towns left, but Marie certainly believed there were ghosts: specters who persisted in haunting their old hangouts. A shade lingering in the lengthening shadows, Marie thought. That's all I am.

Unfolding her deck chair, Marie sat down and looked out at the ocean. There was no haze today. The September clarity was over the water. The air was cool and dry, and peppery with pollen from the goldenrod that was flowering in profusion everywhere. Another summer gone, Marie mused. It always went by so quickly, summer did. Marie remembered that she had half a bottle of Finlandia left in her locker. She was going to get it when she saw Vivian coming toward her.

Vivian was obviously dressed for the road. She was wearing a suit with linebacker shoulders and open-toed Mildred Pierce shoes that looked as though they had been made for a gladiator.

"What are you doing in a bathing suit?" Vivian asked. "I'm all ready to leave."

"But I'm staying here," Marie replied.

"Oh no you're not. You're coming back to the city with me and help me open the shop."

"Forget it, Viv."

"Don't sit down again," Vivian said. "Do as I say. I've got a gun."

Marie looked and saw something pointing at her from inside the pocket of Vivian's suit.

"Go ahead and shoot," Marie said. "See if I care."

In exasperation Vivian took the nail file out of her pocket and threw it.

"Don't ever try and stick up a bank with that," Marie said.

Vivian opened her pocketbook and removed from it a pharmacist's bottle.

"I'm sorry. Am I making you nervous again?" Marie said guiltily.

"No," Vivian replied. "I just want you to witness something." Flipping off the safety cap on the bottle, Vivian emptied its contents into her hand.

"These are the last of my Valiums," she said. "Watch this." Vivian turned to face the breaking waves of the high tide, and casually threw the pills into them.

"There," she said. "There they go. My once precious pills. Maybe, when the winter winds blow, they'll calm the waters a bit. But I doubt it."

"Do you realize how much you're risking?" Marie said. "On a . . . a . . . dress shop."

"I know what the odds are," Vivian replied. "And I'm willing to take the chance. Because I'm betting on myself."

"Well, I wish you luck," Marie said.

"Are you just going to sit there until it snows?"

"Snow isn't so bad. It's freezing rain that really depresses me."

"It's too bad you can afford depression—among your other luxuries."

"But I'm elevating my depressions lately, Viv. They're becoming contemplations. Before long I'll have a whole philosophy worked out. Now, you can't tell me that's a waste of time."

"Try logical positivism. The tenet of that philosophy is get out there and *sell*."

"That's also a religion, isn't it? The gospel according to Amway Products. But I'm afraid I can't see it as my salvation, honey."

"You can't do anything for people who won't do anything for themselves," Vivian said. Sighing, she turned around and walked out of the club.

"Be careful not to catch one of those heels between the boards," Marie called after her.

Marie sat down again. Closing her eyes, she rested her head against the canvas of her deck chair. You can't stretch the season very far, she thought. You have just so long. And then it's fall. And then winter. The leaves all off the trees and so much gray in your hair you have to start coloring it. It can't be September already, can it? I can't be thirty, can I? Oh, my God, *forty*. How can *I* possibly be fifty? I don't feel fifty. Marie wondered if eighty came as a surprise, too. Maybe not, if you stretched the early years out far enough. Then maybe something would snap in your head and at eighty you'd be ten again, looking around for your favorite uncle.

Opening her eyes once more, Marie gazed at the ocean. Why was it so hypnotic? Why did people want to live next to it and watch it repeating its rhythms, over and over? Was it some basic response to the origins of your own breath and heartbeat that drew you to the water's edge? It was as though you could see out there the elements of your own body freed from its small compass and far-flung. It was almost as if you could lie in the seabed and touch with one hand Maine and with the other Ireland.

Alone in her canvas chair, at the far end of the empty deck, Marie began to feel pangs of isolation. What longing the ocean could call up; here, at the tip of land, you could sense earth separated from earth, the drifting continents aching to rejoin at the ragged edges where they had parted.

Marie wondered if drifting might not be the natural state of things. Out on the water, she saw a whitened root rising and falling in the waves. Once it had been able to hold on somewhere, once it had a grip on solid ground, but now it was just drifting. And it was lonely. Pushed around in circles by random winds and currents. A large wave broke over the solitary piece of driftwood, and Marie lost sight of it in the flurry of foam. Then it reappeared, washed up on the sand.

Even driftwood finds its way back eventually, Marie thought. Maybe because it just keeps moving. *Moving*, Marie thought. Moving. Yes, the summer really is over. Yes, I really am forty. I'm past forty. And I have to move on.

Marie got out of her chair.

Hurrying across the deck, she went into the manager's office and asked the Harvard boy who was putting sheets over the wicker chairs if she could use the telephone.

"Go right ahead," he said.

Marie dialed Vivian's number.

When Vivian answered, Marie said, "Got room in your car for another aspiring saleswoman?"

At the other end of the line there was a shriek that sounded as if it might have been coming from a child's birthday party.

"I'll do my best," Marie went on, "and I'm one employee you won't have to provide any incentives for. Because I have my own incentive. I don't want to spend another summer sitting on this deck."

Before Vivian could reply to that, Marie said, "I'll see you in a few minutes," and hung up. She went back to her chair, folded it, and took it to her locker. She closed the door on the chair and the bottle of Finlandia. And locked it.

Marie looked at the key for a moment. Then she looked at the pool. And then she tossed the key into the pool.

As Marie was walking out of the Bath Club, the solitary Styrofoam cup that had been rolling across the deck slipped through the space where a rotted board had been removed. The cup would remain there, in the darkness under the deck, with the Popsicle sticks and the cigarette butts, all winter long.